Silver Girl

Silver Girl

A Novel

Elin Hilderbrand

A REAGAN ARTHUR BOOK

LITTLE, BROWN AND COMPANY

NEW YORK   BOSTON   LONDON

Reagan Arthur Books / Little, Brown and Company
Hachette Book Group
237 Park Avenue, New York, NY 10017
www.hachettebookgroup.com

First Edition: June 2011

Reagan Arthur Books is an imprint of Little, Brown and Company, a division of Hachette Book Group, Inc. The Reagan Arthur Books name and logo are trademarks of Hachette Book Group, Inc.

Library of Congress Cataloging-in-Publication Data
Hilderbrand, Elin.
  Silver girl : a novel / Elin Hilderbrand.—1st ed.
    p. cm.
  "A Reagan Arthur book."
  ISBN 978-0-316-09966-0 (HC) / 978-0-316-19042-8 (Can. edition)
  1. Female friendship—Fiction. 2. Women—Massachusetts—Nantucket Island—Fiction. 3. Nantucket Island (Mass.)—Fiction. 4. Man–woman relationships—Fiction. I. Title.
  PS3558.I384355S55 2011
  813'.54—dc22

                                                          2011002750

              10 9 8 7 6 5 4 3 2 1

                        RRD-C

              Printed in the United States of America

For my daughter, Shelby Katharine Cunningham.
I am at a loss for the words to describe you.
Graceful? Vivacious? Captivating?
All of these, yes, my love, and more.

PART ONE

MEREDITH MARTIN DELINN

They had agreed not to speak about anything meaningful until Meredith was safely inside the house on Nantucket. First, they had the highway to face. Meredith knew it too well, just like every other American with a home (or, in her case, three homes) between Maine and Florida. There were the ninety-three tedious exits of Connecticut before they crossed into Rhode Island and, a scant hour later, Massachusetts. As they drove over the Sagamore Bridge, the sun came up, giving the Cape Cod Canal a cheerful pink glaze that hurt Meredith's eyes. There was no traffic on the bridge even though it was the first of July; that was why Connie liked to do the drive overnight.

Finally, they arrived in Hyannis: a town Meredith had visited once with her parents in the early 1970s. She remembered her mother, Deidre Martin, insisting they drive by the Kennedy Compound. There had been guards; it was just a few years after Bobby's assassination. Meredith remembered her father, Chick Martin, encouraging her to eat a lobster roll. She had been only eight years old, but Chick Martin had confidence in Meredith's sophistication. *Brilliant and talented,* Chick used to brag shamelessly. *The girl can do no wrong.* Meredith had tasted the lobster salad and spit it out, then felt embarrassed. Her father had shrugged and finished the sandwich himself.

Even all these years later, the memory of Hyannis filled Meredith with a sense of shame, which lay on top of the disgrace Meredith had been feeling since her husband, Freddy Delinn, had been indicted. Hyannis was a place where Meredith had disappointed her father.

Thank God he couldn't see her now.

Although they had agreed not to talk about anything meaningful, Meredith turned to Connie, who had decided—against her better judgment—to shelter Meredith, at least for the time being, and said, "Thank God my father can't see me now."

Connie, who was pulling into the parking lot of the Steamship Authority, let out a sigh and said, "Oh, Meredith."

Meredith couldn't read Connie's tone. *Oh, Meredith, you're right; it's a blessing Chick has been dead for thirty years and didn't have to witness your meteoric rise and your even more spectacular fall.* Or: *Oh, Meredith, stop feeling sorry for yourself.* Or: *Oh, Meredith, I thought we agreed we wouldn't talk until we got to the house. We laid ground rules, and you're trampling them.*

Or: *Oh, Meredith, please shut up.*

Indeed, Connie's tone since she'd rescued Meredith at two in the morning was one of barely concealed...what? Anger? Fear? Consternation? And could Meredith blame her? She and Connie hadn't spoken in nearly three years, and in their last conversation, they had said despicable things to each other; they had taken a blowtorch to the ironclad chain of their friendship. Or: *Oh, Meredith, what have I done? Why are you here? I wanted a quiet summer. I wanted peace. And now I have you, a stinky international scandal, in my front seat.*

Meredith decided to give Connie the benefit of the doubt. "Oh, Meredith" was a quasi-sympathetic non-answer. Connie was pulling up to the gatehouse and showing the attendant her ferry ticket; she was distracted. Meredith wore her son Carver's baseball hat from Choate and her last remaining pair of prescription sun-glasses, which fortunately were big, round, and very dark. Meredith turned her face away from the attendant. She couldn't let anyone recognize her.

Connie pulled up the ramp, into the ferry's hold. Cars were packed like Matchbox models in a snug little suitcase. It was the first of July; even at this early hour, the mood on the boat was fes-tive. Jeeps were laden with beach towels and hibachi grills; the car parked in front of Connie's was a vintage Wagoneer with at least sixteen beach stickers, in every color of the rainbow, lining the bumper. Meredith's heart was bruised, battered, and broken. She told herself not to think about the boys, but all that led to was her thinking about the boys. She remembered how she used to load up the Range Rover with bags of their bathing suits and surf shirts and flip-flops, and their baseball gloves and cleats, the aluminum case that held the badminton set, fresh decks of cards, and packs of D batteries for the flashlights. Meredith would load the dog into his crate and strap Carver's surfboard to the top of the car, and off they'd go — bravely into the traffic jam that lasted from Freeport all the way to Southampton. Inevitably, they timed it badly and got stuck behind the jitney. But it had been fun. The boys took turns with the radio — Leo liked folk rock, the Count-ing Crows were his favorite, and Carver liked the headbanger stuff that would make the dog howl — and Meredith always felt that the hotter and slower the drive was, the happier they were to arrive in Southampton. Sun, sand, ocean. Take your shoes off, open the windows. Freddy did the drive on the weekends, and in later years, he arrived in a helicopter.

As Meredith looked on the summer revelers now, she thought, *Leo! Carver! Leo. Poor Leo.* For all of the years of their growing up, Leo had taken care of Carver. Protected him, schooled him, included him. And now, Carver was the one who would be supporting Leo, propping him up. Meredith prayed he was doing a good job.

A voice came over the loudspeaker, announcing the rules and

regulations of the boat. The foghorn sounded, and Meredith heard distant clapping. The good, fortunate souls headed to Nantucket Island on this fine morning were applauding the start of their summer. Meanwhile, Meredith felt like she was still three states away. At that very moment, federal marshals would be entering Meredith's penthouse apartment on Park Avenue and seizing her belongings. Meredith wondered with a curious detachment what this seizing would be like. To go with Connie, Meredith had packed one duffel bag of simple summer clothes, and one cardboard box of personal effects—photographs, her marriage license, the boys' birth certificates, a few of her favorite paperback novels, one particular spiral-bound notebook from her freshman year at Princeton, and one record album—the original 1970 release of Simon and Garfunkel's *Bridge Over Troubled Water,* which Meredith had no hope of ever listening to, but which she couldn't bring herself to leave behind.

She'd been permitted to take her eyeglasses, her prescription sunglasses, and her four-karat diamond engagement ring. The ring had been inherited from her grandmother, Annabeth Martin, and not bought with dirty money. There was a strand of pearls from Meredith's mother, a present on Meredith's graduation from Princeton, which fell into the same category, but Meredith had no use for pearls now. She couldn't wear pearls in jail. With a little forethought, she might have pawned them and added the money to the paltry sum she had left.

But what of her other possessions? Meredith imagined grim, strapping men in black uniforms with handguns concealed in their waistbands. One might lift the delicate Shalimar bottle off her dressing table and, unable to help himself, inhale the scent. One would strip her Aurora linens from Schweitzer off the bed. Those sheets were worth thousands of dollars, but what would the marshals do with them? Launder them, fold them, sell them off? They would take her Hostetler sculpture and the Andrew Wyeth sketches; they would clip the Calder mobile from the ceiling in the living room. They would go through Meredith's closet and box up the Louboutins and the Sergio Rossis; they would carry off her everyday dresses—Diane von Furstenberg, Phillip Lim—and her gowns—the Dior, the Chanel, the Caroline Herreras. The Feds had told Meredith that her belongings would be sold at auction and the proceeds funneled into a restitution fund for the fleeced investors. Meredith thought of her baby-blue Dior gown, which she had paid $19,000 for—a fact that, now, made her want to gag with disgust—and wondered who would own it next. Someone petite—Meredith was only five foot one and weighed a hundred pounds. That gown had been custom-tailored for her by John Galliano himself. Who would end up with Meredith's copper All-Clad sauté pans (never used, except occasionally by Leo's girlfriend, Anais, who thought it was a sin that Meredith didn't cook in her gleaming gourmet kitchen). Who would end up with the cut crystal whiskey decanter that Freddy had never poured a drink from, except in the final days before his exposure to the world. (It was the sight of Freddy throwing back three successive shots of a 1926 Macallan that put Meredith on high alert. A Pandora's box of accusations had cracked open in her mind: *No one knows how he does it. He says it's black magic, but it can't be legal. He's breaking the law. He's going to get caught.*)

Meredith knew the Feds would be most interested in what they found in Freddy's home office. Freddy had always kept the door to his office locked, a practice that began when the children were young and he wanted to keep them from interrupting him on the phone, though it continued into later years. The door had remained locked—both when he was in the office and when he wasn't—even against Meredith. If she wanted entry, she had to knock. She had testified to this in her deposition, but the authorities didn't believe her. Her fingerprints (literal) were on the doorknob. And her fingerprints (figurative) had been found on one illegal transaction. Three days before the collapse of Delinn Enterprises, Meredith had transferred $15 million from the company's "slush fund" into the personal brokerage account she and Freddy shared.

The federal marshals would also be interested in Freddy's den. Their decorator, Samantha Deuce, had masterminded the "gentleman's library" look with shelves of books on finance, antique piggy banks, and baseball memorabilia from Babe Ruth's stint with the Yankees. Freddy wasn't even a Yankees fan, but Samantha had likened him to Babe Ruth because, she said, they were both iconic men of their times. *Iconic men of their times.* Meredith had believed Samantha to be a maestro of overstatement.

Freddy had nearly always enjoyed his den alone; Meredith was hard-pressed to remember anyone else relaxing in the deep suede club chairs or watching the fifty-two-inch television. The boys didn't like hanging out in that room; even when the ball game was on, they preferred to watch in the kitchen with Meredith. There was a hidden dartboard in the back of the den that Meredith was sure had never been used; the darts were still in the bubble wrap.

The only person that Meredith could remember ever seeing in Freddy's den was Samantha. Meredith had come across Freddy and Samantha in that room a few years earlier. They had been standing side by side admiring a hunting print that Samantha had bought at Christie's. (The choice of this print was ironic, since Freddy didn't hunt and hated guns: his brother had been killed by an errant bullet in a training exercise in the army.) Freddy had been resting his hand on Samantha's lower back. When Meredith walked in, Freddy whipped his hand away so quickly that it called attention to the fact that he had been touching Samantha in the first place. Meredith thought of that moment often. Freddy's hand on Samantha's lower back: No big deal, right? Samantha had been their decorator for years. Freddy and Samantha were friends, chummy and affectionate. If Freddy had simply left his hand there, Meredith wouldn't have thought a thing about it. It was his startled reaction that made Meredith wonder. Freddy never got startled.

The ferry lurched forward. Connie had wedged her hunter-green Escalade between a Stop & Shop semi and a black Range Rover not so different from the one that Meredith used to drive to the Hamptons. Connie got out of the car, slamming her door.

Meredith panicked. "Where are you going?" she asked.

Connie didn't answer. She opened the back door of the Escalade and climbed in. She foraged in the way-back for a pillow, and lay across the backseat.

"I'm tired," she said.

"Of course," Meredith said. Connie had left her house at eight o'clock the night before, a scant four hours after receiving Meredith's phone call. She had driven six hours to Manhattan and had idled in the dark alley behind 824 Park Avenue, waiting for Meredith to emerge. There had been a reporter standing behind a Dumpster, but he had been smoking a cigarette and hadn't gotten his camera ready until Meredith was in the car and Connie was screeching out of the alley in reverse, like a bank robber in a heist movie. Meredith had ducked her head below the dashboard.

"Jesus, Meredith," Connie said. "And have you seen the *front* of the building?"

Meredith knew it was swarming with reporters, television lights, and satellite trucks. They had been there on the day Freddy was led out of the apartment in handcuffs, then again on the morning that Meredith had gone to visit Freddy in jail, and they had gathered a third time nearly two days earlier in anticipation of Meredith's removal from the building by federal marshals. What the public wanted to know was, where does the wife of the biggest financial criminal in history go when she is turned out of her Park Avenue penthouse?

Meredith had two attorneys. Her lead attorney's name was Burton Penn; he asked Meredith to call him Burt. He was new to her. Freddy had taken their longtime family lawyer, Richard Cassel. Goddamned Freddy, taking the best, leaving Meredith with prematurely balding thirty-six-year-old Burton Penn. Though he had, at least, gone to Yale Law School.

The other attorney was even younger, with dark shaggy hair

and pointy incisors, like one of those teen vampires. He wore glasses, and in passing, he'd told Meredith that he had an astigmatism. "Yes, so do I," Meredith said; she had worn horn-rimmed glasses since she was thirteen years old. Meredith had bonded more closely with this second attorney. His name was Devon Kasper. He asked her to call him Dev. Dev told Meredith the truth about things, but he sounded sorry about it. He had sounded sorry when he told Meredith that, because she had transferred the $15 million into her and Freddy's shared brokerage account, she was under investigation, and it was possible she would be charged with conspiracy and sent to prison. He had sounded sorry when he told Meredith that her son Leo was also under investigation, because he had worked with Freddy at Delinn Enterprises.

Leo was twenty-six years old. He worked for the legitimate trading division of Delinn Enterprises.

So why, then, were the Feds investigating Leo? Meredith didn't understand, and she was trying not to panic—panic wouldn't serve her—but this was her child. He was her responsible son, the one who got into Dartmouth and was captain of the lacrosse team and vice president of the Dartmouth chapter of Amnesty International; he was the one who had a steady girlfriend; he was the one who, to Meredith's knowledge, had never once broken the law— had never shoplifted a pack of gum, had never taken a drink underage, had never gotten a parking ticket.

"Why are they investigating Leo?" Meredith had asked, her bruised heart racing. Her child in danger, as surely as a three-year-old running out into traffic.

Well, Dev said, they were investigating Leo because another trader—a well-respected, ten-year veteran on the legitimate floor named Deacon Rapp—had told the SEC and the FBI that Leo was involved in his father's Ponzi scheme. Deacon testified that Leo was in "constant contact" with colleagues on the seventeenth floor, which was where the Ponzi scheme was headquartered. Freddy had a small office on the seventeenth floor, as well as a secretary. This came as a shock to Meredith. She had known nothing about the existence of the seventeenth floor, nor the secretary, a Mrs. Edith Misurelli. The Feds couldn't question Mrs. Misurelli because she had apparently been due months of vacation time and had left for Italy the day before the scandal broke. No one knew how to reach her.

Dev sounded especially sorry when he told Meredith that she absolutely could not be in contact with either of her sons until the investigation was cleared up. Any conversation between Leo and Meredith might be seen as evidence of their mutual conspiracy. And because Carver and Leo were living together in an old Victorian that Carver was renovating in Greenwich, Meredith couldn't call Carver, either. Burt and Dev had met with Leo's counsel, and both parties agreed there was too much chance for cross-contamination. Meredith should remain in one camp, the boys in another. For the time being.

"I'm sorry, Meredith."

Dev said this often.

Meredith peered at Connie, who had scrunched her long, lean form to fit across the backseat. Her head was sunk into the pillow, her strawberry-blond hair fell across her face, her eyes were closed. She looked older, and sadder, to Meredith—her husband, Wolf, had died two and a half years earlier of brain cancer—but she was still Connie, Constance Flute, née O'Brien, Meredith's oldest, and once her closest, friend. Her friend since the beginning of time.

Meredith had called Connie to ask if she could stay with her "for a while" in Bethesda. Connie had artfully dodged the request by saying that she was headed up to Nantucket for the summer. Of course, Nantucket. July was now upon them—a fact that had effectively escaped Meredith, trapped as she was in her apartment—and Meredith's hopes tanked.

"Can you call someone else?" Connie asked.

"There isn't anyone else," Meredith said. She said this not to invoke Connie's pity, but because it was true. It astounded her how alone she was, how forsaken by everyone who had been in her life. Connie was her one and only hope. Despite the fact that they hadn't spoken in three years, she was the closest thing to family that Meredith had.

"You could turn to the church," Connie said. "Join a convent."

A convent, yes. Meredith had considered this when casting about for options. There were convents, she was pretty sure, out on Long Island; she and the boys used to pass one on their way to the Hamptons, set back from the highway among rolling hills. She would start out as a novice scrubbing floors until her knees bled, but maybe someday she'd be able to teach.

"Meredith," Connie said. "I'm kidding."

"Oh," Meredith said. Of course, she was kidding. Meredith and Connie had attended Catholic schools together all through their childhood, but Connie had never been particularly devout.

"I guess I could pick you up on my way," Connie said.

"And do what?" Meredith said. "Take me to Nantucket?"

"You do owe me a visit," Connie said. "You've owed me a visit since nineteen eighty-two."

Meredith had laughed. It sounded strange to her own ears, the laugh. It had been so long.

Connie said, "You can stay a couple of weeks, maybe longer. We'll see how it goes. I can't make any promises."

"Thank you," Meredith had whispered, weak with gratitude.

"You realize you haven't called me in three years," Connie said.

Yes, Meredith realized that. What Connie really meant was: *You never called to apologize for what you said about Wolf, or to give me your condolences in person. But you call me now, when you're in heaps of trouble and have nowhere else to go.*

"I'm sorry," Meredith said. She didn't say: *You didn't call me, either. You never apologized for calling Freddy a crook.* Now, of course, there was no need to apologize. Connie had been proved right: Freddy was a crook. "Will you still come get me?"

"I'll come get you," Connie said.

Now, Meredith wanted to wake Connie up and ask her: Can you please forgive me for the things I said? Can we make things right between us?

Meredith wondered what the federal marshals would think about the mirror she'd smashed in the master bath. In a fit of rage, she'd thrown her mug of peppermint tea at it; she had savored the smack and shatter of the glass. Her reflection had splintered and fallen away, onto the granite countertop, into Freddy's sink. *Goddamn you, Freddy,* Meredith thought, for the zillionth time. The ferry rocked on the waves, and Meredith's eyes drifted closed. If there were beating hearts beneath the federal marshals' black uniforms, then she supposed they would understand.

CONSTANCE O'BRIEN FLUTE

They had agreed not to speak about anything meaningful until Meredith was safely inside the house on Nantucket. Connie needed time to digest what she'd done. *What had she done?* She had six hours in the car from Bethesda to Manhattan to repeatedly ask herself. The roads were clear of traffic; on the radio, Connie listened to Delilah. The heart-wrenching stories of the callers boosted Connie's spirits. She knew about loss. Wolf had been dead for two and a half years, and Connie was still waiting for the pain to subside. It had been nearly as long since Connie had spoken to their daughter, Ashlyn, though Connie called Ashlyn's cell phone every Sunday, hoping that one time she might answer.

Connie sent Ashlyn flowers on her birthday and a gift certificate to J. Crew at Christmas. Did Ashlyn tear up the gift certificate, throw the flowers in the trash? Connie had no way of knowing.

And now look what she'd done. She had agreed to go to Manhattan to pick up her ex–best friend, Meredith Delinn. Connie thought *ex-friend,* but inside Connie knew that she and Meredith would always be tethered together. They had grown up on the Main Line in Philadelphia. They attended Tarleton in the 1960s, then grammar school, then high school at Merion Mercy Academy. They had been as close as sisters. For two years in high school, Meredith had dated Connie's brother, Toby.

Connie fingered her cell phone, which rested in the console of her car. She considered calling Toby now and telling him what she was doing. He was the only person who had known Meredith as long as Connie had; he was the only one who might understand. But Toby and Meredith had a complicated history. Toby had broken Meredith's heart in high school, and over the years, Meredith had asked Connie about him, the way a woman asks about her first true love. Connie had been the one to tell Meredith about Toby's voyages around the world captaining megayachts, his hard-partying lifestyle that landed him in rehab twice, the women he met, married, and abandoned along the way, and his ten-year-old son who was destined to become as charming and dangerous as Toby himself. Meredith and Toby hadn't seen each other since the funeral of Connie and Toby's mother, Veronica, six years earlier. Something had happened between Meredith and Toby at the funeral that ended with Meredith climbing into her waiting car and driving away before the reception.

"I can't be around him," Meredith had said to Connie later. "It's too painful."

Connie hadn't been gutsy enough to ask Meredith exactly what had happened. But she decided it would be wisest not to call Toby, as tempting as it was.

Connie had seen Meredith on CNN back in April, on the day

that Meredith went to visit Freddy in jail. Meredith had looked gray haired and haggard, nothing like the blond, Dior-wearing socialite that Connie had most recently seen in the society pages of the *New York Times*. Meredith had been wearing jeans and a white button-down shirt and a trench coat; she had been ducking into a cab, but a reporter caught her before she closed the door and asked her, "Mrs. Delinn, do you ever cry about the way things have turned out?"

Meredith looked up, and Connie had felt a sharp rush of recognition. Meredith's expression was feisty. This was the Meredith Connie had known in high school—the competitive field-hockey player, the champion diver, the National Merit Scholarship finalist.

"No," Meredith said.

And Connie thought, *Oh, Meredith, wrong answer.*

She had meant to call Meredith in the days following. The press was brutal. (The headline of the *New York Post* read, *JESUS WEPT. BUT NOT MRS. DELINN.*) Connie had wanted to reach out and offer some kind of support, but she hadn't picked up the phone. She was still bitter that Meredith had allowed money to sink their friendship. And besides, Connie was too involved with her own melancholy to take on Meredith's problems.

Connie had seen a picture of Meredith, peering from one of her penthouse windows, published in *People*. The caption read, *At daybreak, Meredith Delinn gazes out at a world that will no longer have her.*

The paparazzi had caught her in her nightgown at the crack of dawn. *Poor Meredith!* Again, Connie considered calling, but she didn't.

Connie then saw the article on the front page of the *New York Times* Style section entitled "The Loneliest Woman in New York." It told the story of Meredith's ill-fated trip to the Pascal Blanc salon, where she'd been getting her hair colored for fifteen years. The newspaper reported that Meredith had been calling for an appointment at the salon for weeks, but she kept getting put off by the receptionist. Finally, the owner of the salon, Jean-Pierre, called Meredith back and explained that he couldn't risk offending his other patrons, many of whom were former Delinn investors, by having her in the salon. The article said that Meredith asked for an after-hours appointment, and he said no. Meredith asked if the woman who normally colored her hair could come to her apartment—Meredith would pay her in cash—and Jean-Pierre said no. The article also stated that Meredith was no longer welcome at Rinaldo's, the Italian restaurant where she and Freddy had dined at least twice a week for eight years. "They always sat at the same table," Dante Rinaldo was quoted as saying. "Mrs. Delinn always ordered a glass of the Ruffino Chianti, but Mr. Delinn drank nothing, ever. Now, I can't let Mrs. Delinn come to eat, or no one else will come to eat." The article had made one thing perfectly clear: everyone in New York City hated Meredith, and if she were to show her face in public, she would be shunned.

Awful, Connie thought. *Poor Meredith.* After she read the article, she picked up the phone, and, with numb fingers, dialed the number of Meredith's Park Avenue apartment. She was promptly informed by an operator that the number had been changed and that the new number was unlisted.

Of course.

Connie hung up, thinking, *Well, I tried.*

And then that very day, at one o'clock, Connie had been watching Fox News as she packed her suitcases for Nantucket. It was the day of Freddy's sentencing. The talking heads at Fox were predicting a sentence of twenty-five to thirty years, although Tucker Carlson mentioned how savvy and experienced Freddy's counsel was.

"His attorney, Richard Cassel," Carlson said, "is asking for seventeen years, which could become twelve years with good behavior."

And Connie thought, *Ha! Richard Cassel!* Connie had done beer bongs with Richard Cassel when she'd gone to visit Meredith at Princeton. Richard had tried to lure Connie back to his suite, but she had turned him down. He was such a casual aristocrat in his button-down shirt with the frayed collar, and his scuffed penny loafers. Hadn't Meredith told Connie that Richard once cheated on an exam? He was a fitting attorney for Freddy.

Connie's memories of Richard Cassel were interrupted by the announcement that Frederick Xavier Delinn had been sentenced to 150 years in federal prison.

Connie sat down for that. *A hundred and fifty years?* She thought, *The judge is making an example of him.* Well, Connie hated to say this, but Freddy deserved it. So many people had been left penniless; futures had been destroyed, kids were forced to drop out of college, family homes had been foreclosed on, eighty-year-old women had to get by living on Social Security, eating from cans. *A hundred and fifty years.* Connie thought, *Poor Meredith.*

Connie was angry with Meredith for her own personal reasons, but unlike everyone else, she didn't blame Meredith for Freddy's crimes. Meredith couldn't have known what Freddy was doing. (*Had* she? Okay, there was always room for doubt.) But when Connie closed her eyes and searched inside of herself for an answer, she thought, *There is no way Meredith knew.* There was *no way* Meredith would accept fraud in her life. She was a straight arrow. Connie should know: growing up, it had driven her crazy. And still, Connie wondered, just as the rest of the world wondered, how could she *not* have known? Meredith was a smart woman—she had been the class salutatorian at Merion Mercy, she had gone to Princeton. How could she be blind to the crimes going on under her own roof? So, she knew. But no, she couldn't have.

Connie had opened her eyes in time to see Freddy, looking gaunt and nauseous and wearing an ill-fitting suit, being led from the courthouse, back to his dungeon.

You bastard, she thought.

It was a few hours later that the phone had rung. The caller ID said, *NUMBER UNAVAILABLE,* which always stirred up hope in Connie, because any unidentified number might be Ashlyn calling.

Connie picked up. "Hello?"

"Connie? Con?" It was a woman's voice, so familiar, though Connie was slow to identify it. It wasn't her daughter, it wasn't Ashlyn, so there was an immediate stab of disappointment to experience before she realized... that the woman on the phone was Meredith.

"Meredith?" Connie said.

Meredith said, "Thank God you answered."

What had she done? Why had she said yes? The truth was, Meredith had been on Connie's mind for months. The truth was, Connie felt sorry for Meredith. The truth was, Connie had been closer to Meredith than to any other woman in her entire life — her own mother included, her own daughter included. The truth was, Connie was lonely. She yearned for another person in the room, someone who knew her, who understood her. The truth was, Connie didn't know why she had agreed, but she had agreed.

Connie had balked when she saw the throng of reporters outside Meredith's building. She had nearly cruised on past, but she knew Meredith would be waiting for her in the dark alley behind the building and that to abandon her there would be cruel.

When Connie pulled up, Meredith ran from the back door and leapt into the car. She was wearing the same white button-down blouse, jeans, and flats that Connie had seen her photographed in months earlier when she went to visit Freddy in jail. Connie barely waited for Meredith to shut the door before she hit the gas and reversed out. A photographer got a shot of the car departing; thankfully, Meredith's head had been down. Connie floored it up Park Avenue, although she didn't feel safe until they were off the FDR and on I-95. That was when Meredith had wanted to talk, but Connie had held up her palm and said, "Let's not discuss anything until we're safely in the house on Nantucket."

Though there was much, of course, that she wanted to know.

*   *   *

When the announcement came over the loudspeaker that the ferry was pulling into Nantucket harbor, Connie startled awake. Meredith was in the front seat, and there were two steaming cups of coffee—light, with sugar—snug in the console. Connie and Meredith drank their coffee the same way, a habit learned together at age six during tea parties with Meredith's grandmother, Anna-beth Martin, who unorthodoxly served the little girls real coffee from a silver pot.

Meredith was wearing a baseball hat and sunglasses. When she saw that Connie was awake, she said, "I got coffee. A guy in line stared me down, but he was a foreigner, I think. I heard him speaking Russian."

Connie said, "I don't want to burst your bubble…"

Meredith said, "Believe me, there is no bubble."

Connie said, "You're going to have to be incredibly careful. No one can know you're here with me. No one Russian, no one Swed-ish, I mean no one."

"Except for my attorneys." Meredith took a sip of her coffee. "They have to know where I am. Because I'm still under investiga-tion. Me, and Leo, too."

"Oh, Meredith," Connie said. Connie found herself feeling both concerned and annoyed. Meredith should have told her this before she asked Connie to come get her, right? Would that have changed Connie's mind? And poor Leo, Connie's own godson, one of the greatest kids she had ever known. Still under investiga-tion? But why? Connie refrained from asking the obvious: *Do they have anything to charge you with? Am I going to become some kind of accessory to conspiracy?* Instead, she said, "I almost called Toby last night, to tell him I was bringing you here."

"Toby?" Meredith said.

"Toby, yes."

"Do you mind if I ask where he is?"

Connie metered her breath. She said, "He's in Annapolis, running a wildly successful charter sail business. In the winter, he takes off and barefoots through the Caribbean."

"Meaning he sleeps with models half his age in Saint Barth's," Meredith said.

Connie couldn't tell if Meredith was being playful or bitter. She decided to go with playful. "I'm sure that's correct," Connie said. "He's never really grown up. But that's what we love about him, right?"

Meredith bleated. *Ha.* Connie felt the old ambivalence about Meredith and Toby's long-ago relationship return. There was jealousy—once Meredith had fallen in love with Toby, he had become far more important to Meredith than Connie was; there was guilt that Toby had so mercilessly trampled Meredith's feelings; there was disbelief that all these years later, Meredith still cared about him. Even after Meredith was married to Freddy and ludicrously wealthy with her twenty houses and her fleet of Rolls-Royces and a private jet for every day of the week, she always asked: How is Toby? Is he still married? Dating anyone? Does he ever ask about me?

"Listen," Connie said. It was weird having Meredith next to her like this. There was so much shared history—years and years and years, and many of those years they had been together every single day—and yet so much had changed. "I know you don't have anywhere else to go. But it's possible that this won't work. I'll be miserable, you'll be miserable, we won't be able to mend the friendship. You're under investigation, but *I* can't be under investigation. You understand that? If anything happens that I'm not comfortable with, you'll have to leave. You'll have to find your own way."

Meredith nodded solemnly, and Connie hated herself for sounding harsh.

"But I want to try it," Connie said. "I want to give you a place to rest your mind. I want to spend time with you. I'm not completely selfless, Meredith. I'm lonely, too. I've been lonely every hour of every day since Wolf died. Ashlyn has made herself a stranger to

me. We don't speak. There was a misunderstanding at the funeral."
Connie shook her head. She didn't want to think about that. "She
has no idea how cruel she's being. She won't understand until she
has children of her own."

"I'm sorry," Meredith said. "If it makes you feel any better, I'm
not allowed to contact either of the boys because of the ongoing
investigation. And although Freddy isn't dead, he might as well be."

There was symmetry in their situations, but Connie didn't want
to contrast and compare to determine whose situation was worse.
Thankfully, at that moment, the cars in front of hers started pulling off the ferry, and Connie edged the Escalade forward. As she
did so, the panorama of Nantucket in the morning sun was
revealed: blue sky, gray-shingled houses, the gold-domed clock
tower of the Unitarian Church. Meredith had owned homes in
glamorous places—before their falling out, Connie had been to
visit her in Palm Beach and Cap d'Antibes—but for Connie, the
vista of Nantucket Island was the most breathtaking in the world.

"Wow," Meredith whispered.

"Get down," Connie advised. "Just in case."

There were no cameras, no satellite trucks, no reporters—just
the relaxed pace of a Friday morning in early July on Nantucket.
There were tourists on Steamship Wharf and the usual crowd on
"the strip"—people ordering sandwiches for the beach, renting
bicycles, getting their surfboards waxed at Indian Summer. Connie drove past the Nantucket Whaling Museum. Wolf had loved
the whaling museum; he had been a maritime buff, reading all of
Nathaniel Philbrick's books and everything by Patrick O'Brian.
Wolf's family had owned the land on Nantucket for generations,
and when Connie and Wolf had the money, they tore down the
simple cottage that sat on three acres of beachfront land and built
a proper house.

The house was located in the hinterlands of Tom Nevers. When
Wolf and Connie mentioned that they lived in Tom Nevers, people
who knew the island said, "Really? All the way *out there?*"

It was true that Tom Nevers was "out there" by island standards. It was a six-mile journey down the Milestone Road, and it wasn't as chic as the village of Sconset, nor was it as prestigious as owning a home that fronted the harbor. Tom Nevers had no restaurants and no shopping; to get coffee and the paper, Connie had to drive to Sconset. Because Tom Nevers faced southeast, it was frequently blanketed in fog, even when the rest of the island was bright and sunny. But Connie loved the peace and quiet, the rugged, deserted beach, and the friendly seal that swam offshore. She loved the low horizon and the simplicity of the other houses. Tom Nevers wasn't glamorous, but it was home.

As soon as Connie turned into their long, dirt driveway (marked by a weathered wooden plank that said "Flute") she told Meredith it was okay to sit up.

"Wow," Meredith said again. The driveway was bordered on either side by eelgrass and wind-flattened Spanish olive trees. They drove on, and Connie wondered what Meredith was thinking. It had been a sensitive topic—long before the thing with Wolf and the money—that Meredith and Freddy had never deigned to visit Wolf and Connie here on Nantucket. Meredith had promised to visit the summer after she graduated from college; she had been on her way with her bus and boat tickets already booked, but she'd canceled at the last minute because of Freddy. And then once Meredith and Freddy were married, Meredith became wrapped up with her fabulous life in the Hamptons.

The house came into view, and the ocean beyond.

Meredith said, "My God, Connie, it's *huge*. It's *magnificent*."

Connie felt a bloom of pride, which she knew she should usher away. They had learned, hadn't they, that material things were evanescent. Meredith had once had everything in the world; now, she had nothing. And yet, Connie couldn't help feeling a certain satisfaction. It had forever been the case that Connie was considered the pretty one, Meredith the smart one. Connie had been given a life filled with love; Meredith had been given a life filled with fortune: money, places, things, and experiences beyond one's wildest dreams. Meredith's home in Palm Beach had once been owned by the Pulitzers. Meredith had hosted Donald and Ivanka for dinner; Jimmy Buffett had sung to her on her fortieth birthday. It was rumored that she even had a star in the heavens named for her.

In the face of this, wasn't it okay for Connie to feel pleasure that Meredith was impressed by the house? It *was* huge; it *was* magnificent.

It was, alas, empty.

That was the thought that met Connie when she opened the front door. Connie's footsteps echoed in the two-story foyer. The floors were made from white tumbled marble, and there was a curved staircase to the right that swept up the wall like the inside of a nautilus shell. The house had been Wolf's design.

Wolf was dead. He would never walk into this house again. This reality hit Connie anew in a way that felt unfair. It had been two and a half years; friends and acquaintances had told Connie that life would get incrementally easier, her sorrow would fade, but that day hadn't come.

Connie struggled for a breath. Beside her, Meredith looked very small and overwhelmed, and Connie thought, *We're a couple of basket cases. Me, once voted "Prettiest and Most Popular." Meredith, once voted "Most Likely to Succeed."*

Connie said, "Let me show you around."

She led Meredith through the foyer into the great room, which ran the whole length of the house, and flooded with rosy light at dawn. To the left was the kitchen: maple cabinets fronted with glass, countertops fashioned from blue granite. The kitchen had every bell and whistle because Connie was a gourmet cook. There was an eight-burner Garland stove, a porcelain farmer's sink, a wine refrigerator, double ovens, a custom-made extra-wide dish-washer, a backsplash of cobalt and white Italian tile that she and Wolf had found on their trek through Cinque Terre. The kitchen flowed into the dining room, which was furnished with a glossy cherrywood table and twelve chairs. Beyond a break for the double doors that led to the back deck was the living area, also decorated in white and blue. At the end of the room was a white brick fireplace with a massive mantel made of driftwood that Wolf's grandfather had found on their beach after Hurricane Donna in 1960.

"It's wonderful," Meredith said. "Who decorated?"

"I did," Connie said.

"I never decorated a thing in my life," Meredith said. "We always had Samantha." She wandered to the far end of the living room, where Wolf's barometer collection lined the shelves. "That always felt like a privilege, you know, to have Samantha pick things out for us, put things together, create a style for us. But it was phony, like everything else." She touched the spines of Wolf's books. "I like this so much better. This room is you and Wolf and Ashlyn."

"Yes," Connie said. "It is. It was. It's hard, you know." She smiled wistfully. She was happy not to be alone, but it was excruciating to hear Meredith repeating the things that Connie found it impossible to say. "Shall we go down to the water?"

It was particularly hard to be on the beach, because that was where she'd scattered Wolf's ashes two summers earlier in the presence of Wolf's brother, Jake, and his wife, Iris, and Toby, who had used the memorial on Nantucket as an opportunity for his last ridiculous bender. As Connie and Meredith left footprints in the wet sand—the tide was low—Connie wondered where the remains of Wolfgang Charles Flute were now. He had been a whole, warm, loving man with impressive height—Wolf was nearly six foot seven—and a baritone voice, a keen intellect, a crackerjack eye. He had been the owner of an architectural firm that built civic office buildings in Washington that were considered innovative, yet traditional enough to hold their own against the monuments. He had been a busy man, an important man, if not particularly powerful by Washington standards or wealthy by Wall Street standards. The best thing about Wolf had been the balanced attention he gave to every aspect of his life. He'd helped Ashlyn make the most dazzling school projects; he had mixed a shockingly cold and delicious martini; he had been a fanatic about the unicycle (which he learned to ride as an undergraduate at Brown) as well as paddleball, tennis, and sailing. He had collected antique sextants and barometers. He had studied astronomy and believed the placement of the stars in the sky could teach man about terrestrial design. Wolf had always been emotionally present in Connie's life, even when he was working on deadline. On days he had to work late—and there had been two or three a month—he sent flowers, or he invited Connie to come to his office for a candlelight dinner of Indian take-out. When Connie went out with her women friends, he always sent wine to the table and the other women cooed about how lucky Connie was.

But where was he now? He had died of brain cancer, and Connie had followed his wish to be cremated and have his ashes scattered off the beach in Tom Nevers. The ashes had broken down, disintegrated; they had become molecules suspended in seawater. The body that Wolf had inhabited, therefore, was gone; it had been absorbed back into the earth. But Connie thought of him as here somewhere, here in this water swirling around her ankles.

Meredith waded to midshin. The water was still too cold for Connie, but Meredith seemed to be enjoying it. The expression on her face fell somewhere between rapture and devastation. She spoke in a voice full of tears, though as the *New York Post* promised, her eyes remained dry.

"I never thought I'd put my feet in the ocean again."

Connie nodded once.

Meredith said, "How do I thank you for this? I have nothing."

Connie hugged Meredith. She was tiny, like a doll. Once, in high school, they had gotten drunk at a party at Villanova, and Connie had carried Meredith home on her back. "I want nothing," Connie said.

That was a lovely little *Beaches* moment down by the water, Connie thought, and it did feel good to have company and it did feel good to have Meredith indebted to her for life, but the magnitude of what Connie had done was now sinking in. Her best friend from childhood was married to the biggest crook the world had ever known. Meredith was *persona non grata* everywhere. She had millions of disapprovers and thousands of enemies. She was "still under investigation." The "still" made it seem like being under investigation was a temporary condition that would be cleared up, but what if it wasn't? What if Meredith was found guilty? What if Meredith *was* guilty?

What have I done? Connie thought. *What have I done?*

Meredith settled into her room—a simple guest room with white wainscoting and a small private bath. Both bedroom and bath were done in pinks, decorated by Connie herself with help from Wolf and the woman at Marine Home Center. The bedroom had French doors that opened onto a tight, Romeo-and-Juliet-type balcony. Meredith said she loved the room.

"My room is down the hall," Connie said. The "room" she was speaking of was the master suite, which comprised the western half of the second floor. There was the bedroom with its California king bed that faced the ocean; there was a bathroom with a deep Jacuzzi tub, glassed-in rainfall shower, dual sinks, water closet, heated tiles in the floor, a wall of mirrors, and a scale that generously dropped a pound or two. There were two enormous closets. (Last summer, Connie had finally taken Wolf's summer clothes to the hospital thrift shop.) And there was Wolf's study, complete with drafting table, framed oceanographic maps, and a telescope that had been positioned to view the most interesting summer constellations. Connie didn't have the emotional strength to show Meredith the master suite, and the fact of the matter was, she hadn't spent a single night in her own bed since Wolf died. Every night she had been on Nantucket, she had fallen asleep, with the aid of two or three chardonnays, on the sofa downstairs— or, when she had houseguests, on the bottom bunk of the third-floor bedroom, which she was pointlessly preserving for future grandchildren.

She didn't want to sleep in the bed without Wolf. The same held true at home. She couldn't explain it. She had read somewhere that the death of a spouse was number one on a list of things that caused stress—and what had she done that morning but invited more stress into her life?

"I have to go to the grocery store," Connie said.

Meredith said, "Would it be all right if I came along?"

Connie watched Meredith bouncing on her toes, as she used to on the end of a diving board.

"Okay," Connie said. "But you have to wear your hat and glasses." Connie was terrified of getting caught. What would happen if someone discovered that Meredith Delinn was *here*, living with *Connie?*

"Hat and glasses," Meredith said.

Connie drove the six miles to Stop & Shop while Meredith made a list on a pad of paper braced against her thigh. Connie's fear subsided and a sense of well-being sneaked up on her, which she normally only experienced after a very good massage and three glasses of chardonnay. She opened the sunroof, and fresh air rushed in as she turned up the radio—Queen, singing "We Are the Champions," the victory song of the Merion Mercy field-hockey team, which she and Meredith had both played on for four years. Connie grinned and Meredith turned her face toward the sun, and the car was a happy place for a moment.

In the store, Connie sent Meredith for whole-wheat tortillas and Greek yogurt while she waited at the deli counter. She sent Meredith for laundry detergent, rubber gloves, and sponges, but then Meredith was gone for so long that Connie panicked. She raced through the store with her cart, dodging the other shoppers and their small children, everyone moving at a snail's pace, drugged by the effects of the sea air and sun. Where was Meredith? Connie was hesitant to call out her name. It was unlikely that she'd left the store, so what was Connie afraid of? She was afraid that Meredith had been handcuffed by FBI agents. Meredith should rightly be in the aisle with the Windex and the paper towels, but she wasn't there, nor was she in the next aisle, nor the next. Connie had only had her old friend back for a matter of hours, and now she was missing. And Connie wasn't even sure that she wanted Meredith to stay—so why was she now panicking that Meredith was gone?

Connie found Meredith standing in the bread aisle, holding a bag of kaiser rolls.

Connie flooded with relief, then thought, *This is ridiculous. I have to get a grip.* "Oh, good," she said. "I thought I'd lost you."

Meredith said, "There was a *USA Today* photographer who staked out the Gristedes by my house, and there was a guy from the *National Enquirer* who frequented the D'Agostino down the street. I couldn't go shopping for eggs. Or toothpaste."

Connie took the rolls from Meredith's hands and dropped them in the cart. "Well, no one's following you here."

"Yet," Meredith said, adjusting her sunglasses.

"Right. Let's not press our luck." Connie headed for the checkout. She was grateful not to know anyone in the store. She and Wolf had made a conscious decision not to engage in Nantucket's social scene. They attended parties and benefits and dinners at home in Washington all year long, and Nantucket was a break from that, although Wolf still had a few friends on Nantucket from summers growing up. His parents and grandparents had belonged to the Nantucket Yacht Club, and once or twice a summer Wolf was called on to sail, or he and Connie were invited to a cocktail party or barbecue in the garden of a friend's ancestral summer cottage. But for the most part, Connie and Wolf kept to themselves. Although she had been coming to Nantucket for over twenty years, Connie often felt anonymous. She knew no one and no one knew her.

As they stood in line, Meredith handed Connie three twenty-dollar bills. "I'd like to chip in for expenses."

Connie considered waving the money away. The television

reporters had made it clear that—unless there was a cache of funds at some offshore bank—Meredith Delinn had been left penniless. "Do what you can," Connie said. "But there's no pressure."

"Okay," Meredith whispered.

On their way back to Tom Nevers, Connie noticed a commotion at the rotary. News vans were clustered in the parking lot of the *Inquirer and Mirror,* the island newspaper. Connie did a double take. *Were* those news vans?

"Get down," Connie said. "Those are reporters." She checked the rearview mirror. "CNN, ABC."

Meredith bent in half; she was as low as the seatbelt would allow. "You're kidding," she said.

"I kid you not."

"I can't believe this," Meredith said. "I can't believe they care where I am. Well, of course they care where I am. Of course the whole world needs to know that I am now summering on Nantucket. So they can make me look bad. So they can make it seem like I'm still living a life of luxury."

"Which you are," Connie said, trying to smile.

"Why couldn't you live someplace awful?" Meredith said. "Why couldn't you live in East Saint Louis? Why couldn't they be reporting that Mrs. Delinn was spending the summer in hot and dangerous East Saint Louis?"

"This isn't funny," Connie said. She checked her rearview mirror. The road behind them was clear. Connie checked again. "Well, guess what. They're not following us."

"They're not?"

Connie motored on. She felt the teensiest bit disappointed. "False alarm, I guess." She tried to think why there would have been TV vans at the rotary, and then she remembered a third- or fourth-tier news story, buried way beneath the sentencing of Freddy Delinn. "Oh, that's right!" she said. "The president is here this weekend!"

Meredith sat up. "You scared me." She was doing some audible

Lamaze breathing to calm herself down, and Connie remembered when Meredith was in the hospital after giving birth to Leo. Connie had taken two-year-old Ashlyn to the hospital to see Meredith and the baby. Freddy had been as proud as a goddamned rooster, handing out expensive (not to mention illegal) Cuban cigars; he'd pushed one on Connie, saying, "Go home and give it to Wolf. He's going to love it." Connie remembered feeling jealous that giving birth had come so easily for Meredith (Connie had slogged through twenty-three hours of labor with Ashlyn and she'd suffered a uterine rupture, which precluded her from having any more children). Meredith had said, "Thank God, Freddy got his boy and the hallowed Delinn name will live on." This had upset Connie; she had felt defensive that Ashlyn was a girl and that there would be no more children to carry on the hallowed Flute name. Feeling bad about this led to resentment that, while Connie had made the trip from Bethesda to New York to see Meredith in the hospital, Meredith hadn't made the reverse trip two years earlier when Ashlyn was born. It was amazing how memories intruded like that. It was amazing how Connie's mind held the good and the bad of every interaction, swirled together like children's paints. Meredith might only remember happiness that Connie had come, or recall the cute outfit that Connie had brought. When Meredith thought of Leo being born, she might only think, *Leo is under investigation.*

Connie turned into her driveway and parked in front of the house. Meredith scrambled to get the groceries out of the car.

"You go in and relax," Meredith said. "I'll get these."

Connie laughed. "You're not an indentured servant," she said. "But thank you for the help."

She flashed back to that day at the hospital. Meredith had allowed Ashlyn to hold her hours-old infant, even though the head nurse strongly advised against it. *It'll be fine!* Meredith had said. *Connie and I will be right here.* Meredith had snapped the pictures herself. She'd had one framed and sent it to Connie. And then, of course, she'd asked Connie to be Leo's godmother.

"It's nice to have someone else around," Connie said.

"Even me?" Meredith said.

"Even you," Connie said.

MEREDITH

At ten minutes to five, Meredith couldn't put it off any longer: she had to call her attorneys and give them her coordinates. She was still under investigation. She wasn't allowed to leave the country; the Feds had her passport. Burt and Dev needed to know where she was.

She sat on her bed and turned on her cell phone. This had become a suspenseful moment in Meredith's daily routine: Had anyone called her? Had anyone texted her? Would Carver and Leo break the rules and text her the *I love you* that she so desperately needed? Had any of Meredith's former friends found enough compassion in their hearts to reach out? Would she hear from Samantha? Had Burt or Dev called? Did they have good news or bad news? How bad was the bad news? Would this be the moment when Meredith received the worst news? Indeed, the reason Meredith kept her phone turned off was to limit the torture to this one moment, instead of living with it all day long.

There were no messages and no texts. This presented its own kind of misery.

She dialed the law firm and said a Hail Mary, which was what she always did when she dialed the law firm. She could hear the sounds of Connie making dinner downstairs.

Meredith had thought she might feel safer on Nantucket, but she was plagued by a low-grade terror. Nantucket was an *island,* thirty miles out to sea. What if she needed to escape? There would be no hopping in a cab uptown or downtown or across the bridge or through the tunnel into New Jersey. There would be no high-tailing it to Connecticut if Leo or Carver needed her. She felt both exiled and trapped.

Meredith had $46,000 of her own money. This was the savings that she'd tucked away in a CD earning 1.5 percent, from her teaching job in the 1980s. (Freddy had ridiculed her for this. *Let me invest it,* he'd said. *I'll double it in six months.*) But Meredith had kept rolling over the money in that CD for no reason other than personal pride—and how relieved she was now! She had something to live on, actual legitimate money that she'd earned and banked. Forty-six thousand dollars would seem a fortune to many people, she knew, but to her it felt like a pittance. She had run through that much in an afternoon of antiques shopping. *Disgusting!* she thought as the phone rang. *How had she become that person?*

The receptionist answered.

"May I speak with Burton Penn, please?" Meredith asked.

"May I ask who's calling?" the receptionist said.

Meredith cringed. She hated identifying herself. "Meredith Delinn."

The receptionist didn't respond. The receptionist never responded, though Meredith had called and spoken to this self-same receptionist dozens of times.

The phone rang. Although Meredith had asked for Burt, the person who answered the phone was Dev.

"Hi Dev," Meredith said. "It's Meredith."

"Thank God," Dev said. "I was just about to call your cell. Where are you?"

"I'm on Nantucket," Meredith said.

"Nantucket?" Dev said, "What are you doing on Nantucket?"

"I'm with a friend," Meredith said.

Dev made a noise of surprise. Clearly, he had been under the impression that Meredith didn't have any friends. And he was right. But Meredith had Connie. Was Connie her friend? Connie was something; Meredith wasn't sure what.

"What's the address there?" Dev asked.

"I have no idea."

"Phone number? Please, Meredith, give me *something.* The Feds want us to have contact information for you on the ground."

Meredith had written down the phone number at the house. She recited it to Dev.

He said, "First things first. I'm glad you're safe." Meredith smiled. Dev was one person, aside from her sons, who didn't want to see her jump off the George Washington Bridge. Her other attorney, Burt, would never have expressed this kind of sentiment. Burt didn't dislike Meredith, but he was detached. She was a case, a legal problem. She was work.

Dev said, "I heard from Warden Carmell at the MCC, and he said Mr. Delinn was shipped out on the bus at noon. Ten hours down to Butner. He's due to arrive tonight."

Meredith closed her eyes. When her attorneys had called her to tell her Freddy had been given the maximum sentence, Meredith hadn't been sure what they meant. She had turned on the TV and saw Freddy being led out of the courtroom in his light-gray suit, which no longer fit. The banner across the bottom of the screen read: *Delinn sentenced to 150 years.* Meredith had run for the kitchen sink, where she vomited up the half cup of tea she'd managed to ingest that morning. She heard a noise and she thought it was the TV, but it was the phone. She'd dropped the phone on the ground, and Burt was calling out, "Meredith, are you there? Hello? Hello?" Meredith hung up the phone and shut off the TV. She was done.

She had gone into her bedroom and fallen back onto her king-size bed. She had sixteen hours until federal marshals came to escort her from her home and she would have to give up the sheets, which were as crisp as paper, the luscious silk quilt, the sumptuous down-filled duvet.

One hundred and fifty years.

Meredith had understood then that Freddy had taken her hand

at the edge of a giant hole, and he had asked her to jump with him, and she had agreed. She'd jumped without knowing how deep the hole was or what would happen when they hit the bottom.

"Okay," Meredith said to Dev now, although obviously the fact that Freddy was going to prison for two or three lifetimes wasn't okay. She was so angry with Freddy that she wanted to rip her hair out, but the thought of him on that bus crushed her.

"The sticking point with your investigation..."

"I know the sticking point."

"They can't seem to get past it," Dev said. "Do you have anything to add?"

"Nothing to add," Meredith said.

"Anything to amend?"

"Nothing to amend."

"You know how bad it looks?" Dev said. "Fifteen million dollars is a lot of money, Meredith."

"I have nothing to add or amend," Meredith said. "I told it all in my deposition. Do they think I *lied* in my deposition?"

"They think you lied in your deposition," Dev said. "Lots of people do."

"Well, I didn't," Meredith said.

"Okay," Dev said, but he didn't sound convinced. "If you think of anything you want to add or amend, just call. Otherwise, we'll be in touch."

"What about Leo?" Meredith said. "Please tell me about Leo."

"I didn't hear from Julie today," Dev said. Julie Schwarz was Leo's attorney. It was her job, now, to help federal investigators find Mrs. Misurelli, and to prove that Deacon Rapp was lying. "And days that I don't hear from Julie are good days, much as I love her. It just means there's no news. And as they say, no news is..."

"Right," Meredith said. She wasn't going to utter the words "good news." Not until she and Leo and Carver were free and clear. And together.

Goddamn you, Freddy! she thought (zillionth and first).

A voice rang out from downstairs: it was Connie, calling her for dinner.

They sat at a round teak table on the deck and gazed out at the indifferent ocean. The ocean didn't care whether mankind lived or died or cheated or stole; it just kept rolling and tumbling over itself, encroaching, then receding.

Connie had poured herself a glass of wine. She said, "Meredith, do you want wine?"

"Do you have any red?"

"Of course I have red," Connie said, standing up.

"No, wait. I don't want it," Meredith said. The chicken was cooking on the grill, and it smelled far more delicious than anything Meredith had eaten in months. Meredith would have loved a glass of red to go with the chicken and the fresh, delicious salad that they were now eating—Connie had whipped up the vinaigrette while Meredith looked on, astonished—but drinking a glass of red wine would put Meredith right back at her usual table at Rinaldo's, next to Freddy.

"You're sure?"

"I'm sure." Meredith squinted out at the water. She saw a sleek, black head out about twenty yards. "Do you have seals?"

"That's Harold," Connie said. "Our seal. He's always here."

Meredith watched Harold swim through the breaking waves, then she noticed Connie's downcast eyes.

"Are you okay?" Meredith asked.

Connie took a sip of her wine and nodded, but her eyes were shining. *Our seal:* she was thinking about Wolf. Meredith wanted to take Connie's hand, but she wasn't sure how that kind of gesture would be received.

Connie sniffed. "Tell me something."

"What?" Meredith said.

"I don't know. Anything," Connie said. "We have to start somewhere."

Instinctively, Meredith checked her wrist. For her birthday in October, Freddy had given her a tiger-striped Cartier watch, but Meredith had been required to leave behind any personal effects purchased in the past twelve months worth more than three hundred dollars. She said, "Well, as we speak, Freddy is on the bus for Butner. He'll get there at ten o'clock tonight."

"Jesus," Connie said.

"What he did was awful," Meredith said. She swallowed, and wished for that wine, but she took a sip of ice water instead. Her glass of ice water had a paper-thin slice of lemon in it. Things at Connie's house were nice like that. What had Meredith done to deserve this? Freddy was, at that very moment, on some bus to North Carolina, his hands and feet shackled in heavy iron cuffs. The bus driver probably stopped for bathroom breaks every four hours or so. If Freddy couldn't hold it, he would wet himself, and the other prisoners would love that. Meredith tensed with worry, as she might have for one of her children. Freddy suffered from a weak bladder. Recently, Meredith wondered if this had been a side effect from carrying around so much stress, fear, and guilt. Maybe now that he'd confessed, his bladder was sturdier. "I went to see him in jail."

"I know," Connie said. "I saw it on TV. I mean, I saw you headed down there."

"It was a disaster," Meredith said. "In retrospect, I shouldn't have gone. But I wanted to see him."

After the police hauled Freddy away on the afternoon of December 8, Meredith had found herself thinking of him in the past tense, as though he were dead—but he was alive, only a few miles away at the Metropolitan Correctional Center, which was connected to the federal courthouse by an underground tunnel. Meredith could go visit him. But should she? As the weeks passed, she went back and forth on this question. Absolutely not. But yes, she had to; there were so many things to ask. She wasn't sure how it would look to the rest of the world. She couldn't decide. She asked her attorneys.

"Should I go see Freddy in jail?" she said. "Or should I follow my sons' example and cut him out of my life?"

They stumbled over each other trying to answer. Dev, she could tell, wanted her to forsake the old man. *What can he do for you now? He's ruined you along with everyone else.* Burt, on the other hand, was more orthodox.

"I'm not your publicist," Burt said. "I'm your attorney. So it's my job to tell you that you have a legal right to visit your husband." He handed her a sheet of paper. "Visiting hours are Mondays between nine and eleven. The visit can last up to an hour."

"Can I bring him anything? What does he need?"

Burt cleared his throat. "They're pretty strict about what will make it through security down there." The way he said this sounded vague. It sounded as if there were pages and pages of regulations, but Burt had yet to grow familiar with them. Had Burt ever *had* a client in jail before? Meredith wouldn't embarrass him by asking point-blank. "Quarters are good."

"Quarters?"

"Rolls of quarters," Burt said. "For the vending machines."

"For the vending machines," Meredith repeated. She thought about Freddy selecting a bag of Doritos or a package of Twinkies from a vending machine, and a part of her died. But what did she think he was eating in there? Salad caprese?

She decided not to go. The only way she could ever hope to save herself was to do what her children had done: denounce Freddy and the life they'd led together. When Leo and Carver found out about Freddy's crimes, they had roared in anger, and Freddy sat impassively, offering them nothing to combat the fact that they were the sons of a thief and a pathological liar. They had stormed out of the apartment, and Meredith understood now, though she hadn't at the time, that the boys had expected her to go with them. But she had stayed by Freddy's side, because that was where her rut had been dug for the past thirty years. She couldn't leave Freddy until this was figured out. Leo had said, *What precisely do you need to figure out, Mom? Dad is a thief. He's a criminal! He has committed financial genocide!* Carver said, *We're changing our name. You should, too.*

Meredith knew she should make a statement, do an interview with Barbara Walters, if Barbara would have her. Explain the truth as she understood it, even though nobody on God's green earth would believe her.

Weeks passed, then months. Meredith stuck to her resolve. Don't think about Freddy. Pretend Freddy is dead. But as the evidence materialized against her, and then against Leo, Meredith realized her best hope lay in going to see him. She needed answers. There was the matter of the money: The money the Feds knew about, and the money they didn't. He had to give it back—all of it. He understood this, right? How long had the Ponzi scheme been going on? Since the beginning? Had Delinn Enterprises *ever* been fully legitimate? Wasn't there some way to prove that Leo was innocent, that Deacon Rapp was lying about Leo? Couldn't Freddy give up the names of the people who had conspired with him in order to save his son? Meredith started scribbling out a list of questions. She had eighty-four. Eighty-four questions that required answers, including a question about why Freddy had been touching Samantha's back that day.

To the jail, Meredith had worn jeans and a white button-down shirt and suede flats and her trench coat, and she carried a clutch purse with two rolls of quarters inside. Her hair hadn't been colored in months, and there had been no trips to Palm Beach, so she was graying and her skin was the color of paste. She wore no makeup—she couldn't insult the American public by bothering with mascara—although she knew that by not prettying herself, she would invite the press to comment on how worn-out she looked. Well, she *was* worn-out. The mob of photographers and reporters was waiting for her, snapping pictures, sticking microphones in her face, but Burt and Dev were there to fend them off and hail her a cab.

Later, she would wish she'd stayed in the relative safety of her apartment.

There had been a terrific wait to get in to see Freddy, during which Meredith experienced thirty-one flavors of anxiety. Burt and Dev were with her—together, they were costing her nine hundred dollars an hour, though how she would ever pay them, she had no idea. Burt checked his BlackBerry with a compulsivity that unsettled Meredith. Dev paged restlessly through an outdated *National Geographic* from the sad, wobbly lounge table that was scarred with other people's initials. He then set the magazine down and studied the other denizens of the waiting room—the men and women who looked even more hopeless and lost than Meredith felt—as though he were going to put them in a novel. They didn't speak until Meredith was called to go through security, when both Burt and Dev wished her luck. They weren't going in with her. Security was another long and arduous process where Meredith and her clutch and trench coat were subjected to scrutiny. Meredith was patted down—roughly—by a female officer twice her size. The woman did everything but pick Meredith up, turn her upside down, and shake her. She didn't say so, but she must have recognized Meredith and felt the predictable contempt. At the end, she shoved Meredith, just for fun.

Meredith didn't protest. She was too nervous to protest because she was being escorted through locked doors and down long, stark hallways, to see Freddy. Meredith had promised herself she wouldn't break down. She would fight off sentimentality and longing. She would simply ask Freddy the questions she needed the answers to, maybe not all eighty-four—there wouldn't be time for that—but the top two or three: Where was the rest of the money? What could they do to clear Leo's name? How could she prove to the world she was innocent? At this point, Freddy was the only person who could help her.

When she finally did see Freddy, she lost her legs. The guard had her firmly by the arm and kept her upright.

Freddy! A voice inside her head was echoing down a long tunnel.

He was wearing an orange jumpsuit, just like the prisoners they'd seen on countless reruns of *Law & Order;* his hands were cuffed behind his back. His hair, which had been salt-and-pepper curls, was shaved down to the scalp, and nearly white. He was fifty-two; he looked seventy-five. But it was him just the same, the boy who had accosted her in the stacks of the Princeton bookstore. They had been enrolled in the same anthropology course, and Meredith had picked up the last used textbook, thinking she would save her parents some money. Freddy had begged her for it. He'd said, *I can't afford a new textbook, so if you buy that one, I'll have to go without, and if I go without, I'll fail the course. You don't want me to fail the course, do you?* And she'd said, *Who are you?* And he'd said, *I'm Freddy Delinn. Who are you?*

She'd told him her name was Meredith Martin.

He said, *You're very pretty, Meredith Martin, but that's not why I'm asking you for the book. I'm asking you because I'm here on six different scholarships, my mother works at a bottling plant during the day and at Kmart as a cashier at night, and I need that used book.*

Meredith had nodded, taken aback by his candor. Growing up on the Main Line, she had never heard anyone admit to poverty before. She liked his black hair and blue eyes and his pale, smooth skin. She would have mistaken him for just another beautiful, ass-holish upperclassman had it not been for his humility, which pierced her. Meredith had found him instantly intriguing. And he had called her pretty! Toby had broken up with Meredith only a few months earlier, and he had so decimated her self-esteem that she'd been certain no one would ever call her "pretty" again.

She handed Freddy the used book and took a new book, at more than double the price, for herself.

This entire memory was encapsulated in a single moment as she looked at Freddy. Meredith thought, *I never should have given him that book. I should have said, "Tough luck," and walked away.*

The warden released Freddy's wrists from the cuffs so he could talk to Meredith on the phone.

Meredith found herself unable to speak. She didn't pick up the phone and neither did he. He had always believed that Meredith was smarter than he was—true—that she was classier, better bred, more refined. He had always treated her like a rare, one-of-a-kind treasure; he had lived in awe of her. Deep in her heart, she worried—God, how she worried—that he had started all of this as a way to impress her.

She picked up the phone. "Fred."

The guard standing behind Freddy helped him pick up the phone and put it to his ear.

"Fred, it's Meredith." Saying this made her feel idiotic, but she wasn't sure he recognized her. She had pictured him crying, apologizing; she had, at the very least, pictured him expressing his undying love.

He regarded her coolly. She tried to get the guard's attention to ask "Is he okay?" but the guard was staring off into middle space, perhaps willfully, and Meredith couldn't snag him.

"Fred," Meredith said. "I need you to listen to me. I'm in trouble and Leo's in trouble. They're trying to get me on a conspiracy charge." She swallowed. "They think I *knew* about it!" Freddy seemed to be listening, but he didn't respond. "And they think Leo was working with you on the seventeenth floor. Someone named Deacon Rapp told them this." Meredith watched Freddy's face for a flicker of recognition or interest. "Where is the rest of the money, Fred?" She had the list of eighty-four questions in her clutch purse—no one from security had even bothered to look at it—but if he could just tell her this one thing, then she could turn the information over to the Feds, and maybe that would get them off the hook. Even if there wasn't very much left—a few billion or hundreds of millions—to give the Feds this information would help her and Leo. There would be no helping Freddy at this point. "Please tell me where the rest of the money is. An offshore account? Switzerland? The Middle East? It does nobody any good hidden, Freddy."

Freddy removed the receiver from his ear and looked at it like it was something he might eat. Then he set the receiver down on the counter in front of him.

She said, "Freddy, wait! They're going to prosecute me. They're going to prosecute Leo. Our son." Maybe Freddy didn't care about Meredith; she had to acknowledge the possibility that, along with lying about everything else, he had been lying about his devotion to her. But he would never knowingly allow Leo to go to prison.

He stared at her. The Plexiglas between them reminded Meredith of being at the zoo. Freddy was watching her like she was some curious specimen of wildlife.

She tried another tack. "I brought you quarters," she said. "For the vending machines." She held up the quarters, the only thing she had to bargain with.

He tilted his head but said nothing.

"He had no intention of talking to me," Meredith said to Connie. "He wasn't going to explain himself, he wasn't going to give me any answers. He wasn't going to give me anything. He didn't care if I went to prison. He didn't care if Leo went to prison."

Connie said, "He's a bastard, Meredith."

Meredith nodded. She had heard people say this again and again. Her attorneys had said it. Even Freddy's attorney, Richard Cassel, had said it to Meredith, out in the hallway before Meredith's deposition: *You knew he was a bastard when you married him.* But it wasn't that easy. Freddy had been many things during the thirty years of their marriage and a bastard wasn't one of them. Freddy was smart and charming and driven to succeed like nobody Meredith had ever known. And he had made it clear that Meredith was part of his success. How many times had he said it? She was his winning lottery ticket. Without her, he was nothing. She, in turn, had done what any devoted wife would do: she had defended him.

He had returns of 29 percent in good years. Meredith reminded people that he had been the star of the economics department at Princeton. He delivered returns of 8 percent in down years, and people were even happier. Meredith said, "Freddy's got the magic. He understands the stock market like nobody else."

But those who weren't invited to invest with Delinn Enterprises had been jealous, then suspicious. He's lying. He's cheating. He's breaking the law. He's got to be; you just can't deliver returns like that in this economy. Although it was difficult, Meredith learned to snub these people. She took them off the lists of the benefits she was chairing; she had them blackballed from clubs. These actions, now, seemed abominable, but at the time, she had only been defending her husband.

Was Freddy a bastard? Yes—God, yes! Meredith knew it now but didn't understand it. She didn't understand how she had lived with the man for thirty years without knowing him. He had always been generous to a fault; he made good things happen for people. He called the dean of admissions at Princeton to get his secretary's son off the waiting list. He gave a pregnant woman his seat in first class, while he took her seat in coach—on a transatlantic flight! He sent Meredith's mother orchids every year on her birthday without a reminder from Meredith. Was he a bastard? Yes, but he had hidden it well. And that was part of the allure of Freddy Delinn—he came across as mysterious and unknowable. What was it Freddy was hiding in the deep recesses of his mind, behind his kind and generous facade?

Now, of course, Meredith knew. Everyone knew.

Things at the jail had ended badly. Freddy didn't say a single word. He stood up and offered his wrists to the guard like a well-trained monkey—and the guard, without so much as a glance at Meredith, shackled him back up.

"Wait!" Meredith said. She jumped up abruptly, knocking her chair over, and she slapped her palms against the Plexiglas.

"Freddy, wait! Don't leave. Don't you dare leave!" She felt a force on her arms, the guards grabbed her, and she struggled to break free. She shouted, "They're going to throw us in jail, Fred! Your family! You have to fix this! You have to tell them we're innocent!" The guard had her bent over in a half nelson. She screamed. "Freddy! Goddamn it, Fred, tell them!"

The guard led Freddy away. It was no use; there was no getting him back. He was going to let them drown. Meredith's body went limp in the guard's grip; she clapped her mouth shut. She had never, ever raised her voice in public. She thought, *He's drugged.* Or they'd given him a lobotomy or shock treatment. He'd been sitting right there, but he hadn't been himself. He would never willfully let his wife and son go to the gallows.

Would he?

As Meredith was led back down the depressing hallways from whence she'd come, she had to admit: she didn't know.

"So you still haven't spoken to him?" Connie said. "You haven't gotten any answers?"

"No answers," Meredith said. "My attorneys told me that Freddy has stopped speaking altogether. They're diagnosing it as a type of post-traumatic stress disorder."

"Give me a break," Connie said. "Freddy?"

It seemed unlikely. Freddy was tough. He had come from nothing. His father had left the family when Fred was in diapers, then Fred lost his only brother, but he had shored himself up. He didn't believe in things like PTSD. He was a pull-yourself-up-by-your-bootstraps kind of guy. He was a nothing's-gonna-happen-until-you-make-it-happen kind of guy. He had been so hard on the boys, Meredith remembered; they'd had to earn Fred's respect. There were no excuses for bad grades or bad behavior or a missed fly ball. There were no excuses if they forgot a "please" or a "thank you," or if they neglected to hold the door for their mother. *You kids have it so much easier than I had it. You don't even know. You don't know a thing.*

Burt and Dev had confirmed with prison officials that Freddy Delinn had completely shut down. He was spending time in psych, but they couldn't make him talk. He spoke to no one.

"Sometimes prisoners use this as a form of control over their captors," Burt said. "He's like that Indian in *One Flew Over the Cuckoo's Nest*."

So he was being willfully mute, Meredith thought. Which should not be confused with PTSD. He was pulling a Chief Bromden. Had Freddy even read *Cuckoo's Nest*?

"I don't know what to do," Meredith said to Connie. "Freddy is the only one who can save me, and he won't do it."

"Forget Freddy," Connie said. "You're going to have to save yourself."

That night, Meredith didn't sleep. *Goddamn you, Freddy,* she thought (zillionth and second). But she was sick with worry about him. By now, he would be getting adjusted to the horrors of his new, incredibly permanent home. What did it look like? What did it smell like? What did they feed him? Where did he go to the bathroom? Where did he shower?

And how were the boys? Meredith had seen some of the houses that Carver renovated—he favored glorious old Victorians in sad, sagging disrepair. He yanked out carpet and sanded down the long-hidden wood floors beneath. He drove around to architectural salvage places looking for glass doorknobs and stained glass windows. In Meredith's imagination, the boys were living in such a house; it smelled like polyurethane; every surface was coated with sawdust. Carver hung doors while Leo lay across a high-backed sofa, talking to Julie Schwarz on the phone. Meredith knew the Feds had seized his computer and were trying to back up Deacon Rapp's claims and link Leo to the bandits on the seventeenth floor. The Feds were still trying to track down Mrs. Misurelli in Italy so they could depose her. She, apparently, had been the gatekeeper upstairs. In this case, being "under investigation"

for Leo was a lot of sit around and wait. Maybe in his spare time—
and there would now be much of it—Leo helped Carver paint
bedrooms or shingle the roof or repoint the brickwork of the eight
fireplaces. Meredith was certain Anais was around; she had
remained steadfast. She would cook her famous veggie enchiladas
for Leo and Carver, and she would grow jealous about how much
time Leo was spending on the phone with Julie Schwarz.

Meredith was okay picturing the boys like this, although Leo was
a worrier and she knew he'd be having night sweats. For years when
he was a child, Leo had wandered into Meredith and Freddy's bedroom, afraid of the dark. He had a recurring dream about a scary
pelican. Now the scary pelican was real: It was Deacon Rapp, it was
the FBI, it was Freddy. Meredith couldn't stop the unbidden flashes
of Leo in prison, his head shaved, the other men coming after him
day and night with their sick desires. Leo was only twenty-six.

Fear gripped her like hands around the neck, the way it could
only happen in an unfamiliar room in the pitch black of night.
Take me if you must, Meredith thought. *But do not take my son.*

Connie had been right about one thing: Meredith was going to
have to save them herself.

But how? How?

In the morning, Connie said, "I'm going to the Sconset Market for
some muffins and the newspaper. And I'm going to the package
store for a case of wine."

Meredith nodded and tried not to seem like an eager, panting
dog. *Don't leave me here alone,* she thought. *Please.*

"I know you want to come with me," Connie said. "But Sconset
is a tiny village, and everyone who summers there has summered
there forever. Strangers are scrutinized. Someone will ask you
who you are, guaranteed. The Sconset Market is microscopic. So
you're going to have to stay here. We don't want anyone..."

"Right," Meredith whispered. "I know."

"I won't be gone long," Connie said.

*   *   *

Meredith took an old book-club selection of Connie's out onto the deck. She would read in the sun; this was what people did in the summertime. This was what Meredith had done for days on end all those years in Southampton. She had read by her pool, walked to the ocean, swam with the boys and watched them surf; she had pitched the Wiffle ball to them and chased after their grounders. She had thrown the Frisbee to the dog. She had cut flowers from the garden and had given instructions to their housekeeper, Louisa. She had invited people for dinner, and made reservations at Nick and Toni's, and dealt with the details of the various fundraisers she was chairing. Her life had been disgustingly easy; it had, in so many ways, been beneath her. *Brilliant and talented,* her father used to say. And yet, what had she done with it?

Goddamn you, Freddy, she thought (zillionth and third). She tried to concentrate on the words on the page of her book — it was about a woman in a small town who is murdered — but Meredith's mind was squawking. She lived with a bullhorn in her head, loudly announcing and reannouncing her fears; it was the internal soundtrack of extreme anxiety. There was medication for it, perhaps. Meredith wondered if Connie had anything. She didn't want to snoop, but a few minutes after Connie left the house, Meredith padded upstairs to the master suite. She just wanted to see it.

The door that led to the suite was closed tight, and Meredith wouldn't have been surprised or insulted if the door had been locked. After all, Connie was now rooming with the wife of the biggest crook in history. But the door was open, and Meredith tiptoed through the rooms. The bedroom had an arresting view of the ocean, and the bed was made up with Frette linens (Meredith checked, she couldn't help herself, though she knew she shouldn't care about things like thread count anymore). The closets were roomy. Wolf's closet was completely empty except for some padded hangers and a thick, nubby fisherman's sweater folded on the dresser. Meredith touched the sweater, then felt she had, somehow, crossed a line. She didn't look in Connie's closet, though she would have liked to—even as a schoolgirl, Connie had had a flair for fashion. However, Meredith couldn't help from peeking in the master bath—and that was when she saw the prescription bottles. There were four or five of them, and Meredith was sure that one of those prescriptions would help her. She eyed the brown bottles for a long, hot moment, then she made herself retrace her steps and leave the suite, shutting the door behind her.

She wondered if it was a bad thing that Connie had brought her to this beautiful house where she had nothing to do but think. If she had been scrounging half-eaten Big Macs out of a Dumpster, consumed with worry about her daily survival, she wouldn't have this much time to think.

And that might have been better.

Back on the deck, Meredith tried to read. The woman in her novel was worse off than she was; she had been murdered in the woods. The mother of that woman was worse off than she was. But then Meredith realized she *was* that woman. If Leo went to prison, he would be raped, beaten, and eventually killed. She was sure of it. But she had to stop thinking like this. The bullhorn blared in her head. Freddy was in Butner for all eternity. Meredith was here. How had she gotten here?

Before Meredith graduated from high school and attended Princeton and fatefully met Freddy Delinn in the stacks of the campus bookstore, there had been one presiding fact in Meredith's life, and that was that she loved her parents. She had loved her mother, Deidre, certainly, but she had been especially devoted to her father.

Meredith's father's name was Charles Robert Martin, but everybody called him Chick. Chick Martin was a respected lawyer in the downtown Philadelphia firm of Saul, Ewing, Remick, and Saul; he worked on the thirty-eighth floor of the high-rise known throughout the city as the "clothespin building," because of the Claes Oldenburg sculpture out front. Chick specialized in the laws of arbitrage, and although Meredith loved her father to distraction, she had never learned exactly what arbitrage was. (Fred had claimed to understand arbitrage inside out, but it was safe to say he had been bluffing about that.) The way her father explained it, he had very specialized knowledge about a certain portion of the tax code, and his law partners came to him with intricate and tricky questions that he would, after hours of research, produce the answers to.

Chick Martin made a handsome salary. The Martins had an impressive home in Villanova with white columns and black shutters and a wide green lawn in front and back. Inside the house, there were beautiful crown moldings, five working fireplaces, a butler's pantry, and a dumbwaiter that ran from the kitchen to the basement.

Chick Martin was a golfer—the family belonged to the Aronimink Country Club—and a rabid Philadelphia sports fan. He had season tickets to the Eagles, and he would very often be given box seats to see the Phillies at the Vet, or the Flyers or Sixers at the Spectrum. He once took Meredith to a car dealership to shake hands with Dr. J, and the two things that Meredith remembered about that event were that Dr. J's hand was so large it spread halfway up her forearm, and Chick Martin, whom Meredith had believed was the most important man in Philadelphia, had been rendered speechless by the presence of Julius Erving. Meredith had wanted to intervene on her father's behalf and tell Dr. J that her father was a tax attorney who specialized in the difficult, mysterious world of arbitrage, and that it should be Dr. J who was in awe of Chick Martin and not the other way around. Her father had brought a basketball for Dr. J to sign, which he had, in a sprawling script without even really paying attention, but Meredith's father was delighted. He mounted it on a pedestal in his office.

Chick Martin was a guy's guy. There were always other men

around the house at night and on the weekends—other attorneys and executives and business owners who played golf with Chick, or who accepted tickets to the Eagles, or who came over to the house on the last Thursday of every month for poker. Poker in the Martin household was a sacred affair that occurred in the game room and involved cigar smoking and subs delivered from Minella's Diner. On poker nights, Meredith's mother read in her bedroom with the door closed, and Meredith was supposed to do her homework upstairs and go straight to bed. Meredith always broke this rule. She wandered down to the game room, and her father would let her sit on his lap and munch on the dill pickle that accompanied his eggplant parm sub, while he played his hand. When she got older, he pulled up a chair for her and taught her how to read the cards.

The other men accepted Meredith's presence in the room, though she could tell they didn't love it, so she never stayed for more than three hands, and she never asked to play.

Once, when she was just out of the room, the door closing behind her, she heard Mr. Lewis, who was an estate attorney for Blank, Rome, say, "That's a good-looking daughter you got there, Chick."

And Meredith's father said, "Watch your mouth."

And George Wayne, who was a big shot at PSFS and a descendant of General Anthony Wayne, said, "Do you ever wish you'd had a boy, Chickie?"

And Meredith's father said, "Hell, no. I wouldn't trade Meredith in for a hundred boys. That girl is perfection. That girl owns my heart."

Hearing her father speak those words confirmed what Meredith already knew: she was safe. Her father's love was both a cocoon and a rabbit's foot. She would live a happy life.

And, indeed, she did. Her grades were excellent, and she was a natural athlete: she played field hockey and lacrosse, and she was a champion diver. As a diver, she made it to the finals in State College her junior and senior years; in her senior year, she placed third. She'd had interest from Big Ten schools, but she didn't want to carry the burden that a Division I athletic scholarship entailed. She wanted to be well rounded. She edited the yearbook and was a lector during morning chapel. She was *that girl* at Merion Mercy, the girl everyone admired and talked about with near-embarrassing praise.

Meredith was safe, too, because she'd had a best friend since the beginning of time, and that friend was Constance O'Brien. They met at preschool at Tarleton, although Meredith didn't actually remember *meeting* Connie. By the time their synapses connected time and circumstance in a meaningful way, they had already been friends for years, and so it seemed to both girls that they had always been together. They grew up a half mile from each other in the same kind of house, which is to say, Catholic, upper-middle class, civilized but not snobbish. The only difference between the two homes was that Connie's mother, Veronica, drank. And the way Meredith knew that Veronica O'Brien drank was because her own parents talked about it: Veronica went to the Mastersons' party, picked a fight with her husband, Bill, and battled it out with him on the front lawn. Veronica fell down and bruised her hip. She forgot to pay the neighborhood babysitter so many times that the babysitter refused to work there anymore. When Meredith was older, she heard about Veronica O'Brien's drinking from Connie. Her mother left a bottle of vodka in the second fridge in the garage and did three shots before Bill O'Brien came home from work. Veronica committed minor offenses like throwing away Connie's paper on Mark Twain, and major offenses like setting the kitchen drapes on fire. Connie and Toby had learned to keep their friends out of the house. But they took advantage of the money and the freedom their mother bestowed on them while drinking, and when they reached a certain age, they burgled their mother's wine and · vodka and gin and drank it themselves.

Veronica O'Brien's drinking — though it did manifest itself in more insidious ways eventually — did little to hamper Meredith and Connie's childhood happiness together. They were twins, sisters, soul mates. As they got older, however, the peace was harder to keep. They were growing and changing; things grew nuanced. There was one twenty-four-hour period when Meredith and Connie didn't speak. This was right after Meredith told Connie that she, Meredith, had kissed Connie's brother, Toby, on the way home from Wendy Thurber's late-night pool party.

Meredith had dutifully reported every detail to Connie by 8 a.m., just as she would have if Toby had been any other boy—but this time, Connie was disgusted. Meredith and Toby? It was appalling.

Meredith had felt ashamed and confused. She had expected Connie to be happy. But Connie slammed the phone down on Meredith, and when Meredith called back, the phone rang and rang. Meredith kept calling until Veronica answered and pleasantly and soberly explained that Connie didn't want to talk right that second. Meredith should call back later, after Connie had had a chance to calm down.

Meredith was stunned. She hung up the phone and looked out her bedroom window down the street toward Connie's house. She would forfeit Toby, then. She would give him up. It wasn't worth ruining her friendship with Connie.

But here, Meredith faltered. She was a hostage to her feelings and, stronger still, her hormones. She had known Toby O'Brien just as long as she had known Connie, essentially her entire life. They had thrown water balloons at each other in the O'Briens' backyard on hot afternoons, and they had watched horror movies side by side in the O'Briens' shag-carpeted den, eating Jiffy Pop and Jax cheese doodles. Whenever they went somewhere in the O'Briens' Ford Country Squire—to Shakey's for pizza or to the King of Prussia Mall or downtown to Wanamaker's to see the light show at Christmas—Connie, Meredith, and Toby had sat three across in the backseat, and sometimes Meredith's and Toby's knees had knocked, but it had never meant a thing.

How to explain what happened? It was like a switch had flipped and in an instant the world had changed, there in the deep end of Wendy Thurber's pool. There had been a bunch of kids at the party — Wendy, Wendy's brother Hank, Matt Klein, whom Connie was dating (though secretly, because Matt was Jewish and Connie feared her parents would object), Connie, Toby, Meredith, a girl from the field-hockey team named Nadine Dexter, who was chunky and a little butch, and Wendy's runty next-door neighbor Caleb Burns. There was the usual splashing and roughhousing and dunking; all of the kids were in the pool except for Connie, who claimed the water was too cold. She lounged in a chaise wearing her petal-pink Lilly Pulitzer cover-up, and she braided and rebraided her strawberry-blond hair. Meredith impressed everyone with her dives. She had just perfected her front one and half somersault with one and half twists, which was a crowd pleaser.

As the party was starting to wind down, Meredith encountered Toby in the deep end. He had, as a joke, pulled at the string of her bikini top, the top had come loose, and her newly formed breasts — so new they were tender to the touch — were set free, bobbing for a second in the chlorinated water. Meredith yelped and struggled to retie her top while treading water. Toby laughed wickedly. He swam up behind her and grabbed her, and she could feel his erection against her backside, though it took a second to figure out what was happening. Her mind was racing, reconciling what she had learned in health class, what she had read in Judy Blume novels, and the fact that Toby was a seventeen-year-old boy who might just be turned on by her newly formed breasts. Immediately, there was a surge of arousal. In that instant, Meredith became a sexual being. She felt momentarily sorry for her father and her mother, because she was lost to them forever. There was, she understood, no going back.

Connie left the party with Matt Klein. They were off to make out and push at the boundaries of Connie's virginity, though Connie had said she was determined to stay chaste until her sixteenth birthday. Connie talked about her sex life all the time, and up to that point, Meredith had bobbed her head at what felt like the appropriate moments, not having a clue what Connie was talking about but not wanting to admit it. Now, suddenly, she *got* it. Desire.

She dried off and put her shorts and T-shirt back on, then a sweatshirt because it was nighttime and chilly. She took a chip off the snack table but refrained from the onion dip. Caleb Burns's mother called out from next door that it was time for him to go home. Wendy's brother Hank, who was friends with Toby, wanted Toby to stick around, hang out in his room, and listen to Led Zeppelin.

Toby was bare chested with a towel wrapped around his waist. Meredith was afraid to look at him too closely. She was dazzled by how he had suddenly become a different person.

Toby said, "Sorry, man. I have to head out." He and Hank did some kind of complicated handshake that they had either learned from watching *Good Times* on channel 17 or from hanging out on South Street on the weekends. Meredith knew that Toby would walk home—his house was nearby, hers a half a mile farther— not an impossible walk but not convenient either, in the dark. Meredith's parents had said, as always, *Just call if you need a ride home.* But if Meredith called for a ride, she would be missing a critical opportunity.

She said to Wendy and Nadine, who were both attacking the bowl of chips, "I'm going to go, too."

"Really?" Wendy said. She sounded disappointed, but Meredith had expected this. Wendy was a bit of a hanger-on; she was constantly peering over the proverbial fence at Meredith and Connie's friendship. "Where did Connie go?"

"Where do you *think?*" Nadine asked slyly. "She went to get it on with Matt."

Wendy's eyes widened and Meredith shrugged. Wendy had clearly not been introduced to her own sexuality yet, though Nadine had, in whatever form that had taken. (Another girl? Someone from the camp she went to in Michigan?)

Meredith kissed Wendy's cheek like an adult leaving a cocktail party and said, "Thanks for having me."

"You're walking?" Wendy said, sounding worried. "My dad can probably drive you."

"No, I'll walk," Meredith said.

"I can ask him."

"I'm fine," Meredith said. She hurried to the gate. Toby was strolling across the Thurbers' front lawn. He hadn't waited for her and she hadn't gotten out before him. She wondered if she had been imagining his erection, or if she had been flattering herself that the desire had been aimed at her. But if not her, then who? Not pathetic Wendy, and certainly not Nadine with her blocky shoulders and faint mustache. Meredith waved to the other girls and took off down Robinhood Road, trying to seem nonchalant. All this posturing! She wished Toby was behind her. Now it would look like she was chasing him.

When they were three houses away from the Thurbers' and four houses away from the O'Briens', Toby turned around and pretended to be surprised to find Meredith behind him.

"Hey," he called out in a kind of whisper.

She was at a loss for words. She waved. Her hair was damp and when she touched it, she could feel that it held comb marks. The streetlights were on, so there were pools of light followed by abysses of darkness. Across the street, a man walked a golden retriever. It was Frank diStefano, the roofer, a friend of Meredith's father. Oh, boy. But he didn't see her.

Toby stopped in one of the dark spots to wait for her. Her heart was tripping over itself like two left feet. She was excited, scared, nearly breathless. Something was going to *happen* between her and Toby O'Brien. But no, that wasn't possible. Toby was unfathomably cool, a good student and a great athlete, and he was as beautiful as Connie. He had dated the most alluring girl at Radnor—Divinity Michaels—and they had had an end-of-the-year breakup that was as spectacular as a Broadway show, where Divinity threatened to kill herself, and the school counselors and the state police were called in. (There had been simultaneous rumors circulating about Toby and the young French teacher, Mademoiselle Esme, which Connie called "completely idiotic, and yet not beyond Toby.") Earlier that summer, Toby had started "hanging out" with an Indian girl named Ravi, who was a junior at Bryn Mawr. Compared to those girls, what did Meredith have to offer? She was his kid sister's best friend, a completely known quantity, a giant yawn.

And yet...?

Meredith walked along the strip of lawn between the street and the sidewalk, and her feet were coated with grass clippings. She had her flip-flops in her hand and she stopped to put them on, partly as a stall tactic. She kept walking. Toby was leaning up against a tree that was in the front yard of a house where, clearly, no one was home.

"Hey," Toby said, as she approached. "Meredith, come here."

She went to him. He was the same person—sandy hair, green eyes, freckles—but he was new to her.

He seemed nervous, too, but with all of his experience with women, this was impossible.

He said, "Are you walking all the way home?"

She nodded.

He said, "Have you seen Connie?"

"No," Meredith said, gazing down the street. "She went somewhere with Matt."

"I don't know why she doesn't just tell my parents about him," Toby said.

"It's because he's..."

"Jewish," Toby said. "I know. But my parents won't care."

"I told her that," Meredith said. "She doesn't listen."

Toby put both his hands on Meredith's shoulders. "She doesn't listen to you? Her best friend?"

Meredith looked at Toby. This was, for sure, the first time she'd ever seen him. Everything had changed. She shook her head, pretending that she was caught up in the drama of Connie and Matt Klein, though she couldn't have cared less. Just as she was wondering if she should take a step closer to Toby, he pulled her in, as if for a friendly hug.

"Meredith," he said into her hair. Then he said, "Sorry about the pool. About pulling on your suit, I mean."

She could feel his erection again. Again, she thought about health class, Judy Blume, what she had heard other girls say. She was sick with desire. "Oh," she said. "That's okay."

He fumbled with her head, like it was a ball he was trying to get the correct grip on. Then he had one hand on her ear, and he was kissing her, deeply and desperately. And she thought, *Oh, my God, yes! Yes!*

They stood against the tree kissing for twenty minutes? Thirty minutes? They kissed until Toby's hands fell to her hips, he pulled her against him and groaned, and he played with the bottom edge of her sweatshirt as if considering whether or not to lift it, and although Meredith was thinking, *Yes, lift it, lift it,* she pulled away.

She said, "I really have to go. I have a long way to walk."

He said, "Will you go with me tomorrow night to see *Animal House*?"

"Yes," she said.

"Just you and me?" he said. "A date."

"Yes," she said.

He smiled at her and she saw his teeth, straight and white. She had known him through three years of braces and rubber bands. She had known him when his teeth fell out and he left them under his pillow for the tooth fairy. She waved and backed away and he said, "I'll pick you up at seven!"

"Okay!" she said. And she ran all the way home.

But then Connie was mad and wouldn't speak to Meredith on the phone. Meredith considered calling the O'Brien house again, asking to speak to Toby, and telling him the date was off. But Meredith couldn't make herself do that. She was in the grip of a romantic and sexual urge that wouldn't be denied. She liked Toby, and Connie would have to wrap her mind around that. Connie had Matt Klein; they had gone to third base, or nearly. Connie couldn't have Matt and expect Meredith to have nobody; that was unfair. Meredith was sorry it was Toby, but this was a matter of the heart, one beyond her control.

Meredith's eyes drifted closed. It was a welcome change to be thinking about something else, even if that something was Toby O'Brien. Sailing in Annapolis, seducing in Anguilla. At Connie's wedding, Meredith had been close. At Veronica's funeral, even closer. But Meredith hadn't allowed herself to get sucked back in. She had been lucky.

When Meredith woke up, Connie was lying in the chaise next to her, reading.

Meredith thought, *Oh, thank God. She came back.*

They went for a walk on the beach.

Meredith said, "I was thinking about Nadine Dexter and Wendy Thurber. Do you remember the night of Wendy's pool party?"

"Wendy *who?*" Connie said.

Meredith didn't say, *I was remembering the night I first kissed your brother.*

Meredith said, "I'm going in the water."

"Suit yourself," Connie said. "It's too cold for me."

Later, they took outdoor showers, and Meredith put on white shorts and a navy Trina Turk tunic, refugees from her Hamptons closet circa 2007. She went downstairs with her hair still damp. Connie was pouring herself a glass of wine. It was five o'clock. A day hadn't passed that quickly for Meredith since long before Freddy's arrest — but this mere thought triggered a heaviness. She pictured Leo and

Carver with plaster dust sugaring their hair and clothes, sitting on the wide front porch of the imaginary house, drinking a beer. They were okay, Meredith told herself. They were fine.

"Glass of wine?" Connie asked.

Meredith decided she would have a glass of wine; maybe it would help her sleep.

"White or red?" Connie said.

"White, please," Meredith said. She didn't want to think about the Ruffino Chianti, their usual table at Rinaldo's, Freddy saying, *Here comes your poison, Meredith.* Freddy didn't approve of Meredith drinking, and he rarely, if ever, drank himself. He didn't like losing control, he said. Of course, he hadn't always felt that way. He had been a social drinker in college and young adulthood, and then, as his business grew, he had transitioned into abstinence. Now, Meredith knew that you couldn't lie and cheat *and* drink, because what if you let something slip? What if you let the facade crumble? She thought of Freddy throwing back those three shots of Macallan and how shocked she had been. She had known something was wrong then, seventy-two hours before the rest of the world knew. Freddy had turned on her with wild eyes; she had seen the desperation. She thought, *We've lost all our money.* But so what? Easy come, easy go. Freddy had then pulled Meredith into the bedroom and had pushed her down and taken her roughly from behind, as though it were his final act. Meredith remembered feeling raw and panicky and electrified—this was not the perfunctory lovemaking she and Freddy had engaged in for the past decade or so (its lackluster nature owing to the fact, she had assumed, that he was preoccupied with work)—she remembered thinking, *WOW.* They were ruined perhaps, but they still had each other.

That was what she'd thought, then.

Connie handed Meredith a glass of chardonnay and said, "You can go out to the deck."

"Do you need help with dinner?" Meredith asked.

"Don't tell me you've started cooking?" Connie said.

"No," Meredith said. And they laughed. "I ate from cartons every night after Freddy left."

The words "after Freddy left" echoed in the kitchen. Connie poured a stream of olive oil into a stainless steel bowl and started clanging with her whisk.

Meredith said, "I'll go out."

She stepped onto the deck and took a seat at the round teak table. She hadn't heard from Burt and Dev; she never knew if that was good or bad. The sun spangled the water. Let's say good. She might be going to jail, but she wasn't going to jail today.

Out in the water, Meredith saw a sleek, black head, then its body and flippers undulating through the waves. Then she saw a second dark form, moving less gracefully. Meredith squinted; she was wearing her prescription sunglasses, which weren't as strong as her regular horn-rimmed glasses.

She called out to Connie. "Hey, there are two seals today."

"What?" Connie said.

Meredith stood up with her wineglass. She poked her head through the sliding door.

"There are two seals today."

"Really?" Connie said. "I've never seen two before. Only one. Only Harold."

"I saw two," Meredith said. "Harold found a friend."

She smiled at this.

CONNIE

When Connie checked her cell phone in the morning, she saw that she'd missed a phone call during the night. There was no message, just a clattering hang up. Connie checked her display, then gasped. The number itself was unfamiliar, but it was from the 850 area code:

Tallahassee. Which was where Ashlyn practiced medicine. So had Ashlyn called, finally, after twenty-nine months of silence? Connie's hopes were coy, afraid to show themselves. The call had come in at 2:11 a.m., but this told Connie nothing. Ashlyn was a doctor, and doctors kept absurd hours. Connie checked the number again. It was the 850 area code; that was certainly Tallahassee, and Tallahassee was where Ashlyn now lived. So, it was Ashlyn. Was it Ashlyn? Connie was tempted to call the number right back, but it was still early, not quite seven. Should she call at eight? Ten? Should she wait and call tonight? A call at two in the morning might mean Ashlyn was in trouble. Connie decided to call right back, but then she caught herself. This was an opportunity she couldn't afford to blow. She would wait. She would think about it.

Connie stepped out onto the front deck. There was low-lying fog, typical of early July: How many times had the town had to cancel the Fourth of July fireworks? *Ashlyn!* Connie thought. Was it possible? Connie was going out to get muffins and the newspaper from the Sconset Market, a pleasant errand, and now she would think about Ashlyn, a phone call out of the blue.

Connie didn't see the envelope until she had kicked it off the porch and down the stairs. What was it? She picked it up. Manila envelope, closed with a gold clasp, nothing written on it, thin and light, nothing particularly sinister, but Connie got an awful feeling. She thought, *Don't open it!* She thought, *Anthrax!* But that was ridiculous. This was Nantucket; it was a placid, foggy morning. She thought, *An envelope dropped on the porch?* She thought, *Something from the Tom Nevers Neighborhood Association.* They so often left her out because she was a summer resident, whereas most everyone else lived here year-round, but they'd remembered her this time. Potluck dinner or a community yard sale.

She opened the envelope and saw there was a photograph inside, a glossy color photo, five-by-seven, of Meredith, wearing her navy tunic and white shorts, standing on Connie's back porch, holding a glass of wine.

Connie shivered. She looked out at her front yard and thought, *What is this? Who put this here?*

She looked at the photo again. It had been taken the night before. Meredith was turned toward the sliding door and she was smiling.

All day they passed the photograph back and forth between themselves, and when one or the other of them wasn't looking at it, it sat on the dining table like a time bomb.

Meredith had blanched when Connie showed her the photograph. Someone had been out there taking her picture, but where? Meredith thought it was the same guy they'd seen by the Dumpster in the alley behind 824 Park Avenue—he must have followed them all the way from the city!—but Connie made her see this was unlikely, if not impossible. It was someone else.

"The only way they could have gotten that shot of you was from the beach," Connie said. "Did you see anyone walking on the beach?"

"No one," Meredith said.

"Or it could have been taken from the water," Connie said. "Did you see anyone in a boat? Or a kayak?"

"I saw the seals," Meredith said. "That was what I was smiling about, remember? Harold had a friend."

Connie said, "Harold's 'friend' was a photographer in a wet suit. Is that possible?"

"Oh, God," Meredith said. She approached the sliding glass doors, then backed away. "You know what scares me?"

Connie wasn't sure she wanted to know. What scared Connie was the whole thing. Someone taking the picture, someone leaving it for them on the front porch. A person trespassing on her property. Meredith couldn't stay here. She had to go. The whole thing was chilling. Someone was watching them.

"What scares you?" Connie asked.

"If it was just the paparazzi, they wouldn't have left the photograph for us. They would have published it, and we would have woken up this morning, and it would have been splashed across the front of the *Post. HAPPY HOUR FOR MRS. DELINN.*"

"So if it wasn't the paparazzi, who was it?"

"Someone who wants me to know they know I'm here. One of Freddy's enemies. The Russian mob."

"The Russian mob isn't real," Connie said.

"There were Russian investors who lost billions," Meredith said. "There are a lot of people who want Freddy's head. And since they can't get to Freddy, they're coming after me." She looked at Connie. "I'm putting you in danger."

"No," Connie said. "You're not." But she was. She had to go. Connie racked her brain. Meredith had made it clear that she'd lost everybody else in her life. But Connie had friends. Maybe she could ship Meredith quietly off to Bethesda? She could live with Wolf's brother, Jake, and Jake's wife, Iris. Iris was a know-it-all busybody. She had a degree in psychology from the University of Delaware and she was constantly expressing concern over others' "general state of mind," and especially Connie's, since Connie had recently lost her husband and her daughter and, in Iris's estimation, wasn't doing terribly well. Connie would take great pleasure in inflicting Meredith on Iris, but she couldn't bring herself to inflict Iris on Meredith. There was Toby? God, no, that could backfire in any one of a hundred ways. Plus, if Meredith left, Connie would be alone, and the absolute best thing about the past two days was that, for the first time in years, Connie hadn't been alone.

Connie flung open the sliding door, and Meredith scurried to the other side of the room, as though she were a vampire, allergic to daylight. Connie went outside and stood on the deck. The jig was up. Meredith was here. Connie wanted to face the ocean and anyone hiding in it and shout, *She's here! Meredith Delinn is here!* The world could tell Connie she was unstable, insane, or just plain stupid, but at that moment, she made a decision: Meredith was staying.

*   *   *

Meredith was afraid to read on the deck. Meredith was afraid to walk on the beach. Connie sat on the deck herself. She peered at the water. Around noon, Harold appeared, alone. Connie watched him frolic in the waves, then felt lonely. She went inside and made turkey sandwiches.

"Meredith!" she called. "Lunch!"

Meredith didn't answer.

Connie went upstairs and tapped on Meredith's door.

Meredith said, "*Entrez.*"

Connie opened the door. Meredith was lying on her bed wearing her bathing suit and cover-up, reading.

"Come out on the deck and have lunch."

"No," Meredith said.

Connie wondered if Meredith was more frightened of the Russian mob or the FBI.

"No one is trying to hurt you. They're just trying to scare you."

"They succeeded."

"Well, they didn't succeed with me. I've been sitting on the deck all morning and nothing's happened."

Meredith said, "Someone knows I'm here."

Connie sighed. "What can I say? Someone knows you're here. You know, we might feel better if we called the police."

"We can't call the police," Meredith said. "Absolutely not."

"Why not?" Connie said. "You're scared, you feel threatened, you call the police; they write up a report, wave their guns, anyone watching us knows we've called the police, they get intimidated, they leave us alone."

"No one can know I'm here," Meredith said. "Not even the police. If this gets out, everyone's going to hate you."

"No one's going to hate me," Connie said, "and the police would keep it quiet." But she knew Meredith was right: the police talked to the fire department who talked to Santos Rubbish who talked to the guys at Sconset Gardener, and soon everybody on Nantucket knew that Meredith Delinn was hiding out at 1103 Tom Nevers Road. "Okay, we won't call the police. Just please come outside."

"No," Meredith said.

For dinner, Connie made cheeseburgers and salad. The cheeseburgers had to be cooked on the grill, which put Connie out on the deck with her back to the ocean. It was unnerving, she had to admit. She kept whipping around, but when she did, no one was there.

At Meredith's request, they ate inside. They needed a safe topic of conversation, which meant they had to venture pretty far back. Growing up, high school—but not Toby. Meredith again unearthed the names Wendy Thurber and Nadine Dexter, and once Connie had sifted through the archaeological ruins of her mind and figured out who these names belonged to, she hooted. Wendy and Nadine had been good, close friends. They had once been a part of Connie's everyday, though she hadn't seen them in over thirty years. What were Wendy and Nadine doing now? Meredith remembered Wendy as clingy and pathetic, and Nadine as a stout lesbian in the making.

"Yes, so do I," Connie said, although really it had been so long ago and Connie's memory was so poor that she was helpless to do anything but agree.

At nine thirty, Meredith said she was going upstairs. "It's my bedtime," she said, and Connie remembered that both Meredith and Freddy had always stuck to an early bedtime, as though they were children with school in the morning.

"Freddy's not here," Connie said, pouring herself a third glass of wine. "You can stay up with me."

Meredith said, "Are you afraid to stay up by yourself? Admit it, you are."

"I'm not *afraid* to stay up by myself, no. But I'd like company."

Meredith moved toward the stairs, meaning she didn't care that Connie wanted company (and yes, actually, Connie *was* a little afraid). She said, "I wonder what it's like for him."

"Who?"

"Freddy. In prison."

Connie was tempted to say something ungenerous. But instead she said, "I'm sure it's perfectly awful."

"I'm sure it is, too," Meredith said. "But what if 'perfectly awful' is something even worse than you and I can imagine?"

"Do you care?" Connie said.

Meredith didn't answer that.

"Do you still love him?" Connie asked.

"I'm going up," Meredith said, and Connie was glad. They had ventured way off their safe topics.

Connie's mind was on the phone call from Tallahassee. All Connie had to do was call the number back and *find out*—but she was afraid this new number would prove to be a dead end, and her hopes of reconnecting with her daughter would be crushed. The longer she held off calling, the longer the potential for reconciliation lived. And, too, Connie was afraid that she would call the number and Ashlyn would answer, and what would Connie say, after nearly two and a half years of silence? How would Connie keep from breaking down and crying, or breaking out and screaming—and in either case making things worse?

She finished her third glass of wine and then polished off Meredith's unfinished glass of wine as she did the dinner dishes. By that time, her fear had all but dissipated. She checked her cell phone again. The Tallahassee number was on her display. This was the moment.

She pushed the button that dialed the number. Then she steeled herself. One ring, two, three...seven, eight...voice mail. It was a computer-generated voice, one that gave no hint or clue who Connie had called. *Please leave a message.*

Connie took a breath. Leave a message? She left a message each and every Sunday on Ashlyn's cell phone and had never once gotten a response. Why expect that this would be any different?

And yet, she couldn't resist. She said, "Ashlyn, it's Mom. I see that you called. If you want to call me back, I'm here on Nantucket. As I'm sure you realize. If you call me back, I'll tell you something unbelievable." She paused. She couldn't stand using news of Meredith as a bribe, but she didn't have anything else to offer as enticement. "Call me back, please." She looked at the display of her phone, at the seconds ticking off, as if expecting her phone to answer. "Call me," she said again, and then she punched the phone off.

She shouldn't have left a message.

Had she sounded like she'd been drinking? She had slurred a little bit in there with the "As I'm sure you realize." Would Ashlyn notice?

Connie lay down on the sofa. She hated herself.

She didn't see the graffiti until she was in her car the next morning, on her way to the Sconset Market for the newspaper. It was the Fourth of July, and Connie was wondering if Meredith would want to go to see the fireworks that night. Probably not, definitely not, too many people. Then, Connie caught a glimpse of something unexpected, a color. A garish neon green. Huh? Connie looked in her rearview mirror and hit the brake as hard as she might have for an oncoming deer. She closed her eyes and tried to calm herself. She had a headache like a door repeatedly slamming. She opened her eyes. *Oh, my God.* She threw the car in reverse and backed all the way up to the house. She parked. She got out of the car. She studied the damage to her beautiful, beloved house.

Someone had spray painted, in letters that had to be six feet high, in a color that assaulted the eye, that noxious green, the word "*CROOK.*"

Connie couldn't believe it. She had to touch the paint on the gray shingles. The paint was still wet; some of it came off on Connie's fingertips. So, this had been done when? Late last night? Early this morning? Connie felt violated. She felt—if she could say this without sounding melodramatic—like she'd been raped.

Some depraved, hateful person had vandalized her home. He had trespassed onto her property—with extension ladders and what must have been ten cans of spray paint—and graffitied the front of her house.

CROOK. Meredith would be devastated. God, this was a hundred times worse than the photograph. Connie couldn't stand the thought of telling her.

She gave herself a minute to repeat the obvious things in her head: She should have known something like this would happen. The photograph had been a warning: *We know you're here. Now we're coming after you.* Freddy Delinn had enemies, dangerous people who had lost a lot of money. One of them, or a group of them, was behind this.

Connie touched the paint again. It would come off, right?

Inside, she found Meredith wearing a white nightgown, sitting in a chair at the head of the dining-room table as if waiting for a banquet to be served. A banquet of humiliation and sorrow, Connie thought. Meredith wasn't reading or drinking coffee. She was just sitting. Meditating, perhaps. When the screen door slapped shut behind Connie, Meredith startled. She looked up.

"Back already?" she said. "Did you forget something? Your wallet?"

Connie sat in the chair next to Meredith and took Meredith's hands in hers in her best imitation of a grief counselor. She had known this person since she was a child, since before rational thought or lasting memory. She had never imagined having to tell her something like this.

"I have to call the police," Connie said.

Meredith clenched her jaw. She nodded, though barely.

"Someone vandalized the house," Connie said. She tried to swallow, but her mouth was a sandbox. She was parched, hung over, heartsick. Her house! If Wolf had been alive to see this...

"What?" Meredith asked. Her hands were small and very cold.

"Green paint, big letters."

"What does it say?" Meredith asked.

"Crook."

Meredith hid her face in her hands. "Oh, God," she said.

Connie rubbed her back. She was tiny and frail. But no. She *wasn't* frail, and neither was Connie. "So I'm going to call the police."

"Okay," Meredith said.

Connie had thought they would send a lackey in a squad car, someone to witness the damage and write up a cursory report, especially since it was a holiday, but the chief of police came himself. He was a pleasant-looking middle-aged man with a short haircut, brown going gray around his ears. He was tall and impressive in his white uniform shirt, his crisp black pants, radio on his hip. When he climbed out of his car, he greeted Connie first, very kindly keeping his eyes off the vandalism.

"Mrs. Flute?" he said. "I'm Ed Kapenash, chief of police."

"Nice to meet you," she said.

Then he regarded the house. "Wow."

"I know," Connie said.

The chief, too, seemed most immediately interested in touching the paint. "The good news is that this appears to be water based, which is lucky for you. In the city, they have all kinds of nasty oil-based paints that never come out. You'd literally have to reshingle your house to have this gone. As it is, I can give you the name of a good power washer. I can pull some strings and see if I can have him out here today, assuming he hasn't gone fishing or to the beach with the rest of the world."

"Oh," Connie said. "Yes, absolutely. That would be wonderful."

"Okay," the chief said. "Your first priority will be getting the paint off your house, and our first priority will be finding out who did this."

"There's something I should explain," Connie said.

"And what's that?" he asked.

"Meredith Delinn is staying here."

"Meredith Delinn?"

"Yes. She's the wife of..."

"I know who she is," the chief said. "She's staying *here?*"

"She's a friend of mine from growing up," Connie said. "We've been friends forever."

The chief removed a pen from his back pocket and started taking notes. (What would he write? *BFF?*) He said, "Well, that explains things a little bit, doesn't it? Explains them but doesn't excuse them. We'll do what we can to find out who did this and to make sure it doesn't happen again. I'll start by putting a squad car on this road every hour throughout the night. Do you mind if I speak to Mrs. Delinn?"

"Um," Connie said. Meredith was still in her nightgown, and Connie was protective and suspicious. This guy *was* the chief of police, but what if he turned around and sold the story to the *National Enquirer*? "Just a minute. Let me ask her."

The chief nodded. "I'll call my power-washer connection from my car. I take it you'd like him here as soon as possible?"

"Yes," Connie said. "Thank you." She was trying not to look at the front of her house. That poisonous green, the absurd size of the letters, the ugly word. It was a scream, written on her house. *CROOK.* People had called Richard Nixon a crook. John Dillinger had been a crook. Bonnie and Clyde. But none of those people had been a crook like Freddy Delinn.

"Meredith?" Connie said. She saw that Meredith had gone upstairs and changed into what Connie thought of as her Doomsday outfit: her white button-down shirt, now a little wrinkled, jeans, suede flats. Already, it was too warm for the jeans. "The chief of police is here. He has questions for you. Is that okay?"

Meredith nodded.

"You don't have to talk to him," Connie said.

"I will."

Connie beckoned the chief inside, and the three of them sat at the dining-room table.

Connie said to the chief, "Can I get you some coffee?"

The chief held up a hand. "I've already had my three cups."

"Ice water then?"

"I'm all set, thanks," the chief said.

Connie brought a pitcher of ice water and three glasses to the table nonetheless. She poured herself a glass, returned to the counter where she sliced a lemon and put the slices in a shallow bowl. The three of them were sitting in a house that screamed *CROOK,* but there was no reason they couldn't be civilized.

"So," the chief said. "You're in luck. I've gotten hold of a man to do the power washing. He'll be here before noon today, he said."

"Excellent, thank you," Connie said.

The chief lowered his voice to speak to Meredith. He was responding to the situation, or to her pinched face, which was drained of all color. Or he was responding to her diminutive size—five foot one, a hundred pounds. Meredith had complained all her life that her petite stature caused people to treat her like a child.

"Do you have any idea who might have done this?" the chief asked her.

Connie couldn't help herself from interjecting. "Well, yesterday, something happened."

"What happened yesterday?" the chief said.

"Someone left an envelope on my front porch," Connie said. "And in the envelope was this photograph." She slid both the photograph and the envelope across the table.

The chief studied the photograph. "So you don't know who took this?"

Connie shook her head. "It was just left on our porch. Like someone was telling us they knew Meredith was here. It was creepy."

"Creepy," the chief agreed. "You should have called us then."

Connie felt a flash of triumph. Meredith cast her eyes down at the table.

"We figured out it was a photographer dressed as a seal,"

Connie said. "It was taken from the water, night before last, around six o'clock."

"And then it was left on your porch. You found it when?"

"Yesterday morning."

"Yesterday morning. And you didn't call the police. And now this morning you have this vandalism."

Meredith said, "I'm sorry. I should have let Connie call the police. She wanted to. But I didn't want anyone to know I was here."

The chief took a noticeable breath. "You'll forgive me for being indelicate and asking the obvious. Are any of your husband's former investors living on Nantucket that you know of?"

Meredith raised her face to the chief. Her expression was so blank, Connie was scared.

"Mary Rose Garth lost forty million. The Crenshaws lost twenty-six million; Jeremy and Amy Rivers lost nine point two million; the LaRussas lost six million and so did the Crosbys and so did Alan Futenberg. Christopher Darby-Lett lost four and a half million."

The chief scribbled. "These people live on Nantucket?"

"They're summer residents," Meredith said. "The Rosemans lost four point four, the Mancheskis lost three eight, Mrs. Phinney lost three five; the Kincaids, the Winslows, the Becketts, the Carlton Smiths, Linsley Richardson, the Halseys, the Minatows, and the Malcolm Browns all lost between two and three million. The Vaipauls, the McIntoshes, the Kennedys, the Brights, the Worthingtons…"

Connie sucked down a glass of cold water and tried not to let her surprise show. She had no idea so many of Freddy's investors were on this island. She and Meredith were sitting in the heart of enemy territory.

The chief left an hour later with a list of fifty-two names of Nantucket summer residents who had lost over a million dollars in

Freddy's scam. He couldn't question any of them without proba-
ble cause, but it was good to have the list to reference, he said. Of
course, he pointed out, it wasn't certain that the vandal was an
investor; there were all kinds of creeps in the world. The chief was
taking the photograph and the envelope with him. The main
thing, he said, was that Connie and Meredith should try to relax
while remaining vigilant. The house had an alarm system, though
Connie had never felt the need to set it. Nantucket—and Tom
Nevers in particular—was so safe! She would set it tonight; she
would set it from now on.

"And we'll send a squad car out like I promised," the chief said.
"Every hour on the hour throughout the night."

"Thank you," Connie said. She hated to see him go. He was the
first man to help her in this kind of practical way since Wolf had
died. And he was handsome. She checked for a wedding ring. He
wore a solid gold band—of course. Chiefs of police were always
happily married, with a couple of kids at home. That was as it
should be. Still, Connie was pleased with herself for noticing him.
It felt like some kind of progress.

Less than an hour later, there was a knock at the door, and both
Connie and Meredith froze. They were still at the dining-room
table, drinking coffee and letting their bowls of cereal grow soggy.
Meredith was talking in circles—mostly about the investors who
lived on Nantucket. She only knew a few of them personally. She,
of course, knew Mary Rose Garth (net loss $40 million); everyone
in New York society knew Mary Rose Garth, the anorexically
thin, sexually lascivious rubber heiress. She had served on the
board of the Frick Collection with Meredith.

And Jeremy and Amy Rivers (net loss $9.2 million) had been
friends of Meredith's from Palm Beach.

Meredith told Connie that she had met Amy Rivers during a
tennis clinic at the Everglades Club. Amy had a high-powered job
for a global consulting firm; she had gone to Princeton three years

behind Meredith, though Meredith didn't remember her. But they bonded over their equally pathetic backhands and their mutual admiration of the tennis pro's legs, and became casual friends. Amy traveled all the time for business—Hong Kong, Tokyo, Dubai—but when next she was in Palm Beach, she called Meredith to go to lunch. They sat out on the patio at Chuck and Harold's—very casual, very friendly—but at the end of the lunch, Amy bent her head toward Meredith as if to confide something. Meredith was wary. Palm Beach was a vicious gossip town. Meredith was okay with accepting confidences, but she never, ever told any of her women friends a single thing about her personal life.

Amy said, "I have money to invest. In the neighborhood of nine million. Do you think there's any way I could get into your husband's fund? I hear his returns are unbelievable."

"Oh," Meredith said. She felt a bit deflated. She had thought that Amy Rivers had chosen to befriend her because she recognized Meredith as being in a category above the run-of-the-mill Palm Beach matron. While it was true Meredith didn't teach anymore, she was extremely smart and capable. But now it seemed that what Amy had been after, really, was a way into Delinn Enterprises. The fact of the matter was, Meredith had no say in who was chosen to be an investor. People asked her all the time if she could "get them in" with Freddy; even the cashier at Publix, who had inherited money from her great-uncle, had asked. But when Meredith mentioned these people to Freddy, he always said no. He had some secret set of criteria for accepting investors that he wouldn't share with Meredith, and quite frankly, she didn't care. Still, for certain people, she agreed to ask. Although she felt a tiny bit stung by Amy Rivers, Meredith promised to lobby Freddy on her behalf. Amy clapped a hand over her mouth like she had just been named Miss America.

"Oh, thank you!" she said. "Thank you, thank you, thank you! Here's my card. You'll let me know what he says?"

When Meredith talked to Freddy about Amy Rivers, Freddy asked who she was.

Meredith said, "A woman I play tennis with at the Everglades. She's a consultant with Hackman Marr."

"Hackman Marr?" Freddy said, sounding interested.

"Yes," Meredith said. "And she went to Princeton, graduated in eighty-five. I had lunch with her today. I really like her."

"I'm sorry," Freddy said.

"Sorry about what? You mean you won't take her on?"

"No."

"Why not?"

"We don't take investors because we 'really like' them," Freddy said. "We take them on for other reasons."

"What other reasons?" Meredith asked. "She said she has nine million dollars." She handed Freddy Amy's business card. "Will you please think about it? For me, please?"

"For you, please? All right, yes," Freddy said. "I'll think about it."

And voilà! Freddy called Amy Rivers himself and invited her to invest, and Amy sent Meredith a huge bouquet of flowers. They became great friends, playing tennis and meeting for lunch, recommending books, talking about their kids. Amy never again mentioned Delinn Enterprises, Freddy, or her money. And then, of course, there was no money. Amy Rivers lost everything.

Meredith looked at Connie. "I could tell you dozens of stories like that."

Connie wasn't sure how to respond. She and Wolf, too, had been investors. She thought that all this talk about other investors might lead to an uncomfortable discussion of their own situation—but Connie was spared this by the knock at the door. It frightened her at first, and it certainly frightened Meredith, but then Connie realized it must be the power washer, and she hurried to greet him.

The man's name was Danforth Flynn; he told Connie to call him Dan. He was about fifty, with the lean body of a long-distance runner and a permanent sunburn. Again, Connie felt self-conscious.

This was the second time this morning that she had a handsome man show up to help her.

Dan Flynn regarded the front of the house and whistled.

"Did the chief explain?" she asked.

"He did."

"Can you get it off?"

He approached the front of the house and touched a shingle that had been painted. He rubbed his fingers together. "I can," he said. "What I want you to do is to go inside and close and lock all of the windows on this side of the house. This is going to take me a couple of hours, I'd guess. And it's going to be loud."

"No problem," Connie said.

"Okay," Dan Flynn said. "I'll get started. The tank of my truck holds four thousand gallons of water, but this job is so big I may need to hook up to your outdoor spigot to fill my reserve tank. Can you show me where that is?"

"I can," Connie said. "It's around here." She led him to the side of the house and showed him where her garden hose was coiled. He wasn't looking at the house, however—he was looking at the view of the ocean.

"You have quite a spot," he said. "In good old Tom Nevers. I forget how breathtaking it can be out here."

"Yes," she said. "The land had been in my husband's family since the nineteen twenties, but we only built the house fifteen years ago. And then my husband died in two thousand nine, so now it's just me."

"Funny," Dan said, still looking at the water. "My wife died in two thousand nine. Breast cancer."

"Brain cancer," Connie said.

They were quiet for a moment, and Connie couldn't help but think of her friend Lizbet who had, for two and a half years, been encouraging Connie to go to a support group so she could meet people who were going through the same thing she was.

Connie looked at Dan Flynn and smiled. "I'll go take care of those windows," she said.

"Great," he said.

Connie bounded into the house. She felt more energized than she had in months.

She closed the windows on the first floor and watched Dan move around his truck, turning knobs, pulling out a thick blue ridged hose. He was wearing jeans and a T-shirt and running shoes. He had a buzz cut, brown hair turning gray, and a day of growth on his face like that newly retired NFL quarterback, which she found sexy. Sexy? She couldn't believe she was thinking this way.

Connie caught sight of herself in the mirror. She had lost a lot of sparkle in the past two and a half years—but did she really look so bad for fifty? Her hair was still strawberry blond, more strawberry in the winter, more blond in the summer. She had her mother's good genes to thank for that because Veronica had gone to the grave at sixty-eight with a full head of natural red. Connie had green eyes, a light tan, some freckles, some sun spots. Her skin wasn't great; she had never been able to stay out of the sun. She was out of shape although she was very thin from skipping meals. Her nails were a mess, and her eyebrows. She needed to start taking care of herself again. She needed to exercise.

Ha! All this in response to the cute power-washing guy. Meredith was going to die laughing.

Connie went upstairs to close the second-floor windows. Dan had started working. The noise was incredible; it sounded like the house was being attacked by fighter jets. Connie hurried to shut all the windows. She could see Dan Flynn bracing the hose against his hip, shooting a stream of water at the house that was moving so fast, it looked solid. Dan's body was shaking like he was operating a jackhammer; all the muscles in his arms were popping. The whole thing was rather phallic.

"Meredith," Connie said. "Come here, you have to see this."

There was no response. Connie was pretty sure the paint was coming off. There were green puddles in the yard now, the color of radioactive waste.

"Meredith?" Connie called.

Connie finished with the windows facing the front of the house and, just to be safe, she shut the windows on either side of the house, even though those rooms would get murderously hot. The house had central air-conditioning—but, like the alarm system, Connie never turned it on.

She moved into the hallway. The door to Meredith's room was shut. Connie remembered the blank look on her face as she sat at the table, and the way she recited the names of the investors. (She had committed nearly three thousand of the names to memory, she said, as a kind of penance. It was how she'd filled her days in the New York apartment after Freddy had been taken away.)

Connie had a bad feeling. She knocked on the door.

"Meredith?" she said. No answer. She could have been sleeping. Connie really wanted to respect Meredith's privacy, just as she wanted her own privacy respected—it was the only way it was going to work with them living in the house together—but Connie was worried that Meredith would take pills or hang herself or slash her wrists with one of the disposable razors that Connie knew were under the sink in the bathroom.

"Meredith?" Connie said. No answer. Nothing. Just the percussive drone of the power washer.

She opened the door and gasped. Meredith was sitting on her bed, facing the door, wearing that same zombie-like expression. Her Louis Vuitton duffel bag was next to her on the bed.

"Jesus!" Connie said. "You scared me. What are you doing?"

She looked at Connie. "I have to leave."

"No!" Connie said.

"Yes," Meredith said. She stood up, grabbing her bag.

"You are *not* leaving," Connie said. She tried to wrest the leather handles from Meredith, but Meredith held fast. She was small, but she was tough; Connie remembered her on the hockey field, gripping her stick, biting down ferociously on her mouth guard.

"I'm leaving," Meredith said. "Your beautiful house was wrecked because of me!"

"It's not wrecked," Connie said. "Come see—this man named Dan Flynn is outside fixing it. The paint's coming off. We'll never even be able to tell it was there."

"But it *was* there," Meredith said. "*CROOK.* They think I'm him. They think I was in on it. They think I'm the one who stole their money. And I did in a way, didn't I? Because I had four houses, a yacht, a jet, seven cars, jewelry, clothes, antiques—and where did the money for all that come from? Well, technically, I stole it, didn't I?" She blinked, and Connie thought that this might be the thing that made Meredith cry, but behind her glasses, her eyes were dry. "But I had no idea. *No idea.* I thought Freddy was a genius. I thought he was beating the market, again and again and again. I was so..."

"Meredith—"

"Stupid! So blind! And no one believes me, and why should anyone believe me? I'm a smart woman with an Ivy League education. How could I not see something illegal was going on?" She glared at Connie. "Even you tried to tell me."

That was correct; Connie had tried to tell her. But Connie was in too generous a frame of mind to revisit that. "You were blinded," Connie said. "Blinded by love."

"Is that an excuse?" Meredith said. "Is that going to get me off the hook with the FBI, Connie? *Love?*"

Connie didn't know what to say.

"Do *you* believe I'm innocent?" Meredith said.

"Yes, Meredith. I believe you're innocent."

"And why is that? Why are you the *only person in the whole country* who believes I'm innocent?"

"Because I know you."

"I knew Freddy," Meredith said. "I thought I knew Freddy." She raised her head. "I should never have called you to come get me. I've put you in danger. Look what happened to your house. I'm drowning, Connie, but I'm drowning alone. I won't take you with me."

"Meredith!" Connie said. She had to shout to be heard above the din of the power washer. "YOU'RE STAYING. I WANT YOU TO STAY. I'M NOT WILLING TO LET YOU GO." She didn't say, *You have nowhere else to go,* because it wasn't about that. "I need you to stay for me, okay, not for you. I need a friend. I need companionship. And it has to be you. We're going to put what happened behind us; we're going to forget the things we said to each other. We need time for that. And we need to figure out how to prove you're innocent. We need the world to see you as I see you."

Meredith didn't move or speak for what seemed like a long time, but then, Connie watched her exhale. She relaxed her grip on the duffel bag and let Connie take it from her. Connie said, "I want you to come see what Dan the power-washer guy looks like." And she led Meredith to the window.

MEREDITH

Connie came home from the hospital thrift shop a few days later with a dark wig for Meredith, styled in two long pigtails. When Meredith tried it on, she looked like Mary Ann from *Gilligan's Island.*

"It's awful," Meredith said.

"Awful," Connie agreed. "But that's a good thing. We want mousy, and we want anonymous. And we need to do something about your glasses."

"I love my glasses," Meredith protested. "I've had my glasses since the eighth grade."

"I know," Connie said. "I remember the day you got them. But now, they have to go. We aren't going to stay inside all summer, and we aren't going to have you accosted by haters, and so you need to travel incognito. The glasses are a dead giveaway. When women dress up as Meredith Delinn for Halloween, they'll be wearing those glasses."

"Are women going to dress up as me for Halloween?" Meredith said.

Connie smiled sadly. "The glasses have to go."

Connie took Meredith's glasses to Nantucket Eye Center and had a new pair made. While Connie was gone with her glasses, Meredith was left helplessly blind. She desperately wanted to go outside and sit on the deck, but she was terrified to do so without Connie around. She lay upstairs on her bed, but she couldn't read without her glasses. She stared at the blurry surrounds of the pink guest room.

She was still back on the Main Line in the 1970s with her father and Toby.

Meredith's parents had been stunned when she told them about her date with Toby. For Chick Martin, the surprise had been mixed with something else. Jealousy? Possessiveness? Meredith feared her father would react the same way that Connie had. But he rose above whatever qualms he had about Meredith's burgeoning womanhood and acted the role of protective father. When Toby arrived on that first evening to pick Meredith up, Chick asked, "Do you have a clean driving record?"

"Yes, sir," Toby said.

"You will have Meredith home by eleven, please."

"Yes, sir, Mr. Martin," Toby said.

It took Chick a few months to adjust to Meredith's new persona. Meredith was the same on the outside—studious, obedient, loving toward both her parents, respectful of their rules, grateful for all they did for her—but something had changed. To her father, she supposed, it seemed like she was now focused on Toby. But really, she was focused on herself—her body, her emotions, her sexuality, her capacity to love someone other than her parents.

Whoa! Meredith couldn't remember ever feeling as alive as she had that summer she turned sixteen, when her romance with Toby raged in her like a fire. She was hot for him—that had been the popular turn of phrase at the time. Many times they skipped the movies and drove to Valley Forge Park and made out in the car. They touched each other through their clothes, and then the clothes started coming off in stages. And then arrived a night when Meredith was naked and Toby had his jeans at his knees and Meredith straddled him and...he stopped her. It was too soon, she was young, it wasn't time yet. Meredith had cried—partly out of sexual frustration, partly out of anger and jealousy. Toby had had sex with Divinity Michaels and Ravi from Bryn Mawr and probably also the French teacher, Mademoiselle Esme (though Meredith had never been brave enough to ask him)—so why not her?

"This is different," he said. "This is special. I want to take it slow. I want it to last."

"Plus," he said, "I'm afraid of your father."

"Afraid of my *father?*" Meredith wailed.

"He spoke to me," Toby said. "He asked me to respect you. He told me to be a gentleman."

"A gentleman?" Meredith said. She huddled, shivering, against the passenger-side door. The vinyl seats of the Nova were cold. She hunted for her underwear. She didn't want a gentleman. She wanted Toby.

Meredith went on a campaign to keep her father and Toby away from each other. But then Chick invited Toby over to help burn the piles of leaves in the yard, then go inside and watch Notre Dame trounce Boston College, and eat pigs in a blanket that Meredith's mother served along with a dish of spicy brown mustard. At the holidays, Toby was invited to the Martins' annual Christmas party, which was so crowded with reveling adults that Meredith was certain there would be an opportunity to sneak to her bedroom. But Toby would not be coerced upstairs.

Toby was also invited over on New Year's eve, a night that Meredith had traditionally spent alone with her parents. They always ate dinner at the General Wayne Inn and always saw a movie at the cinemas in Frazer, then they always returned home for a bottle of Tattinger champagne (Meredith had been given her first sip at age thirteen) and chocolate truffles while watching Dick Clark in Times Square on TV. Toby came along for all of it—the dinner, the movie, the champagne, the chocolates, and the ball dropping at midnight. At twelve fifteen, Chick shook Toby's hand and said, "I want you out of this house in one hour. Do you understand me?"

"Yes, sir."

"I'm not coming back down, so I'll need your word."

"You have my word, sir."

"Very good," Chick said. "Please tell your parents we say 'happy New Year.'" And he closed the door to the library with a click.

Meredith remembered sitting still as a statue on the library sofa, holding her breath, believing that it was some kind of trick. But then she heard her parents' footsteps on the stairs and their footsteps treading down the second floor hall above them. They were going to bed, leaving Toby and Meredith in the plush comfort of the library for a whole hour.

Toby approached the sofa cautiously. Meredith pulled him down on top of her.

Toby said, "Meredith, stop."

Meredith said, "He basically gave you his *permission*." She would not be deterred. It was a new year, and she was going to lose her virginity—not in the front seat of Toby's '69 Nova, and not in the grass of Valley Forge Park—but right here in her own house by the library fire.

Quietly.

*   *   *

In the spring, Toby graduated, but because he had underper-formed on his SATs, he took a year off to boost his prospects for college. During the summer, he and Meredith went to the O'Briens' summer house in Cape May, where they sailed every day and hung out on the boardwalk at night eating chili dogs and kettle corn. They had their picture taken in a photo booth and kept the strips in the back pockets of their jeans. They bought matching white rope bracelets.

In the fall, Toby took two classes at Delaware County Commu-nity College and worked as a waiter at Minella's Diner. He was around for everything Meredith's senior year, and although Mere-dith's parents grew concerned—was it a good idea for Meredith to be so serious about someone in high school?—they had no grounds for complaint. Meredith was at the top of her class at Merion Mercy, and she was placing first and second in all her diving competitions. She was a National Merit finalist, and everything else besides.

Because he worked at Minella's, Toby was sometimes the one who delivered the subs to the Martin house for Chick's monthly poker games, and one night, Chick invited Toby to come back after his shift and join the game. This night fostered a new bond between Chick and Toby; Meredith figured her father either liked Toby, or he was embracing the if-you-can't-beat-'em-join-'em phi-losophy. Chick invited Toby down to his law offices, and the two of them went out for lunch at the City Tavern. He took Toby and Meredith to Sixers games. He and Deidre and Toby and Meredith went to see the lights at Longwood Gardens at Christmastime, they went to hear the Philadelphia Orchestra at the Academy of Music, they went out to dinner at Bookbinders and to brunch at the Green Room in the Hotel du Pont.

"You do all this old-people stuff," Connie said. "How do you stand it?"

"We like it," Meredith said. She refrained from telling Connie that what she wanted most in the world was to marry Toby. She pictured the two of them having kids and settling down on the Main Line, in a life not so different from that of her own parents.

To this day, Meredith couldn't explain how the whole thing fell apart, but fall apart it did.

Toby broke up with Meredith on the night of her high-school graduation. The O'Briens threw a huge party for Connie; the party was tented and catered and there was free-flowing alcohol for the adults, which inevitably trickled down to the teenagers. Toby was drinking Coke and Wild Turkey, but because Meredith's parents were in attendance, she was sipping lukewarm Tab. Connie was drinking gin and tonics like her mother. She had given up on her romance with Matt Klein and was now dating the star of the Radnor lacrosse team, Drew Van Dyke, who was headed to Johns Hopkins in the fall. Connie and Drew disappeared from the party at ten o'clock, and Toby wanted to ditch, too — he suggested skinny-dipping in the pool at Aronimink, then making love on the rolling hill behind the ninth tee. But this was too dangerous for Meredith; Chick was the president of the board at Aronimink, and if Meredith and Toby got caught, her father would be humiliated, which wasn't something Meredith was willing to risk. She told Toby she wanted to stay and dance to the band.

Toby said, "What are you, a hundred years old?"

It was true that the people remaining at the party were all older, friends of Bill and Veronica O'Brien.

"My parents are dancing," Meredith said. "Let's stay."

"I don't want to stay and dance with your parents," Toby said. "I'm getting kind of sick of your parents."

Meredith was aghast at this statement. She felt her cheeks grow hot.

"I'm nineteen," Toby said. "And you're eighteen. Let's go act our age."

Meredith glanced back at the dance floor. Her mother and father were jitterbugging.

"That looks like so much fun," Meredith said.

"It does not look like fun," Toby said.

Just then, a man approached Meredith. His name was Dustin Leavitt, and he worked with Bill O'Brien at Philco. Dustin Leavitt was a bachelor; he was tall and handsome and polished and charming—he was an *adult*—but he seemed to especially enjoy talking to Meredith. Over the winter, he'd seen her dive against Lower Merion—Dustin's niece swam the butterfly for Lower Merion—and that had been Meredith's best meet. She'd gotten 9's on her reverse one and a half pike and broken the pool record. *You're quite the shooting star,* Dustin Leavitt had said to her in the hallway of the school after the meet.

Since she'd arrived at the party, Meredith had felt Dustin Leavitt looking at her. Even Connie had noticed it. She'd said, "I think Dustin Leavitt has a thing for you."

And Meredith said, "Please shut up."

Connie said, "I'm serious. He's hot. And he's a *man.*"

Meredith knew he was fifteen years her senior. Thirty-three. It seemed impossibly old.

"Hey there, Toby," Dustin Leavitt said. "I'd love to take your girlfriend for a spin. Do you mind?"

Meredith was certain Toby would object, but he just shrugged. "Go for it."

"Meredith?" Dustin Leavitt held out his arms.

Meredith was uncertain. She was flattered by the gesture, certainly, but she didn't want to upset Toby. But she wanted to dance, and Toby was drinking and he was being mean. She let Dustin Leavitt lead her to the dance floor, and it was only when the song was over and Meredith and Dustin were flushed and perspiring, clapping for the band, that Meredith realized that Toby had left the party without her.

Meredith went home with her parents a while later, panicked and heartsick about Toby. She was afraid he'd left because he was mad or upset about her dancing with Dustin Leavitt. But when Meredith finally talked to him—she walked over to the O'Briens' house first thing the next morning, ostensibly to help clean up— he told her that he didn't care about her dancing with Dustin Leavitt. In fact, he said, it had come as kind of a relief.

"What does *that* mean?" Meredith asked. They were in the backyard under the tent. Toby was stacking the folding chairs, and Meredith was picking crumpled cocktail napkins out of the grass.

"I think we should break up," Toby said.

"Break up?" Meredith said. "You're breaking up with me?"

"I think I am," he said. He nodded once, definitively. "I am."

Meredith had sat down in the grass and cried. Toby stretched out beside her and leaned back on his hands. It was like he had changed overnight. He was distant and cool. He was leaving for Cape May in a few days, he said, to work as first mate on a sail-boat; he would be gone all summer, she knew that. Yes, she said, but she was supposed to visit him. Every weekend!

He said, "Right. But I think it would be better if I was free."

"Better for whom?"

"Better for me," he said. He went on to mention that, although he really liked Meredith's parents, he didn't want to *become* Mer-edith's parents. Not yet, anyway, and maybe not ever. "Besides," he said, "you're going to Princeton in the fall. You'll have so many amazing opportunities in front of you..."

"Jesus Christ!" Meredith screamed. She thought of the stories she had heard about Divinity Michaels locking herself in the jani-tor's closet and threatening to drink the ammonia. Now Meredith understood. "Don't patronize me!"

"Okay," Toby said. His expression was one of concern, but probably only because Meredith had taken the Lord's name in vain—which she never did—and he feared she was becoming a psycho like his other ex-girlfriends. "Geez, Meredith, I'm sorry. I can't change how I feel."

*   *   *

Meredith cried in her bedroom, she cried on the phone with Connie (who, if Meredith wasn't mistaken, sounded almost happy about the breakup), she skipped meals and her parents worried. Chick Martin took Meredith to the Villanova parking lot to practice for her driving test, but this turned into hour-long sessions of Meredith crying and Chick attempting to console her.

"I can't stand to see you hurt like this," Chick said. "Your mother and I feel so helpless. Do you want me to talk to Toby?"

"No," Meredith said. Her father could do many magical things, but he couldn't make Toby love her.

It took two days for Meredith's glasses to be ready, and when they were, the transformation was complete. She put on the dark wig with the pigtails and slipped on the new glasses, which had wireless rims. The lenses seemed to float before Meredith's eyes. They offered no definition the way her signature horn-rimmed glasses had.

"That's what you want," Connie said. "Trust me."

It was true that with the wig and the glasses, Meredith looked nothing like herself. From a distance, even Freddy wouldn't recognize her.

On Saturday morning, Connie suggested that they go shopping in town. Meredith declined. "Town" meant other people and she couldn't do other people.

"But you haven't even seen town," Connie said.

"I'll see it another time," Meredith said.

"Like when?" Connie said.

"When it's less populated," Meredith said. She was thinking of midnight in the middle of March. "When there's less chance of being recognized."

Connie argued that the more people were around, the less likely someone would notice Meredith. Plus, she and Wolf had always gone into town shopping on Saturday morning; it was what they did.

"Someone out there is watching me," Meredith said.

"The police checked the area. It's not like someone is watching you twenty-four, seven."

"It feels like it."

"It was a scare tactic, Meredith. That's how they want you to feel. But we're not going to let them win. We're going to live our lives. And if they're watching you today, then they're watching you shop in town."

Meredith had little room to argue, and she was desperate to get out of the house. Once they got to town, Meredith realized Connie was right: There was such a happy buzz on Main Street that no one had time to take notice of her. There were people everywhere—parents with children in strollers, couples holding hands, older men in pink polo shirts walking golden retrievers, women wearing Lilly Pulitzer skirts and carrying shopping bags from Gypsy and Eye of the Needle. Meredith used to be one of those women. Now, of course, she couldn't afford to buy a thing. But it was fun to be part of the crowd. She and Connie stopped at the Bartlett's Farm truck, and Meredith let her eyes feast on the fresh, organic produce nestled into sixteen square boxes on the tilted truck bed. It was a patchwork quilt of color—the purple cabbages, the green zucchini and cucumbers, the red hothouse tomatoes, the yellow summer squash. Connie bought some beautiful, tender lettuce and an armload of bright gladiolus that Meredith offered to carry. She felt lucky to be carrying flowers and shopping at farm trucks. She wondered what the boys were doing. She hoped Leo was with Anais, mountain biking or playing golf, momentarily free from anxiety. Poor Freddy had finished the first week of his one hundred and fifty year sentence. He was staring down an eternity of barbed wire and desolation. For all Meredith knew, this time next year, she would be in prison herself.

But she couldn't let herself think about that.

Connie led her around the corner and down the cobblestone streets to Nantucket Bookworks, where they browsed for a luxurious stretch of time. Meredith stayed away from the nonfiction shelves; already there were books about the evil empire of Delinn Enterprises. These books had been written quickly and must have contained hundreds of inaccuracies and suppositions. Meredith assumed at least one of the books contained background information about Freddy and possibly about her as well. But would they have gotten it right? Would they have written about Meredith's idyllic upbringing on the Main Line? Would they have written about how she adored her father? Would they have written about her good grades, her excellent test scores, her near-perfect reverse one and a half pike? Would they have wondered how a girl with so much on the ball had allowed herself to get mixed up with Freddy Delinn?

Meredith immersed herself in the novels. For some reason, fiction hit on the meaning of life so much more concisely than real life itself did. She browsed Atwood and Morrison, Kingsolver, Russo. She picked up a novel by Laura Kasischke that she'd seen written up in *Town & Country* months before. There was a shelf of classics, too: she could pick up the one Austen she hadn't read yet or *Pale Fire* by Nabokov. There were holes in her canon. One couldn't read everything, though Meredith could try. Now, she had the time. For one second on a sunny Saturday morning in a bookstore in Nantucket, her life seemed good, at least in that one aspect.

Then, she looked up. Connie had bought the new Barefoot Contessa cookbook and was waiting patiently, browsing at the travel section. Meredith had to make a decision. Would she buy anything? Yes, she would buy the Kasischke and *Persuasion.* She put the other books back where they belonged—Meredith wanted to follow the rules in even the smallest things now—and when she turned to the register, she saw Amy Rivers. Amy was holding a copy of Nathaniel Philbrick's *Mayflower,* asking the woman behind the counter if she could get it autographed by the author. Her voice was so familiar that Meredith panicked to the point of absolute stillness. Connie was waiting, they had other places to go, but Meredith couldn't move. Her disguise of wig and glasses wouldn't be enough. If Amy Rivers saw her, she would know her.

Amy Rivers sensed something, perhaps. She turned toward Meredith. Meredith bowed her head. Amy Rivers had left a message on the answering machine in the Delinns' Park Avenue apartment, a screaming, hysterical message in which she'd used the word "fuck" as every part of speech. She could not fucking believe it. Freddy was a lying, criminal bastard, an inexcusable fuck of a human fucking being. Then Amy lit into Meredith. Meredith had fucked her, fucking betrayed her. *And I thought we were fucking friends. What the fuck?* Meredith wanted to call Amy back, to remind Amy that it was *she* who had begged Meredith to get her in with Freddy. Meredith had given Freddy Amy's business card as a favor. Meredith had no idea Freddy was running a Ponzi scheme. She had no clue she was setting Amy up to lose all her money. Amy said herself that the returns were "unbelievable." Things that seemed unbelievable usually were. Amy was smart enough to know that. Where was Amy's due diligence? Why was this *Meredith's* fault?

Meredith felt Amy's eyes on her. She could see Amy's feet and legs. She was wearing her white Tretorns with the pink stripe, the same shoes she'd played tennis in at the Everglades Club. Meredith closed her eyes and counted to twenty. She felt a hand on her arm.

Connie said. "Hey, are you okay?"

Meredith looked up. Amy was gone.

"Yes," she said. And she went to the counter to buy her books.

That run-in was enough to send Meredith back to the refuge of Tom Nevers, but Connie was hot to keep going. They went into Stephanie's gift shop, and Connie read aloud all the funny sayings on the cocktail napkins, and Meredith faked a smile. She had let her guard down in the bookstore, and she'd nearly been assassinated. She had to remain aware at all times; she would never be safe.

They moved on: down the street, they gazed in the window of Patina at the tall, incredibly elegant Ted Muehling candlesticks.

"They're, like, eight hundred dollars apiece," Connie said.

Meredith didn't mention that in her life before, she would have waltzed right in and bought four or six of the candlesticks in different sizes. She would have filled them with the hand-milled beeswax candles that she bought at Printemps in Paris; she would have looked fondly on the candlesticks a dozen times over the next several days, feeling the buzz that buying fine, expensive things gave her. But by the end of the week, the buzz would be gone; the candlesticks would be just one more thing for Louisa to dust, and Meredith would have moved on to wanting something else—buying it, then forgetting it. It had been a shameful way to live, even when she'd believed the money she was spending was her own. She wondered if she would ever buy anything as frivolous as candlesticks again.

On to Vanessa Noel shoes. The shoes were glorious—suede and snakeskin, patent leather and sequined. There were sandals and slides and slingbacks and peep toes. Connie tried on a pair of pink slides decorated across the vamp with striped grosgrain ribbon. They fit perfectly; they made her legs look amazing. She was so tall, so slender. Meredith felt fifty stabs of jealousy, but she was used to feeling jealous about Connie's looks.

Meredith said, "They're fabulous. You should get them."

Connie said, "I think I will. But where will I ever wear them?"

Meredith said, "How about on a date with Dan Flynn?"

Connie looked at Meredith in shock, alarm, anger perhaps. Had Meredith overstepped her bounds? Connie was still singularly devoted to mourning Wolf. Meredith had noticed that Connie had been sleeping each night on the sofa under a blanket, and when Meredith asked her why, she said, "I can't sleep in the bed without him." Meredith found this a little strange. It had been two and a half years! But she'd said nothing. Now, she'd stuck her foot in her mouth.

But then Connie said slyly, "I *am* going to get them!"

While Connie was paying, Meredith picked up a pair of silver heels decorated with milky blue stones. Gorgeous, original—they would have matched a blue silk shutter-pleat dress that Meredith had left in her closet in Cap d'Antibes. These were shoes for a dress she no longer owned. They were on sale for $495.

No.

On the way back home, they stopped at Nantucket Looms where Connie bought a certain kind of wildflower soap that she liked, and then they passed Saint Mary's, the Catholic church. It was a gray-shingled building with white trim—just like every other building on Nantucket—and there was a simple white statue of the Virgin Mary out front. The Virgin held her hands out in a way that seemed to beckon Meredith in.

She said to Connie, "I'm going in to light a candle, okay?"

Connie nodded and took a seat on a bench. "I'll wait here."

Meredith entered the church and inhaled the vague scent of incense; a funeral Mass must have been celebrated that morning. She slipped three dollars into the slot, and even then, she felt a twinge—three precious dollars! She lit the first candle for Leo. It was a parent's job to keep his children safe, and Freddy had failed. He had so wanted the boys to join him in business, although it had been obvious from the beginning that he would only get Leo. Leo had worked preposterous hours, and he had made very little money compared to the people who worked on the abhorrent seventeenth floor. Surely the Feds realized this? If Leo was in on the Ponzi scheme, wouldn't he be rich, too, like the rest of them? Why would Freddy involve Leo in something illegal? How was it any different from giving Leo a handgun and forcing him to hold up a 7-Eleven?

Keep Leo safe, Meredith prayed.

She lit a candle for Carver. Carver was a free spirit; he'd had no interest in an office job, and Freddy, reluctantly, had let him go. Carver had asked Freddy for a loan in order to buy his first renovation project, and Freddy had said no. No handouts. So Carver had gone to the bank himself, and they gave him the loan because his last name was Delinn and nobody turned down a loan to a Delinn. And now, thank God, he wasn't involved; he was a carpenter, and he could keep a roof over his brother's head.

Keep Carver strong, Meredith prayed.

She struggled with the last candle, then decided she would light it for Freddy.

But she couldn't think of a word to say to God on his behalf.

She blessed herself and stepped back out into the sun. She was ready to go home. Her wig was starting to itch.

As they pulled into Connie's driveway, Meredith studied the front of the house. The paint had come off, but the power washing left the ghost of the word behind. If you looked closely, *CROOK* was still there — only instead of hideous green letters, it was marked by shingles that were paler than the others. Dan had come back that morning to do some touch-up work. They had missed him, but there were telltale puddles in the front yard. Dan had promised that, over time, the shingles he'd blasted would weather back to gray. In six months, he said, the damage would be completely gone.

Connie pulled her purchases from the backseat of the Escalade. "Dan was here," she said, eyeing the dripping eaves. "I can't believe we missed him."

Meredith was the first one to the front door. A business card was sticking out of the screen. She plucked it — it was Dan's card. On the back, he'd written, "Connie, call me!" Meredith felt a rush of adolescent excitement.

"Look!" she said. "He left this!"

Connie flipped the card over. Her expression was inscrutable. She said, "It's probably something about the house. Or about the bill."

Meredith felt a twinge of panic. The bill. She would pay it, but how much would it be? Four hundred? Six hundred?

"You're going to call him, though, right?" Meredith said.

"Not right now," Connie said.

Meredith didn't push it. Once inside, she extracted the bobby pins from her head and pulled off her wig. Ahhh. Her real hair, which could now only be described as blondish gray, was matted.

She tried to fix it in the mirror. Her glasses were truly awful. No man would ever leave a business card for her. But that was okay; that was absolutely for the best.

Meredith longed to go for a swim. There was the sunny deck, and there was the beach twenty stairs below. There was the golden sand and the cool, blue water. But unlike the center of town with all its busyness and crowds, being on Connie's property spooked her.

Connie said, "There's Harold."

"Where?" Meredith said.

Connie pointed offshore, and Meredith saw the sleek black head surface, then disappear. Yes, only one seal.

"How long has Harold been around?" Meredith asked.

"I was wondering that the other day," Connie said. "And I figured out this is the fifth summer."

"The fifth? Really?"

"Wolf saw him first when he was fooling around with his binoculars. The next summer, Wolf was sick, but we came here anyway, and Wolf spent a lot of time on the deck, wrapped in a blanket. He couldn't see very well by that point, but I would tell him every time I saw Harold. The following summer, Wolf had died, and we scattered his ashes here. Then last summer. And now this summer. So, five." Connie was quiet for a moment, then she said, "It's amazing how Wolf's death has put everything into two categories: before Wolf died and after Wolf died."

Meredith nodded. She certainly understood that: the before and the after.

"Let's have lunch," Connie said.

Connie wanted to eat on the deck, but Meredith refused.

"You're being ridiculous," Connie said.

"I can't help myself," Meredith said. "I feel exposed."

"You're safe," Connie said. "No one is going to hurt you."

"You don't know that," Meredith said.

Connie was holding two beautiful plates of food. "Okay, I'll eat inside one more time. But after this, I'm eating outside if I want to. I'm lying on the deck, just like I did the other day. I'm going for a swim."

"You won't swim until August," Meredith said. "Admit it, you think the water's too cold."

"The water is too cold," Connie said. "But I'll walk on the beach. And if they want to photograph me walking on the beach, so be it. I'll give them the finger. That's what you have to do, Meredith. Mentally give them the finger. Let them know they don't scare you."

"They do scare me," Meredith said.

Even inside, lunch was delicious: tuna sandwiches with hothouse tomato and the farm lettuce, great globs of mayonnaise, the subtle tang of mustard. They drank cold cans of sparkling Italian lemonade.

Connie had Dan Flynn's business card next to her plate. She said, "I'm sure he just wants to know where to send the bill."

Meredith said, "Call him and find out."

Connie made a face. Then she picked up the phone. Meredith stood to give her friend some privacy, and Connie snapped her fingers and pointed to Meredith's chair.

"Stay," she said. "I can't do this alone."

Meredith sat.

Connie said, in a bright voice, "Hi, Dan? It's Connie Flute calling. From Tom Nevers? Yes, it looks great. I'm so *relieved.* You're a lifesaver!" She paused and her green eyes widened. "Oh? Tonight you mean? Gosh, well…I have other plans tonight, I'm afraid. What about tomorrow night?" She bit her lower lip. "Okay, that sounds great. And would it be okay if Meredith joined us?"

Meredith waved her arms and shook her head so violently, she heard wind in her ears. *NO!*

"I can't leave her here alone," Connie said. "Especially not after what happened."

Meredith mouthed, "You go! I'll stay here!"

"Okay, that sounds perfect. Seven thirty, Company of the Cauldron. Wonderful. You'll come pick us up at six? So early, you're sure? You're sure it's not out of your way? Oh, don't lie—it's out of everyone's way! We could just meet you at the restaurant. Really? You're sure? Okay, okay, fine, drinks sound fun. So... we'll see you at six. Thanks, Dan! Bye-bye." She hung up.

Meredith said, "What the hell are you thinking?"

Connie collapsed in her chair. She fiddled with the bread crusts that were still on her plate. "He asked me out to dinner. To the Company of the Cauldron. Which is the most romantic restaurant on earth."

Meredith groaned. "I'm not going with you."

"You have to," Connie said.

"Oh, come on, Connie. Why?"

Connie massaged her forehead. "I'm not ready to date. Normally, I would have just told this guy I'm not ready—but if you come with us, then it won't be a real date and I'll be okay." Connie's cheeks were flushed and her green eyes were shining. She liked Dan. And why not—he was good-looking, he was the right age, he'd lost his wife. But Meredith knew that if she refused to go, Connie would call Dan back and cancel. How was this any different from Connie insisting that Meredith come with her to Radnor High School three afternoons a week to watch Matt Klein wrestle when they were in the eleventh grade? How was it different from driving with Connie past Drew Van Dyke's house in the middle of the night to make sure his car was in the driveway and not parked in front of Phoebe Duncan's house?

"This is high school all over again," Meredith said.

"That's what life is," Connie said. "It's high school, over and over and over again."

It would be nice if that were true, Meredith thought. In high school, no one died of prostate cancer. In high school, no one was operating a $50 billion Ponzi scheme. The fact that what was happening right now was like high school was something to rejoice about, she supposed.

"All right," Meredith said. "I'll go." She didn't *want* to be left in the house alone; it would absolutely petrify her. "Did he sound upset that you were dragging me along?"

"Not really," Connie said.

Right: men would do anything for Connie, including having dinner with the wife of the biggest robber baron in history.

"And what plans do we have tonight?" Meredith asked.

"Plans?"

"You told Dan you had plans tonight."

"Of course I did," Connie said. She stood to clear the table. "I couldn't let him believe we were *staying home.* Don't you know anything?"

Their "plans" for Saturday night included eating a goat cheese soufflé and Caesar salad for dinner—it was like something Meredith used to order at Pastis, and Connie had whipped it up herself. And after dinner, Connie invited Meredith upstairs to Wolf's study to look at the stars through Wolf's telescope.

"Wolf knew all of the constellations," Connie said. She pointed the telescope out the window. "I only know Orion, the Big Dipper, and Cassiopeia."

"I can find the Little Dipper," Meredith said. "And the Pleiades. And I know what the Southern Cross looks like." Meredith had seen the Southern Cross on a trip she and Freddy had taken to Australia. They had been staying in the northwestern seaside town of Broome, which was the remotest place Meredith had ever visited. Freddy had a friend from business school named Michael Arrow who owned a huge pearl farm in Broome. Michael had been an investor; he had lost the pearl farm, which had been in his family since 1870. Michael had been a good guy, open and likable; he had been a friend. Meredith wondered how Freddy felt about cheating Michael Arrow. *Goddamn you, Freddy!* she thought (zillionth and fourth).

What Meredith remembered about Broome was the open-air

movie theater Michael had taken them to. They had sat on swings and watched a movie under the stars. Meredith couldn't remember what movie they'd seen, but she remembered Michael saying, "And that beauty there? That's our Southern Cross."

Meredith wondered if she'd ever see the Southern Cross again. Freddy, most certainly, would not.

Through the telescope, the stars looked closer, though they were still just stars, just points of light that were millions of miles away.

Connie said, "Freddy bought you a star, didn't he?"

Meredith nodded but said nothing. Freddy had bought Meredith a star and named it Silver Girl, after the lyrics of a song that Meredith's father used to sing her. *Sail on Silvergirl, Sail on by, Your time has come to shine, All your dreams are on their way, See how they shine.* The song was "Bridge Over Troubled Water." Every time it came on the radio, Chick Martin would reach for Meredith's hand. *Oh, if you need a friend, I'm sailing right behind.* Chick Martin had bought the album for Meredith's birthday. He played the song before each of her swim meets. They had slow-danced to the song in the living room in the hour before Meredith's graduation. He had played the song on a cassette during every driving lesson after Toby broke up with her and left town for the summer. Meredith had played the song on her turntable again and again in the cold, lonely days after Chick Martin dropped dead of a brain aneurysm. She had the old album upstairs in her sole cardboard box; it was now, and always had been, her most precious possession. Even though technology had rendered the album all but useless, she couldn't bear to part with it.

Meredith had explained the meaning of the song to Freddy, and, years later, when NASA made it possible for private citizens to buy and name stars, Freddy had bought a star for Meredith and named it Silver Girl.

Whoa. That was hard to think about, for many reasons.

Meredith excused herself for bed.

*   *   *

Connie was so excited about the date with Dan Flynn that Meredith felt herself growing excited by osmosis. Connie spent all day on the deck in the sun, diligently applying SPF 15 to her face and keeping cucumber slices over her eyes like a movie star. Meredith watched Connie from the safety of the living-room sofa, where she lay reading a book. More than anything, she wanted to be outside, but she couldn't relax while worrying that someone might photograph her. The paparazzi in New York had been relentless, swarming the awning of Meredith's building for days. But this was more insidious—the hidden camera, the secret, gazing eye recording Meredith's every move. Whether or not there was anyone out there watching her didn't matter. Meredith felt self-conscious; she felt guilty. She didn't belong on a sunny deck on Nantucket.

She wanted to call Dev to see if he had any further news from Julie Schwarz about Leo's case. Had they discredited Deacon Rapp? Had they found Mrs. Misurelli? Meredith switched on her cell phone and held her breath as she waited for calls or texts to come in. Nothing. Then she realized it was Sunday and even Dev, as hard as he worked, wouldn't be in the office. He would be on a lake fishing somewhere, or strolling in Central Park. Hell, even the Feds—the nameless, faceless Feds—would be enjoying summertime today.

Meredith was borrowing a white linen dress from Connie; it was too long, it hit her midknee, but what could she do? She wished her skin had a little bit of color. She slipped on the dress first, then did her makeup, then put on her wig. It didn't matter what she looked like, she reminded herself. She was the sidekick here, the tagalong. She was Rhoda to Connie's Mary Tyler Moore. She was Mary Ann to Connie's Ginger.

Connie looked absolutely drop-dead gorgeous in a celadon-green silk sheath. She looked like a mermaid who lured sailors to their death. She had on sparkly silver Manolos (Meredith had once owned a nearly identical pair) and she wore Guerlain Champs-

Élysées and smelled like a garden in Provence. *Oh, perfume!* Meredith nearly asked Connie for a spritz, but she refrained. It didn't matter how she smelled.

There was a knock at the door, and Dan Flynn materialized in the foyer. He was a very handsome man to begin with, and he cleaned up incredibly well. He wore creased white pants with expensive-looking loafers and a blue-patterned Robert Graham shirt.

Connie floated down the hallway. From her perch on the stairs, Meredith could see Dan's eyes pop. It gave Meredith a vicarious thrill, watching Dan feast on the vision of her lovely friend. They embraced awkwardly, and Meredith suppressed a smile. Then Dan noticed Meredith and said, "And here comes my second date. Am I lucky or what?"

Connie and Meredith climbed into Dan Flynn's strawberry-red Jeep. The soft black top was accordioned down, and Dan said, "Here we go! Hold on to your hair!" This was a joke about Meredith's wig— and surprise!—Meredith laughed. She did, indeed, hold on to her hair. The wind and the sun in her face were intoxicating. Dan played some Robert Cray. Meredith felt relaxed for the first time in months. She had made a deal with herself in the upstairs bathroom that she wouldn't spend the evening musing about what the boys were doing, or about Freddy. Freddy, she had to assume, was fending for himself, and she, Meredith, was left to do the same. She was determined to be a sparkling dinner companion, witty and interesting—and not the complete downer that Dan Flynn, no doubt, expected.

"We're starting with drinks!" Dan said. "Champagne!" Yes, Meredith loved champagne, although it gave her a regrettable headache. They arrived at the Galley Restaurant, which looked out over Nantucket Sound; they took their champagne onto the sand, where they lounged across low-slung wicker furniture covered with creamy linen pillows. It was a scene straight from the south of France. Meredith listened to Connie and Dan talk about Nantucket—the way it was now, the way it used to be. Dan Flynn had been born and raised on the island, and his father before him and his father...back five generations. At one time, he said, his family had owned nearly a tenth of the land on the island, but they had sold some of it off and donated some to conservation. Dan was a fisherman and a clammer and the owner of twenty-five lobster traps. He owned the power-washing business, and he managed his family's fourteen properties, though his real job, he said, was to know everyone on the island and everything that was going on. In the off-season, he traveled. Just like the whalers of the 1800s, Dan Flynn had seen the world. He had ridden a motorcycle through China; he had backpacked through India, contracted malaria, and spent months convalescing, with the help of some psychedelic drugs, on the beach in Goa. He had hiked with his wife and three sons to see Machu Picchu.

Connie was beaming, and it looked like real Connie beaming and not fake, polite Connie beaming. Dan was a charmer and a gentleman. When Meredith tried to slip him a twenty-dollar bill for the drinks, he said, "Put that away. Everything tonight is my treat." Meredith felt a relief she would have found absurd only a year before: she didn't have to worry about money.

They left the Galley and stopped for another round of drinks at 21 Federal. Even Meredith, who knew next to nothing about Nantucket, had heard of 21 Federal—which meant she had to be on high alert. She would see someone she knew—but, she reassured herself, no one would recognize her. The wig, the glasses. Dan had been instructed to introduce her as Meredith Martin.

Dan knew everyone at the bar at 21 Federal, including both of the bartenders. He ordered more champagne. The bar was dark and sophisticated; the clientele was attractive and convivial. But it was in gracious, genteel places like this that the Delinn name got kicked around. These were the people who had lost money or who knew people who lost money. *We're changing our last name,* Carver had said. *You should, too.*

Meredith wondered if the boys had followed through with this.

Would Leo be able to change his name while under investigation? She worried that if they did change their name, they would slip away from her, and how would she ever find them?

She had to bring herself back. Stay present, no musing! The people next to her were talking about horses. Dan and Connie were talking about sailing.

Connie said, "My husband used to sail. And my brother, Toby, is a sailor."

Toby, Meredith thought. God, she remembered when Toby had seemed like the dangerous one.

Meredith excused herself for the ladies' room, even though this meant walking past people seated for dinner, people who might recognize her. She glanced surreptitiously at faces: she knew no one. She eyed the door to the ladies' room warily. Amy Rivers could be on the other side of that door.

She wondered if she would ever outlive this particular anxiety.

The ladies' room was empty. Meredith peed gratefully, washed her hands, adjusted her wig, and briefly studied herself in the full-length mirror. Somewhere in this disguise was a girl who had been able to execute a flawless reverse one and a half pike, a woman who had read all of Jane Austen's novels except for one, a daughter and a wife and a mother who had always acted out of love. She was a good person, though no one would ever see her that way again.

Goddamn you, Freddy Delinn, she thought (zillionth and fifth). Then she took it back, because that was how she was.

The Company of the Cauldron was, as Connie had promised, the most romantic restaurant on earth. The room was small, charming, cozy. It was lit only by candles and decorated with dried flowers, copper pots, antique farm implements, and kitchen utensils. There was a harp player, and the sound of the music made Meredith think that even if everything she'd been told about heaven turned out to be false, there had better still be a harp player. Dan knew the owners of the restaurant, and so they were given the table in the front window, where they could look across the cobblestone street. Connie and Meredith sat next to each other, and Dan sat across from them. There was a rustic loaf of bread on the table, and a dish of garlicky white-bean dip. Dan ordered a bottle of wine, and when the waiter left to fetch it, Dan reached for Connie's hand. Connie and Dan were holding hands, this was their date that Meredith was crashing, and yet Meredith didn't want to be anywhere else.

As their food arrived, the conversation grew more serious. Dan talked about his wife and her ten-year battle with breast cancer. Her name was Nicole, she found a lump when she was forty years old and her youngest child was four. She went through chemo, and then a double mastectomy, and then five years on tamoxifen. Nicole had taken every possible precaution, including putting herself on what Dan called "a nasty macrobiotic diet," and just when they thought she'd beat it—she was in great shape, doing long breast-cancer walks across the state—they found the cancer had metastasized to her liver. She was dead in two months.

"I'm so sorry," Connie said. Her eyes were shining with tears.

"The kids?" Meredith said.

"It was paralyzing for the boys," Dan said. "Especially my oldest. He ditched his plans for college, stole my old pickup truck, and lit out for California. I hardly ever hear from him."

That makes three of us who aren't in touch with our kids, Meredith thought.

Connie took a breath. "My husband died of prostate cancer that metastasized to the brain," she said. "But I can't talk about it. I'm just trying to survive each day."

Dan raised his wine glass. "To survival."

Amen, thought Meredith.

The three of them touched glasses.

The evening might have ended with the tiny, seductive chocolates that came with the bill, but Dan Flynn was one of those people who never stopped. (Freddy had always been in bed by ten o'clock, and preferably nine thirty. *The stress!* he used to say, when Meredith begged him to stay out later. *There's no way you'd understand!*) Dan pulled Connie and Meredith down the street to the Club Car. There was more champagne ordered for the ladies, while Dan drank a glass of port. Meredith was tentative at first — again, scanning the old Pullman car for people she knew. (On the way, Dan had told Meredith that this Pullman car had once been part of the train that ran from Nantucket town out to Sconset.) But Meredith was drawn to the back end of the car where a man played the piano and people gathered around him singing "Sweet Caroline" and "Ob-La-Di Ob-La-Da." At one point, Meredith caught sight of Dan nuzzling Connie's neck at the bar. This was the romantic end of their date; they would both want to be rid of Meredith soon. The piano player launched into "I Guess That's Why They Call It the Blues," and Meredith belted it out, thinking of Sister Delphine at Merion Mercy, who had trained Meredith's voice for four years in the madrigal choir. Now here she was, a rather drunk torch singer.

The piano player turned to Meredith. "You have a great voice," he said. "What's your name?"

She had to make up a name. She touched her wig. "Mary Ann," she said.

"Okay, Mary Ann, you pick the next song," he said.

She picked "I Will Survive" by Gloria Gaynor, since survival had become a sort of theme for the evening. A theme for the summer.

CONNIE

On Monday morning, Connie woke up and didn't know where she was.

Then she laughed, uneasily.

She was in her bed.

She was in her own bed, tucked between the crisp white sheets, her head sunk into a cloud of a pillow. Light spilled in through the windows. The ocean seemed so close it felt like the waves were lapping at the bottom of the bed.

Connie's head was heavy but not throbbing. She noticed water in the glass carafe on her night table, with a thin slice of lemon, just as she liked it. She had no recollection of fixing it herself. She looked circumspectly over her shoulder to make sure the other side of the bed was unoccupied.

Okay.

Her clock said 5:30. God love Nantucket, the Far East of the United States. Morning came early. Connie put a second pillow over her head, and closed her eyes.

When she reawoke at ten minutes to eight, she thought, *My God, I'm in my bedroom! I'm in my bed!*

She had done it. She had faced down some kind of demon and slept in her own bed. But this pride was quickly replaced by guilt. She had slept in her own bed when *not* sleeping in it had been a tribute, of sorts, to Wolf.

Connie pulled a feather pillow to her chest as memories of the previous night came back to her. She had held hands with Dan Flynn, and just that act—holding hands with a man—had felt sinfully good. All her life she had had boyfriends; in high school and college she left one for the next. She hadn't been alone for five minutes, she realized, until Wolf died. That she had survived for so long without male attention seemed amazing, like going without hot food or good books. At the Club Car, Dan had put his mouth on her neck, and something inside of her stirred, as if returning from the dead. She had to shake off the chill, but she was doing it; she was warming up! How long since she had given her physicality any thought? With Dan, all she wanted to be was a body.

Once they were home and Meredith had stumbled up to bed, Dan and Connie had gone into the kitchen—ostensibly for a nightcap—though what Dan had asked for was water. Connie didn't remember water, what she remembered was soft, deep kissing that sent her into the stratosphere.

And Dan, the gentleman, had kept it to just kissing. Connie had cried, she remembered that now, when she told Dan that she hadn't kissed a man since Wolf died. She had believed that her days of being kissed were over. Dan didn't offer a parallel sentiment. He didn't say that Connie had been the first woman he'd kissed since Nicole died, which probably meant he'd stanched the bleeding of his heart with the kindnesses proffered by other women. He'd had sex with a woman from Nicole's yoga class when she brought over a brown-rice casserole, or he'd allowed himself to be seduced by the children's twenty-one-year-old nanny. Men were different creatures. If Connie had been the one who had died, Wolf would never have spent two and a half years sleeping on the sofa. He would already be remarried to some younger, prettier, less seasoned version of Connie. Of that she was sure.

Connie drank down the water and slipped out of bed. She would leave it unmade; she liked the way it looked rumpled. Finally, the bedroom looked inhabited.

She brushed her teeth, washed her face, inspected her skin in the mirror. She was still pretty. Big whoop. She had always been pretty, but this morning she was grateful for her looks. Dan Flynn had kissed her. He had left it at kissing—maybe because he wanted to take it slow, or maybe because today was Monday and he was scheduled to work at a house on Pocomo Point at 8 a.m.

Yes, that was it. That was what he'd told her.

It was *Monday.*

Connie gasped. Oh, my God. Oh, my God. Oh, my God. She... she couldn't even say it. A realization came to her that was so slippery, it shot right out of her grip, ricocheted around, bounced, and oozed before landing with a big, ugly, stinky splat on the floor of her mind.

She hadn't called Ashlyn yesterday. It had been Sunday, and she hadn't called.

Connie looked at herself in the mirror with wide eyes. Her eyelashes stuck together with clumps of the previous night's mascara. She had gone on a date with another man, she had kissed that man, she had slept in her own bed for the first time in two and a half years. This was all noteworthy. Indeed, startling.

But overshadowing these developments: she had forgotten to call her daughter.

After the initial panic passed, Connie thought, *I wonder if Ashlyn noticed. And if she did notice, I wonder if she cared.*

Connie hadn't spoken to her daughter since ten days after Wolf's funeral, on the day that they settled Wolf's estate and took care of the accounting at their lawyer's office in Georgetown. Ashlyn had received a trust fund filled with stocks and government bonds—it was a portfolio that Wolf had been building for her for years—that was now worth between $600,000 and $700,000. And she had inherited Wolf's navy-blue Aston Martin convertible. Ashlyn had been able to contain her seething anger and bitterness until she had the money in hand and was seated behind the wheel of the car—and then she drove out of Connie's life.

Part of it was the curse of having a daughter who was a doctor. When Wolf was diagnosed with prostate cancer, Ashlyn had just graduated from Johns Hopkins University School of Medicine, and she was doing her residency in pediatric oncology at the Washington Cancer Institute at WHC. Wolf had been suffering from symptoms and ignoring them; he was too busy with work, and although beaming with pride about the accomplishments of his daughter, he himself didn't like to go to the doctor. He liked to allow his body to heal itself, no matter the suffering. This had been true through the decades that Connie had been married to him, with stomach bugs, ear infections, colds. The problem with Wolf's prostate had presented itself a little differently, interfering as it did with their sex life. Connie had been relieved when Wolf made an appointment with a urologist, and then when he got the news of irregularities with his prostate, she was alarmed. But the first oncologist they saw was a placid man who assured them that radiation would take care of the problem. Wolf would be tired; for a while, he would be incontinent and their sex life would be put on hold.

Ashlyn had been privy to what the doctors had told Wolf, and she had agreed with their treatment plan. She and Wolf had private phone conversations about his illness, and that was fine. Ashlyn had a shiny new medical degree and she wanted to show it off. She knew far more about cancerous cells than Connie did, even though cancer of the prostate wasn't something Ashlyn saw in ped onc. Connie and Ashlyn didn't discuss Wolf's illness except in the most general terms because it was *prostate* cancer, and despite the fact that Ashlyn was a doctor, Connie still believed Wolf's privacy should be respected.

As predicted, the cancer went away following radiation treatment. Wolf wore adult diapers for twelve weeks or so; when they went to the theater, Connie would carry a spare diaper in her purse and slip it to Wolf like a contraband package before he went to the men's room. It was a humbling time for Wolf, but a small price to pay for a clean bill of health.

And then life went back to normal. Wolf was given an Institute Honor Award from the AIA for a student union building he designed at Catholic University, and three enormous commissions followed, including a federal commission to design and build a new VA building in downtown D.C. Wolf had never been busier, but both he and Connie recognized the work and its compensation as a golden sunburst that would mark the pinnacle of his career. They had nearly $3 million in investments with Delinn Enterprises, and that money was growing exponentially—one month they had a return of 29 percent—and this, along with the award, the commissions, and Wolf's restored health, secured their sense of good fortune and well-being.

Wolf started experiencing splotchy vision at the same time that

Ashlyn brought a friend home for her parents to meet, a woman named Bridget.

Ashlyn and Bridget both lived in Adams Morgan, less than thirty minutes away from Wolf and Connie in Bethesda, but they decided to come and stay for the weekend. Connie, initially believing this to be a "country escape" for two overworked, stressed-out residents, took great pains to make the house welcoming. She made up the beds in both guest rooms and put dahlias in glass vases on the nightstands. She baked cranberry muffins and braised short ribs to serve with a mushroom stroganoff. She filled the Aston Martin with gas and mapped out the drive to the biggest pumpkin patch in the state of Maryland. She had bought two novels lauded in *Washington Post Book World* and had rented a handful of new releases from the video store.

What Connie *hadn't* done was to think about what this visit from Ashlyn and her closest friend might *mean* — until she saw them walking hand in hand, with their duffel bags, from the Metro station. Until she saw them stop in the middle of the brick path that led to Connie and Wolf's front door and face each other and share an intimate, whispered moment — Ashlyn was clearly reassuring Bridget that the weekend would be fine; her parents were open-minded, tolerant, liberal people, registered Democrats, pro-choice, anti-war — and then kiss.

Connie was watching them from the front window. She had been anticipating their arrival. And quite honestly, it was as if her heart were a teacup that fell to the floor and shattered.

Ashlyn and Bridget were lovers. The reason that Ashlyn had wanted to come spend the weekend wasn't to tell her parents this but, rather, to show them.

Connie straightened her spine. She tried a couple of smiles before she opened the front door. She needed to talk to Wolf, but he was on-site. The commissions had kept Wolf at work for ridiculously long hours, and although Connie hadn't complained, she now felt abandoned and resentful. She needed Wolf here. He should have been paying attention; he might have prepared Connie for this possibility. Was her daughter, her only child, a lesbian? Yes, it appeared so. Although girls, Connie thought, were more apt to experiment sexually, weren't they? Time to ruminate was running out; Connie could hear the girls' footsteps on the stairs leading to the front door. She could hear Ashlyn giggling. This didn't mean there would never be a wedding at the house on Nantucket as Connie had always dreamed. This didn't mean there would never be grandchildren. Connie *was* liberal; she *was* tolerant. She had taken women's studies classes at Villanova; she had read Audre Lorde and Angela Carter and Simone de Beauvoir. But was it still okay for Connie to say that this *wasn't* how she wanted things to turn out? This—Connie opened the door and saw Ashlyn and Bridget side by side, grinning nervously—wasn't what she wanted at all.

She got an A+ for trying in her own estimation. Connie smiled and hugged Bridget and fawned over her as though she were an adorable kitten Ashlyn had brought home. Bridget was Irish, from County Mayo, and she had an elfin quality about her—a pixie cut of black hair, freckles, and that accent, which stirred delight in Connie despite the circumstances. She was witty and, from what Ashlyn said, wickedly brilliant. She was exactly the kind of girl Connie would have wanted a son to bring home.

Connie plied the girls with oatmeal chocolate chip cookies—Ashlyn's childhood favorite—and a pot of tea—the lover was Irish—and she chattered like an idiot. An idiot mother who hadn't guessed her own child's sexual preference. (Had there been clues Connie had missed? In high school and college and even in medical school, Ashlyn had had *boyfriends*. Wolf had caught one young man climbing the rose trellis up to Ashlyn's bedroom in the middle of the night. And, as Wolf had shouted angrily at the time, that boy hadn't come to play tiddlywinks!) Connie knew she was transparent—at least to Ashlyn—and she was grateful when Ashlyn said that she and Bridget were going up to "their" room to unpack. This gave Connie a chance to escape to the sanctuary of her bedroom where she called Wolf to break the news.

He listened, but didn't comment. He said, "I know this is going to sound like a complete non sequitur, but I have a crushing headache. The pressure in my skull is so intense, it feels like I'm growing horns. Can this wait until I get home?"

That night, the four of them sat around the dining-room table eating the sumptuous meal that Connie had prepared, and Ashlyn and Bridget talked about the trip they were planning to London, Wales, Scotland, and finally to Ireland to visit Bridget's family.

So another mother can have her dreams trampled, Connie thought.

But what she said was, "That sounds terrific, girls!"

Ashlyn scowled, probably at the use of the term "girls." Why infantilize them? Why not refer to them as women or, better still, people? But Connie found it helpful to think of them as innocent girls: Ashlyn with her long, pale hair left loose except for a braid that framed her face and made her look like a Renaissance maiden, and Bridget with her shiny cap of black hair and her implike smile. They weren't so different from Connie and Meredith in high school — always together, palling around, being funny and affectionate with each other — were they?

Wolf didn't say much of anything during dinner. His head, he complained. And he'd already taken six hundred milligrams of ibuprofen. He excused himself before dessert. The girls settled on the couch to watch one of the DVDs Connie had rented and to eat apple brown betty and make some jokes about the whipped cream that Connie pretended not to hear as she cleaned up in the kitchen. She reminded herself that this was probably a phase. She prayed to God that she wouldn't be woken up by any female cries of ecstasy, and she cursed Wolf for being so self-absorbed. When she got upstairs, he was already in bed with the light off, a washcloth folded over his eyes.

Connie said, "I honestly can't believe it."

Wolf said, "I'm going blind, Con. I can't see a thing."

*   *   *

In the morning, Ashlyn took one look at her father and suggested he call his primary care physician. But it was Saturday, so that meant the emergency room. Wolf resisted. He would just take some more ibuprofen and lie down.

Ashlyn said, "Dad, your right pupil is dilated."

Wolf said, "I just need rest. I've been working like a demon."

And Ashlyn, caught up in the throes of romance, didn't push him the way she might have normally. She and Bridget were, at Connie's suggestion, off to the pumpkin patch in the Aston Martin. They were taking a picnic.

By two o'clock, Wolf was moaning. By three, he asked Connie to call an ambulance.

Connie changed into shorts and a T-shirt. She pulled her hair back into a ponytail. The house was still; Meredith was sleeping. Connie would go get the newspaper. She would drive around and clear her head. She would decide whether to call Ashlyn this morning or wait and see what happened. In her heart, however, Connie knew that nothing would happen. She could call or not call—it didn't matter.

Wolf had been diagnosed with prostate cancer that had metastasized to the brain. He had two tumors located in the frontal lobe and so, the oncologist said, Wolf's analogy about "growing horns" was apt. One of the tumors was operable; one was inoperable. The inoperable tumor was spread out, like a spilled drink on a table. They would give Wolf chemo and try to shrink the inoperable tumor. If they got it to a stage where it could be contained, they could go in and scoop out both tumors at once.

Wolf, over the course of the weekend, had seemed to accept his own mortality. "What if I decline chemo? What if I just let them be?"

The doctor said, "Severe headaches, which we can manage with medication. Blotchy vision, ditto. Depending on how aggressive the cancer is, you might have one year; you might have three."

Wolf squeezed Connie's hand. "Okay," he said.

"Chemo," Connie said.

"Let me think about it," he said.

Connie sat on the edge of the unmade bed. At dinner at the Company of the Cauldron the night before, Dan Flynn had told them about his wife's death. The basics of her illness were similar to Wolf's. The cancer disappeared then resurfaced—the same cancer—in a different place. Nicole had breast cancer travel to her liver. Wolf had prostate cancer travel to his brain. It seemed so unfair: the doctor declared you "clean," said you'd "beat it," and then one random, renegade cell traveled to a more hospitable location and decided to multiply.

Connie had never been able to share Wolf's story with anyone who hadn't lived through it with her. It was too Byzantine; it didn't make sense.

Wolf had refused chemo.

Part of this was because of the three commissions he was working on, including the new VA building. These buildings would, presumably, stand for decades and possibly centuries. It was architecture, he was the architect, and if he bailed out now because of debilitating treatment, he would lose control. The buildings would become something else—someone else's—even if they used his plans.

"It would be like Picasso handing his palette to his assistant, or to some other artist—Matisse, say—and asking that person to finish *Guernica*. You understand that, don't you, Connie?"

What Connie understood was that Wolf thought he was Picasso. So it was about ego.

"Not ego," Wolf said. "Legacy. I can finish these three buildings and complete my legacy, or I can go in for chemo and let my legacy slip down the drain. And there's no saying the chemo will save me. The chemo might shrink my tumor to an operable size, and then I'll die on the table."

"You have to have faith," Connie said.

"I have faith that I can finish the buildings," he said. "I can finish my life's work."

"And what about me?" Connie said.

"I love you," Wolf said.

He loved her but not enough to fight the disease. The work was what was important. His legacy. This was his argument, and Connie also knew that deep down, he was afraid. He didn't like doctors, he was distrustful of the health-care system, he feared chemo, and he feared having his head shaved, his skull cracked open, and his brain scooped out like orange sherbet or rocky road. Better to bury himself in the work and pretend like nothing was wrong. Numb his pain with Percocet and, later, morphine, and hope that his body healed itself. Connie had been married to Wolf for twenty-five years, but she, ultimately, had no say or sway in the matter. It was his body, his illness, his decision. She could either fight him or back him. She backed him.

Ashlyn was furious. She was, in turn, incredulous and disconsolate. She stormed Wolf's office, then his work sites, and lectured him. She set up an appointment for a second opinion that he agreed to go to and then skipped at the last minute because of a problem with his head mason. Ashlyn stormed the house and screamed at Connie.

"You're just going to stand by and let him die!"

Wolf died seventeen months later. He had gotten two of his commissions done and the third—the spectacular, complicated VA building—into its final phase.

Connie couldn't believe she had all but lost her only child over Wolf's death, but the fact was, Ashlyn had always been an intense, tricky kid. She was all or nothing. She loved you or hated you;

there was never any middle ground. Connie herself had grown up scattered, disorganized, fun loving, laid back. None of these words applied to Ashlyn. Ashlyn didn't accept compromise; she didn't take it easy on herself or others. Connie and Wolf had once met with a school psychologist who was concerned that Ashlyn was "preoccupied with perfection." She was eight years old, and when she held a crayon, a vein bulged in her forehead.

After Wolf died, Ashlyn's anger consumed her. Ashlyn *became* her anger. During the days when there was still dialogue, Connie had heard it all.

Ashlyn said, "You didn't encourage him to fight. If you're diagnosed with an illness like his—which was certainly treatable, if not curable—you battle it. You do whatever you can, you take the clinical trials, you go through seventeen rounds of chemo, you do what you have to do to stay alive."

"But you know your father didn't feel that way. His work..."

"His work!" Ashlyn screamed. Her eyes flashed in a way that frightened Connie, and Connie reminded herself that Ashlyn was hurting. All her life, Ashlyn had favored her father. She sought his attention and love as though they were the only attention and love that mattered. Connie had often been treated as the enemy, and if not an enemy then an obstacle that had been placed between Ashlyn and Wolf. Connie had remained steadfast, and sure enough, in college and medical school, Ashlyn had come back to her. There had been lunches and shopping trips and spa vacations (though no real heart-to-hearts, Connie saw now, there had been no chance for Ashlyn to reveal her emotional life). Ashlyn had remained closer with Wolf and that was fine. If anything, Connie had counted on Wolf agreeing to treatment for Ashlyn's sake. She had expected Ashlyn to save Wolf for both of them.

Connie said, "Your father was a thoughtful man. He made the choice that felt right to him. Surely, in your work you've seen other patients who refused treatment?"

"Those patients weren't my father."

Fair enough. Connie said, "I loved your father deeply. You know I did. I chose to respect his decision because I loved him, but don't you think it was hard for me, too? Don't you think it was damn near impossible for me to watch him slip away?"

"He chose his work," Ashlyn said. "Not you, not me."

"He was afraid of hospitals," Connie said. "He didn't even like putting on a Band-Aid. I couldn't imagine him hooked up to forty machines, lines sticking out of him, pumping him full of poison. I couldn't imagine him strapped to a table while they sawed open his skull."

"He would have done it if he loved us," Ashlyn said.

"That's not true," Connie said. "Because he did love us. He loved me, and he loved you."

"Yeah, but you know what it feels like?" Ashlyn said. She had been crying so hard that the half-moons under her eyes were pink, and her nostrils were raw and chafed. Such pale skin, pale hair, pale eyes. Ashlyn had fair and delicate looks, and people always assumed on meeting her that she would have a mild, milky way about her, but they were wrong. She was a force, driven, determined, and focused. Even in childbirth, she had wanted out. "It feels like he gave up on me because of how I am. Because of Bridget—"

"Honey!" Connie said. "No!"

"He gave up on me. Because there won't be a big wedding or an investment banker son-in-law. Because there won't be grandchildren. And you let him."

"Ashlyn, stop! That had *nothing* to do with it."

"For twenty-six years I strived to make you proud of me. High school, college, medical school—"

"We are proud of you—"

"But I can't help how I feel. I can't help *who I am*—"

Connie had tried to make Ashlyn see that Wolf's decision was just that—Wolf's decision. It had been supremely selfish, yes. But he had wanted to live and die on his own terms. It had nothing to do with Ashlyn or her relationship with Bridget. It might seem that way because of the timing, but no.

"But yes!" Ashlyn said. She wasn't going to back down. She was raging at Connie, and Connie felt a flash of anger at Wolf for leaving her behind to be raged at. After all, she had lost him, too. She was suffering, too. Connie should have backed off—she'd had twenty-six years of dealing with her daughter to know this was true—but instead Connie said, "You think Daddy didn't want to fight because he found out you were gay? You know what that sounds like to me, Ashlyn? That sounds like a heap of self-loathing."

Ashlyn reached out to smack Connie, but Connie caught her hand and held it tight. She was Veronica O'Brien's daughter, after all. She said, "Come to peace with yourself, Ashlyn, and then you'll be able to come to peace with your father's decision."

Connie didn't regret saying any of this, although she did regret what she said later, after the funeral. And she regretted not doing more when Ashlyn climbed into the Aston Martin. Connie should have laid her body down in front of the car. She should have chased after her.

Connie had found out—through Jake and Iris—that Ashlyn had taken a job with a hospital in Tallahassee. She had moved down there with Bridget. Jake and Iris claimed they only heard from Ashlyn sporadically, and they promised that when they had important news, they would let Connie know. (Most of the reason Connie didn't like Iris was because Iris knew more about her daughter than she did.) Connie continued to call Ashlyn's cell phone every week, and every week she was treated to voice mail.

The call that came to Connie's phone on the day the photograph of Meredith was left on the porch was the most promising lead Connie had had since Ashlyn drove away in the Aston Martin.

Connie descended the stairs to the front door. That she hadn't called Ashlyn yesterday now seemed like it might be a positive thing. *How can I miss you when you won't go away?* Ashlyn would, at the very least, be curious about her mother's lapsed communication. And maybe even worried.

Connie would wait a few days, then try again with the new phone number.

That decided, Connie felt better. She was moving on with her life, finally. She had experienced two Julys and two Augusts since Wolf died, but only now, today, did she feel like it was actually summertime. She would go to the Sconset Market and get the paper and some snickerdoodle coffee and freshly baked peach muffins. When Connie got back, Meredith would be awake, and they could deconstruct the night before minute by minute.

If nothing else, it was a wonderful distraction.

Connie stepped outside and knew immediately that something was wrong. Something with her car. It was parked in front of the house, the windows were intact, the body work was unscathed, at least on the side facing the house. But the car looked sick. It was sunken, listing.

Connie moved closer to inspect. "Oh," she whispered.

The tires had been slashed.

They had been sliced open in ragged gashes. And then Connie noticed a piece of paper tucked under the windshield wiper. She plucked it out, opened it up, read it.

In black marker it said, "Theif, go home."

Connie's first instinct was to crumple the note and throw it away, but they would need it as evidence for the police. The police again. Oh, her poor car. Connie spun around and surveyed her property. The day was bright and sunny, with enough breeze to make the eelgrass dance. This spot was idyllic. It had been safe, until she brought Meredith here. Now they were under attack.

Theif, go home.

Whoever wrote the note didn't know how to spell. So it was somebody young, or somebody stupid, or somebody foreign.

Or was it Connie who was being stupid? First her house, now her car. What would be next? Meredith and Connie had bull's-eyes painted on their backs. What if this escalated? What if they got hurt? Connie was placing her well-being on the line for Meredith's sake. But Meredith was her friend. They hadn't spoken for three years—those had been awful, lonely years—and now Connie had her back.

Theif, go home. Connie was assaulted by contradictory thoughts. Meredith had said horrible things to her; Meredith had put Freddy and his contemptible dealings before her lifelong friendship with Connie. Meredith was still under investigation—she knew more than she was telling, that was for damn sure. But Meredith had never stolen or cheated in her life. She was the only senior girl who never sneaked sips of the Communion wine; she was the only one who didn't cheat on her Good Friday fast—not a single Ritz cracker, not one chocolate chip from the bag her mother kept in the baking cabinet. Connie had watched Meredith march up the steps of Saint Mary's the other day, and she'd thought, *There is a woman who still believes in God. How does she do it?* Meredith's number one glaring fault was that she had always been so goddamned perfect, and nobody liked a perfect person. *Pull the stick out of your ass!* How many times had Connie wanted to shout *that* out over the years? Now that Meredith's perfection had come to a screeching halt, Connie loved her more. Just last night, Meredith had sung at the bar; she had been terrific fun, a good sport, and Connie had been shocked. She remembered Meredith's face as she belted out the song: shining with sweat, her glasses slipping to the end of her nose.

Theif, go home.

As far as Connie was concerned, Meredith *was* home.

Connie regarded her shredded tires. She understood how they had gotten to this point, but that didn't make it any easier.

She went back inside to wake up Meredith.

MEREDITH

Chief Kapenash inspected the four slashed tires, took the note as evidence, and gave Connie and Meredith his sincere apology. He'd had a squad car scheduled to cruise the road every hour, and last night it had made the run between midnight and 4 a.m. Before midnight, that particular officer had been called to break up a party of underage drinkers on the beach, and after four that officer had been called to a domestic dispute all the way out in Madaket. So the vandalism had taken place either while Connie and Meredith were out on the town or in the early-morning hours.

It didn't matter. Either way, Meredith was scared. Slashed tires: it seemed so violent. When she asked the chief what kind of tool could slash a tire, he'd said, "In this case, it looks like a hunting knife." And then there was the matter of the note. *Theif, go home.* It had been written in block letters, making it impossible to identify a male or female hand. (Meredith had secretly checked the handwriting against the handwriting on the back of Dan Flynn's business card. She liked Dan, and it seemed that Dan liked her, but in the world that Meredith now knew to be hiding all kinds of secrets, she wondered if Dan was asking Connie out so he could hurt Meredith. Thankfully, the handwriting didn't match up.) *Theif, go home.* The only clue they had to go on was the misspelling.

Dan showed up and changed all four tires. The labor for that was gratis, but Meredith offered to pay for the tires, which had cost six hundred dollars, and while she was at it, she threw in four hundred dollars for the power washing. She held out a thousand dollars in cash to Connie, her hand trembling.

Connie looked at the money and said, "Put it away."

"Please, Connie. You have to let me pay."

"We're in this together," Connie said. She then confided that, while changing the tires, Dan had invited her out on his boat on

Thursday. They were going to cruise around the harbor and check the lobster pots. "And you're coming with us."

"No," Meredith said flatly. "I'm not."

"You have to," Connie said.

"The man wants you to himself," Meredith said. "Last night was fine, but I'm not going to be a tagalong all summer."

"Well, I can't leave you here by yourself," Connie said. "Not after what happened this morning."

"I'm a big girl," Meredith said. "I'll be fine."

Connie grinned. It was amazing what a little romance did for a person. Her tires had been slashed with a hunting knife, and yet Connie was floating. Meredith thought she might insist one more time that Meredith come along, and if she had, Meredith would have agreed. She liked the sound of a boat ride—out on the open water, Meredith wouldn't be confronted with anyone she knew. And she was afraid to be left home by herself. She would spend the day behind locked doors, huddled on the floor of her closet.

But Connie didn't insist, and Meredith figured that Connie was ready to be alone with Dan. The phone in the house rang just then, and Meredith nearly jumped out of her skin. Connie hurried to get it—she may have thought it was Dan, or the police with a suspect. A few seconds later, she said, "Meredith? It's for you."

Leo! Meredith thought. *Carver!* But then Meredith chastised herself. She had to stop thinking like that. It was hope, ultimately, that would bring her down.

"Who is it?" Meredith asked.

"Some fifteen-year-old boy who says he's your attorney," Connie said.

Meredith took the phone. She felt a surge of jangly nerves. Good news? Bad news? Bad news, she decided. It was always bad news.

"Meredith?" the voice said. It was Dev. Meredith pictured his shaggy black hair, his vampire teeth, his rimless glasses. She hadn't made the connection before, but she realized she now wore the same kind of glasses as Dev. They looked far better on him.

"Dev?" she said.

"Hey," he said. His tone was soft, nearly tender. "How's it going?"

"Oh," she said. She thought for a moment that Dev had heard about the slashed tires and was calling to offer her some legal counsel—but that was impossible. "It goes."

"Listen," Dev said. "Burt and I had a meeting with the Feds. They're now convinced there is upwards of ten billion dollars stashed somewhere overseas. Freddy's still not talking. The Feds are willing to hold off pressing conspiracy charges on you, and possibly Leo also, if they get your cooperation."

Meredith sank into one of the dining-room chairs. From there, she could see the blue of the ocean. It was a dark, Yankee blue, different from the turquoise water in Palm Beach or the azure water of Cap d'Antibes. "What kind of cooperation?" Meredith said. She sighed. "I've already told you everything."

"I need ideas about where that money might be," Dev said.

"I thought I was clear," Meredith said. She took a metered breath. "I don't know."

"Meredith."

"I don't know!" Meredith said. She stood up and walked over to the window. "You were very kind to me back in New York. And I repaid you by being honest. I told the Feds the truth. Now they're trying to bribe me with my own freedom and, worse still, my son's freedom, which we deserve anyway, because I didn't know the first thing about what was going on. And you know and I know and Julie Schwarz knows that Leo didn't either. I wasn't privy to any of Freddy's business deals. They didn't interest me. I'm not a numbers person. I majored in American literature. I read Hemingway and Frost, okay? I did my thesis on Edith Wharton. I can give you a detailed explanation on the use of the outsider in *The Age of Innocence,* but I don't know what a derivative is. I don't properly know what a hedge fund is."

"Meredith."

"I don't know where Freddy put his money." Meredith was

screaming now, though in a low voice, so as not to alarm Connie. "There was an office in London. Have you checked there?"

"The Feds are investigating the people in London."

"I never once visited the London office. I didn't know *a single person* who worked there. And those were the bad guys, right?"

"Those were some of the bad guys," Dev said.

"I don't even know their names," Meredith said. "I was never introduced. I couldn't pick them out of a crowd of two. Freddy took me to London three times, and the first time we were college kids, backpacking. The other two times Freddy visited the office, and do you know where I went? I went to the Tate Gallery to see the Turners and the Constables. I went to Westminster blinking Abbey."

"What the Feds are looking for are buzzwords," Dev said. "Phrases. People's names. Things Freddy repeated that might not have made sense. One of the words that turned up in the files is 'dial.' Do you know the meaning of the word 'dial'?"

Meredith gave a short laugh. "That was the name of Fred's eating club at Princeton."

"Really?" Dev said. He sounded like he'd discovered a gold nugget in his sieve.

"Really," said Meredith. Freddy had been the king of the pool table at Dial. He had wooed Meredith with his dead eye, twelve ball in the right corner pocket. They used to get drunk on keg beer and raid the kitchen at Dial late at night, and Freddy would whip up his specialty—a fried chicken patty with a slice of tomato and Russian dressing. Nothing Meredith had eaten before or since had tasted better. Freddy had been able to let loose back then—drink too much, stay up late. He had those incredible looks—the black hair, the clear blue eyes. Meredith remembered asking him if he resembled his father or his mother. *I don't look like my mother,* he said. *And I never met my father, so I couldn't say.* What kind of name was Delinn, anyway? Meredith asked. Because it sounded French. *It's a French name,* Freddy said. *But my mother always said the old man was Irish. I didn't grow up the way you grew up, Mere-dith. I don't have a pedigree. Just pretend like I hatched from an egg.*

Devon said, "What about the word 'buttons'?"

"Our dog," Meredith said. Buttons had been a gift for the boys when they were ten and eight. Freddy had an investor who owned a kennel upstate, where the dogs consistently won awards. Freddy wanted a golden retriever. Meredith had lobbied to give the puppy a literary name—Kafka or Fitzgerald—but Freddy said it was only right to let the kids name the dog, and they named him Buttons. Meredith could still picture the boys and that tiny, impossibly cute butterscotch-colored puppy. Freddy had snapped pictures with this silly grin on his face. That night in bed, he'd said to her, *We'll give them cars on their sixteenth birthday and Rolexes when they turn twenty-one, but no present will ever beat the one we gave them today.*

And Meredith had to agree.

"Could it be a code word?" Dev asked.

"I suppose," Meredith said. "Freddy was very fond of the dog. He took him to work. They walked there, they walked home. Sometimes they detoured through the park. I used to take the dog to Southampton for the summer, and Freddy would get very depressed. Not without us, mind you, but without the dog."

"Really?" Dev said. Another gold nugget.

Meredith shook her head. This was a wild-goose chase. There was most certainly money hidden; Freddy was too cunning not to have buried millions, or even billions, but he would have hidden it where it would absolutely never be found.

"What about the word 'champ'?" Dev said. "That was a word that turned up frequently."

Oh, God. Meredith coughed, and fought off the urge to spit. *Champ? Frequently? How frequently?* "Champ" was Freddy's nick-name for their decorator, Samantha, because her maiden name was Champion. (Meredith had always thought that the nickname was meant to be a jab at Samantha's husband, Trent Deuce, whom Freddy disliked and dismissed.)

" 'Champ'?" Dev asked again. "Ring a bell?"

Meredith paused. "Where did this word 'champ' turn up? I'm curious. In his date book? His diary?"

"I really can't say," Dev said.

Right, Meredith thought. The information flowed only one way.

"Does the word mean anything to you?" Dev asked.

Meredith thought back to the day when she'd come across Freddy with his hand on Samantha's back. She remembered how he'd whipped his hand away when he saw Meredith. She could still see the expression on his face: What was it? Guilt? Fear? Despite this memory, which always made Meredith uneasy, she didn't want to turn Samantha over to the FBI. Samantha was Meredith's friend, or she had been. Plus, she was a decorator; she had nothing to do with Freddy's business or the Ponzi scheme.

Still, Dev was asking. She wasn't going to be the woman the media thought she was: a woman who lied to her lawyer. And there was Leo to think of. Leo!

" 'Champ' was Freddy's nickname for our decorator. Samantha Champion Deuce."

"Oh, boy," Dev said quietly.

"She was a friend of Freddy's, but a better friend of mine," Meredith said. "She was our decorator for years."

"How many years?"

"Ten years? Twelve?"

"So there are lots of reasons why her name might turn up," Dev said. "Reasons that have nothing to do with the business."

"I guarantee you, Samantha didn't know a single thing about Freddy's business," Meredith said. "She used to call where he worked the 'money shop.' Like he was dealing in ice cream or bicycles."

"But now you understand what we're looking for?" Dev asked. "Words that have meaning. They might be a clue, a contact, a password. The money could be anywhere in the world. I spoke to Julie Schwarz…"

"You did?" Meredith said.

"Leo is making a list of words, and so is Carver. But they said we should ask you. They said Freddy talked only to you, confided only in you..."

"He was my husband," Meredith said. "But there are a lot of things I didn't know about him. He was a private person." For example, Freddy never told Meredith who he voted for in an election. She didn't know the name of the tailor in London who made his suits. She didn't know the password on his phone or his computer; she had only known that there was a password. Everything was locked up all the time, including the door to his home office.

"I understand," Dev said.

How could he understand? Meredith thought. Dev wasn't married. He hadn't slept beside someone for thirty years only to discover they were somebody else.

"This could help you, Meredith," Dev said. "This could save you. It could keep you out of prison. In a year or two, when all this is in the past, you could resume normal life."

Resume normal life? What did that even *mean?* Meredith was tempted to tell Dev about Connie's slashed tires, but she refrained. She was afraid it would sound like a cry for pity, and the image Meredith needed to convey now was one of strength. She would come up with the answer. She would save herself.

"I can't think of anything now," Meredith said. "You've caught me unprepared. But I'll try. I'll...make a list."

"Please," Dev said.

That night, Meredith was too afraid to sleep. She kept picturing a man with a hunting knife hiding in the eelgrass. Meredith rose from bed, crept into the hallway, and peered out one of the windows that faced the front yard and the road. The yard was empty, quiet. The eelgrass swayed. There was a waxing gibbous moon that disappeared behind puffy nighttime clouds, then reemerged. At three fifteen, a pair of headlights appeared on the road. Meredith tensed. The headlights slowed down at the start of Connie's driveway, paused, then rolled on. It was the police. The squad car parked in the public lot for a few minutes, then backed up and drove away.

She would make a list of words, the way Dev had asked. *Resume normal life* meant life with Leo and Carver. Leo would be safe and free, and the three of them—including Anais, and whatever young woman Carver fancied at the moment—would have dinner together at the sturdy oak table in Carver's imaginary house.

Meredith would come up with the answer.

Atkinson: the name of the professor who taught the anthropology class that brought her and Freddy together.

Meredith had given Freddy the used textbook. With that bond between them, they gravitated toward each other on the first day of class. Meredith and her roommate, a girl from backwater Alabama named Gwen Marbury, sat with Freddy and his roommate, a boy from Shaker Heights, Ohio, named Richard Cassel. The four of them became something of a merry band, though they hung out together only in that one class. When Meredith saw Freddy elsewhere on campus, he was usually in the presence of a stunning, dark-haired girl. His girlfriend, Meredith assumed, another upperclassman. It figured. Freddy was too funny and smart, and too beautiful himself, to be available. Through Gwen Marbury, who was far more interested in the social politics of Princeton than in her studies, Meredith learned that the girl's name was Trina Didem, and that she was from Istanbul, Turkey. Trina was a dual major in economics and political science. Again, it figured: ravishing, exotic, and brilliant, someone destined to be a far-flung correspondent on CNN or the head of the Brookings Institution or secretary of state. Meredith's crush on Freddy intensified the more she learned about Trina, although Meredith realized that what she was experiencing was nothing more than a freshman crush on a particularly cool upperclassman. It was also a way to stop thinking about Toby at the College of Charleston drinking yards of beer with all the sweet, blond southern girls. But Meredith cherished her time in class with Freddy and Richard and Gwen—the three of them cracked jokes about the clicking language of the Khoisan tribe, and they speculated on the advantages of a matriarchal society—and when class was over, Meredith continued her anthropological study of Trina Didem. Trina waited for Freddy outside on the stone steps of the building so she could smoke her clove cigarettes. She, Trina, wore a black suede choker at all times, as well as dangly earrings made from multicolored stones. She wore tight, faded jeans, and she carried a buttery soft Italian leather bag. Really, Meredith thought, she probably had a crush on Trina as well as Freddy. Trina was a woman, whereas Meredith was a girl trying to become a woman.

At the beginning of December, a knock came on the door of the anthropology classroom. Professor Atkinson stopped lecturing and swooped over to answer the door with a perplexed look on her face, as though this were her home and these were unexpected guests. Standing at the door was Trina Didem. Professor Atkinson looked first to Freddy, perhaps thinking there was going to be some kind of lovers' spat right in the middle of their discussion of Dunbar's number. But Trina, it seemed, was there on official business. She read off a slip of paper, in her lilting English. She was looking for Meredith Martin.

Meredith stood up, confused. She thought perhaps Trina had learned of her crush on Freddy and had come to call her out. But a second later, Trina explained that Meredith was needed in the Student Life Office. Meredith collected her books. Freddy reached for her hand as she left. It was the first time he'd ever touched her.

Meredith followed Trina out of the building. She was so starstruck in Trina's presence that she was unable to ask the obvious questions: *Why did you pull me out of class? Where are we going?* It looked, from the path they were taking, like they were headed for the office of the dean of students, which differed slightly from the Student Life Office that she'd been promised. Or maybe they were one and the same—Meredith was still too new to campus to know. Trina took the occasion of being outside in the cold, crystalline air to light a clove cigarette. Because she was a step or two ahead of Meredith, the smoke blew in Meredith's face. Somehow, this snapped Meredith back to her senses. She said, "You're Freddy's girlfriend, right?"

Trina barked once, then blew out her smoke. "Not girlfriend. Freddy is my English tutor." She blew out more smoke. "And my economics tutor. I pay him."

Meredith felt her own lungs fill up with the cloying, noxious smoke—it tasted to Meredith like burning molasses, and her grandmother's gingerbread cookies, which she detested—but she didn't care because she was so excited. Freddy was Trina's *tutor!* She *paid* him! Meredith couldn't wait to tell Gwen.

Meredith's elation was short-lived. Once they were in the plush office belonging to the dean of students, which was empty but for the two of them, Trina closed the door. Meredith remembered an Oriental rug under her feet; she remembered the brassy song of a grandfather clock. She noted that Trina had extinguished her cigarette, but an aura of smoke still clung to her. Up close, she could see that Trina had speckles of mascara on her upper eyelids.

What's going on? Meredith wondered. But she wasn't brave enough to ask. It was definitely something bad. She fleetingly thought of how ironic it would be if she got kicked out of school right at the moment that she had learned Freddy was unattached.

Trina said, "The dean is in a meeting across campus. I'm an intern here, so they sent me to tell you."

Tell me what? Meredith thought. But her voice didn't work.

"Your mother called," Trina said. "Your father had a brain aneurysm. He died."

Meredith screamed. Trina moved to touch her, but Meredith swatted her away. She could remember being embarrassed about her screaming. She was screaming in front of Trina, whom she had considered a paragon of Ivy League womanhood. And what news had Trina, of all people, just delivered her? Her father was dead. Chick Martin, of the eggplant parm subs and the monthly poker games; Chick Martin, the partner at Saul, Ewing who specialized in the laws of arbitrage; Chick Martin, who had believed his daughter to be brilliant and talented. He had suffered a brain aneurysm at work. So arbitrage had killed him. Arbitrage was tricky; it had a million rules and loopholes, and while trying to decipher the code that would bring him to his answer, Chick Martin's brain had short-circuited. He was dead.

But no, that wasn't possible. Meredith had just been home for Thanksgiving break. Her father had been waiting for her at the Villanova train station. He had wanted to come get her at the university, but Meredith had insisted on taking the train — New Jersey Transit to 30th Street Station, SEPTA to Villanova. *That's what college kids do, Daddy!* Meredith had said. *They take the train!*

Both of her parents had coddled her over break. Her mother brought her poached eggs in bed; her father gave her forty dollars for the informal class reunion that was taking place on Wednesday night at the Barleycorn Inn. Her parents brought her along to the annual cocktail party at the Donovers' house on Friday night, and as a concession to her new adult status, her father handed her a glass of Chablis. He introduced her to couples she had known her whole life as though she were a brand-new person: *My daughter, Meredith, a freshman at Princeton!*

Chick Martin, Meredith's first and best champion, the only champion she'd ever needed, was gone.

Meredith stopped screaming long enough to look at Trina, thinking how she *hated* her, *hated* the smell of clove cigarettes, *hated* the city of Istanbul, *hated* the beauty and sophistication that was masking the sadism required to deliver this kind of news. Meredith said, "No, you're wrong."

Trina said, "I'll walk you back to your suite so you can pack your things. We've called for a car to take you home."

The world had stopped being safe on that day. As happy as Meredith had ever been in her life, she had never been *truly* happy again.

Her father was gone; her father's love for her was gone. She thought back to the driving lessons in the university parking lot, her father saying, *I can't stand to see you hurt like this.* The pain Toby had caused Meredith was one thing. This pain, now, was quite another.

Seven hundred and fifty people attended Chick Martin's funeral—his law partners, his poker buddies, friends, neighbors, Meredith's teachers, everyone she had ever known, it seemed. Connie was there and Connie's parents, but not Toby—he was entering finals at the College of Charleston and said he couldn't get away.

Dustin Leavitt came to the funeral.

Dustin Leavitt? Meredith saw him approaching the church as she waited for the hearse out front with her mother and grandmother. There were so many people from so many parts of Meredith's past in attendance that she had a problem pinning names to faces. When she saw Dustin Leavitt, she registered his good looks and she thought he was someone she knew from Princeton—a professor? a graduate student? then it came to her—Dustin Leavitt, thirty-three-year-old coworker of Mr. O'Brien's at Philco, whom she had danced with at Connie's graduation party. She had forgotten all about him.

He took her hands. Despite the fact that so many people had held, pressed, or squeezed Meredith's hands, they were ice cold. Meredith hadn't given a thought to her appearance in days, and now she worried that she looked like a red-nosed, wild-haired troll. She didn't own a black dress, so she was wearing a black cashmere turtleneck and a gray pinstriped skirt. Black tights, awful black flats. She had stupidly put on mascara, which now trailed in sooty streaks down her face.

"Hi!" Meredith said, trying to sound normal, as though she had come across Dustin Leavitt sitting at a booth in Minella's Diner and not on the steps of Saint Thomas of Villanova on the occasion of her father's funeral. She felt embarrassed by her situation, and then ashamed about her embarrassment.

Dustin Leavitt said, "I'm sorry for your loss, Meredith. Every-one knows how much your father loved you."

"Oh," Meredith said. She welled with fresh, hot tears. Dustin Leavitt hesitated. Meredith knew she was making him uncom-fortable, so she tried to smile and wave him on. He squeezed her bicep—it seemed to her he had also done this after the Lower Merion swim meet—and then he disappeared into the dark mouth of the church.

Meredith saw him later at the reception at Aronimink, and still later, at the after-reception, which was an impromptu event held at the O'Briens' house. Meredith's mother and grandmother had gone home, but Meredith had stuck with Connie, and Veronica and Bill O'Brien, and the other mourners who were for the most part all drunk, but because of the early hour—six o'clock—and because of the meager, WASPy offerings of the luncheon at Aron-imink, thought that more drinks and pizza and cheese steaks at the O'Briens' sounded better than going home. Meredith had lit-tle recollection of anything that had transpired that day—she had taken a pill at 9 a.m. to settle her nerves—and by the time she reached the O'Briens', she was drunker than either Connie or Veronica, which was saying something. She believed she finally understood alcohol's true purpose—to eradicate conscious and deliberate thought when such thought was too agonizing. Dustin Leavitt did his part in providing comfort by bringing Meredith a tall flute of very cold champagne.

"People think champagne is best for celebrating," he said. "But I like it for misery, myself."

Meredith knew she had a witty response to that somewhere inside her, but it was buried beneath a pile of her broken child-hood memories, and she couldn't snatch it out. She raised her glass to Dustin Leavitt's handsome but increasingly blurry face and said, "To misery."

They touched glasses. They drank. In the dining room, where the table was laden with pizza boxes and foil-wrapped subs and cardboard boats of curly fries, Connie was huddled in the arms of Drew Van Dyke, who had come home from Johns Hopkins in order to be with Connie during her time of need. After all, her best friend's father had died. Meredith felt a surge of confusion. Certainly Connie had loved Chick Martin; because Meredith and Connie were so close, Connie had been like an adopted daughter to Chick. But Meredith suspected that for Connie and Drew, this funeral was just a bonus opportunity to travel the two hours to see each other and have sex. And why did Connie have someone here to comfort her, but not Meredith?

Toby should be here, Meredith thought. He should be here for her father. He should be here for her.

Meredith looked at Dustin Leavitt. "Get me out of here," she said.

"Gladly," he said.

They walked out the front door together without explanation or excuse, and no one fussed. Meredith had the leeway granted to the newly bereaved, maybe — or maybe nobody noticed.

She followed Dustin Leavitt out to his car, a Peugeot sedan. He opened the door for her. She got in, humbled once again by her hideous outfit, and to make matters worse, over the course of the day she'd worked a hole into the foot of her tights so that her big toe stuck through the material. This bothered her the way a ragged fingernail or loose tooth might.

Dustin said, "Any place special you want to go?"

Meredith shrugged.

He said, "My place okay?"

"Sure," she said.

She watched out the window as they drove. The town of Villanova looked the same as it had her whole life, but it was different now because her father was gone. They passed the train station where, until the day before, Chick Martin's car had remained in the parking lot, as if waiting for him to come home. How many times had Meredith ridden the bus home from school and seen her father's bronze Mercedes in that parking lot?

Dustin Leavitt took roads that led them to the expressway, and Meredith felt the first stirrings of panic. "Where do you live?" she asked.

"In King of Prussia," he said. "Over by the mall."

The mall, okay, yes the mall was familiar, but in her childhood naïveté, Meredith had thought that King of Prussia *was* the mall. She hadn't realized it was also a place people might live.

She had no energy or desire for conversation; she didn't want to ask Dustin Leavitt about his family or his job or his hobbies, and she certainly didn't want to talk about herself.

He pulled into an apartment complex. Three tall buildings, twenty or thirty stories, formed a semi-circle. They walked into the center building. On the ground floor was a Chinese restaurant. Through the window, Meredith saw people whose fathers had *not* died that week drinking electric-blue cocktails out of fishbowls.

Dustin Leavitt pulled out his keys, opened his mailbox, removed a sheaf of letters, and flipped through them. This simple, everyday act jolted Meredith like ice cubes down her back. What was she doing here? Who was this man? What would happen next?

Next, they would get into the elevator. Dustin Leavitt would push the button for the eighteenth floor. Dustin would step off. What choice did Meredith have now but to follow? The hallway was carpeted in maroon wall-to-wall that held the paths of the vacuum cleaner. It smelled like cigarettes and litter boxes and soy sauce. Meredith was disgusted. Her drunkenness started to assert itself. She feared she was going to vomit. Dustin Leavitt unlocked the door to apartment 1804. The apartment was dark.

Dustin said, "Good, my roommate isn't home."

Roommate? thought Meredith. She was the one with a roommate. Gwen Marbury. Meredith hadn't known what to expect from Dustin Leavitt; she supposed she'd expected that he would own a house, like Mr. O'Brien, minus the wife and children. Dustin was thirty-three years old. She certainly hadn't expected a crummy apartment and a roommate.

He opened his refrigerator, and it illuminated the kitchen. He said, "Would you like a beer?"

"Sure," Meredith said.

He handed her a bottle of St. Pauli Girl. She took the tiniest sip, mainly to block the ambient smells of the apartment. Dustin opened a beer for himself, loosened his tie, and walked down the dark hall. Meredith faltered. Now, it seemed, would be the time to excuse herself. But she had *asked* him to take her away from the O'Briens' house, and when he said, "My place okay?" she had said yes. She was far from home with no way back. She followed.

The next thing she knew, they were kissing on the bed. Dustin Leavitt was on top of her. His hands were fighting to get her tights down. Her shoes had fallen off, her big toe was protruding from the foot of her tights. Meredith couldn't decide whether to help Dustin or resist him. Meredith wished she were anywhere else. How could she stop him? She had asked for this.

He yanked off her tights. He put his finger in her. It hurt. She hadn't been with anyone since Toby, way back in June.

"Tight," he said.

Meredith was afraid she was going to vomit. Dustin Leavitt put on a condom; Meredith breathed in and out through her mouth, willing herself not to get sick. She would not think about the cheese steaks with cold, congealed onions on the O'Briens' dining-room table. She would not think about cat turds lying in kitty litter. She would not think about her father, collapsed on his desk, bleeding from one eye.

Dustin Leavitt entered her.

This, Meredith thought, *is what happens when a girl loses her father. She gets date raped.*

And then blames herself.

*   *   *

Meredith stayed home through Christmas, playing and replaying "Bridge Over Troubled Water" on her turntable. *If you need a friend, I'm sailing right behind.* Relatives and neighbors came to put up the Christmas tree and fix lovely meals that Meredith and her mother didn't eat. The holiday was a brightly wrapped box with nothing inside. Toby called, but Meredith refused to talk to him. She asked her mother to take a message.

"He sends his condolences," her mother said. "He said he loved Chick and will remember him fondly."

Condolences? Fondly? What kind of lexicon was this? Toby loved Chick, but he no longer loved Meredith. Meredith was furious. She thought about calling Toby back and telling him she'd slept with Dustin Leavitt. Would he care?

Meredith asked Connie about this when they met for beers at Bennigan's. Connie was noncommittal and dismissive about Toby.

"Try to forget about him," Connie said. "He's a lost cause."

Meredith would try to forget about him. To distract herself, she studied. In a rare form of torture, Princeton held finals after Christmas. Meredith went back to campus and, despite the fact that she was a shadow of her former self, she slayed her exams: A's across the board.

Freddy approached her in the first week of the new semester.

"I heard about your father," he said. "I'm sorry."

This was said with more gravitas than Meredith was used to encountering in her peers. Connie had hugged her and listened to her at home, and her roommate, Gwen, had hugged her and listened to her here, but Meredith could tell they didn't get it. She felt their pity, but not their empathy. They treated her like she had an illness. And Gwen, who hated her own father, even sounded a little envious.

But when Freddy spoke, Meredith sensed a deeper well.

"Thank you," she said. "Trina told you?"

"Gwen, actually," he said. "But when Trina showed up at class,

I knew it wasn't good news. She's pretty much known as the Grim Reaper around here."

"Yeah," Meredith said. She would be only too glad if she never saw Trina again. She remembered back a few weeks when Trina's clothes and accessories and mannerisms had been of the utmost interest to her—it was amazing how that had changed. Even Meredith's attraction to Freddy had paled when compared to the real love of Meredith's life. The steady, unconditional, fortifying love of Meredith's father was gone forever. It wasn't fucking fair, it was *not* fucking fair! Meredith, that week, had been alternating between devastated melancholy and door-kicking, hair-pulling anger.

Meredith and Freddy walked together for a while in silence. Meredith didn't know where Freddy was going, but she was headed to the east side of campus to the Mental Health Services building where students could receive free counseling. Meredith saw a woman named Elise, and did little more than sob through her fifty-minute sessions.

Freddy said, "My brother, David, died last year. He was in the army, and he was shot during training. A total, pointless mistake. Some complete asshole discharged his weapon when he wasn't supposed to, and my brother is dead."

"Oh, God," Meredith said. She had heard dozens of stories of untimely deaths in the weeks since her father died, and she had yet to figure out how to respond. She knew people were trying to create some kind of interpersonal connection by sharing their own losses, but Meredith took self-indulgent pleasure in believing that her loss was unique—and far worse—than anyone else's. But Freddy's story did indeed sound both sad and bad. A brother shot accidentally while training to defend our country? Shot by one of his own? Meredith wanted to say the right thing, but she didn't know what that was. She decided to give him a question he could answer. "How old was he?"

"Twenty-three."

"That's really young. Were you close?"

Freddy shrugged. "Not really. But he was, you know, my *brother*."

"That must have been hard," Meredith said, then hated herself. She sounded just like Connie, or Gwen Marbury!

Freddy didn't respond and Meredith didn't blame him, but he did walk Meredith all the way to the Mental Health Services building. She thought of detouring so he wouldn't guess where she was headed, but then she decided it didn't matter if he knew. As soon as her destination became clear, he said, "I came here a lot last year. It helped. Is it helping you?"

"No," Meredith said.

"It takes a while," Freddy said. He locked eyes with her, and only then did Meredith remember that he had reached for her hand as she was called from the classroom. And in that moment, she recognized Freddy, much the way she thought the Virgin Mary must have recognized the angel Gabriel; it felt no less mystical. Freddy was a different person from the cool upperclassman she'd had a crush on. He was the person who had been sent to collect her. As Freddy held her gaze outside the dour and depressing Mental Health Services building, Meredith thought, *I'm yours. Take me.*

"I'll come back and pick you up in an hour?" Freddy asked.

"Yes," she said.

They had been inseparable from that point forward.

For many years, Meredith had believed that Freddy had been sent to her by her father. She had believed this right up until December of last year, when she, with the rest of the world, learned of Freddy's crimes. Even now, when she thought about Freddy's betrayal, it took her breath away. Other people had lost money. Meredith had lost faith in the one person she believed had been sent to save her. He, Freddy Delinn, was Dustin Leavitt, a man who would rape a drunk eighteen-year-old girl who had just lost her father. He was the man with the hunting knife. He was not an emissary from her guardian angel–father, but rather an emissary of the devil, come to ruin her life.

Meredith heard a door open down the hall.

Connie said, "Meredith, is that you?"

"Yes."

"Are you all right?"

All right? She would be all right if she didn't think, if she didn't remember. She felt a hand on her shoulder. Connie was there, her long hair tangled and even more beautiful in sleep.

"Meredith?"

"Yes," Meredith said. And she let Connie lead her back to bed.

CONNIE

Connie spent all morning trying to convince Meredith to come along. It was a brilliant day—sun, blue sky, a touch of a breeze. Days didn't get any better than this.

"Nothing you can say will change my mind," Meredith said. "I'm not going."

"I don't want to go alone," Connie said. She gazed at the ocean. "I'm scared."

"There, you admitted it," Meredith said. "Do you feel better?"

"No," Connie said. "I want you to come. If you come, I'll feel better."

"How are you going to know how you feel about this guy if you never spend time alone with him?"

"I'm not ready for time alone with him," Connie said. She thought about the kissing. It had been wonderful, but that, some-how, only added to her fear. "I'm going to cancel."

"No, you're not," Meredith said.

"I'll tell him we can picnic here, on the deck," Connie said. "I'll tell him we can swim here, on this beach, with Harold."

"No," Meredith said.

"That way we can all be together."

"No!" Meredith said.

"Meredith," Connie said. "I haven't asked you for anything since we've been here."

"Okay, wait," Meredith said. "Are you really going to play that card?"

Connie could barely believe it herself. "Yes," she said.

"Well, then, I can't say no, can I?" Meredith said. "You saved my life. You brought me here. You're sheltering me despite physical damage to your house and your car. I'm indebted to you. And so I *have* to go with you on your date." She put her hands on her hips. She was tiny in stature but imperious. Connie could tell she was trying not to smile.

"Yes," Connie said. "Thank you."

Meredith said, "I'll go put on my wig."

While Meredith was upstairs, there was a knock at the door. Connie practically ran to open it. She was *so* much more relaxed now that Meredith had agreed to come along, emotional arm twisting notwithstanding. Connie's fear and anxiety floated away. They were going on Dan's boat. They were going to have fun!

Connie flung open the door. Dan was holding a bunch of wildflowers that Connie recognized as coming off one of the farm trucks that parked on Main Street.

"For you," he said, handing her the flowers.

"Thank you!" she said. "That's sweet."

He smiled. He was so handsome with his sunglasses perched in his short, ruffled hair. Connie leaned in to kiss him. She meant it to be a quick, thank-you-for-the-flowers kiss, but he closed his eyes and made it a longer kiss. And even as Connie was liking it, loving it, she thought, *No, I can't do this. I'm not ready for this.*

She pulled away. She said, "Meredith has decided to come with us today."

"Oh," Dan said. "Terrific."

"It's not terrific," Meredith said, coming down the stairs. She was securing her wig with bobby pins. Connie threw her a warning look. Meredith was coming with them because Connie needed her, but she couldn't let Dan know she was coming because Connie needed her. This was the logic of high school, Connie knew, but just because they were older didn't mean they had outgrown the rules.

Meredith said, "I'm an egregious interloper. A third wheel. But the fact is, I don't feel safe alone in the house all day." She smiled sheepishly at Dan. "I'm sorry."

"Don't be sorry," Dan said. "It's fine."

"Just fine," Connie said.

It was one of those days that made you feel lucky to be alive—no matter if you'd lost a spouse to cancer, no matter if your only child no longer acknowledged your existence, no matter if your husband had lost $50 billion in a Ponzi scheme and you were hated by everyone in America. The back of Dan's red Jeep was loaded with life jackets and fishing poles, and Connie wedged in her cooler, which contained a couple bottles of wine and enough picnic lunch for ten people. Connie sat up front next to Dan, and Meredith stretched out in the backseat and closed her eyes in the sun. Dan played Marshall Tucker's "Heard It in a Love Song," and they all belted out the words at the tops of their lungs.

Dan pulled into the parking lot at Children's Beach. Children's Beach was a green park with a band shell, a playground, and an ice-cream shack fronted by a small beach right on the harbor. Connie tried to keep her emotions in check. She hadn't been to Children's Beach since Ashlyn was a little girl. There had been a few summers when Connie had brought Ashlyn here every day— Ashlyn had gone down the slides, complaining if the metal was too hot on her legs, and Connie had pushed Ashlyn on the swings, back and forth a thousand times. In those days, the ice-cream shack had been a breakfast joint with the best doughnuts on the island. God, it hurt to think about it. Connie had brought Ashlyn here on days that Wolf had been asked to sail, and then they'd walked to the Yacht Club to meet him for lunch, and Connie's only worry had been that Ashlyn might misbehave.

Dan sprang into action, and Connie and Meredith followed suit. He took the fishing poles, the beach towels, a gas can. Connie took one end of the cooler and Meredith took the other. Meredith, too, had an eye on the action at Children's Beach—the mothers trying to get their toddlers to eat one more bite of peanut butter and jelly, the kids building sandcastles, the orthopedist's dream that was a twenty-foot-high cone-shaped climbing structure on the beach—but she snapped out of her reverie. Was she thinking about Leo? Meredith took three life jackets in her free hand. Connie grabbed her beach bag.

Dan's boat was moored along the dock. They walked down to the boardwalk in front of the White Elephant Hotel and climbed aboard.

It was a beautiful boat, a Boston Whaler Outrage with dual engines off the back. Connie fell in love with it immediately. It had a horseshoe of cushioned seating in the back and up front, and room for two behind the controls under a bimini. Toby was a sailor—a skill learned in summer camp in Cape May and then honed at the College of Charleston—and Wolf had been a sailor as well, but Connie had never warmed to the sport. Sailing was so much work, a combination of physical work and intellectual work, and it required luck. Connie loved being out on the water, but it was much easier to do it Dan's way—turn a key and inhale those exhaust fumes.

Connie helped Dan gather the rope that tethered them to the slip. He guided the boat out into the harbor. Meredith was sitting up front, waving to the people on other boats. Connie joined her.

Meredith was beaming. Beaming! She felt comfortable enough to wave to people.

Connie said, "You're glad you came, aren't you?"

"Shut up," Meredith said. She raised her face to the sun and grinned.

"Where do you want to go?" Dan asked. Connie was sitting next to him behind the controls.

"Anywhere," Connie said. "Everywhere." She was happy-giddy, if a teensy bit uncomfortable to be sitting next to him in the girl-friend seat. But it was nice, too, to be able to just go where they wanted as fast as they wanted without worrying about the main-sail or the jib. She had never sat next to Wolf on a boat. When they sailed, he was always moving, always monitoring.

They cruised up harbor, past the huge homes of Monomoy and the huger homes on Shawkemo Point. Dan singled out certain houses and told Connie who owned them—this famous author, that captain of industry. The island looked especially verdant and inviting today. The houses seemed to be stage sets for summer: flags were snapping, beach towels hung from railings. Meredith scanned the land, one hand shielding her eyes, and then lay back in the sun with her glasses off and her eyes closed.

They tooled up to Pocomo Point, where they came across a fleet of Sunfish with white sails—kids learning the basics.

Dan said, "As soon as we're out of their way, we'll anchor and go for a swim."

He stopped the boat in a beautiful, wide-open spot. Great Point Lighthouse was visible to the northwest and the handsome Wau-winet hotel was due north. Without the noise of the engine, the only sound was that of the waves slapping the side of the boat, and Connie suddenly felt anxious.

"Let me pull out the wine," she said.

"It's dazzling here," Meredith said.

"We'll swim," Dan said. "And then we can have lunch." He looked at Meredith. "Do you swim?"

"Yes," she said. "I do."

Connie pulled the cork from a cold bottle of chardonnay. She felt her blood quicken. She couldn't pour fast enough. She wasn't sure what was wrong with her. "Meredith was a champion diver in high school. She came in third at the state finals our senior year."

"Really?" Dan said. "Well, then, I have a surprise for you."

Connie filled a red Solo cup with chardonnay and guzzled the top third of it down. A cool burn slid down her throat, and she felt her muscles go slack.

"Wine?" she asked Dan.

He was moving the cooler and rearranging some other things at the stern and he said, "I'll get a beer, in a minute."

Typical man with his beer, Connie thought. Wolf had been a wine drinker. It had been one of the many elegant things about him. Connie took another sip. How often did men like Wolf come along?

"Meredith, wine?" Connie asked.

"No, thank you," Meredith said.

Dan pulled something out of the back of the boat—a long white springboard. A diving board.

"There we go," he said proudly.

"Oh, my God!" Connie said. "Meredith, a diving board!"

Meredith made her way to the back of the boat. She saw the springboard and put her hand to her mouth.

Dan said, "I got it for my kids. They love it." He climbed up onto it, stripped off his T-shirt, which he threw into the well, and took a couple of test bounces. Then he approached the end of the board and did a soaring swan dive. He surfaced and rubbed at his eyes. "Your turn!" he called to Meredith.

Meredith looked at Connie. "I haven't dived in years."

"You were the best at Merion Mercy," Connie said. "You held all those records."

Meredith was pulling the bobby pins out of her head—off came the wig. Meredith's real hair was matted underneath, and she shook it out.

"I can't believe I'm going to dive," she said. "Will I remember how?"

"Isn't it like riding a bike?" Connie asked. She drank some more, and a feeling of well-being settled over her. Her arms tingled; there was a golden glow in her chest.

"I guess we'll see," Meredith said. She shed her cover-up and climbed onto the board. She walked to the end, then walked back. She gave it a few test bounces. Then, she composed herself at the back of the board, and, like a gymnast, she took one, two, three choreographed steps, bounced impossibly high, and folded her body into a perfectly straight up-and-down front dive. It was a thing of beauty. Connie blinked. She had gone to all of Meredith's home meets in high school, and what struck her watching Meredith dive now was the time warp.

Dan whistled and clapped and shouted. Meredith surfaced, her hair wet and slick, and swam easily over to the ladder on the side of the boat.

Meredith said, "Just like riding a bike."

Connie said, "Do another one. Do something fancy. Really show him." She remembered Meredith once telling a reporter from the *Main Line Times* that a simple front dive or a reverse dive was the hardest to execute because her body wanted to flip and twist. Her body, she said, craved degree of difficulty.

Meredith climbed back up onto the board. She did a front one and a half pike. Her pike wasn't as tight as it had been in high school, but that was to be expected.

Dan grabbed a towel and sat next to Connie. "Man," he said. "Did you see that?"

"I told you," Connie said. She drank her wine. She had two inches or so left in her cup. Another glass like that and she'd be ready for some food.

Meredith climbed back up onto the board. She walked out to the end with regal bearing and turned around.

Back dive. Her entry was perfect, her toes pointed, though she didn't get the height she'd gotten in high school. God, Connie could remember the way Meredith had seemed to float in the air, the way she had seemed to fly.

"Do another one!" Connie said.

"I don't know," Meredith said. She mounted the board and did a backflip with a half twist.

Dan put his fingers in his mouth and whistled.

Connie said, "That was too easy!" Connie remembered Meredith stretching on the blue mats that the coaches laid out alongside the diving well. Meredith could put her face flush to her knees, her arms wrapped around her thighs. It hurt now just thinking about it.

Meredith did a simple inward dive. Then a reverse dive. Then, without any warning, she approached the end of the board and whipped into a front two and a half somersault, tuck. Dan hooted, and Connie wondered if she should feel jealous. She had been an aggressive field-hockey player in high school, but that didn't inspire this kind of admiration. Connie touched Dan's shoulder, to remind him that she was still there. "Are you ready for that beer?"

He said, "Aren't you going to try?"

She filled her cup with wine—glug, glug, glug—and didn't quite catch his meaning. Meredith executed something else; Connie only looked up in time to see Meredith's legs enter the water. The key to a good entry was as little splash as possible.

Connie said, "Excuse me?" She corked the wine and stuck it back in the cooler.

"Aren't you going to take a turn on the board?" Dan asked.

"Oh," Connie said. "I don't dive like that."

"Come on," Meredith said. "The water's nice."

"Come on," Dan said, standing up. He climbed onto the board. "You must be hot."

She was kind of hot, yes, but she didn't like being pressured into things. And she still found the water too cold for swimming. But now if she said no, she would seem prissy and high maintenance or, worse, she would seem old. She would jump off the board once, she decided, and then she would drink that wine.

Dan did another swan dive and waited, treading water, for Connie to have a turn. Connie bounced on the board, testing it, as she'd seen Dan and Meredith do, but the board had more spring than she anticipated—either that or her legs weren't as steady as theirs—and she lost her balance and had to windmill her arms like some vaudeville act just to keep from falling.

"Whoa!" she said. "Okay." She steadied herself and proceeded to the end of the board. In the distance, she saw Great Point Light. Seagulls flew overhead, a few wispy clouds scudded by. She didn't want to jump. She liked it here, perched over the water, surveying.

She bounced, placed her arms over her head, and dove, hitting the water much sooner than she expected, and harder. Her chest, where she'd been holding that golden chardonnay glow, stung. And she had water up her nose. Her nasal passages buzzed and burned, and the burn trickled down her throat. Connie wiped her eyes, adjusted her bathing-suit top, pawed at her hair.

"There you go!" Dan said. "Great job!" But Connie felt he was being patronizing.

"The water's freezing," Connie said, though it wasn't, really. She wanted to get back on the boat. But here came Meredith again.

She said, "Okay, last one."

"What's it going to be?" Dan asked.

Meredith ran for the end of the board, bounced, and launched herself into another front one and a half pike, though her pike was loose, and she entered early, making a big splash. Despite this, Connie gave Meredith two hands up: a ten. Meredith jerked her head toward her shoulder. "Water in my ear," she said.

It was only swimming back to the ladder that Connie noticed the name of the boat written in gold script. *Nicky.*

Nicky? Connie thought. And then she realized: Nicole, the wife. Nicky.

She felt ten kinds of sad as she pulled herself aboard.

It was nothing a second and then a third glass of wine couldn't cure. Dan cracked a beer, and Meredith drank a diet Nantucket Nectars iced tea. Connie didn't love the fact that she had been bullied into the water, but she did love drying in the sun and feeling the saltwater evaporate off her skin.

Meredith's wig lay on the seat next to Connie like some kind of poor, abandoned animal. Connie held it up with two fingers.

"I wish you didn't have to wear this," Connie said.

"Here, give it to me," Meredith said.

"I wish people would just leave you alone," Connie said. She could feel the wine circulating around her brain, embalming it. "Leave *us* alone."

There was an awkward silence. Meredith jerked her head again, still trying to drain her ear. Connie hoped she hadn't heard; the words had come out wrong.

Dan said, "I don't know about you, but I'm ready for lunch."

Lunch, yes! Connie enthusiastically pulled lunch from the cooler. There were two kinds of sandwiches: chicken salad on wheat, or roast beef and Swiss with horseradish mayo on rye. There was potato salad that Connie had made from scratch, as well as a chilled cucumber soup with dill. There was a fruit salad of watermelon, strawberries, and blueberries. There were chocolate cupcakes with peanut-butter icing.

"Amazing," Dan said. He had one of each kind of sandwich, a whopping portion of potato salad, a cup of soup. "You made all this yourself?"

"Meredith dives," Connie said, "and I cook." She felt like perhaps this evened things out. She took a bite of her chicken-salad sandwich. "Did your wife like this boat?"

Dan nodded. "Loved it."

"You named it for her?" Connie asked. Her voice sounded con-frontational to her own ears, though she wasn't sure why. Clearly the boat was named for his wife, and why should that matter? It was his boat, he'd had it a long time, longer than the past ten days, which was how long he'd known Connie. And there was nothing between him and Connie anyway except for a handful of great kisses. But still, wasn't it a little weird to take a woman that you'd kissed a few times out on a boat named for your dead wife?

"We used to have a boat," Meredith said wistfully. She said this without irony, as if everyone in America hadn't heard about Fred-dy's megayacht, *Bebe,* which had cost him $7 million of his clients' money. She smiled at Dan. "But it didn't have a diving board!"

In the afternoon, they motored to the end of the jetty. There were seals lounging on the black rocks, and Connie thought of Harold.

Dan said, "We're going out to check the lobster pots."

"Oh, yes," Connie said. She had finished one bottle of wine by herself and had eaten only part of half a sandwich, so she was pleasantly buzzed. She had achieved a perfect state of equilibrium. She was happy and lighthearted, without a care in the world. She debated opening a second bottle of wine but decided against it—she was, after all, the only one drinking. Dan had drunk one beer and Meredith had stuck to diet iced tea. But when Dan pulled back on the throttle and the horsepower kicked in, Connie wished she had a drink. If she stopped drinking now, in this sun, she might fall asleep, and if she fell asleep, she'd wake up with a head-ache. The boat was ripping along, skimming the water, and when they encountered wake from the high-speed ferry, which passed them on their starboard side, the front of the boat slammed against the chop, and a fine mist splashed over the side. Meredith was facing front, as still and alert as the maidenhead on a whaling ship; she hadn't replaced her wig, and her glasses were off. She didn't seem to mind getting wet.

Connie had been sitting next to Dan behind the controls, but she made a move to the stern to see if reaching into the cooler was feasible. But as soon as she stood up, the boat hit a wave and Connie fell against the gritty floor of the deck and scraped her knee. There was blood. She crawled to the safety of the cushioned seats and held on to the back rail for dear life. Dan hadn't noticed her fall, which was a good thing, though he would notice the blood on his deck. She inspected her knee. It stung. They crossed the wake of another, bigger power yacht, and the front of the boat slammed again; there was more spray up front. Connie couldn't reach the cooler; it was wedged under the seat, and even if she could get to it, the motor skills required to open the wine were beyond her under the circumstances. She would have to wait until they stopped or slowed down.

Their speed was breathtaking. Connie squinted at the boat's speedometer: one hundred knots, or nearly. Was that equivalent to a hundred miles an hour? She couldn't remember. Dan was a cowboy behind the wheel of a boat, whereas Wolf, while sailing, had been an orchestra conductor. But, Connie reminded herself, she wasn't looking to replace Wolf. She wasn't looking for anything except a respite from her misery. She liked motor boats, she reminded herself. Up front, Meredith seemed completely unfazed by the speed. Connie needed to loosen up.

And then, suddenly, Dan downshifted, and the boat slowed. Sticking out of the sparkling water, Connie saw tall buoys on stakes. Dan maneuvered the boat toward the buoys and cut the engine.

"Okay!" he shouted. He scrambled for the ropes and, like an experienced rodeo hand, lassoed a buoy with a green stripe. He seemed busy, so Connie made a move for the cooler, feeling like a pirate trying to pilfer from the treasure chest. She unwedged the cooler and had just gotten the second bottle of chardonnay in her hands when Dan said, "Quick! I need help here!" He was barking orders, just as Wolf tended to when he sailed. *Men,* Connie thought. She had her eyes on Dan—did he really expect *her* to help him with the lobster traps?—but her hands were rummaging for the corkscrew.

"Help!" Dan called again.

Meredith appeared beside him to help him pull up the ropes. Connie could see she was needed as well, so she abandoned the wine in the cooler and hurried over. Heave, ho—they yanked and rested and yanked and rested. Dan's forearms were straining with the effort, and Connie got the feeling that she and Meredith weren't contributing much in the way of strength. Finally, the heavy wooden trap broke the surface of the green water and Dan said, "Back up!" He hauled the trap up over the side of the boat and Connie and Meredith helped him maneuver it onto the deck.

Dan exhaled and wiped at his forehead. He looked at Connie and thought to smile. He was handsome, he had kissed her, but he was a complete stranger to her. She was glad Meredith was here.

"Wow," Meredith said. She crouched down to inspect the contents of the trap, but Connie didn't want to get too close. She could see thirty or forty blackish-green lobsters crawling all over in a panicked frenzy, like kids at a rock concert. The shells clicked against one another and some of the antennae stuck out of the slats. Lobsters were a lot like cockroaches, Connie decided, with their armored carapaces and their prehistoric ugliness. Still, she thought, delicious. She loved lobster salad, steamed and cracked lobsters with drawn butter, lobster bisque...

"So many!" Connie said admiringly. "What will you do with them?"

"Well, three lucky ones will be our dinner tonight," Dan said. "And the rest I'll sell to Bill at East Coast Seafood."

Meredith said, "I feel sorry for them."

Dan nodded. "Typical female answer. My wife felt sorry for them, too. She used to beg me to let them go."

Connie felt like she should chime in with her own expression of sympathy on the crustaceans' behalf, but she didn't care. She said, "Do you need our help?"

"No," Dan said. "But I have to band these guys and put them in coolers. And then I'm going to fish for a few minutes. Are you ladies okay to kick back here for a little while?"

"God, yes," Connie said. Now that he had basically given her permission, she opened the wine and poured herself a hefty cup. She said, "Meredith, do you want wine?"

"No, thanks," Meredith said. She was standing by the trap, watching Dan as he put on heavy work gloves and pulled the lobsters out one by one, securing thick blue rubber bands on each claw. He then set the disenfranchised lobsters in an industrial-size white cooler that he had pulled out from the hold. Meredith seemed mesmerized by this work. Well, it wasn't anything she would have seen on the French Riviera.

Connie took her wine up to the bow, and lay back in the sun.

Despite her best intentions, she must have fallen asleep because when she next looked up, the lobster trap was gone and the cooler with the lobsters had been tucked under the seats at the stern. Dan had his fishing pole out, and Connie saw that Meredith held the other fishing pole; she was standing next to Dan, reeling in her line.

Connie sat up. She had to pee.

She heard Meredith say, "So there was one time at the pool at Princeton where I dove like that for Freddy, only I was better then because I was younger and I had just been in training. And I was thinking that Freddy would be impressed, that he would think I was so talented, so athletic, so limber—I mean, even from a *sexual* standpoint it should have turned him on, right? But instead of being impressed, he...well, I didn't really understand his reaction. He was nonplussed. He didn't like watching me dive for some reason. And so I stopped doing it. There were times in subsequent years when we were at someone's pool and there was a diving board and I would whip out a front two and a half like I did today—it's a deceptively easy dive—and Freddy would seethe.

He accused me of showing off. He was threatened by my diving. I should have seen that as a sign." Meredith cast her line back out; her reel whizzed. "Why didn't I see that as a sign?"

Dan laughed. "Hindsight," he said.

"Hindsight in my case was worth about fifty billion dollars," Meredith said.

Connie reached for her wine. It was warm. She ditched it over the side and stumbled to the back of the boat for more.

Dan and Meredith were so deep in conversation that they didn't even notice she was awake. She poured another cup of wine and wondered if Dan *liked* Meredith, then decided not. All their lives, boys had enjoyed talking to Meredith—she was smart, quick, funny—but Connie was beautiful and that had always trumped smart.

Even Freddy Delinn had once—yes, he had once made a pass at her. Connie had banished that memory—she thought, permanently—from her mind.

She secured her wine in one of the round cup holders situated conveniently around the boat, then she climbed up onto the side and dove in. Smack! Again, the water came too fast. Her chest burned and her scraped knee stung. She let herself drift down into the cool depths and she peed, sweet release. She knew there was sea life below her—all of those lobsters for starters and probably a lot of other sinister creatures. That far out, maybe even sharks. But the wine and the nap gave Connie a lethargy that made her want to float beneath the surface for a minute.

Seven or eight years earlier, Freddy had brought Connie a cocktail on the deck of the house in Cap d'Antibes. Wolf had been out jogging, and Meredith had run into town to an antiques store to take a second look at something she'd wanted to buy. That part of the story made sense in Connie's memory, but Freddy bringing her a cocktail—a very cold, very crisp gin and tonic with lots of lime—had been a surprise, because Freddy didn't drink. So the drink was a flirtation; Connie had sensed that right away. And there was something about the look on Freddy's face when he brought it to her. Connie had always felt insecure when visiting the Delinns—in Manhattan, in Palm Beach, in France—because of money, she supposed. It was impossible, in the face of all that money, to feel that one measured up. And so, to compensate, Connie flaunted her beauty. On the evening that Freddy brought her the drink, she was already dressed for dinner. She was wearing a long patio dress in an orange and pink paisley; the dress had a plunging neckline, putting her breasts on display. At home in America, Connie would only have worn that dress privately, for Wolf. But this was the south of France, where everyone seemed determined to show off what they had.

Freddy was still in his robe. He had looked appreciatively at Connie's breasts, and he let Connie catch him looking, which seemed a brazen thing to do. He gave her the drink, she sipped it, they leaned together on the railing that looked down the cliff over the Mediterranean.

Then he turned toward her and she meant, as a grasp at light conversation, to ask him what his ethnic background was. The name "Delinn" was French, right? But just then, Freddy said, "You're an incredibly beautiful woman, Constance."

Connie was rendered speechless. She nodded, though barely. She wasn't struck by Freddy's actual words—people had been telling her she was beautiful her whole life—but by how he said it. He had said it with *intent,* as though he meant to carry her up to his bedroom and make love to her right that second. He had used her full name, Constance, which made her feel sophisticated. And then he leaned in and kissed her, and with one deft hand, he cupped her breast, which was thinly sheathed behind the silk of her dress. She felt a stab of arousal and she made a gasping noise. She and Freddy separated and stared at each other for a fierce, hot second, then Connie left the deck. She took her drink up to the guest room, where she sat on the bed, waiting for Wolf to return.

Even now, what struck Connie about that encounter was Freddy's confidence, his authority, his sense of entitlement as he reached out to kiss her and touch her body. He had no qualms about putting his hands on something that did not belong to him.

Connie felt arms close in around her, and she squirmed, confused and afraid. She was being pulled to the surface.

"What?" she choked.

Dan was in the water next to her, holding her roughly under one arm. "Thank God," he said. "I thought you were drowning."

"Drowning?" she said.

"You fell in dangerously close to our lines," he said.

From the side of the boat, Meredith waved. "Are you okay?"

"I didn't fall," Connie said. "I dove in."

"All I saw was the splash," Dan admitted. "But you've had so much wine, I was worried."

So much wine? Connie thought.

"I'm fine," Connie assured him. She swam away from him, toward the ladder on the back of the boat. There was the name again. *Nicky.* What a weird afternoon.

They stayed on the water until well after five o'clock. The sun mellowed in its slant, and Connie, despite the fact that she was being watched like a teenager, finished off the second bottle of chardonnay, though not by herself. As they motored back into the harbor, Meredith agreed to a glass. Connie and Meredith sat in the bow of the boat together, and Dan turned on some Jimmy Buffett, and the gold dome of the Unitarian Church glinted in the sun, and Connie decided that it had been a good day.

Meredith turned to Connie as Dan was tying the boat up in the slip and said, "You were right. I'm glad I came."

Once on land, they made a plan. Dan would drop them at home and return at seven o'clock for a lobster dinner.

Connie liked this idea. What she liked, she realized, was being back on her home turf. She started by making herself a very tall, very cold, very citrusy gin and tonic—reminiscent of the one prepared for her by Freddy Delinn—and carried it with her into the outdoor shower. When designing the shower, Wolf had built a special shelf for Connie's dressing drink, a feature that was, in her mind, the utmost in civility. She took a long shower, then wrapped herself in a towel, freshened her drink in the kitchen, and headed upstairs to dress.

Meredith popped out of her room and said, "I checked around the house and the car. Nothing happened while we were gone."

Connie waved a dismissive hand. "Of course not."

She put on a white cotton sundress and let her hair dry naturally. She moisturized her face—she had gotten a lot of sun—and applied mascara. Her hand wobbled with the wand, and the makeup smudged, and Connie cursed and got a cotton ball to wipe the mess away and start over.

Downstairs, in the kitchen, she put out crackers and Brie and a hunk of good cheddar and a jar of truffled honey. She poked a fork into three baking potatoes and accidentally stabbed her palm. She turned on the oven, though she hated to do it on such a warm evening. She refreshed her drink, and Meredith appeared and Connie said brightly, "Tanqueray and tonic?"

Meredith said, "I'll stick to wine."

Connie realized there was still a bottle in the cooler. She hadn't emptied the cooler; the picnic things were still in there, now sitting in two inches of water. She pulled out the container of potato salad and the thermos of soup. Were the sandwiches okay? Veronica, Connie's mother, would have tossed them. She couldn't abide leftovers, especially not in the form of sandwiches that, however well wrapped, would be a touch soggy. But Wolf had been raised in a more abstemious household with parents from the Depression era, and he never threw food away. So, in Wolf's honor, Connie put the sandwiches in the fridge.

She said to Meredith, "I wish we had blueberry pie. One should always have blueberry pie with a lobster dinner, but I don't have time to run out and get a pie now. So we'll have to eat these cupcakes for dessert." Connie pulled the plastic wrap off the top of the cupcakes, and the icing smeared. She wondered briefly what her mascara looked like. *You're an incredibly beautiful woman, Constance;* that was what Freddy had said so many years earlier, but no woman was beautiful with smudged makeup. Freddy's voice had been serious and stagy, as though he were a movie star born and bred, instead of some poor kid from upstate New York. The icing on the cupcakes — peanut-butter icing — was an unfortunate shade of brown, Connie realized now. It looked like...

She still had to shuck the corn, put on water for both the corn and the lobsters, tear greens for a salad, whip up a dressing, and clarify three sticks of butter. She gulped the rest of her drink and poured another and squeezed what was left of the lime into it. She heard someone say, *Really, Connie, another drink?* And she looked up, thinking it was Meredith, but Meredith was at the back door watching Harold frolic in the waves. Meredith had washed her hair and put on her white shorts and navy tunic. She hadn't worn that outfit since the evening she'd been photographed in it, so Connie was happy that she felt okay putting it on, and besides, she looked good. The sun lit her up like a statue. This had been Wolf's favorite time of day. The room was starting to spin, but no, Connie didn't have time. Water for lobsters and corn, salad dressing, set the table. Find the lobster crackers and picks. She wished they had blueberry pie.

At the stroke of seven, there was a knock at the door. Dan was one of those prompt people. Wolf, too, had strived for promptness, but Connie consistently made him late. She came by it honestly; her parents had been late to absolutely everything. *Late to my own funeral,* Veronica used to say. Wolf would get so mad, and as much as Connie didn't like to think about it, she and Wolf had fought.

Connie took a fortifying gulp of her drink despite the fact that her vision was blurring and her heels kept slipping off the backs of her espadrilles. The water for both the corn and the lobsters was boiling — too early, if they were to enjoy a proper cocktail hour — but the salad looked crisp and fresh, and the salad dressing was complete, though Connie's fingertips now smelled like garlic. Meredith had set the table for three.

Dan knocked again. Connie hurried to the front door and nearly turned her ankle. Stupid shoes.

She opened the door and there was Dan, showered and handsome in a white shirt and jeans, which was Connie's favorite outfit on any man. He was holding a bakery box in one hand and a large paper bag that contained the lobsters in the other hand. He held out the bakery box.

"For dessert," he said.

Connie took the box. It was a blueberry pie.

"Oh!" she said. She looked at Dan, thinking, *This is incredible, the man read my mind.* It was more than a lucky guess; it had to be fate. They were simpatico. Dan knew that a lobster dinner needed blueberry pie. "Thank you!"

She took a stutter step backward and nearly lost her balance, but Dan grabbed her arm. She said, "Whoa, geez, these shoes. I'd better take them off before I break my neck. Come in, hello." She moved in to kiss him, hoping for a kiss like the one he'd given her that morning, but this kiss was perfunctory and dry. He seemed somewhat less enchanted by her than when he'd arrived to pick them up for the boat trip. Quite possibly, Connie thought, he didn't even want to be here. Quite possibly, he'd only come out of a sense of obligation, because he had the lobsters.

As Connie headed back into the kitchen, she tried to figure out what she'd done that day to put him off. Maybe he'd decided he just didn't like her. She liked *him;* she liked that he was prompt. She liked that he had brought blueberry pie.

She said, "Can I get you a drink?"

He said, "Sure. Do you have any beer?"

Beer again. Connie hadn't thought about beer. She checked the fridge and found two green bottles of Heineken in the back, thank God, bought by one of her houseguests, probably Toby, before he quit for good. Toby used to drink beer even after his first try at rehab, because he claimed beer wasn't alcohol. Drinking beer was like drinking juice, Toby said. It was like drinking milk. Toby was an alcoholic, as purely and classically as their mother, Veronica, had been, but he'd beaten it now. He was sober. Connie pulled a beer out, opened it, poured it into a glass and watched it foam all over her counter.

Dan was out on the deck with Meredith, admiring the water. Meredith pointed out Harold's dark head. She said something and Dan laughed. Connie wondered again if Dan liked Meredith. Maybe they would be a better couple. But that was silly. Connie was glad to see Meredith outside on the deck. She hadn't ventured out to the deck since the photograph. Connie supposed she felt safer with Dan around. A man.

Connie joined them outside. She handed Dan his beer, and the three of them did a cheers.

"Thank you for a perfect day," Meredith said.

Connie took a breath to chime in but she couldn't think of what to add, so she just smiled. At Merion Mercy Academy, it had been popular to practice walking with a textbook balanced on one's head to promote good posture. Connie felt like she had a book balanced on her head now, one that was in danger of sliding off and hitting the ground. Or maybe it was her head that was threatening to fall off.

Dan said, "Well, thank you for joining me. It wouldn't have been much fun alone."

Connie nodded. Yep. She realized she was still holding her gin and tonic. She thought she had switched to wine. Meredith's wine glass was empty; she needed a refill. Connie would fetch the bottle.

Dan said, "I think the highlight was watching you dive!"

Connie nodded. Yep. Great watching Meredith dive. Meredith was a fantastic diver — champion, had been.

Meredith said, "That *was* fun! Of course, I used to be much better."

"When you were younger," Connie said. Her voice sounded funny to her own ears. Had those words made sense? Meredith and Dan were both looking at her now. "I used to go to all of Meredith's meets. Every one, every meet, every single meet."

They were still looking at her. Okay, what? She didn't want to know. She wanted to go get the bottle of wine. She would pour her gin and tonic down the sink. She picked up a cracker and cut a messy piece of Brie. Food! Connie devoured it. She'd had nothing to eat since the half of the half sandwich on the boat.

Dan said, "Do you need help with the lobsters?"

"No, no," Connie said, her mouth still full. She made some hand motions indicating *I've got it, I'll go in now and take care of things, you two stay here.*

The two pots on the stove were at such a rolling boil that their lids chattered. The bag with the lobsters was on the counter. Connie didn't want to do the lobsters, she realized. Wolf had always done the lobsters, and last summer, Toby had done them. Wolf, Toby, Freddy Delinn. How long would the lobsters take? Should she get Dan or just drop them in herself? She needed to clarify the butter. Meredith and Dan looked happy out on the deck; they were talking. They were enjoying their cocktail hour. So what if Connie was slaving in the hot kitchen? So what if Meredith was a great diver? Graceful and all that? Sexually limber. Who had said that? Connie took off her shoes. Ahhh, now that was a good idea. Wine. Connie poured herself a glass of wine and she should refill Meredith's glass also. She would, as soon as she was done with the butter. She went to pour her gin and tonic down the drain, but there was only a scant inch left, so she drank it.

She put the butter in the pan and turned on the burner.

Late for my own funeral, Veronica used to say. Veronica had died of cirrhosis of the liver. This had surprised no one. And then, at her funeral, something had happened between Meredith and Toby; Connie was sure of it.

Toby, Wolf, Freddy Delinn, Dan. Danforth Flynn, that was a nice name.

The butter was melting and Connie decided she would just do it: She dumped the lobsters into the boiling water. One, two, three. She secured the lid. There was a barely discernible high-pitched noise: the lobsters screaming. But no, that was a myth. It was the sound of air escaping the shells, or something.

Wine for Meredith. The butter was melting. What about the corn? The corn would only take five minutes.

And then Connie remembered her cell phone. She hadn't checked her cell phone since early that morning, before Dan arrived. What if Ashlyn had called?

Connie hurried up to her bedroom to grab her phone. Danforth Flynn, Freddy Delinn, Wolf, Toby. Her phone showed no missed calls. No missed call from Ashlyn. Never a call from her headstrong daughter, but why not?

Connie checked her texts: there was one unread text, which probably meant her cell-phone carrier had sent her a reminder that her bill was overdue. Connie held her arm straight out so she could read the display. The text was from Toby. It said: *Sold the boat to the man from Nantucket. Will be on island in 3 weeks, OK?*

Toby would be on island in three weeks? The man from Nantucket? Who was that? It was a joke, but Connie had forgotten the punch line. Toby was coming in three weeks! Her handsome, funny-fun-fun brother! Sold the boat? That just wasn't possible, unless he was buying a bigger boat or a faster boat.

Connie pushed the buttons that would reply to Toby. She had never really gotten the hang of texting, but maybe she should, maybe if she texted Ashlyn, Ashlyn would respond.

OK? he asked. Connie punched in: *OK!* Then she remembered about Meredith. She couldn't let him walk into that surprise party unwarned. What she wanted to say was *You won't believe this but Meredith Delinn called me up and asked me to throw her a lifeline, and I did, and guess what? It's been great. Except for the paint on the house. And the slashed tires.* But that was far too long for a text, especially when Connie couldn't see the buttons clearly. While she was getting Meredith's glasses replaced, she should have picked up a pair for herself. Connie left the text at *OK!* But then she thought to add *LOL!* which her friend Lizbet had told her meant "laugh out loud."

Connie sent the text. Then she hurried downstairs. She had a lot of pots on the stove.

The kitchen was hot. Connie rescued the butter from the stove. She dropped the corn into the second steaming pot and turned off the heat under the lobsters. She drizzled the dressing over the greens and tossed them. She poured the butter into a small ceramic pitcher. Her bare feet felt good against the cool floor. She had to pour Meredith more wine.

She hadn't lost anything, she reminded herself. There was no Ashlyn now, but there had been no Ashlyn before. She would try texting.

"Okay, we're ready!" Connie said.

Why was the kitchen so hot? The oven was on, that was why. But Connie had forgotten to put in the potatoes. Goddamn it— there they sat on the counter, in plain sight. She'd just overlooked them. *Laugh out loud,* she thought. But tears sprung to her eyes.

Meredith came in from the deck and said, "What can we do to help?"

Connie dissolved in sobs.

Meredith said, "Connie, what's wrong?" She sounded genuinely alarmed. But she wouldn't understand. Meredith, quite famously, had made it through a national crisis without shedding a single tear.

"I forgot to put in the potatoes," Connie said.

*   *   *

Connie recalled only snippets of dinner. She allowed Dan to lead her to her chair, and he cracked open her lobster and pulled the meat from it, as though she were a child. Her corn lay on her plate untouched. Her shoulders caved in, like her bones were melting, and Meredith rose and brought her a sweater. There was bright banter between Dan and Meredith, on what topic, Connie couldn't tell. The salad was weepy with dressing. Connie could only manage one bite.

"Eat!" Meredith implored her.

In the place where Connie expected to find her wine was a glass of ice water with a slice of lemon. She drank it gratefully, remembering how they used to pull this very same trick with her own mother and how Veronica usually fell for it, but one time spit the water all over the table and demanded her gin. Connie's eyes were closing, her head bobbed forward like it used to sometimes in the movie theater, when Wolf took her to the long, harrowing arthouse films he liked. She was hoping that either Meredith or Dan would have the foresight to put the blueberry pie in the oven to warm it up, though she was doubtful about this. She was the only one who thought of such things. But she was far too tired to stand up and tend to it herself.

Ashlyn didn't realize how cruel she was being. She wouldn't understand until she had children of her own. She may not have any children of her own, ever. And whereas this would be a shame, it would also be a blessing. Wolf, Toby, Freddy Delinn, Danforth Flynn. Connie's head fell forward to her plate, but she snapped it up again, alert and conscious. She stared at Meredith. Did Meredith know what Freddy had said and done to Connie in Cap d'Antibes? Certainly not. That man told her nothing.

Connie felt a pressure in her armpits. She felt herself being lifted. She was in Dan's arms. She could smell him; she could feel the weave of his white shirt. Linen. Who ironed for him, she wondered, now that his wife was dead? She was floating, much the way she'd been floating in the water today.

She heard the words "a lot to drink."

Meredith said, "And she barely ate anything."

She landed in softness, too novel yet to be familiar. Her bed, as lovely and luxurious as a bed in a five-star hotel. She felt a kiss on her cheek, but the kiss was feminine. It was Meredith.

Connie's eyes fluttered open. It was still light outside. There was something Connie wanted to tell Meredith, but Connie couldn't stay awake another second.

She said, "Wolf's dead." The words sounded funny, garbled. Had they made sense?

Meredith said, "I know, honey. I'm sorry."

MEREDITH

When Meredith awoke the morning after the boat ride, her body ached. Specifically, her torso: the spaces between her ribs were stretched and sore.

The diving.

Meredith felt guilty even thinking it, but yesterday had been a good day. Was this possible, really, considering her current circumstances? Certainly not. But yes. Yes. It had been a day when Meredith had been present in every moment. She had thoughts about Freddy but those thoughts had been intentional; they hadn't sneaked up on her. She had thought about the boys, too, but the day had been so brilliant in its every aspect that Meredith's thoughts about Leo were more optimistic than usual. She wondered what Leo and Carver were doing and decided that they were most likely enjoying the weather and not wasting their precious hours thinking about Deacon Rapp.

The good times had started with the diving board. Meredith had felt herself transform as she pulled off her wig and climbed onto that board. She hadn't taken a dive in years—decades—and while she expressed doubts to Connie about her ability to flip and twist and enter the water headfirst, inside she knew she could do it. There were dives still trapped inside of her, dives that had been waiting for thirty years to get out.

Meredith had been meant to dive at Princeton; it was one of the things that led to her admission. Coach Dempsey had one other diver—a junior named Caroline Free who came from California and who was breaking all kinds of Ivy League records. But Caroline Free would graduate, and Coach Dempsey wanted to bring Meredith up in her wake. But when Meredith's father died, Meredith lost all interest in diving. It was amazing how one of the most important things in her life suddenly seemed so pointless. Coach Dempsey understood, but he came right back to her sophomore year. By sophomore year, Meredith was ready. She had gained ten pounds her freshman year from the beer and the starchy food in the dining hall and the late-night fried chicken sandwiches with Russian dressing that Freddy made for her in the Dial kitchen. Back home in Villanova for the summer, she had returned to the Aronimink pool and swum laps alongside her mother, wearing one of her mother's hideous bathing caps festooned with lavender rubber flowers over the right ear. The laps had worked; Meredith was back to her slender, petite self, and she meant to stay that way. Plus, she wanted to dive. She missed it; it was part of who she was.

When she told Freddy, he went straight to work talking her out of it. If she dove for the Princeton team, he said, it would be all-consuming. There would be early-morning conditioning practices and regular afternoon practices. There would be home meets and, more sinisterly, *away* meets—whole weekends at Penn and Columbia and Yale with the squeaky-skinned, green-haired members of the swim team. He predicted that Meredith would miss the Dial holiday formal—a look at the team's schedule confirmed this—and with Meredith gone, Freddy would have to find another date.

Meredith took the opportunity to ask him who he'd taken to the formal the year before.

He said, "Oh, Trina."

"Trina?" Meredith said.

Freddy studied her to see if there were going to be any mildly annoying follow-up questions. They had, of course, talked about Trina early on in their relationship, and Freddy had corroborated Trina's story—though it had felt to Meredith like the *corroboration of a story*—that Trina was his tutoring student and not much else. Those had been Fred's exact words, "not much else." Now, Meredith found he had taken her to last year's formal! She didn't think she even needed to ask the annoying follow-up questions.

He said, "I didn't have anyone else to ask, and she was good for things like that. She presents well."

Meredith knew she shouldn't care about something as frivolous as the Dial holiday formal, but she did. Holiday formals at the eating clubs were glamorous events with twinkling lights and French champagne and sixteen-piece orchestras playing Frank Sinatra. The prospect of missing the formal and of Freddy going, instead, with Trina was enough to seal the deal: Meredith met with Coach Dempsey and gave him her regrets. He begged her to reconsider. Princeton *needed* her, he said. Meredith nearly buckled. She loved the university with near-militant ferocity; if Princeton needed her, she would serve. But Freddy laughed and said that Dempsey was being manipulative. Freddy was the one who needed her. This was his senior year. He wanted to spend every second of it with Meredith.

Meredith gave up the diving. Her mother, as it turned out, was happy. She had feared that diving would distract Meredith from her studies.

Meredith hadn't dived in any structured or serious way again. Freddy didn't like her to. He was jealous that she excelled at something that had nothing to do with him. He wanted Meredith to focus on sports they could do together—swimming, running, tennis.

And so, that was where Meredith put her energies. She and Freddy swam together in the Hamptons, in Palm Beach, in the south of France—which really meant that Meredith swam in the ocean or did laps in their sapphire-blue, infinity-edge pools while Freddy talked to London on his cell phone. They had played tennis regularly for a while, but ten years into the marriage, Freddy was far too busy to ever make a court time, and Meredith had been left to play tennis with women like Amy Rivers.

Diving from Dan's boat the day before had been a pleasure long overdue. How many other forty-nine-year-old women could pull off a front two and a half somersault? Meredith could have gone even further; she had been tempted to do her front one and a half with one and a half twists, but she didn't want to seem like a show-off, and she didn't want to injure herself. Dan Flynn had been impressed by her diving, which was gratifying, and Connie, reverting to high-school type, had been proud and proprietary. *I used to go to all of Meredith's meets.* It was fun to remember those meets, especially home meets where Connie always occupied the same seat in the pool balcony and used hand signals to assess Meredith's entry into the water. *A little over. A little short.* Two palms showing meant *Perfect 10!* There had been one meet when they had been down a judge, and after much conferring, Meredith convinced both team coaches to allow Connie to fill in. Connie knew the dives inside and out, and Meredith knew Connie would be fair. Connie had ended up being harder on Meredith than the other two judges, but Meredith won anyway.

To dive again had been to return to her real, deep-down, pre-Freddy self. But there had been other great things about yesterday— the sun, the water, the boat, the lunch. Meredith had loved being on the boat, feeling its speed and power, enjoying the salty mist on her face. She was, for the first time since everything happened, buffered from the outside world. She had enjoyed talking with Dan about lobstering, and he had asked her if she wanted to fish with him. Yes, certainly—she wasn't going to let a single opportunity get past her. At the end of the afternoon when the sun was mellow and golden and the water sparkled and Meredith was enjoying a cold glass of wine with Connie and there was the promise of a real, true lobster dinner ahead, Meredith had realized that she could experience happiness. Fleeting, perhaps, but real.

Even dinner was lovely—to a point. Dan appeared with the lobsters and a blueberry pie—he'd granted Connie's one wish without realizing it—and when they were out on the deck, Meredith couldn't thank him enough.

While Connie was in the kitchen pulling dinner together, Dan said, "I hope you won't think I'm too forward in saying this, but you're nothing like I thought you'd be."

This might have suggested a thorny conversation ahead, but Meredith had spent enough time with Dan to know that he wouldn't try to stick it to her. The bizarre thing was being faced with her own notoriety. Freddy had turned her into a public persona. People like Dan Flynn, a power washer on Nantucket Island, had formed an impression of "Meredith Delinn" without knowing her. Everyone in America had.

She cocked her head and said, "Oh, really? And how did you think I'd be? Tell me the truth."

Dan said, "I thought you'd be a society bitch. A fallen society bitch. I thought you'd be materialistic, demanding, entitled. I thought, at the very least, that you'd be bitter. Self-absorbed. A fun-sucker."

"A fun-sucker?" Meredith said. "Me?"

"Now, I'm not going to pretend I *know you* know you. I mean, we've only been on two dates, right? Sunday night and today."

Meredith glanced back at Connie in the kitchen. "Those weren't properly *our* dates..."

"Point taken," he said. "But I got to know you a little bit, right? And I think you're a wonderful woman, Meredith. You're smart, you're interesting, and you're a hell of a good sport."

"Well, thank you," Meredith said.

"You're an accomplished diver, you can cast a fishing line...does the world know this about you? No, the world sees you as...what? The wife of Freddy Delinn. A possible conspirator in his crimes..."

"I wasn't a conspirator," Meredith said. She hated herself for even having to say this. "I knew nothing about his crimes, and neither did my sons. But there are still people I have to convince of that."

"I believe you," Dan said. "I more than believe you. I know you're innocent in this. I can tell...because of how you are."

"Well, thank you," Meredith said. She said this to end the conversation while things were still relatively light. But she was tempted to remind him that he *didn't* know her and that he couldn't accurately tell anything about her. She was tempted to say that none of us knows anyone else—not really. If there was one person Meredith had thought she had known in this world, it was Freddy Delinn, and she had been wrong.

As soon as they settled at the table, it became clear that Connie was drunk. Dan glanced at Meredith, and Meredith made a helpless face. She felt responsible and embarrassed. She had noticed Connie drinking wine on the boat, a lot of wine, two bottles minus the one glass that Meredith had had, but she'd said nothing. What would she have said? Connie was a grown woman and she liked her wine. Some women were like that; they drank chardonnay like water, and it had no obvious effect. Meredith was comforted by the fact that Connie drank wine. Connie's mother, Veronica, had been an abuser of gin and could be found at any time of day with a Tervis tumbler at her elbow. There were always half-filled bottles of tonic around the kitchen and lime wedges in various stages of desiccation on the cutting board and in the sink drain.

Of course, Connie liked her gin, too. (Meredith decided there must be an inherited predilection for the juniper berry, because no one would have grown up watching Veronica destroy herself like she did and then voluntarily *choose* to drink gin.) Meredith had watched Connie pour herself a gin and tonic at the kitchen counter, but she didn't comment. It was, after all, cocktail hour. Furthermore, Meredith was in no position to judge or scold. Connie had saved Meredith's life; she had brought Meredith to this place and had put her in a position to have a wonderful time today. If Connie wanted to drink, Meredith wasn't going to pester her.

Now, though, Meredith felt negligent. Dan helped Connie into her chair, and she slumped. He pulled the meat from her lobster. Meredith pulled the meat from her own lobster thinking that the best idea was to act normal and see if they could make it through the meal. Meredith fetched Connie a glass of ice water with a paper-thin slice of lemon, the way she liked it. Then she helped herself to an ear of corn and some salad. She was impressed that Connie had been able to pull dinner together in her condition. Meredith could take a few pointers from Connie in the kitchen. There would come a day in the not-too-distant future when she would have to prepare her own meals, and she had never learned to cook. She was ashamed of this. Her mother had been a classic housewife of her era — veal saltimbocca, chicken and dumplings on Sundays, the best tuna salad Meredith had ever eaten. Meredith could microwave hot dogs, and she could fry or scramble an egg; that was how she'd managed when Leo and Carver were small. And then, magically, overnight it seemed, there was money to go to restaurants every night and hire a cook for breakfast, lunch, snacks, and any dinner party that Meredith wanted to throw.

But Meredith couldn't let her mind veer off this way. The meal before her was enticing, yet simple. Surely with a little instruction, Meredith could one day manage this?

"Cheers!" Meredith said.

Dan met her glass with a clink, and Connie, too, reached for her glass, but hesitated, realizing it was ice water. She succumbed, picking up the water and touching glasses with both Dan and Meredith.

"This looks delicious!" Dan said. He was using the too-loud, overly cheerful voice that one used with the infirm.

Connie made a move on her salad. Meredith said, "Eat!"

Meredith dug into her lobster. Her face was pleasantly warm and tight from the sun. There was no conversation, but that seemed okay. They were all busy eating.

Meredith said, "Boy, being out on the water really gave me an appetite!" She eyed Connie. Connie cut a piece of lobster, dragged it long and lavishly through the clarified butter, then left it impaled on the end of her fork, dripping onto the tablecloth.

"Eat up, Connie!" Meredith said. She felt like she was talking to a five-year-old.

Dan was eating ravenously, probably trying to get as much food in him as he could before this dinner came to its untimely end. Meredith wanted to say something that would ensure Dan would come back.

She said, "So what else should I do while I'm here on Nantucket?"

"Well, you have to go to Great Point," Dan said.

"How do I do that?"

"You need a four-wheel drive—the Escalade would work— and a beach sticker."

"Do you go to Great Point?" Meredith asked.

"Every chance I get," Dan said. "The fishing is great. And the clamming on Coatue."

"I'd love to go clamming," Meredith said.

"I'll take you sometime," Dan said.

"That'll be fun," Meredith said. "Won't it, Con? Clamming with Dan?"

Connie's head fell forward, and at first Meredith thought Connie was agreeing with her, but Connie's head dropped dangerously close to her plate before she caught herself and snapped her neck back. She came to for a second, though her eyes were glazed over and, Meredith noticed, she had salad dressing in her hair. Okay, Meredith hated to be a fun-sucker, but she was going to call the game.

She gave Dan a look, and Dan nodded. He picked Connie up, and together they delivered Connie to her bedroom. She sighed as she hit the mattress. Dan retreated, but Meredith stayed to tuck Connie in.

By the time Meredith got downstairs, Dan was standing by the front door, ready to leave.

"Don't you want to stay and finish your dinner?" Meredith said.

"I'd better go," he said. "It's been a long day."

She couldn't argue with him about that. "Do you want to take the pie, or...?"

"No, no, no," he said. "You ladies enjoy it."

Something about the way he said this made Meredith worry they would never see him again. She panicked. She said, "I know Connie really likes you. She's just...going through some stuff. Her grief, you know...and then, as if that's not enough, *I* show up. And all of the things that have happened since we've been here. She's under a lot of pressure."

He held up his palms. "I get it," he said. "I've been there."

Oh, no, Meredith thought. He was slipping away. This was upsetting. Meredith wanted him to stay—and if he had to leave, then she wanted to make sure he'd come back. For Connie's sake, certainly, but also for her own. He'd become sort of like a friend.

Meredith opened the door for him. She said, "Well, thank you again. For everything. It was...the best day I've had in a long, *long* time."

These words weren't lost on him. He smiled. "You're welcome, Meredith. You're very welcome." He moved in to hug her, and as he pulled away, he said, "Keep your chin up."

Oh, no! That sounded like a permanent good-bye. Dan stepped outside. Meredith didn't know what to say, so she said, "Okay, I will." Once he was in his Jeep, she closed the door.

Now, Meredith touched the sore muscles between her ribs and decided she needed some Advil. But Connie would be feeling way worse this morning than Meredith did. Meredith eased herself out of bed and headed downstairs to see about her friend.

* * *

Dan didn't call for three days, and then four. Connie was pretending not to notice, but Meredith was certain she did. She asked Meredith how humiliating her behavior had been at dinner. The last thing she remembered, she said, was taking a bite of salad. "And it was overdressed!"

As if soggy salad was the problem.

Meredith tempered her response, though she felt flashes of fury: Dan Flynn was a quality person who could probably do them both a lot of good, and Connie had frightened him away.

She said, "Not humiliating at all. You were tired."

"I was drunk."

"You have a lot on your plate," Meredith said. "Emotionally speaking."

"True," Connie said. "Do you think Dan realizes that? Do you think he'll give me a free pass for one shabby drunken night?"

"Of course I do," Meredith said.

But the phone didn't ring. Meredith and Connie went about their days quietly. Meredith got a little braver. She ventured out onto the deck for half-hour stretches, she went for short walks on the beach with Connie. She took her first incredibly delightful outdoor shower and stayed in until the hot water ran out. On Saturday morning, Meredith and Connie went into town, and Meredith could tell Connie was hoping they'd run into Dan. Meredith found she wanted to run into Dan herself. Imagine that! Instead of fearing a chance encounter, she was seeking one out. She and Connie walked along with their eyes peeled. When they passed 21 Federal, they fell into a glum, respectful silence, as if for the newly deceased.

Then Connie said, "You know, I think Dan liked *you.*"

"What?" Meredith said.

"I think he liked you."

"Connie," Meredith said. "I am the least desirable woman in all the world." She lowered her voice to a whisper. "First of all, I am married to Freddy Delinn. Second of all, look at me." She was glad her point would be underscored by the fact that she was wearing her thrift-shop wig, which was growing ratty. "No one *likes* me. No one will ever *like* me again."

"I think Dan liked you," Connie said. "As a person. I think he liked the way you were."

"I think he liked the way *you* were," Meredith said.

"Then why isn't he calling?" Connie asked.

Connie came up with an answer. Dan wasn't calling because she, Connie, was a hag. Since Wolf died, she had let herself go. She needed her nails done, she needed her eyebrows and bikini line waxed.

"We're going to the salon," she said.

"I can't," Meredith said.

"Of course you can," Connie said. "Wear your wig."

"It's not that easy," Meredith said.

"Of course it's that easy. We've been out to places a lot more public than the salon, and you've been fine."

"I know," Meredith said. "But I can't go to the salon." The salon was the equivalent of swimming in shark-infested waters. It was like negotiating a minefield on a pogo stick on Friday the thirteenth. The Pascal Blanc salon had been the first place to publicly denounce Meredith—and it didn't get much more public than the front page of the *New York Times* Style section. Surely Connie had seen the article?

"In case you haven't gotten it by now," Connie said, "I don't like going places without you."

"I'm going to have to beg your indulgence here," Meredith said. "I can't do the salon."

"You have to get back up on the horse," Connie said.

"So you saw the article?"

"I saw the article," Connie said. "And do you know what I thought when I read it? I thought, 'Meredith Martin is the best woman your salon has ever seen. It's your loss, Pascal Blanc.'"

"Really, it was my loss," Meredith said. "I'm as gray as Whistler's mother, and the salon got to broadcast how morally superior they were by keeping me out in the name of protecting their other clients, who might be upset by the sight of me."

"Don't you want to get your hair done?" Connie asked.

God, the answer to that question was yes. Since she'd started to go gray at forty, every six weeks she'd had her hair restored to the natural color of her youth—soft baby blond. This was, she knew, unspeakably vain of her—though it had more to do with how she felt inside, and especially now. The real Meredith Martin was blond. She was a brilliant and talented eighteen-year-old girl with an impossibly bright future.

"I can't get my hair done," Meredith said. "If I go to the salon, I'll have to wear my wig."

"So you'll go with me, then," Connie said. "And wear your wig. You can get a manicure and a pedicure. My treat."

"It's not about the money, Con." Though it was about the money, in addition to everything else. In Palm Beach, Meredith used to get a manicure and pedicure every week to the tune of $125. And she always left a $50 tip. So, $175 on her nails, $100 on a weekly massage, and $250 every six weeks for hair. All that money, and she hadn't blinked an eye. She was shamed by it now.

"It's not about the money," Connie said, "because it's *my treat.* Manicure and pedicure. Please? It's no fun going to the salon alone."

"I can't," Meredith said. "Women who are under investigation don't go to the salon. Women whose children are under investigation don't go to the salon. Women whose husbands are serving one hundred and fifty years in federal prison do not go to the salon."

"I understand you feel that way," Connie said. "But it's not that big a deal. It's a manicure and a pedicure. Something to make you feel pretty. Something to take your mind off things. I can go alone, but I really want you with me. And no one's going to hurt you, I promise."

* * *

Connie secured appointments for Friday afternoon. In the car, Meredith thought she might hyperventilate. She used her Lamaze breathing; it had been much more helpful for her Freddy-induced anxiety than it ever had for the births of her two children. Connie eyeballed her.

"Do you just want to bag and go home?" Connie said.

"No," Meredith said. "We're going." It had become some kind of stupid hurdle she now felt she had to jump. It was a test. And, Meredith reminded herself, she had never failed a test in her life.

The RJ Miller salon was inviting and unpretentious. There was jazz music playing, and the place smelled deliciously of hair product, acetone, cappuccino. It was a hive of activity, and Meredith quickly ascertained that this might work in her favor. The women who were lined up in the chairs were all glamorous—as glamorous as the women in Palm Beach or Southampton. They were suntanned and Botoxed; they wore Lilly Pulitzer skirts and Jack Rogers sandals. The type was familiar—it was Meredith's type, her exact genus and species—but she didn't recognize a soul. And no one turned to look at Meredith in her ugly wig and boring glasses. She was as exciting as a reference-room librarian. More than a few women turned to gaze at Connie; she was bewitching that way.

Connie checked them in with the receptionist, who had a cascade of sumptuous golden ringlets. She introduced Meredith as "Mary Ann Martin." The receptionist barely took notice of her, except perhaps to secretly wonder why Meredith wasn't there to have something done about her atrocious hair. It was a relief to be overlooked, but Meredith couldn't help reflecting on the Pascal Blanc salon in the days when Freddy's fund was returning at nearly 30 percent. When Meredith walked in, the room all but burst into applause. Meredith had been grounded enough to know that the ass-kissing had nothing to do with her and everything to do with money, but even so, she'd believed that the staff of the salon had liked her. She was a real person, despite her many millions. And yet, not a single one of the salon staff or the women she befriended at the salon had stood up for her. She had to admit, it had surprised her that, apparently, in the thirty years that she'd been with Freddy, she hadn't made one true friend; she hadn't forged one single human connection that could withstand the seismic aftershocks of Freddy's collapse. Absolutely everyone had forsaken her—except Connie.

"This way," the receptionist said. She led them into the spa room and showed them each to a pedicure tub. Meredith started to climb up on a perch, then realized she had forgotten to pick a color. She chose a dark purple. *Paris at Midnight.*

Meredith had experienced Paris at midnight more than once— any time they flew to Cap d'Antibes, they flew to Paris and then drove down to the coast in a Triumph Spitfire that Freddy kept in the hangar at Orly. Often, Meredith had shopping to do in Paris— she liked to stop at Printemps for candles and table linens, and at Pierre Hermé for boxes of colorful macarons.

Her life had been one of disgusting consumption. How had she not seen that?

The nail technician appeared. She introduced herself as Gabriella. She asked Meredith—whom she called "Marion"—if she would like a cappuccino. Meredith, feeling courageous, said yes.

Gabriella had some kind of accent, Eastern European or Russian. Meredith had known the names and life stories of all of the girls who had worked at Pascal Blanc. Her regular manicurist, Maria José, had a son named Victor who went to public school in Brooklyn. Meredith had once gone to see Victor in his high-school musical; he played Mr. Applegate in *Damn Yankees.* Meredith went because she loved Maria José and she wanted to be supportive, but Maria José was so ecstatic that *Meredith Delinn* would travel all the way to Red Hook to see Victor that Meredith's presence overshadowed Victor's performance, and Meredith ended up feeling guilty. When Meredith had explained this to Freddy, he'd kissed her cheek and said, *Ah, yes, I know. It's hard being Meredith Delinn.*

Here, at RJ Miller, Meredith didn't talk to Gabriella. She hid behind a copy of *Vogue*—which was filled with the cool and lovely things she could no longer afford—and tried to enjoy the pampering. She monitored the comings and goings of the salon over the top of the magazine. Every time a woman entered the salon, a chime sounded, and Meredith seized up in fear. Once, she jerked her foot, and Gabriella said, "Oh, no! I hurt you?"

"No, no," Meredith said. She closed her eyes and leaned back, listening to the sticky, slapping sound of Gabriella rubbing lotion into her feet and calves.

Next to her, Connie was blissed out. She said, "This is sublime, is it not?"

"Mmm," Meredith said. It was sublime in theory, though Meredith couldn't relax. She wanted to get it over with and get the hell out of there. She bent forward in anticipation, watching the final steps of her pedicure like she was watching a horse race. Gabriella slid Meredith's feet into the ridiculously thin foam-rubber flip-flops and gently inserted the stiff cardboard toe separators. She painted Meredith's nails with two coats of Paris at Midnight and a shiny top coat. Finished!

Meredith practically jumped off her perch. Gabriella said, "You in hurry?"

Meredith gazed at Connie, whose eyes were at half mast, like some college kid who had smoked too much dope.

"No," Meredith said guiltily.

Gabriella invited Meredith—again calling her "Marion"; Meredith almost didn't respond—over to the manicure table. The manicure table was trickier. There were no magazines to hide behind; it was face-to-face business. Gabriella started working on Meredith's hands and tried to make small talk.

"I like your ring," Gabriella said, fingering Meredith's diamond. Freddy had been dirt poor when they got married, too poor to buy a ring, so he'd been happy about Annabeth Martin's enormous diamond. There had been times, in those early years, when Meredith had overheard Freddy telling people that he'd bought it for her, or letting them assume so.

"Thank you," Meredith said. "It was my grandmother's."

"Are you married?" Gabriella asked.

"Yes," Meredith said. "No. Well, yes, but I'm separated."

Gabriella took this news in stride. She didn't even look up. Maybe she didn't understand "separated." She certainly didn't understand the kind of separated Meredith was talking about.

"So you live on the island, or you just visiting?"

"Just visiting," Meredith said.

"From where? Where you live?"

Meredith didn't know what to say. She defaulted. "New York."

Gabriella brightened. "Yes? New York City? We have many clients from New York City."

"Not New York City," Meredith said quickly. "I live upstate."

Gabriella nodded. She pushed at Meredith's cuticles. Since everything that had happened with Freddy, Meredith had reverted to her childhood habit of biting her nails. She remembered her grandmother dipping her fingertips in cayenne pepper to get her to stop. This would certainly be considered child abuse now.

Gabriella said, "Upstate? Where upstate?"

Meredith didn't want to answer. Gabriella couldn't have cared. Upstate had none of the sex appeal that the city had; they were like two different nations. But the question had been asked in earnest, and it required some kind of answer.

Meredith defaulted again. "Utica," she said. This had been the town where Freddy grew up, though he hadn't been well off enough to live in Utica proper. He had been raised — if you could call it that — in the sticks outside of Utica.

"Really?" Gabriella said. This came out as "Rilly!" Gabriella's voice was loud enough that conversation in that part of the salon came to a momentary halt. "My boyfriend, *he* come from Utica.

Perhaps you know him? His name is Ethan Proctor." She said his name carefully as though she had practiced long hours to pronounce it correctly.

"No, I'm sorry," Meredith said. "I don't know Ethan Proctor."

"But same, from Utica, yes?" Gabriella asked.

"Yes," Meredith said. Gabriella was transforming Meredith's nails from ragged, splintery edges to smooth half-moons. Her hands needed this, but Meredith had to turn the conversation around so that Gabriella was the one talking about herself, otherwise Meredith was going to find herself in trouble.

Gabriella leaned forward and lowered her voice, in the perfect stereotype of gossiping manicurist. "Of course you know who used to live in Utica long time ago?"

No, thought Meredith. *No!*

"Who?" she whispered.

"Freddy Delinn."

Meredith felt her nose twitch, and she thought she might sneeze. This was her goddamned stupid idiotic fault for saying Utica instead of making up the name of a town. Pluto, New York. Why hadn't she said Pluto?

"You know who I mean, Freddy Delinn?" Gabriella asked. "Monster psychopath, steal everybody's money?"

Meredith nodded. Monster psychopath, curled up next to Meredith in bed by nine thirty every night, buying the children a golden retriever puppy, resting his hand on Samantha's back, then snatching it away as though it had never been where it was not supposed to be. This was the boy who had walked her to Mental Health Services and had offered to come back and pick her up. He had talked her out of diving for the Princeton swim team so she could be his date at the holiday formal. He had been master of the fried chicken sandwich, king of the pool table. When, exactly, had he become a monster psychopath? The Feds thought 1991 or 1992, so when the kids were eight and six, right around the time Meredith was set free from the kitchen. No more making mac and cheese from a box.

They could go out for dinner—to Rinaldo's or Mezzaluna or Rosa Mexicano—every single night! Monster psychopath stealing everyone's money. Meredith thought it might be hard to hear Freddy called a monster psychopath by Gabriella the Bulgarian or Croatian manicurist, but all Meredith could think was that it was true.

"Where are *you* from, Gabriella?" Meredith asked.

Gabriella didn't answer. Gabriella hadn't heard her because Meredith's voice was nothing more than a strangled whisper. She may not have spoken at all, in fact; she may have only been thinking those words, desperate to change the subject, but had not actually managed to utter them.

Gabriella said, "There is girl? Here on Nantucket? Like me, also from Minsk?"

Minsk, Meredith thought. *Belarus.*

"She clean houses. She ask her boss, man who own house where she is cleaning, if he can invest her money with Freddy Delinn because man has account with Freddy Delinn, and man says, 'Okay, sure,' he will ask if she can also invest. And Mr. Delinn say, 'Yeah, sure.' So my friend invest her *life savings*—one hundred thirty-seven thousand dollar—with Freddy Delinn and now, all of it gone."

Meredith nodded, then shook her head. The nod was meant to acknowledge the story; the shake was meant to say: *That is a hideous, awful, sickening tragedy, caused by my husband. That money, your friend's life savings, that hundred and thirty-seven thousand dollars, could have been the same money I spent at Printemps on hand-milled candles. It could have been used to put gas in the Spitfire on the way to Cap d'Antibes. But what you have to understand, Gabriella, is that although I am guilty of spending the money in lavish and inexcusable ways, I didn't know where it came from.*

I thought Freddy had earned it.

Gabriella, perhaps picking up on something in Meredith's body language, or in the pheromones she was giving off, which were broadcasting FEAR, said, "Did you know Freddy Delinn?"

"No," Meredith said. The denial came easily and automatically, the same way it must have come to the disciple Peter. Meredith tried to convince herself that she wasn't lying. She didn't know Freddy; she had never known Freddy.

She met up with Connie again as they sat side by side at the nail dryers. Connie still seemed a little dazed, and Meredith wondered briefly if she was drunk. Had she been drinking at home before they left? Meredith didn't think so, but then again, Meredith was oblivious. She should have made a vow to *pay attention* to the next person she became close to, but she hadn't dreamed there would ever be such a person. She would pay closer attention to Connie, starting right now.

"Isn't this *heavenly?*" Connie said. She wasn't drunk, Meredith decided. She just had the nature of an addict, and the whole calming, peaceful, restorative atmosphere of the salon had permeated her skin and made her high.

"My nails look better," Meredith said matter-of-factly. She wouldn't tell Connie about her conversation with Gabriella, she decided. It was Meredith's own fault for mentioning Utica. Freddy was so infamous now that the details of his life were known to everyone. The story about the housekeeper losing her life savings had gutted Meredith—that was how she felt every time, like she was being sliced open—although Meredith wondered about the mysterious relationship between housekeeper and man of the house. What kind of person would go to Delinn Enterprises on behalf of his housekeeper? Was it the same as Meredith going to see the school play of her manicurist's son, a show of interest, a way of proving to himself that there was no class difference between him and his housekeeper—they could both invest with Freddy Delinn?

"I still have to get waxed," Connie said.

"Oh," Meredith said. She desperately wanted to leave.

"It should be quick," Connie said.

*　　*　　*

Meredith decided the safest thing would be to wait for Connie in the car. She told Connie this, and Connie said, "What are you, a dog? Wait right here and read *Cosmo*. I'll be out in a minute."

"I'd feel safer in the car," Meredith said.

"Okay, fine," Connie said. "Do you want to make an appointment for hair?"

Yes, Meredith thought. *But no.* This visit had gone fine — sort of — though her manicurist had called Freddy a monster psychopath to her face and Meredith had had to deny knowing him and she'd been force-fed that unsettling story about the housekeeper.

Could she do hair?

Vanity won out over fear: she made a hair appointment. The receptionist with the ringlet curls said, "You want cut and color?"

"I do," Meredith said. She touched her wig. The receptionist watched her. The receptionist certainly realized Meredith was wearing a wig, but she punched Meredith's information into the computer anyway and handed her a little card. Tuesday at four o'clock.

Connie disappeared into the waxing room. Meredith gave Gabriella a tiny manila envelope that held twenty dollars. This, she reassured herself, was her own money earned years before, *not* the money Freddy had pilfered from the housekeeper.

Meredith headed out of the salon. She was moving down the steps, watching her feet as she went. Paris at Midnight was a dynamite color. Her feet hadn't looked this good in months.

She raised her head, searching for Connie's car in the parking lot. She often caught herself looking for one of her own cars — the black Range Rover they drove to Southampton, or the Jaguar convertible that they drove in Palm Beach, a car that most closely resembled a woman's shoe. She didn't miss the cars at all; she wondered if Freddy did. She decided not. Freddy, ironically, hadn't cared much for material things, only the money and the power it brought. He liked being able to buy a $70,000 Range Rover, but he didn't love the Range Rover itself.

Meredith was so caught up in this thought—if she explained it to Connie or Dan, would they understand?—that she had to stop in the middle of the parking lot and remind herself: green Escalade. She spotted the car, but she was distracted by the sight of a woman chaining up a classic turquoise and white Schwinn at the bike rack while smoking a cigarette. Something familiar about the woman.

The woman turned, plucked the cigarette from her mouth, and blew smoke in Meredith's direction.

Amy Rivers.

Meredith started to shake. She backed up a few steps, thinking it was possible that Amy hadn't seen her, although there had been one split second of what Meredith feared was mutual recognition. Meredith spun back toward the salon and hurried up the stairs. In her haste, one of her flimsy flip-flops ripped off her foot. She had one bare foot, but she didn't care. She went back into the sweet-smelling, air-conditioned cool of the salon and thought, *Get Connie.* Was there another way out of this place? There was a front door. Meredith could walk out the front door, and Connie could drive around and pick her up.

The receptionist noticed Meredith and said, "Oh, did you forget your shoes?"

Yes, all of a sudden, Meredith realized she *had* forgotten her shoes, a fact that was only going to slow her down. Gabriella walked out of the spa room holding Meredith's suede flats, the same shoes she had gone to visit Freddy in—they were now, officially, bad-luck shoes—and at the same time, Meredith heard the chiming noise that meant someone was entering the salon. She was so nervous she feared she would pee all over the salon floor.

A voice said, "Meredith?"

And Meredith thought, *DO NOT TURN AROUND.*

But forty-nine years of Pavlov-like conditioning prevailed, and Meredith responded automatically and found herself face to face with Amy Rivers.

Amy was wearing a light-blue polo shirt and white shorts and her Tretorns. Her hair was in a ponytail; she was tan. The strange thing was how *familiar* she was to Meredith. It didn't seem right that someone so familiar—Meredith had eaten lunch with this woman countless times; she had hit thousands of tennis balls beside her—should be so threatening. She had been Meredith's *friend.* But that was how the world worked. It wasn't the bogeyman in the closet you had to fear; the people you liked and cared about could hurt you much worse.

"Nice wig," Amy said. She reached out to touch it—possibly, to tear it off—but Meredith backed away.

Meredith said nothing. Gabriella was still holding Meredith's shoes. Very slowly, like she had a gun trained on her, Meredith reached out for her shoes. Amy's eyes flickered to Meredith's feet, then over to Gabriella.

"You gave this woman a pedicure?"

"Yes," Gabriella said, a touch of Russian moxie in her voice.

"Do you know who she is?"

Gabriella shrugged, now seeming less certain. "Marion?" she said.

"Ha!" Amy said, announcing Gabriella's gullibility. Turning back to Meredith, she said, "Did you get the message I left you?"

Meredith nodded.

"Your husband stole all my money," Amy said. "Over *nine million* dollars. And I'm one of the lucky ones because I still have a job and Jeremy has a job, but we had to sell the house in Palm Beach, and we had to pull Madison out of Hotchkiss."

"I'm sorry," Meredith whispered.

"But like I said, I'm one of the lucky ones. I honestly don't know how you can move about like a regular human being—summering on *Nantucket,* getting *pedicures*—when you have ruined so many lives. People are *broke* because of you, Meredith, and not only broke but *broken.* Our neighbor in Palm Beach, Kirby Delarest, blew his brains out. He had three little girls."

Meredith closed her eyes. She knew Kirby Delarest. He was an

investor with Freddy; he and Freddy had been friendly acquaintances, if not actually friends, because Freddy didn't have any
friends. But Kirby Delarest had swung by the house on occasion.
Meredith had once happened on Freddy and Kirby barbecuing
steaks by the pool midday, drinking a rare and expensive bottle of
wine that Kirby had bought at auction, and smoking Cohibas.
Meredith had found this odd because Freddy never drank and
certainly not midday during the week, but Freddy had been effusive on that day, saying that he and Kirby were celebrating. *Celebrating what?* Meredith had asked. Because of the cigars, she
thought maybe Kirby's wife, Janine, was expecting another baby.
Meredith had said, *Is there something I should know?* Freddy had
taken Meredith in his arms and waltzed her around the flagstone
patio, and he said, *Just dance with me, woman. Love me. You are
my winning lottery ticket. You are my lucky charm.* Meredith had
been curious, bordering on suspicious, but she decided to just
enjoy it. She didn't ask anything else. She supposed Freddy and
Kirby were toasting the occasion of yet more money, a good deal, a
correct gamble, some more unbelievable returns. Kirby had been
a tall, lean man with white-blond hair, and he had an accent she
couldn't place. It sounded European — Dutch, maybe — but when
she asked him, he claimed he hailed from Menasha, Wisconsin,
which did explain his amiable nature and his Scandinavian good
looks, as well as Freddy's affinity for him. Fred loved midwesterners. He said he found them to be the most honest people on earth.

Meredith hadn't heard the news that Kirby Delarest shot himself, because there was no one to tell her. Samantha had decorated
for Kirby and Janine Delarest; Freddy and Meredith had made the
introduction. Meredith wondered if Samantha knew.

Gabriella and the receptionist stood watching. Meredith then
realized the salon was silent, except for Billie Holiday crooning.

"I'm sorry," Meredith said. "I had no idea."

"No *idea?*" Amy said. She took a step toward Meredith, and
Meredith could smell the cigarette smoke on her. Meredith hadn't

known Amy was a smoker; possibly it was a stress-induced habit, caused by Freddy.

"No," Meredith said. "No idea. About any of it."

"You expect me to believe that?" Amy said. "Everyone knows you and Freddy were connected at the hip. Everyone knows you two were living out some kind of sick love story."

Sick love story? Meredith had no response for that.

"And your son?" Amy said.

Meredith snapped her head up. "Don't," she said. What she wanted to say was, *Don't you dare say one word about Leo.*

"They have hundreds of pieces of evidence against him," Amy said. "Someone in my company knows that cute little lawyer of his, and supposedly even she says it's a lost cause. Your son is going to spend the rest of his life in prison."

"No," Meredith said. She closed her eyes and shook her head. No, there weren't hundreds of pieces of evidence against Leo. Julie Schwarz was a superstar; she would never have spoken out against her case, her client. *Leo!* If there were hundreds of pieces of evidence against Leo, Dev would have told Meredith.

"Yes," Amy said. "Yes, absolutely. My sources are reliable. Your family is going to be flushed away, Meredith. Like turds."

Meredith opened her mouth to speak—and say what? *You're wrong. Leave me alone.* Or again, *I'm sorry*—but the receptionist took the occasion of Meredith's loss for words to step in. "Are you ready to be shampooed, Mrs. Rivers? We have to keep things moving or we'll get backed up."

Amy laughed. "Do you know who this woman is?"

The receptionist seemed baffled. Gabriella said in a weaker voice, "Marion?"

"It's Meredith Delinn," Amy said.

That night, Meredith went up to her room without any dinner. Connie protested. She had salmon steaks marinating and ready to grill, and corn on the cob from Bartlett's Farm. "You have to eat something. I'm going to make you a winner dinner."

The winner dinner was the problem. The dazzling house overlooking the ocean was the problem. The beautiful life Connie had allowed Meredith to share was the problem. Amy Rivers was correct: How could she continue to live a life of privilege when so many people had lost everything? Kirby Delarest—the kindhearted midwesterner whose three little blond girls always wore matching Bonpoint outfits to dinner at the Everglades Club—had shot himself. Meredith occasionally took solace in the fact that Freddy hadn't murdered or raped anyone. But now Kirby Delarest's blood was on his hands. Seen through Amy's eyes, Fred's crimes seemed more reprehensible—as though Meredith had opened a basement door and found thirteen thousand dead bodies stacked one on top of the other.

She couldn't eat a winner dinner.

"I can't eat," she said.

Connie said, "Come on, you've just had a bad day."

A bad day. A bad day was when Meredith got an A- on her French quiz and her mother made chicken à la king with tinned mushrooms for dinner. A bad day was when it was raining and Meredith had both boys in the apartment pulling each other's hair and ripping pages out of their picture books and refusing to go down for a nap. What had happened with Amy Rivers in the salon hadn't been a *bad day.* It had been a moment Meredith would never forget. Amy had forced Meredith's face to the mirror and shown her the truth: She was ugly. She could try to hide, but once people discovered who she really was, they would all agree. Meredith was a despicable human being, responsible for the downfall of thousands. Responsible for the trajectory of the nation's economy into the Dumpster. Gabriella, on hearing the name *Meredith Delinn,* had blanched and said, "But you told me you not *know* Freddy Delinn! Now you say he your husband?"

"She lies," Amy said. "Lies, lies, lies."

The receptionist had backed away from Meredith slowly, as though there were a tarantula sitting on her shoulder.

Meredith whispered, "Cancel my hair appointment, please."

The receptionist nodded; her face showed obvious relief. She banged on the computer keyboard with hard, eager strokes, deleting Mary Ann Martin.

As Meredith moved to the door, Amy said, "You can enjoy your Nantucket summer vacation, Meredith, but you'll pay. The other investors are clamoring for your head. You and your son are going to end up just like Freddy, moldering in jail where you belong."

Meredith had sat in the scorching hot interior of Connie's car like a dog—a dog that would have expired if he'd been left in the car for the length of this appointment—but Meredith had made no move to put down the window or turn on the AC. She didn't care if her brain boiled. She didn't care if she died.

Moldering in jail where you belong. You and your son.

Amy was right: On some level, it *was* Meredith's fault. She was, at the very least, responsible for Amy's loss. She had begged Freddy to take Amy on as a client. *For me, please?* And Freddy had said, *For you, please? All right, yes.* But Meredith hadn't known. They could surgically remove her brain and scour its nooks and crannies, and only then would they realize she hadn't known a thing. Back at the very beginning, Meredith had offered to take a polygraph test, but Burt had told her that with certain kinds of people, polygraph tests didn't work. Meredith didn't understand.

"With pathological liars, for example," Burt had said. "They are so convinced their lies are the truth that nine out of ten times they beat the machine."

Was he calling Meredith a pathological liar? No, no, he insisted. But there had been no polygraph test to announce her innocence.

And there *were* certain things Meredith was guilty of: She was a coward; she had lived a life of submission. She had never asked

Freddy where the money was coming from. Or rather, at a certain stage, she had asked him, and he hadn't given her a straight answer or any answer at all, and she hadn't demanded one. She hadn't picked the lock to his home office under the cover of darkness and gone through his books with a fine-tooth comb the way she should have.

Eleanor Charnes, the mother of Alexander, Leo's friend from Saint Bernard's, had put a rumor out through the school that Freddy's business was crooked, and Meredith had subtly seen to it that Eleanor wasn't invited to the Frick benefit or to the Costume Institute Gala at the Met.

Phyllis Rossi had insisted her husband pull $25 million out of Delinn Enterprises because she'd chatted with Freddy at the Flagler Museum in Palm Beach, and she said she found his answers about his business "evasive." Meredith had blackballed Phyllis for membership to the Everglades Club.

And then, of course, there was what she'd done to Connie.

Meredith was guilty of those things. But Leo—Leo wasn't guilty. (Was he? Oh, God. Oh, God. *Hundreds of pieces of evidence.* From which "reliable sources" had Amy heard this? What did this mean?) When Amy had said Leo's name, Meredith wanted to bare her teeth and snarl. *Don't you tell lies about my son.* Amy Rivers was another scary pelican from the nightmares of Leo's childhood.

Meredith's vision started to splotch. She was going to pass out, but she didn't care.

Connie came rushing out of the salon. When she opened the door, clean, fresh air blew into the car.

"Jesus!" Connie said. "What *happened?*"

Meredith told her, sparing no detail.

Connie said, "This is the woman you told me about? The one from Palm Beach?"

"Yes. I knew she was on the island. I saw her at the bookstore, but I didn't think she recognized me."

"Those things she said about Leo?" Connie asked. "They're not true, are they?"

"They're not true," Meredith whispered. They couldn't be true. They couldn't be.

"I'd like to go back in there and rip her face off," Connie said.

Meredith stared out the window. They were on Milestone Road, on their way home to Tom Nevers. There were trees and more trees. People riding bicycles. Normal people.

"The wig didn't work," Meredith said. "She knew me instantly."

"Because you used to be friends," Connie said. "Let me ask you this: Do you think she's the one who took your picture? Vandalized the house? Slashed my tires?"

The thought had crossed Meredith's mind. Amy was certainly angry enough to do those things, but the spray painting especially seemed juvenile and beneath her. The first word that Meredith would use to describe Amy Rivers was: "busy." She was always rushing from one commitment to another. Her day was overscheduled. When she had lunch with Meredith, she always left ten minutes early and was already five minutes late for the next thing. Seeing Amy on a bicycle had thrown Meredith. In Palm Beach, she whipped her black Audi into the parking lot of the Everglades Club and screeched out. In Meredith's mind, Amy Rivers was too busy to plan and execute that kind of vandalism. Surely she had bigger things to worry about?

But maybe not.

She would never have misspelled the word "thief." Unless she was trying to throw the police off her trail.

Possible?

"I don't know," Meredith said.

Once Meredith retreated to her room, she dialed Dev at the law firm, while praying a Hail Mary. It was six o'clock on a Friday evening. What were the chances Dev would be at his desk? Meredith got the firm's recording, which meant the miserable receptionist had left for the weekend. She was probably already in her seat aboard the Hampton Jitney. Meredith entered Dev's extension. He answered.

"It's Meredith."

"Hey, Meredith—"

Meredith launched into what Amy Rivers had said. It wasn't true, was it? There weren't hundreds of pieces of evidence against Leo?

Dev was quiet. Meredith felt like she was free-falling.

"I'm not Leo's attorney," Dev said. "Honestly, I'm not sure what kind of evidence is amassed against him. There's something, Meredith. I mean, we knew that, right? Otherwise he wouldn't be under investigation. But right now, from the sounds of it, nothing they have is strong enough to stand up in court—otherwise, they would have charged him. And he hasn't been charged. Julie is hunting down this Misurelli woman, the secretary. She said she'd fly to Padua herself if she had to. Julie has a phenomenal legal mind. And she has the eye of the tiger. Leo is in good hands, Meredith. There's nothing you can do except tell yourself that Leo hasn't been charged and he's in good hands." Meredith heard Dev swallow. "Okay?"

"Okay," Meredith said. Dev promised he would talk to her after the weekend, but if she needed him in the meantime, she had his cell number.

Meredith said good-bye and hung up, then turned off her phone. Deep breath: Not charged with anything. In good hands. Phenomenal legal mind. Amy Rivers was lying. *Your family is going to be flushed away. Like turds.*

My God, Meredith thought.

Later, Connie grilled the salmon, and the smoke floated in the open balcony doors and made Meredith's stomach rumble. She should just go down; she was being childish. Without Meredith downstairs, Connie might drink too much. She might obsess about the reason Dan hadn't called, or she might fall deeper into self-pity about Wolf and Ashlyn.

Meredith should go down. But she couldn't.

A little while later, Meredith heard a rustling outside her room. A piece of paper shot under the door.

It said, "Your dinner, Madame."

Meredith opened the door and despite her prevailing sentiment that all she should be eating was stale bread smeared with rat guts, she took the beautiful plate—rosy salmon glazed with some kind of mustard dill sauce, grilled asparagus, and a pearly ear of Bartlett's Farm corn already buttered and salted—and sat on her bed and devoured everything.

Meredith flipped the note over and wrote, "It was delicious. Thank you." She wanted to add, *I love you,* but she and Connie hadn't completely cleared the air between them yet. Soon, maybe. Meredith left the note out in the hallway, then shut her door and lay on her bed. It was still light outside, and her book was right there, but she couldn't read. She hadn't shut herself away to block out Connie. She had shut herself away because she needed to think.

Hundreds of pieces of evidence. Eye of the tiger. In good hands. Hasn't been charged. Fly to Padua. Spend the rest of his life in prison.

Sick love story. That was another phrase that bothered Meredith.

If Meredith were very honest with herself, she would admit that, in some way, the beginning of her love affair with Freddy had been entangled with the end of her love affair with Toby. Meredith had spent her first semester at Princeton seeking out the "amazing opportunities" Toby had promised she would have when he broke up with her. She had wanted Toby to be right. She had wanted Princeton to be so scintillating that she forgot she ever knew a boy named Toby O'Brien. And the person she fixed her attentions on was Freddy. Then her father died, and Toby missed the funeral, and Meredith had allowed herself to be used by Dustin Leavitt. And when Meredith returned to school feeling as lonely as she ever had in her life, there was Freddy. Her answer. He was a pool, and she dove in.

Freddy became the president of Dial his senior year while Meredith moved into a suite with Gwen Marbury and born-again-Christian twins Hope and Faith Gleeburgen, who had been matched with Meredith and Gwen because there had been no other choices for either pair. The Gleeburgens seemed perfectly nice. Although what did Meredith know; she was never in the suite. She spent every night with Freddy.

Meredith didn't have friends other than Gwen Marbury, though Gwen, too, fell away. Gwen had dated Richard Cassel for a while in an attempt to remain close with Meredith and Freddy; she had entertained notions, perhaps, of *becoming* Meredith and Freddy, but Gwen and Richard weren't a good match and they broke up. Richard later told Freddy, "You can take the girl out of the trailer park, but you can't take the trailer park out of the girl," which was a hideous thing to say — but that was Richard Cassel for you: an unapologetic snob.

After Freddy graduated, he received a job offer from Prudential Securities in Manhattan. Meredith couldn't stand the thought of being without Freddy; she couldn't stand the thought of Freddy in Manhattan with all the professional women in their snug power suits, meeting for drinks at the South Street Seaport after work. He would turn his blue gaze on someone else; this new girl would light up, fall at his feet, do his bidding. It made Meredith physically ill to think about. She started vomiting after nearly every meal in the spring of her sophomore year. Freddy thought she was bulimic — but no, she insisted, she was just sick with worry about losing him. They went to Mental Health Services together and saw a counselor, like a married couple. The counselor thought some separation would be good for both of them, but for Meredith in particular.

"It seems like you're in danger of losing yourself," the counselor said. "Freddy has basically subsumed you."

"That's bullshit," Freddy said. "We don't need separation." If he had been thinking the same thing when he walked in there, hearing the words come out of the therapist's mouth propelled him in the opposite direction.

"Then why are you leaving?" Meredith asked.

Well, Freddy pointed out, he had loans to pay back, lots of loans, which was something that Meredith, coming from her privileged background, would know nothing about. The Prudential job paid good money; he couldn't just walk away from it.

"Fine," Meredith said. "Then I'll drop out of school and come to Manhattan with you."

"Now, do you see how self-destructive that is?" the therapist asked.

The solution arrived in the form of a well-paying internship, offered to Freddy by the head of the economics department, who was writing a new textbook and needed a research assistant. Freddy, in his years at Princeton, had been known as an econ whiz. He understood the way money worked, what drove the markets, what slowed them down. He had been watching the stock market, he said, since he was twelve years old. At Dial, he was voted "Most Likely to Become a Wall Street Legend."

Now, Meredith blinked. She was sitting on the edge of her bed, watching the sun sink into the ocean. *Most Likely to Become a Wall Street Legend.* Well, that prediction had come true, hadn't it?

The summer between Meredith's sophomore and junior year, Meredith convinced Freddy to go backpacking through Europe. They rode the Eurail; they slept in cheap hotels and pensiones. Meredith had planned their itinerary of cities—Madrid, Barcelona, Paris, Venice, Florence, Vienna, Salzburg, Munich, Amsterdam, London—as well as the itinerary within each city. She wanted to see the churches and the art museums and every place that had literary significance—Anne Frank's house in Amsterdam, Shakespeare and Company in Paris. Meredith explained to Freddy the importance of Giotto's frescoes and the difference between the Gothic and the Romanesque. Freddy took notes in a tiny reporter's pad. At first, Meredith thought he was making fun of her, but as they squeezed into a twin bed at night, he insisted his interest was sincere. She was the one who had read the Yeats and taken the art-history courses; she was the one who could speak French. He was just an uncultured kid from a house with pasteboard walls in upstate New York, trying to keep up with her.

Before they left, Freddy had told Meredith that he had no money for such a trip. He had put all of his graduation money—which consisted of a check for a hundred dollars from his mother, a thousand-dollar cash award from the economics department, and a thousand-dollar leadership award from the alumni of Dial— toward his student loans. Meredith had assured him that she had enough money for both of them. And, true to his word, Freddy ran out of money right away. He spent the bulk of what he'd brought at a nightclub in Barcelona. Neither Freddy nor Meredith had wanted to go to a nightclub, but they'd met some chic Catalan university students on the Rambles who had talked them into it. Once they were in the club and were charged an exorbitant sixteen dollars for two beers, Meredith suggested they leave, but Freddy decided he wanted to stay. The university students secured a table near the dance floor and ordered several bottles of Cava. Meredith and Freddy danced awkwardly to the house music, and then sat back down at the table, talking to the university students in English. Freddy reverted to his tutoring days, correcting everyone's tenses. Meredith grew drunk and combative—she wanted to leave—but Freddy kept putting her off. One of the students was a dark-haired girl who looked like Trina. This girl asked Freddy to dance. Freddy glanced at Meredith and quickly said no, but Meredith felt compelled to say, "Don't be stupid, Fred. Go dance with her." So Freddy and the girl danced, and Meredith excused herself for the ladies' room—where everyone was snorting cocaine or shooting it into their ankles—and threw up. She rested her face against the grimy tiles of the floor by the evil-smelling toilet and decided that this was the lowest point of her life, short of her hour in Dustin Leavitt's apartment. She hadn't thought such a base feeling was possible when she was with Freddy, but there it was, and furthermore, she was pretty sure she was going to lose Freddy to the Spanish girl. He would marry her and enjoy a life in the Catalan countryside helping the girl's father with his olive farm. Meredith was only roused from the floor by someone aggressively kicking the door to her stall and bellowing something in German. When Meredith got back to the table, Freddy was standing. They were leaving, he said. Meredith had never been so relieved.

When they got outside, however, Freddy told Meredith that he'd paid the bill and that the bill had been three hundred dollars, and that he was, at that point, effectively broke.

Meredith wasn't used to being angry with Freddy. Upset, frustrated, jealous, yes, but not angry. She didn't know how to express what she was feeling.

She said, "Why did you pay the bill? Did they *ask* you to?"

He shrugged. "No. I wanted to."

"But now you have no money."

He gave her a hangdog expression. "I know."

And she thought, *I can't believe you, Freddy. How irresponsible!*

And she thought, *He did it to impress the girl who looked like Trina.*

Then she thought, softening, because there was something about Freddy that always made her excuse him, *He did it because he's naturally generous and he wanted to make those strangers happy.*

She did not think at the time (though she certainly thought it now), *He wanted their admiration, he wanted control. He wanted to walk out of there a big man.*

When Meredith became a senior in college, Freddy left Princeton. He had taken one year off to stay with Meredith, but he couldn't take two. Prudential had come back to him with another job offer at a bigger salary. It seemed that saying no to them and working with a famous economist had boosted his value, and Freddy couldn't turn them down again. His loans beckoned.

Meredith wasn't happy, but she agreed that he should go. It was only one year. She could make it.

She scheduled all of her classes on Monday, Tuesday, and Wednesday, so that by Wednesday night, she could be on a train headed for the city. Freddy, as a perk in the package Prudential had offered him, was living in a condo on East 71st Street. The condo was well beyond his means; it was, essentially, a free sublet from another Prudential trader who was spending a year with a Swiss bank in Zurich.

Meredith gasped. That trader had *remained* in Zurich; he had become a higher-up with a Swiss bank. A Swiss bank, where, possibly, Freddy had hidden money. Which bank was it? She'd asked, but had Freddy ever told her? She needed to remember so she could tell Dev. And what had that trader's name been? *Thorlo* was the name that popped into Meredith's mind, but that wasn't quite right. *Ortho?* No. Meredith had spent a large chunk of her senior year living among this man's possessions. She remembered that he had a Danish mother who had filled his apartment with sleek, modern furniture. She remembered a tall Norfolk pine that it had become her responsibility to keep watered; she remembered a rocking chair made from smooth, blond wood. She remembered a folk statue of a little man with a funny Alpine hat, his hair fashioned from gray cotton. The statue's name had been Otto—was that the name Meredith was remembering? But what, then, had the trader's name been? She racked her brain. This might be the name that could save her. *Thorlo, Ortho.* She had *lived* in this man's apartment. She had chopped celery with his special, sharp knives and had stuck the celery in the Bloody Marys she made for herself and Freddy every Sunday morning. Back in those days, she and Freddy had gone out on the weekends. They went to bars, they danced. Freddy had once gotten so drunk that he climbed up on the bar, gyrating his hips to "I Love the Nightlife." That had been a fun year, Meredith's senior year of college, though college had nothing to do with it; it was her life in the city with Freddy that mattered. Half the time, they enjoyed doing adult things: every Sunday, Meredith would make Bloody Marys and they would get bagels and lox from H&H and they would read the *Times*. And the other half of the time, they were drunk at the Mill on 85th Street. Meredith threw "cocktail parties" for the guys from Dial who had graduated with Freddy and were now living in the city with their various girlfriends. Meredith served shrimp cocktail and Armenian string cheese and pigs in a blanket with spicy brown mustard, just like her own mother had.

She remembered entertaining Richard Cassel and his new girl-friend Astrid, who worked as an editorial assistant at *Harper's Bazaar*. Astrid had shown up wearing a Diane von Furstenberg wrap dress, one of the originals, and a pair of Oleg Cassini heels. A familiar insecurity returned to haunt Meredith, who was wear-ing a khaki skirt and a cable-knit cardigan sweater. Astrid, like Trina, was sophisticated in a way that Meredith feared she would never be. And to boot, the night Richard and Astrid came to the apartment was the night that Richard planned to propose. He had a ring from Tiffany's in his jacket pocket; he was going to present it to Astrid after their dinner at Lutèce. It was all so exactly what Meredith wanted for herself that she had been overcome by nau-seating jealousy. (The coda to that story was that Richard and Astrid did get married, did have five children, the second of whom was born with cerebral palsy, and Richard did step out of the mar-riage, having a long affair with an unhappy married socialite, whom he then married and divorced in short order.)

There was something incomparably romantic about an engage-ment, Meredith thought, which didn't translate to marriage.

She and Freddy had had a lot of crazy sex that year on the impeccable white sheets of the Danish bed. Meredith had slept on this trader's sheets, and still she couldn't remember his name.

Thorlo. No, that was the brand of thick socks that she and Freddy had worn while hiking in the Alps. She was getting confused.

*　　*　　*

The night purpled. Meredith heard water gurgling through the pipes; Connie was running the dishwasher. Meredith's dirty dishes sat on her dresser. She would take them down in the morning and wash them herself. She brushed her teeth and changed into her nightgown. She listened to the waves. She had done so much thinking that Amy Rivers now seemed very far away. Amy Rivers was decades in Meredith's future.

Meredith graduated from Princeton with honors, but not Phi Beta Kappa as she had hoped. She had studied on the train between Princeton and New York, and all day Thursday and Friday while Freddy was at work—but she was away from the precious resource of the Firestone Library, and there had been times when she had been quick or lazy with a paper because she wanted to be with Freddy, or she was hung over from too much fun in the city. Still, her mother beamed with pride, and she had the news of Meredith's graduation from Princeton published in the *Main Line Times* and the Aronimink newsletter. She took Meredith to dinner at the Nassau Inn and gave her a string of pearls and a check for $5,000. A week after graduation, Meredith found that she had been chosen for a teaching program which placed top university graduates into failing school systems and that there were openings in Appalachia, Brownsville, Texas, and New York City. Meredith would go to New York, no question. If there hadn't been a position in New York, she would have abandoned the idea of the teaching program altogether, even though teaching English was all she'd ever wanted to do.

But, thankfully, she didn't have to worry. She had her degree and a job in New York City. She would be with Freddy!

There was more rustling outside the door. Meredith heard Connie sigh at her note. Another note floated under the door. Again, Meredith waited until she heard Connie retreat. The note said, "Your dessert, madame. Sweet dreams!"

Meredith opened the door. A square of something creamy on a graham cracker crust. Cheesecake? She brought the dessert to bed with her, tucked herself under the summer blanket, and tasted a forkful. It was tart: key lime. Key lime put Meredith back in Palm Beach with Amy Rivers, but no, she wouldn't let herself travel that mental highway. Stay present, find the answer. What was the name of that trader?

Meredith wanted Freddy to propose. It was all she thought about. Why? She wondered now. Why, why, why? What about him had been so irresistible? So impossible to let go? His blue eyes? His cutting wit? His natural, easy confidence despite the fact that he came from absolutely nothing? His brilliance in economics? His early success in the financial world? His innate generosity? His burning desire to be the man who took care of things, who solved problems, who made people happy? Was it the way he held Meredith, touched her, talked to her? Yes, now she was getting closer. It was the way he believed her to be a delicate treasure, no less precious than the crown jewels that they had seen together at the Tower of London. Freddy was devoted to her. He wasn't going to leave her the way Toby had. He wasn't going to sail off into the sunset in search of his freedom. He didn't see the allure of a different woman every night. He was singular in his desire. He wanted Meredith. It was intoxicating.

And then, just as soon as Meredith became cozy and secure in Freddy's constancy, Prudential sent Freddy on a two-week trip to Hong Kong. He let it slip that there was talk of moving him permanently to Hong Kong. This gave Meredith emotional seizures. She had just moved into Freddy's sublet, very much against her mother's wishes. (Her mother didn't like how it "looked," the two of them living together.) Meredith would begin her teaching job in September. What would she do if Freddy moved to Hong Kong?

She would move to Hong Kong as well.

She had wanted to go with him on the trip—she could use her

graduation money—but Freddy said no, this was work. This was something he had to do himself. Girlfriends weren't welcome.

"How do you know?" Meredith said. "Did you ask?"

"I just know."

Meredith spent two weeks in the hot, dirty, miserable city while Freddy was in Hong Kong. Connie called and invited Meredith to Nantucket. Connie had just begun dating a man named Wolf Flute, whose family had a cottage on the beach. The place was simple but it had four bedrooms. Meredith could stay for a week, or longer.

Meredith had said no.

She stayed in the apartment, she ordered in Chinese food, she read books in the blond wood rocking chair (*Sophie's Choice; Goodbye, Columbus*); she pined for Freddy. Freddy called three times, but the connection was bad. Meredith heard the words "Victoria Peak," "Hollywood Road," "the Peninsula Hotel." She heard the excitement in his voice. One of the partners had taken Freddy on a junk to another island where they had gone to a seafood restaurant. They picked a fish out of the tank, and twenty minutes later it was sautéed, sauced, and garnished in front of them. Freddy had never been anywhere like Hong Kong. Before meeting Meredith, he had never been anywhere at all.

Meredith hated Freddy, she decided. He was going to leave her behind just the way Toby had, but she wasn't going to let that happen. She was going to preempt him. The next time the phone rang and Meredith suspected it was him, she didn't answer. The phone stopped ringing, then started up again. Meredith smiled vengefully but didn't pick up. She left the apartment for the first time in days. She would go for a walk in the park, then take herself to the Belgian place for *moules et frites*. When she walked out of the apartment, the phone was still ringing.

She calmed down, then revved up again. She screamed at the folk statue named Otto. She lunged at Otto with one of the sharp Danish knives. She wrote "Fuck you" in soap on the bathroom mirror; Freddy would find it when he returned, but Meredith wouldn't be around to witness his reaction. She was going to Nantucket to visit Connie after all. Connie had told her about a party called the Madequecham Jam — hundreds of people partying on the beach! All Meredith needed to bring was a bikini.

Meredith packed a bag. She was taking the Chinatown bus to Boston, and a second bus from Boston to Hyannis, and a two-hour ferry from Hyannis to Nantucket. It was a longer journey than Meredith had anticipated; the mere thought of it exhausted her, but at least she wouldn't be sitting around the apartment, *waiting,* when Freddy got home.

She had been at the door, she remembered, ready to leave for the bus station, when there was a knock. She peered through the peephole. It was Western Union, with a telegram.

"Meredith Martin?" the man said.

She accepted the telegram, her hands shaking. She had never received a telegram before. The only people she had known to receive telegrams were mothers whose sons had died in Vietnam. So this said what? That Freddy had died? He'd been hit by a bus while crossing the street in opposite-side traffic? Or maybe it was a telegram *from* Freddy, saying he wasn't coming back. They were placing him permanently in Hong Kong, and he wanted Meredith to send his things. Maybe he'd meant to tell her this over the phone, but she hadn't answered.

Whatever the telegram said, it wasn't good.

She thought about leaving the telegram behind in the apartment. But what kind of person had the willpower to leave an envelope like this — a telegram just screamed urgency — unopened?

She opened it by the front door. It said:

MEREDITH STOP I CAN'T LIVE WITHOUT YOU STOP
WILL YOU MARRY ME? STOP
FREDDY

She read it again, then a third time, her heart lifting like a balloon. She jumped up and down and whooped. She was laughing and crying and thinking, *Goddamn it, someone should be here,* but no, this was better somehow. He'd surprised her, really shocked her, snatched her from despair, saved her from going to Nantucket, and, most likely, doing something regrettable.

This was the right thing. This was absolutely the only thing. There was no decision. The answer was yes.

There had only been one bump in the road before Meredith and Freddy got married, and that arrived in the form of Connie's own shotgun wedding, which was thrown together in December once Connie learned she was pregnant.

Meredith had been the maid of honor. She wore a red velvet cocktail dress, red stiletto heels, and Annabeth Martin's diamond engagement ring. She and Freddy were living together in the sublet apartment; Meredith was in the throes of her first year of teaching at Gompers. Meredith knew she would see Toby at the wedding, but she was ready for him.

But then Freddy couldn't go. Work needed him. He was low man on the totem pole at Prudential; he had no choice.

And so, Meredith faced Toby alone. Toby was tan from having sailed somewhere impossibly glamorous—Ibiza or Monaco— and he'd brought, as a date, a girl from his crew. The girl's name was Pamela; she was taller than Meredith, and beefier, and she had red, calloused hands. Meredith found her pushy; she offered to help Connie with her train and her bouquet when they had just met the day before.

Connie had said, *Oh, don't you worry about it. I have Meredith here to help me.*

Meredith had thought, All right, Pamela was cute enough, friendly enough, but not the person she'd expected Toby to choose. Toby was effusive with his attention toward his sister and his mother and Pamela; for the ceremony and the first part of the reception, he ignored Meredith completely. She, meanwhile, couldn't keep her eyes off him. He exuded his usual healthy, outdoorsy energy; the tuxedo seemed to be reining him in. The green satin bow tie he'd chosen made his eyes seem greener. Inwardly, Meredith cursed him. Goddamn him for being so luminous all the time. He spun Pamela around the dance floor. He gave a very sweet and funny toast to Wolf and Connie, and Meredith had to admit that freedom did suit him.

The band played "The Best of Times" by Styx, which was Meredith and Toby's number one song as a couple, and Meredith realized she had a choice: she could go to the bar for another fuzzy navel, or she could hide in the ladies' room and cry.

Toby intercepted her on the way to the ladies' room.

"Dance with me," he said.

"You haven't talked to me once all night," Meredith said.

"I know," he said. "I'm sorry. Dance with me."

Meredith thought back to the night of their breakup. She nearly said, *I thought you didn't like to dance.* But instead she let Toby lead her to the dance floor. She fit right into his arms in a way that felt unholy. *Freddy,* she thought. *I am engaged to Freddy.*

Toby hummed in her ear. They used to listen to this song in Toby's Nova when they made love. A long time ago. But not so long: five years. Meredith said, "It's weird that they're playing this song."

Toby said, "I made a request."

Meredith pulled away. Toby had requested their song to the band?

"What about Pamela?" she said.

"She's just a friend. And she doesn't seem to mind."

Meredith craned her neck. Pamela was at the bar, draped all over Wolf's brother.

"I don't get it," Meredith said. "You know I'm engaged? You know I'm getting married in June?"

"I know. I heard," Toby said. "But I just thought..."

"Thought what?" Meredith said.

"I needed a way to break the ice," he said.

"Break the *ice?*" Meredith said. "When I hear this song, Toby, I *hurt.*"

"I know," Toby said. "I hurt, too."

"Why would *you* hurt?" she asked. "*You* broke up with *me.*"

"Meet me later," Toby said. "Please, Meredith? Meet me at the Wayne Hotel."

She glared at him. "You have *got* to be kidding me."

"At the bar," he said. "So we can talk?"

"About what?" she said. But he didn't respond. He tightened his grip on her. He was humming again. *The best of times are when I'm alone with you.*

Meredith had half a mind to storm off the dance floor, but she couldn't make a scene at Connie's wedding; Connie's wedding was shrouded in enough scandal as it was. So she finished out the dance with Toby. The horrible truth was, she still had feelings for him; the horrible truth was, he did have the first and best piece of her heart; the horrible truth was, it felt electrifying to be in his arms. But would Meredith meet him at the Wayne Hotel? She hesitated. One second, two seconds, ten seconds. Then she thought, *No way. I won't do it.* The next song, she returned to her seat, and Wolf's brother, Jake, asked her to dance. Meredith watched Toby and Pamela throw back shots of tequila at the bar.

Meredith thought, *I have to get back to New York. I have to get back to Freddy.*

Freddy and Meredith got married the following June at Saint Thomas of Villanova, the same church where Chick Martin's funeral Mass had been held. There were a hundred and fifty people in attendance, and if Meredith had one complaint, it was that the church looked empty compared to the crowd that had packed in to pay their respects to her father.

Connie served as Meredith's matron of honor, even though

Ashlyn had been born in April and Connie was still nursing her. Richard Cassel had served as Freddy's best man. Bill and Veronica O'Brien were there, though Toby had declined. It had taken courage for Meredith to invite him, but after what had happened at Connie's wedding, she decided it would be a good idea for Toby to watch her getting married to somebody else. Surely, she wasn't the only bride to feel this way? Toby sent a note that said, "Sailing in the Lesser Antilles! Wishing you the very best!" Meredith was disappointed, but she realized he probably wouldn't have come if he'd been down the street.

Annabeth Martin came in a wheelchair and was tended to most of the night by Meredith's mother, both of them glowing with happiness. This was as it should be; Meredith married right out of college—just as they both had—to a man who was going places.

Freddy's mother came to the ceremony but didn't stay for the reception. She claimed she had to get back to Utica that night so she could get to work in the morning.

"Work?" Meredith said. "On Sunday?"

"At the store," Freddy said. He meant Kmart.

Meredith had only met Mrs. Delinn for the first time earlier that day. She was soft bodied, and her skin was the blue-white of an undercooked egg. Her hair was thinning and had been badly dyed the color of Bing cherries. She had watery blue eyes—lacking the intense cobalt pigment of Freddy's eyes. Generally Meredith thought Mrs. Delinn seemed worn out and run down, as though the effort of making it to this moment in her life had nearly killed her. She was oddly deferential to Meredith and kept saying how much she appreciated being invited.

"Of course," Meredith said. "You're Freddy's mother."

"You'll take care of him," Mrs. Delinn said. It was a statement, not a question. "You'll love him. He'll pretend like he can get along without it, but he can't. Freddy needs his love."

Meredith walked down the aisle by herself. She felt the absence of her father; her whole left side was numb. Everyone in the church was beaming at her. She was glad they were there, but the only person who mattered was the man at the altar, his eyes flashing, his face radiating promise. When she was ten steps or so from the altar, he came for her; he took her by the arm and walked her the rest of the way. The crowd in the church gasped at first, and then ahhhed.

Freddy leaned in and whispered, "You looked lonely."

She said, "Yes, but not anymore."

He said, "Never again."

Meredith set down her dessert plate. The ache in her heart could not be described.

She was tired, and in many ways, she was defeated, but she was still herself, Meredith Martin, so she slid out of bed and went into the bathroom to brush her teeth a second time.

She fell asleep remembering the dancing at her wedding. She and Freddy had taken lessons in the city, and they had been synchronized in the way they moved together. It had been a great party—at one point, every single guest had been out on the dance floor. Even Annabeth Martin in her wheelchair; even Wolf holding tiny baby Ashlyn. At one point, Meredith had been in a circle of Freddy's friends—the old guys from Dial, the new guys from Prudential—and now, as Meredith pictured it in her mind, there was someone she didn't recognize in the circle, a tall, lean man with the white-blond hair of a Scandinavian. Meredith turned to Gwen Marbury, while at the same time thinking, *Gwen Marbury wasn't at my wedding,* and asked, "Who is that guy?"

"That guy?" Gwen said. "That's Thad Orlo."

Meredith startled awake. Her eyes snapped open. *Thad Orlo!*

Meredith woke up at daybreak and wondered what time she could reasonably expect Dev to answer his cell phone. Eight o'clock? Seven o'clock? She didn't want to be the lunatic client who called him at dawn. But she wanted to tell him about Thad Orlo. It was something real; it was the name of a Swiss banker. She took a measured breath. She couldn't tell if she was anxious because she was sure this information would help, or if she was worried it wouldn't help. She had to find the answer. *The other investors are clamoring for your head. Your family is going to be flushed away.* She needed to find the key that would set her and Leo free.

She turned on her cell phone and waited with the predictable anxiety to see if anyone had called overnight. Amy Rivers had her number. It was conceivable that she had left an abusive voice mail, elaborating on the hateful things she'd said the day before. But the phone booted up silently, giving Meredith nothing but the time. It was 6:09. Unable to wait another minute, she dialed Dev, and he picked up on the first ring.

"Allo?" he said. He sounded funny, but of course he sounded funny, it was still basically the middle of the night.

"Dev, it's Meredith."

"Hello, Meredith." He sounded out of breath.

"Did I wake you?" Meredith asked.

"No," he said. "I'm running. Riverside Park."

Riverside Park was in the same city where Meredith had spent most of her adult life, but she hadn't been there in twenty years or more, since one of the boys had a little friend from school who lived on the Upper West Side, and the other mother (whose name was lost to Meredith) and Meredith would take the boys to the playground there. Meredith liked thinking of Dev running on those paths by the Hudson. She liked thinking of him unchained from his desk.

"I'm sorry to bug you," Meredith said.

"Is everything okay?" Dev asked.

"I'm calling because I thought of something that might help," Meredith said.

"Oh, yeah?" Dev said.

"A million years ago," she said, "and I'm talking nineteen eighty-two, nineteen eighty-three..."

Dev laughed. Meredith counted back to make sure that Dev would have been *alive* in those years.

"It was my senior year at Princeton, and Freddy was living in New York City working for Prudential Securities."

"Which division?" Dev asked.

"Oh, God, I have no idea," Meredith said. Even as much as she had loved Freddy back then, she hadn't bothered to find out exactly what he did for work. She didn't care; she had never cared, just as Freddy had never cared about the distaff family lines in Faulkner. "Trading? Derivatives? Don't you guys have that kind of information at your fingertips?"

"I don't," Dev said. "The SEC might, though."

"We lived in a sublet of a man named Thad Orlo." She paused. She could hear the thwack of Dev's sneakers on the pavement, a siren, taxi horns, a barking dog. "Has that name come up in the investigation?"

"I'm not supposed to say," Dev said. "But no, I don't think so."

"Thad Orlo was working for Prudential, but he was spending a year in Switzerland, at some Swiss bank, perhaps a bank affiliated with Prudential? Anyway, I never actually *met* him because while we were in New York, he was in Switzerland—that was the whole idea—but I asked Freddy about him from time to time in subsequent years. Freddy told me that Thad Orlo had stayed on with the bank in Switzerland, but when I asked which bank it was, Freddy said he couldn't remember. Now, what this really meant was that he didn't *want* to tell me because if there was one thing about Freddy, he remembered *everything*. And then there was another time—" this, Meredith remembered just as she was saying the words—"when I asked Freddy what had ever happened to Thad Orlo. I was asking because we had, you know, *lived* in his apartment with all of his furniture and all of his stuff—every

time I saw a certain kind of Danish design, I thought of him—
and at first Freddy pretended not to know who he was at all, which
was absurd, and then once he copped to the fact that he did
remember him, he started asking *me* in this paranoid way about
why I wanted to know about Thad Orlo. And I can remember saying, 'Freddy, I'm sorry. I was just wondering!' "

Dev was breathing hard. Maybe he was crushed at how underwhelming this tip was. Maybe he was wondering why she hadn't
just waited until he was in the office. But the more Meredith
thought about it, the more convinced she became.

"Yes," she said. "He was defensive and angry when I asked him
about Thad Orlo. You should check it out. You should find Thad
Orlo."

"But you don't know which bank?"

"I don't. Freddy most certainly does, even though he lied and
told me he didn't."

"But Freddy's not speaking. At all."

"Still?" Meredith said. She didn't want any news about Freddy.
But she did. .

"Still."

"Well, can't you find him anyway?" Meredith said. She had figured the SEC had huge databases crammed with names, and con-
nections between those names. It was impossible, in this day and
age, to stay anonymous, right? "Can't you google him?"

"I'll do that first thing on Monday," Dev said. "Do you know
anything else about this guy?"

"His mother was Danish," Meredith said, but then she wondered if she knew this for sure, or if she had just assumed it,
because of the furniture. "I think."

"Where was the apartment?" Dev asked.

"Seventy-first Street," Meredith said. But she couldn't remember if the building had been between Lexington and Third, or
Third and Second, and she certainly didn't remember the number
of the building. She had lived there for nearly two years, but the

address eluded her. She was old enough now that this sometimes happened. The salient details of her past evaporated.

"Okay," Dev said. "I'll check out everything you just told me."

"And you'll tell the Feds?"

"I'll tell the Feds."

"You'll tell them I'm helping? You'll tell Julie Schwarz and Leo I'm helping?"

"Yes, Meredith," Dev said. She couldn't discern if his breathlessness was due to his fast pace or the beauty of the Hudson in the morning light or exasperation. "I'll tell everyone you're helping."

CONNIE

Connie had been certain Dan would call. She knew she had *not* put on a good show that night at dinner; she had been drunk, and Connie had had enough experience with her own mother to know what that looked like. But she hadn't heard from Dan in nearly three weeks. Their relationship had been progressing, and then, boom, it just ended. Connie wasn't good at handling rejection. It was, as her sister-in-law Iris would say, messing with Connie's general state of mind.

She hadn't heard from Ashlyn, either, even though Connie had tried texting. *Please call. It's Mom.*

She had also resumed her habit of leaving messages on Sundays. It was pointless, Connie knew, as pointless as prayer: she was talking to someone who may or may not be listening.

The only person Connie heard from was Toby. He sent a text that said: *I'll be there the 5th or 6th, OK?*

Connie hadn't been quite sure what that text was referring to, until she scrolled back and saw the text saying that Toby had sold the boat to the man from Nantucket, and he would be on island in three weeks, OK? And she had responded, *OK! LOL.*

Connie groaned. Nothing about this was laugh out loud. She had to tell Toby that Meredith was here. She had to tell Meredith that Toby was coming. Which one of them would be more upset? Connie decided to keep quiet about it for now. She was afraid if she told Toby that Meredith was here, he wouldn't show up. And Connie desperately wanted to see him. She was afraid that if she told Meredith that Toby was coming, Meredith would pack her things and leave. Or perhaps worse, she would get her hopes up, and then at the last minute, Toby would call to say that he wasn't selling the boat after all but was, instead, sailing down to Venezuela to meet some girl named Evelina for a cup of coffee.

Connie looked at the text again. The fifth or sixth? Well, they had nothing going on. They never had anything going on. She responded, *OK.* But left off the *LOL.*

Connie decided to ambush Dan at Stop & Shop. He had told her in passing that when the island got crazy-busy in August, he went to the grocery store midweek at six o'clock in the morning.

Connie hadn't expected to bump into him on her first attempt. "Midweek" could mean Tuesday or Wednesday or Thursday. And "six o'clock" could mean six thirty or seven. But when Connie pulled into the parking lot at ten minutes past six on Wednesday morning, the strawberry Jeep was there. Connie felt a jolt of nervous excitement and an irrational sense of collusion: the mere fact that Dan was here when he said he would be seemed like a good sign. Connie began muttering to herself. *Calm down. Hurry up! You have to catch him before he leaves. This is so obvious, but only to you. He'll think it's a random coincidence; everyone has to go to the store. He gave you the tip for the best time to go, why wouldn't you take him up on it?* She grabbed a cart, she had a list; this was a legitimate trip to the store. Connie had invited Meredith along the night before saying, *Hey, I'm going to the store bright and early if you want to come.* But Meredith had said no; she had said no to every outing since that woman had accosted her at RJ Miller. Connie said, *Meredith you just can't spend the rest of the summer in the house. It's August now, the best month.* And Meredith said, *No, it's not safe.* Connie said, *But it is safe. The vandalism has stopped. You let that woman have her say; that was all she wanted was to have her say. She's not going to do anything else to you. She's not going to stone you.*

But Meredith wouldn't be moved. She was stubborn like that. Connie had not forgotten.

The store was chilly, the produce section like an icebox. Connie was on a mission here. She had to find Dan first, then worry about her groceries. But if she bumped into him in the middle of the store with an empty cart, it would announce the obvious.

Connie tossed a netted bag of limes into her cart.

Connie zipped through the store, checking down each aisle. There was a blond woman with two little boys in their pajamas, a man in a suit and tie—a Jehovah's Witness, perhaps? someone headed to a funeral?—and then she found Dan, looking positively edible in khaki shorts and a T-shirt and flip-flops, standing in front of the healthy cereal. He didn't see her. Connie could back up, retreat to produce, chicken out. But this was her chance. She had gotten up at daybreak to shower and do her hair. She was bright-eyed, she smelled good, she was wearing a pretty pink cotton halter dress.

She pushed her cart forward. "Dan?" she said.

He turned. The expression on his face was...complicated. It was many expressions at once. He looked surprised, happy, wary, perplexed, caught.

He said, "Connie, hey!"

"Hey," she said, trying to sound upbeat, despite his obvious lack of enthusiasm. "Well, I took you up on your tip about the grocery store at this hour, and you were right! The store is empty. It's clean, and everything has been restocked."

"See?" he said. "I told you." He plucked a box of Kashi off the shelf and put it in his cart. Connie looked at his other groceries—taco kit, ground beef, tomatoes, Triscuits, Starbucks coffee, avocados, six boxes of pasta, celery, plums, two large bottles of V8 Splash. She wondered if she had caught him stocking up for a party to which she hadn't been invited, until she remembered that he had teenagers at home.

"So," she said, "what have you been up to?"

Now it was his turn to cast his eyes into her cart, where he saw the lone bag of limes.

Connie wished she had picked something else as her token item.

And sure enough, when he looked at her again, his face said it all—limes for gin. She had been so drunk; she had started drinking on the boat in a way that had quickly become antisocial, and she had continued to drink until she fell face-first into her dinner. And what did she put in her cart to underscore the fact that she was a drunk? A bag of limes. Connie thought she would die of mortification right then and there.

"Oh, you know," he said. "The usual."

The usual: It was such a nonanswer. It was a blow-off. Connie should retreat. She had to accept that this relationship, friendship, whatever it was, was dead in the water. But she didn't want to.

"Have you been out on your boat?" she asked.

"Every Thursday and Sunday," he said. "Have to keep after the lobster traps."

The lobster traps, containing the lobster Connie hadn't eaten, hadn't even tasted.

"Mmm," she said. "What about the Galley? Have you been back to the Galley?"

He didn't answer that question, which meant what? He hadn't been to the Galley, or he'd been to the Galley with another woman?

He said, "How are you doing? How's Meredith?"

Connie wasn't surprised to hear him ask about Meredith. He

loved Meredith. She knew it! But that was her fault. She had dragged Meredith along on both of their dates, and on the second date, Meredith and Dan had bonded over what to do about drunk Connie.

"We're fine," Connie said. "Meredith is good." Lies, all of it lies. They were drowning. They needed someone to save them. "We were wondering why you haven't called." That was good, Connie thought, using the pronoun "we," implicating Meredith as well. Poor Meredith, who refused to leave the house. Connie had even suggested going to Mass so she could light a candle for Leo, but Meredith said no.

Dan smiled. "Why haven't I called?" he said. "Well, you ladies seem to have your hands full."

"We do have our hands full," Connie said. "They're full of despair and grief and loneliness. That's why we miss you. You were fun. I haven't seen Meredith smile like that since..."

"Well, good," he said.

"And I like you, too," Connie said. It felt like a bold admission, but this was a positive—the barrier of small talk had been knocked down. She was going to say what was on her mind. "I thought you'd call; I thought we'd go out again."

"Is that what you want?" Dan said.

"Yes," Connie said.

Dan nodded thoughtfully. "I think you're a beautiful woman, Connie. And I know you've just lost your husband, and I understand the kind of grief you're experiencing..."

"It's my daughter, too," Connie said. "My daughter doesn't speak to me. We had a falling out after Wolf died." Connie couldn't believe she was blurting out True Confessions here in aisle ten of the supermarket. "I think if my daughter hadn't abandoned me, I'd be doing a lot better..."

"I understand that, too," Dan said.

"Do you?"

"My son Joe took off cross-country a few weeks after Nicole

died—he stole my truck—and I've only heard from him once, by e-mail, and he was asking for money. And I sent it to him, despite how infuriated the request and his exodus in general made me. Because he's my son."

Connie nodded.

Dan said, "I told you about Joe at dinner at the Cauldron."

You did? Connie thought.

Dan said, "You don't remember, do you? Because you were drinking, maybe. Well, we were all drinking that night. But your drinking, if I may be so bold, seems to be in defense of something. You're afraid of me, or of intimacy, or the idea of intimacy. You're afraid to start dating someone, you're afraid of talking to someone, and that's why you brought Meredith along both times I asked you out. I get it, Connie: you're not ready. But I'm not ready for someone who's not ready. Does that make sense?"

The store Muzak was playing "Beautiful Day." Before she could talk herself out of it, she said, "Do you want to go somewhere? For coffee, maybe, or a walk on the beach?"

Dan pulled his cell phone out of his back pocket and checked the time. He said, "I have to be in town at eight."

Connie waited.

He said, "Okay, let me finish my shopping. I have time for a walk on the beach. A short walk."

They went to Monomoy, where the sand was thick and marshy and the air smelled of fish and seaweed and things decomposing, though with the sun coming up and the vista before them of the harbor filled with boats, Connie couldn't imagine anyplace more alluring. So she had the setting, and she had the man, temporarily, but she wasn't sure what to do. She was appalled at herself for suggesting this outing. (She wouldn't candy coat it: she had forced him.) Her whole life she had been pursued by boys, then guys, then men. She had been the adored wife of Wolf Flute for more than half her lifetime, but now Wolf was gone, so who was she? It was as though he had taken Connie with him. She was nobody's wife.

She was dangerously close to being nobody's mother.

Connie's feet made a sucking sound as she walked in the wet, dense sand at the shore line. The way Dan had said "a short walk" made her self-conscious. Already Connie thought about turning around so as not to hold this man up any longer. But she was intrigued by what he'd said about his son Joe stealing his truck, taking off for California, e-mailing to ask for money.

"Tell me about Joe," she said. She felt embarrassed that Dan had, apparently, already *told* her about Joe and she had no recollection.

"Oh, man," he said. "We're getting heavy, deep, and real right away?"

"I'm sorry," Connie said. "But I hear the clock ticking. And I really want to know."

"Joe," Dan said. "Joe, Joe, Joe." He was staring out at the water, and this gave Connie a chance to study him. He was so handsome that it made her a little queasy. She liked his short, clipped hair, the brown and the gray; she liked his blue-hazel eyes, the scruff on his face, his Adam's apple, the supple, tense form of his runner's body. Dan took care of his body, Connie could tell. He was going to make it last, and at their age, there was something very appealing about that.

"Just saying the kid's name makes me anxious," Dan admitted.

Connie knew this feeling. God, did she! Every time Connie thought or said the name "Ashlyn," her blood pressure rose. Every time someone else said the name "Ashlyn" — especially someone like Iris — Connie felt like she had a gun trained on her. She was excited to have this phenomenon described by someone else.

"Joe was named for Nicole's dad," Dan said. "So, from the beginning, it was like he belonged to her. Only her." Dan stopped, picked up a round, flat rock, and skipped it a dozen times across the shallows. He grinned at Connie. "I am an excellent skipper of stones."

"Indeed, you are," Connie said. It seemed like he was trying to impress her, which was a good sign.

"If you believe in things like that," Dan said. "That a child can be more aligned with one parent than the other just because of how they're named. I'm not sure I believe it, but I don't know; all three boys were inordinately fond of their mother. On some level, I understood it. She was their *mother,* and she was very nurturing. She was a nutritionist by trade. She worked with the commonwealth on state-mandated school lunches, and locally she worked with the private schools and the Boys & Girls Club and the Boosters. She made sure there was fresh fruit for sale at high-school football games. It sounded ridiculous, but somehow she made it work. It would be a clear autumn afternoon, and next to the snack bar that, by tradition, sold hot dogs and Doritos, there would be a wooden basket of red, crisp apples. Somehow she got the funding for a juice press, and one of the old-timers from the retirement community would be there turning the apples into juice." Dan shook his head. "The kids loved it; the parents loved it. Nicole was written up in the paper. A local hero."

Connie smiled. "So your kids loved her even though she made them eat spinach?"

"They ate spinach for her, they ate kale, they ate *okra,* for God's sake. I used to try to sneak them licorice and Milky Ways, but they would never eat candy. 'Mom would freak out,' they said. I offered them Fritos and Happy Meals. My middle son, Donovan, said to me once, 'Filled with trans fats!' Nicole had them brainwashed; they were her...disciples, and not just about food. About everything. No matter what I did, I couldn't compare. I had a flexible work schedule so I made it to every single one of their ball games, but the only question they asked when they scored the game-winning basket was, 'Did Mom see it?' It used to drive me bonkers, and when I complained to Nicole about it, she accused me of turning our parenting into a competition, which wasn't healthy for anyone."

"So then she got sick..." Connie said.

"Then she got sick," Dan said. "And it was a complete crisis. We didn't tell the kids any more than they needed to know, but they clung to Nicole even tighter. And during the first battle when it looked like we might lose her"—here, Dan stopped talking and drew a few breaths—"I thought that maybe the boys had intuited that illness would claim Nicole, and they were jamming all their love in while they still had a mother to love."

Oh, God. Sad. Tears stung Connie's eyes.

"I mean, Charlie was only four when Nicole got diagnosed, so basically from his earliest memory, he'd been in danger of losing her."

"Right," Connie said.

"This is a long way of saying that all three boys were closely aligned with Nicole—but especially Joe. All three kids had the predictable struggles with Nicole's illness. But the problem with Joe happened when Nicole got diagnosed the second time, with cancer of the liver. The prognosis was bleak. It was, well, it was fucking terminal was what it was, and Nicole knew that, and Joe and Donovan and probably even Charlie knew that. Nicole had always been into holistic medicine and alternative treatments. But the pain with liver cancer took her by surprise. She got a doctor's prescription for..."

"Marijuana," Connie said.

"Marijuana," Dan echoed. "And I'm not going to lie to you. I was surprised Nicole would even consider it. She was such a health nut. She did yoga. Even after the liver diagnosis, I'd find her in downward dog, and she drank these revolting shakes with wheat-grass and God knows what else. But for the pain, she smoked weed. Pure, medical-grade ganja. So her last months with us, she was always high." He cleared his throat. "That might have both-ered me in and of itself. But what really got me was that Joe started smoking it with her."

"He did?" Connie said.

"She allowed it," Dan said. "She encouraged it."

"Encouraged it?"

"She was lonely. She wanted to be less lonely, and having Joe with her in her sick room smoking with her made her feel less lonely. Never mind that the kid was only seventeen, a senior in high school. Never mind that smoking dope for him was illegal. They were communing on a 'higher' level—that was her joke. She made it sound okay, she made it sound beautiful. But for me it was *not* okay, and it was certainly *not* beautiful."

"No," Connie said. "I imagine not."

"It led to some pretty destructive conversations at the end of Nicole's life. She was so worried about the boys. They were her sole focus. What about me, I asked her, your husband of twenty years? She said, 'You'll remarry. You'll find another wife. But the boys will never have another mother.'" Dan looked at Connie. "I can't tell you how that hurt me. I was being dismissed. The boys were her flesh and blood; I wasn't. I was cast as some kind of outsider, and then it occurred to me that I'd always been an outsider." Dan picked up another stone and sent it skipping; it hopped like a bean in a hot pan. "The dying can be so fucking righteous. At some point, Nicole passed into this place where she felt she could say whatever she wanted, no matter who got hurt, because she was going to…"

"Die," Connie said.

"Die," Dan said.

Nicole died, Dan said. (Connie was interested by his tone of voice. He said it like he still couldn't believe it, which was how Connie felt about Wolf.) Donovan and Charlie handled it okay. Joe did not handle it okay. He continued to smoke dope in the house, in front of his brothers, and Charlie was only twelve. Joe had "inherited" a huge stash from Nicole, Dan said. Dan hunted all over the house for it but couldn't turn it up. There were fights. Dan was angry about the marijuana; Joe was angry at Dan for picking fights with Nicole about the marijuana.

"She was dying and you were yelling at her," Joe said.

"What she did was irresponsible," Dan said. "Letting you smoke."

"The marijuana was for the pain," Joe said.

"Her pain," Dan said. "Not your pain."

Joe continued to smoke—though, in a small concession, not in front of his brothers. He had been accepted to Boston College, but after Nicole died, he decided to defer a year. He talked about going to California and working on a campaign to legalize marijuana. Dan told him that no way in hell was Flynn family money going to be spent subsidizing a drug odyssey in California. If Joe wanted to go, that was his choice, but he had to pay his own way.

Joe's answer to this was to steal Dan's pickup truck while Dan was out on his boat. He put it on the ferry and was halfway across the state of New York before Dan figured out what had happened. He could have had Joe tracked down and arrested, but Dan knew Joe was in possession of marijuana, and despite his anger and his hurt, he didn't want to see his kid go to jail.

"And so that was it," Dan said. "He's gone, he's in California, he contacted me the one time for money. He sent a goddamned e-mail. I said to myself, If he has the stones to call and ask me for money, that's one thing, but I will not answer a goddamned e-mail. But then, of course, I did."

"Does he talk to his brothers?" Connie asked.

"He might, but they don't tell me. In our house, his is the name that shall not be spoken."

"But you'd welcome him back?" Connie asked.

"In a heartbeat," Dan said.

They had turned around at the part about Nicole being prescribed marijuana, and now they were headed back. Connie was afraid to ask what time it was. She didn't want this walk to end.

"Do you feel better, telling me?" Connie asked.

"You know?" he said. "I do. You may be the only person I've told the story to that way—start to finish like that. That's the problem with growing up in a place like Nantucket and still living here. Everyone feels like they already know what happened because they were right there watching it. Most people think Joe is a pot-head who stole my truck and lit out to California to live a life even more liberally oriented than his mother's had been. But those people bother me because it wasn't *entirely* Joe's fault. I'm to blame as well, and Nicole is to blame, although *no one* wants to blame Nicole because she's dead. I haven't had a chance to step far enough away from what happened to see it clearly." He laughed sadly. "That's the problem with an island."

"I guess," Connie said.

"So tell me about your daughter," Dan said.

"Isn't one tale of woe enough for one day?" Connie said. "No, I would tell you but I don't want you to be late for work."

"Work can wait," Dan said. He sounded like he meant it, and Connie felt something unfamiliar bloom inside her. Wolf had been the most wonderful man she'd ever known, but those words— *Work can wait*—had never once crossed his lips. Now, if Wolf were here to defend himself, he would point out that power washing and caretaking and lobstering were not the same as being a nationally renowned architect.

Connie ceded this point to him silently while still feeling plea-sure about being put first. "I'll tell you another time," she said.

"No, tell me now. Please," Dan said. "Otherwise I'm going to feel like I failed. Like I didn't allow you to climax."

Connie froze, shocked. Had he really just said that? The idea of her and sexual climax in the same sentence was much more for-eign than it ought to have been. But not wanting to call attention to that fact, Connie laughed.

Dan said, "I'm sorry. That was *very* inappropriate."

She said, "You caught me off guard. But I like that."

"I like that you like that," Dan said, and he took her hand.

They had about a hundred yards of beach left before they reached their shoes, and they were holding hands. Just a little over an hour before, Connie had been sure she was being given the brush off in aisle ten, and now they were holding hands. And Dan had made a joke about bringing Connie to climax. She wasn't sure she had the concentration to proceed.

"Okay, remember what you said about naming Joe after Nicole's father and then feeling like he belonged to her? Well, in my case…" Here, she drifted. She was about to revisit emotional territory she had decided to abandon decades ago. Why go back? Well, on the one hand, Dan had been achingly honest with her, and she wanted to reciprocate. But, on the other hand, she didn't know if she could *be* achingly honest. "I got pregnant with Ashlyn by accident. Wolf and I had been dating for less than six months, and he invited me here to Nantucket for a week, which turned into two weeks. And I'm pretty sure that Ashlyn was conceived in the back of a pickup truck at the Madequecham Jam."

"No way!" Dan said. "You were at the Madequecham Jam? What year are we talking about?"

"Eighty-two," Connie said.

"I was there," Dan said. "I was definitely there. How's that for weird?"

Weird, yes. Though, now that Connie thought about it, it wasn't terribly surprising. Everyone in the universe, it seemed, had been at that beach party. There were hundreds of girls in bikinis and Ray-Ban Wayfarers and guys bare chested wearing board shorts. The soundtrack was Journey and Springsteen and Asia. There were volleyball nets and horseshoes and kegs sitting in tubs of ice, and hibachis with burgers and dogs, and actual dogs catching Frisbees and chasing after tennis balls. There were chicken fights in the water—Connie and Wolf had participated and won handily, Wolf being so tall and Connie so ruthless. The jam had started in the morning and continued on late into the night—there were bonfires and guys strumming guitars and people singing and more beer, all taking place in a miasma of marijuana smoke. Couples drifted off to have sex in the dunes. Wolf and Connie had tried to have sex in the dunes but found them occupied, so they had nestled down in the back of a pickup truck owned by one of Wolf's buddies. Connie didn't remember the sex, though there were things about that night that remained with her—the stars in particular, the obscure constellations that Wolf pointed out: Cygnus, Lyra, Draco. Connie had felt pinned to the earth, one small person, negligible compared to the ocean and the sky, yet she was in love with Wolf Flute, and this made her feel significant in the turning world. Love made her matter. These were deep drunken thoughts. Connie had no idea she was conceiving a child. But yes, looking back, that had been the night. Connie had been nominally "on the pill," though she was lazy about taking it, and she had, in fact, forgotten her pill pack back at her parents' house in Villanova.

The gravity of what had happened that night didn't present itself to Connie until over a month later—Labor Day weekend. She was back on Nantucket with Wolf, only this time his entire family was vacationing at the cottage, as was their tradition. The Flute family believed that the final weekend of summer was superior to all other weekends, and that the last family to leave Nantucket for the season won some kind of intangible prize. (The Flutes regularly stayed until the Tuesday or Wednesday after Labor Day. As a child, Wolf had consistently missed the first day of school, and he'd been two weeks late matriculating at Brown.) In the house that weekend was Wolf's brother, Jake, Wolf's parents, and Wolf's grandparents. It was a weekend that included sailing and badminton, a lobster bake on Saturday, and lobster bisque made from the shells on Sunday. (It was a Yankee household; nothing went to waste.) The Flutes were athletic, hearty, seafaring people, but they weren't drinkers. The only person to have a drink at dinner was Wolf's grandmother, and that drink was a tiny glass of cream sherry. The rest of the family drank ice water or unsweetened iced tea, and Wolf and Connie complied. This being the case, Connie couldn't fathom the reason for her queasy stomach or leaden exhaustion. And yet, as she faced the first incarnation of the lobster and then the second, she had raced to the cottage's lone bathroom—which was no bigger than the bathroom on a ship and had to be shared among the seven of them—and vomited. The times when she wasn't expected at the family table or on a boat or on the beach for some camp game, Connie flopped across her spinsterish single bed in the third-floor guest room originally designed for the governess or nanny, and slept the heavy, sweaty sleep of the dead.

Near the end of the weekend, she awoke to Wolf rubbing her back. "You're sick," Wolf said. "My mother heard you retching in the bathroom. Why didn't you tell me?"

Connie buried her head under the feather pillow. She hadn't said so because she didn't want to ruin Wolf's family vacation or bring light to her infirmities (the fact that Mrs. Flute had heard her "retching" mortified her). She hadn't said so because, part of the time, she felt just fine. She hadn't said so because somewhere inside her, the knowledge lurked: she wasn't sick.

"I'm not sick," she told Wolf.

"You're not?" he said.

"I'm pregnant."

Wolf didn't react one way or another to this news, and Connie was glad. She couldn't handle anger or despair, and she couldn't handle joy. She thought nothing about the situation other than she had finally gotten what she deserved. She had been sleeping with boys since Matt Klein in eleventh grade, and she had never been assiduous about birth control. She had expected the boy-guy-man to be assiduous, and when she discovered they often weren't, it was always during the height of passion and she sometimes—too many times—took her chances. It was amazing she hadn't gotten pregnant before this.

When Wolf finally did speak—it took him so long that Connie had drifted off back to sleep—what he said was, "Wow. Okay. Wow."

The word "wow" bothered her. Connie had no intention of keeping this baby. She was only twenty-two years old, Wolf five years older. Wolf had a job as an architect with a firm in D.C., and he had a small apartment in Dupont Circle, but Connie still lived at home with her parents. She had been renting an apartment in Villanova, but one of her roommate's drunk boyfriends had punched a hole in the plaster and they lost the security deposit and Connie's parents had insisted that she live at home and save money until she proved she was responsible enough to live on her own. She had been working as a waitress at Aronimink and had, in fact, waited on her own drunk parents and her own drunk parents' drunk friends, a situation that Connie found humbling enough to bring her to tears. She couldn't handle caring for her own apartment, and she could barely handle her menial job, so how was she supposed to handle having a baby?

"I didn't want to have a baby," Connie said to Dan now. "I was just a kid; I still had living to do, a lot of living. I wanted to travel to Europe the way Meredith had done; I wanted to be the maid of honor in Meredith's wedding and look hot in my dress. I wanted to discover myself, live up to my potential. I had a degree from Villanova in sociology, and I wanted to prove the people wrong who said such a degree couldn't be put to use. Whatever, I didn't want a baby."

"And your husband?"

"My boyfriend?" Connie said. "Yes, he decided he wanted a baby."

Wolf had been as adamant about having the baby as Connie was adamant about not having the baby. He had been raised Protestant, but the first thing he did was to appeal to Connie's Catholic faith. Hadn't she been taught to believe in the sanctity of life? Yes, of course. But everyone made mistakes, and Connie had reconciled herself to the fact that this abortion was going to be her one grave mistake. She had her own accounting system as far as God was concerned, a system of checks and balances. She had lived cleanly up until that point — premarital sex aside — and she figured that even if she did commit this one mortal sin, she could dedicate the rest of her life to good works and still come out okay.

She would get her MSW and become a social worker on the terrifying streets of North Philadelphia. She could fight homelessness and teen pregnancy.

Wolf said, "I'm not okay with you killing a living thing that God created."

Connie couldn't believe he was taking this kind of hard-line moral position.

"It's an embryo," she said.

"It will turn into a person," Wolf said. "A boy or a girl. A man or a woman. Our child. Our first child, the next generation of my family…The future of the Flutes is *right here*." He rested his hands on her abdomen.

She got it then. Wolf was under the intoxicating influence of the family weekend. He felt the pressure of his parents and his grandparents; he wanted to do his part in sustaining the dynasty, continuing the family line. Connie shook her head, looked away.

They didn't do anything for a week, then another week. Connie returned to Villanova, to her job waiting tables at Aronimink, a job made harder by her condition. The smell of eggs—unavoidable at brunch—made her hurl, and she could no longer join the rest of the staff for late-night benders at the bar. Well, she *could,* she reasoned, since she wasn't keeping the baby. But she didn't.

She and Wolf talked every night on the phone. He said he loved her. He said he wanted to marry her.

"I knew if I had an abortion, I would lose Wolf," Connie said. "And I didn't want to lose Wolf. I was madly in love with him. I wanted to marry him. But I wanted to marry him properly, in good time, and I wanted to be married to him for a while before we had children. I made this argument, but the man would not be moved. He wanted the baby. He was so sure about it that I finally felt secure enough to agree. He promised me everything would be okay. He promised me everything would be better than okay."

Connie and Wolf got married at Christmas in a small ceremony in Villanova. Meredith wore a red velvet cocktail dress and served as maid of honor. Freddy couldn't attend because of a work thing. Toby showed up with a nineteen-year-old girl who had crewed on one of his boats, but there had been one song when Toby had danced with Meredith, and the girl—Connie had forgotten her name—had thrown herself at Wolf's brother, Jake. Overall, however, the wedding was lovely. Connie wore a demure shade of ivory—according to Veronica, anything lighter would have been in poor taste—but what Connie remembered was looking longingly at the flutes of champagne, and longingly at Meredith's twenty-four-inch waist, and wishing that she wasn't pregnant.

Connie and Dan were sitting on the bottom step of the stairs of the public landing. They were still holding hands, and although Connie knew that it must be long past eight, Dan seemed in no hurry to get anywhere. This seemed like true luxury: being with someone who was content to listen. Connie suddenly believed that rehashing the past like this was going to lead her somewhere. But even if it didn't lead her anywhere, it felt good.

"When the baby came, there were complications," Connie said. "Ashlyn rotated during labor, her leg got stuck, I was howling in pain—though just like they all promise, I can only remember the howling, not the pain. At some point during this, my uterus ruptured, and I was rushed into surgery. When this kind of thing happened in the Middle Ages, the baby died and the mother died. But I was at Washington Hospital Center. They were good; they did a Cesarean, pulled Ashlyn out and stopped me from bleeding internally."

"Jesus, Connie," Dan said. He squeezed her hand, and Connie felt a rush of pure ecstasy, then chastised herself for using her most grisly story to get sympathetic attention. But it was true. It had happened; she had survived.

"I was convinced that the complication with the pregnancy was my punishment."

"Punishment for what?" Dan said. "You didn't terminate the pregnancy."

"Punishment, I don't know…for being me, maybe, for all of my transgressions. For *wanting* to terminate the pregnancy."

"Oh, come on, you don't believe that," Dan said.

"I believed it at the time. Ashlyn and I have had a difficult relationship from the get-go. Since her birth. Since conception."

Dan laughed. "You're as insane as I am."

"I know," Connie said. But even when Connie and Ashlyn were getting along, Connie was always holding her breath, waiting for the other shoe to drop. And it always did: Ashlyn said something cutting, cruel, dismissive. If Ashlyn was unhappy, Connie was blamed, and Connie accepted the blame. She would always feel guilty about not wanting to have Ashlyn in the first place.

"Wolf adored Ashlyn," Connie said. "She was his pride and joy. And, in her eyes, he could do no wrong."

Dan said, "Sounds familiar, in a way. Our kids bonded more closely with our spouses than they did with us. But that doesn't mean we failed, Connie."

But Connie *had* failed. She had always given a hundred percent, but there were times when she had resented it. Ashlyn was an amazing, brilliant child, but emotionally, she was made of granite. She was still, today.

Connie decided she would stop there; she didn't want to say anything more. But Dan was curious. "So why the rift?" he said. "What happened?"

"Mmm," Connie said.

She didn't want to tell him what happened.

But this was her chance to speak. Connie started by telling Dan the easy things: high school, college, medical school. Ashlyn excelled on all fronts. They were a happy family. Even when Wolf was diagnosed with prostate cancer, they were united. But then came Ashlyn's trip home with Bridget. The discovery of Ashlyn's sexual orientation converged with the discovery of Wolf's brain tumors. Wolf refused treatment because of his commissions; Ashlyn thought it was a rejection of her. She should have been angry at

Wolf, but she'd directed her fury at Connie, of course, because Connie was the one who remained.

"And then at the funeral..." Connie said. She closed her eyes. Was she going to tell Dan what happened at the funeral? She took a breath of soupy, marshy air. "I was as supportive as I could be about Ashlyn's relationship with Bridget. I mean, I wasn't exactly *happy* about it, but I was happy that Ashlyn was happy. I was happy that Ashlyn had someone, that she wasn't alone."

Still, Connie thought, she should have done a better job acting happy about it. Ashlyn and Bridget had sat together in the front pew of Saint Barnabas Episcopal Church, holding hands. And this had *bothered* Connie. Wolf was dead, Connie was in the worst emotional shape of her life, she had a church filled with everyone she had ever known, as well as many, many people she didn't know, and her daughter was holding hands with another woman in the front pew. Connie had glowered at Ashlyn the same way that her own father had glowered at her when she walked through the King of Prussia Mall with her hand in the back pocket of Drew Van Dyke's Levi's. Connie had wanted to lean over and whisper: *Cool it with the PDA. Reverend Joel is watching. Your great-aunt Bette is watching.* But unlike her own father, who might have made a scene, Connie held her tongue. She was, at that point, proud of herself.

During the reception at Jake and Iris's house in Silver Spring, Ashlyn and Bridget slipped away. Connie noticed them leave the room, still ostentatiously holding hands, but Connie was tied up with a bridge partner of Iris's who had just lost *her* husband to emphysema. Connie discovered Ashlyn and Bridget later, on her way to the bathroom. Connie had headed upstairs in an attempt to escape awkward conversation with the mourners who were standing in line for the first-floor powder room. She found Ashlyn and Bridget standing in the doorway of one of the guest rooms. Bridget had her hands on either side of Ashlyn's face, and they were kissing.

Connie had relived this moment many times in her imagination, wanting the outcome to be different from what it had been. She had seen Ashlyn and Bridget kissing—lips, tongues, hands, shifting bodies—and she had cried out, "Jesus Christ, Ashlyn! Stop it! Stop it right now!"

Ashlyn had turned to her mother, her expression one of humiliation and anger and defiance, and she had raced down the stairs and out of the house. And Bridget had followed her.

Later, Connie tried to apologize. She had called Ashlyn's apartment but got voice mail. She considered contacting Ashlyn at the hospital, but it took her several days to build up the courage to do this. She told herself that the more time she put between her outburst and her inevitable conversation with Ashlyn about it, the better. However, when Connie finally made it to the hospital, she was informed that Dr. Flute had tendered her resignation.

It was only at the lawyer's office when they settled the particulars of Wolf's will that Connie learned that Bridget had been offered a prestigious fellowship at a large university hospital, and that Ashlyn was going with her. Ashlyn refused to say where the hospital was. Ashlyn didn't speak directly to Connie at all, except to laugh spitefully when Connie offered her apology.

"I didn't mean anything by it," Connie said. She had convinced herself that her reaction was no more or less severe than Bill O'Brien's would have been had he found Connie and a boyfriend kissing at the top of the stairs during a funeral reception. (What would he have said? She tried to channel him, channel any parent. *What are you doing up here? This is neither the time nor the place!*) But the slippery, stinky truth of the matter was that the time and the place had little to do with what made Connie react as she did. It had discomfited her to witness her daughter kissing another woman. It had made her...squeamish. Did that make Connie a bad person? Wasn't it, on some level, understandable?

"You two took me by surprise," Connie said. "I didn't expect to find you there. And I was very emotional that day. Ashlyn, I'm sorry."

234   ˢ   *Elin Hilderbrand*

Ashlyn had treated Connie to derisive laughter, and then once in the Aston Martin, a car Wolf had adored, Ashlyn drove away.

"And that's the last I heard from her," Connie told Dan. "I found out that she's practicing medicine in Tallahassee. She's working at some community health clinic, I guess. Her career is secondary to Bridget's. So maybe that's why she won't talk to me, maybe she's ashamed of what she's settled for. Of course, she was angry before the funeral. She holds me responsible for Wolf's death."

Dan put his arm around Connie and squeezed her, but the predictable tears didn't come. It was just like Dan had said: In talking about it, finally, with someone who was essentially a complete stranger to the situation, she was able to gain some distance. She was able to look at herself as someone who had lived through that story. Had it sounded awful to Dan? *Jesus Christ, Ashlyn!* It was nothing Connie hadn't said to her daughter a dozen times over the years in extreme anger or frustration—in response to nail polish spilled on the Persian rug, or a badly broken curfew, or the atrocious state of her bedroom. Had it sounded like the rejection of Ashlyn's sexuality? Had it sounded like a shout-out against tolerance? Did Dan think she was a bigot? Connie had never quite known how to grapple with her outburst—because there had been something in her tone of voice, some emotion that she couldn't name. Anger? Embarrassment? Disgust? Certainly not. But maybe, yes, just a little bit. And now Connie was being punished. She was being punished for not celebrating the fact that her daughter was in love with another woman.

She had learned her lesson. Connie would give anything—her house, her money, her right arm—*just to hear Ashlyn's voice.*

Dan cleared his throat. "That's difficult stuff," he said.

"It's the most difficult stuff I've got," Connie said. She laughed a little. "Remember, you asked for it."

"I'm not sure I know what to say, except I know how you feel. Sort of. I have an inkling."

They sat in silence a few seconds. Connie's mind was racing, she could feel this time coming to an end. She wasn't sure she could just get in her car and drive away after having given this man her most intimate confidence. The sun was high, it was hot, Connie needed water, shade, a swim. But she would sit here and freckle and burn as long as she could be beside Dan.

"You're missing work," she said.

"That I am," Dan said happily. He pulled her up by the hand. "Come on, I'm taking you to lunch."

It was only nine thirty, a little early for lunch they both agreed, though Connie had been up since five, so to her it felt like midday. She left her car in the parking lot there in Monomoy and climbed into Dan's Jeep. She was trembling, either from heat stroke or relief. She had told him the worst of it, and he still wanted to be with her.

"I'd better get these groceries home," he said. "We'll swing by my house, if that's okay with you?"

"Okay with me," Connie said.

They drove back to Milestone Road and Dan turned on to Sheep Commons Lane. He pulled into a circular driveway. The house had gray shingles and white trim, just like Connie's house, and a crisp brick chimney and a front porch with a nice-looking swing, and a ten-speed bike leaning against the railing. Connie gazed into a lush, landscaped side yard with a stone bench among the hostas.

"I'm just going to run in," Dan said, hoisting groceries out of the back.

"Yes," Connie said. In her head, she was singing, *He wants to be with me!* If only she'd known earlier this morning how her trip to the store would pan out, she wouldn't have panicked. If only she'd known the past weeks, when she was moping around the house. Connie couldn't wait to tell Meredith! Then she realized that Meredith had been in the house alone for hours, and that she had no idea where Connie was. Should Connie call? She rummaged through her bag. She didn't have her cell phone; it was in the kitchen, charging.

Meredith would be fine, Connie decided. Meredith wasn't a child.

Dan reappeared. He said, "Good thing you didn't come in. My son Donovan was sitting on the sofa in his underwear eating cereal and watching *Pimp My Ride.* It wasn't something I would have wanted you to see."

Dan drove out the Polpis Road to Sconset, taking meandering detours to travel across the acres of land that belonged to his family. They owned large plots in Squam and Quidnet; there were fourteen homes in the family trust, and Dan was in charge of the rentals and the upkeep. Dan told Connie about the Wampanoag Indian tribes who had populated Nantucket long before the Coffins and Starbucks came aground in the seventeenth century.

"And the Flynns," Connie said.

"In eighteen oh five," Dan said. "We were latecomers."

They ended up at the Summer House for lunch a little before noon. Dan had carte blanche at the restaurant by the pool because he did their power washing every spring. He and Connie sat in chaises in the sun and a waiter came to take their drink order. Dan ordered a beer, leaving Connie open to order wine, which she most definitely wanted, but no, she thought, she wouldn't. She didn't have to. She ordered an iced tea.

Dan delivered Connie back to her house at two thirty. He had blown off his morning appointments, but at three o'clock he had duties that couldn't be ignored. Connie was dizzy with happiness. They had laughed by the pool at the Summer House; they had talked until they both felt drowsy and napped. Dan had, unceremoniously, thrown Connie into the pool—cotton sundress and all—and Connie had found this funny and charming, which meant she must really be crazy about the man, because what fifty-year-old woman enjoyed being thrown into a pool with her clothes on? (And the careful job she did with her hair was ruined.) As they dried off, they ordered soft-shell crab sandwiches and a side of French fries, and they split a crème brûlée for dessert, and Connie thought about how nice it was to be out in the world, among other people. And then she thought about Meredith and felt guilty, and so when Dan said he had to take her home, she was eager.

"But if you're free, I'd like to take you to dinner tonight," he said. "And afterward, I'd like you to spend the night."

Connie nodded. "Yes," she whispered. It was an indication of how mature they were—or did she mean old?—that Dan had made his intentions clear. It eliminated posturing and guesswork. They had both been married before; Connie was going to assume that Dan had had lovers since Nicole's death. He knew what to do and she was grateful.

He dropped her at the front door and she stood on the porch waving until he drove away.

She hadn't had a single drink, but she felt drunk.

She found Meredith lying on the sofa, reading Jane Austen. She was wearing her bathing suit and her cover-up. Her sunglasses were perched on top of her head while she wore her regular glasses, but Connie knew that Meredith hadn't spent one second outside. She was braver now than she'd been that first week, but she wouldn't have ventured outside when she was alone at the house.

"Hey!" Connie said.

Meredith didn't look up. Connie got a sour feeling in her stomach.

"Meredith?"

She didn't move. She didn't tilt her head or twitch her leg. Connie waited. Meredith turned the page. She was near the end of her book. Maybe she was engrossed. Meredith could be such a nerd when it came to books. Then Connie remembered that Meredith had left thirty dollars and the titles of two novels written on a piece of paper on the kitchen counter, and Connie had promised that she would run to Bookworks today to pick them up. Meredith was too afraid to go along, but she really wanted the books; they were important to her. So was that why Meredith was mad, because Connie had forgotten to get the books? Okay, fine, Connie would go right now. She stepped into the kitchen—the money and the list were still there and Connie snapped them up—then she realized that she'd left her car in Monomoy. Shit. Well, she and Dan could remedy that tonight. She could pick up her car after dinner and drive it to Dan's house. Perfect.

Connie said, "Meredith, is everything okay?"

Meredith's head popped up. "You left here at six o'clock this morning saying you were going to the grocery store."

"I know," Connie said. "I'm sorry."

"I was worried, then panicked, then pissed off, because I realized around lunchtime that you must have had other plans and lied to me about them. Am I right?"

"I didn't have other plans," Connie said. "I went to the grocery store." She was speaking very slowly, scrambling in her mind for the right words. She had known Meredith wouldn't take this news well; she had been left in the house alone for almost nine hours. "I bumped into Dan. At the store."

Meredith turned her face toward Connie at the mention of Dan's name, although it was impossible to tell what she was thinking. At this moment, Connie remembered why they hadn't spoken for three years. Meredith was formidable when she was at odds with you. Connie thought back on their fight over the phone. Oh, boy—had they been at odds.

"It was a fluke," Connie said. She sounded like she was insisting. "We talked for a while, and then we went for a walk on the beach, and then we went to lunch at the Summer House, and then he brought me home."

Meredith sniffed, but she wasn't crying. Meredith didn't cry.

"Meredith? Say something."

"It sounds like you had a lovely day."

Connie sat down on the coffee table. She decided she wasn't going to lie to the woman to make her feel better. "It *was* a lovely day. We talked about Ashlyn, and about Dan's son Joe. We went for a drive around the island and ended up at the Summer House. You can have lunch by the pool there and the *Rosa rugosa* are in bloom and you can see the ocean. We had soft-shell crab sandwiches and these French fries that were to die for. Dan threw me in the pool."

"How much wine did you have?" Meredith asked.

Connie paused. It was an unkind question. But Connie wouldn't take the bait. She had learned a thing or two from her other fight with Meredith. Meredith was feeling bad, and she wanted Connie to feel bad, too.

"Are you mad at me?" Connie asked. "Are you mad that I went out with Dan?"

Meredith didn't answer.

"Do you have feelings for Dan, Meredith?" Connie asked. This hadn't crossed Connie's mind before; she had only been worried that Dan had feelings for Meredith.

"No," Meredith said. "I do not have feelings for Dan. Other than thinking he is a very nice guy. And much to my surprise, I've had fun when the three of us were together. The fact that the two of you went out and had fun together without me stings a little, yes. Especially since I didn't know where you were. Now, I get it. You're an adult; this is your house. I'm living here only because you have an open mind and a kind, merciful heart. You can come and go as you please and see who you want, obviously. And I can sit here alone and feel scared shitless and sorry for myself."

"Oh, Meredith," Connie said. Life was, as she continued to believe, high school over and over again. Connie could have gotten snippy and defensive—this *was* Connie's house, she did have every right to act spontaneously without calling home to check in with Meredith; Meredith was living there in the first place because of Connie's good graces—but looking at Meredith now, she got it. "I hate to tell you this, but I'm going out with Dan tonight. For dinner."

"By yourself?" Meredith asked.

Connie nodded.

"Where?"

"The Ships Inn," Connie said. "And Meredith?"

"What?"

"I'm spending the night at Dan's house. He asked me, and I said yes."

Meredith turned back to her book. That was preferable, Connie understood, to Meredith acting shocked and calling her a slut. Connie stood up. She thought, *I'll bike out to Monomoy, get my car, drive to Bookworks and get Meredith those books. She'll have them for tonight.* She thought, *And I'll get the groceries! I'll make something delicious for Meredith's dinner.*

She looked at Meredith, who now had the book tented over her face—though she wasn't crying, never crying—and thought, *How do I fix this?*

MEREDITH

It wasn't until nine o'clock or so that Meredith realized that Connie hadn't gone to the grocery store, or had gone not only to the grocery store. At first, Meredith assumed Connie had tacked on other errands: She went into town to shop at the farm stand or she went to the liquor store. Or she had revisited Vanessa Noel for shoes, or Erica Wilson or David Chase for a new dress or new white jeans or a new pretty top. It made sense that Connie would prefer to go shopping without Meredith. Meredith couldn't afford anything—and she wouldn't leave the house, anyway.

When, at noon, Connie still hadn't returned, Meredith thought, Okay, maybe she went out and did all those other things and then went to Mass (unlikely) or to the Whaling Museum (on such a fine day?). Meredith called Connie's cell phone from the house and another phone rang simultaneously, and Meredith was confused until she realized that Connie's cell phone was right there in the kitchen. Which explained why Connie hadn't called, but this didn't make Meredith feel any better.

At one thirty, Meredith gave in to suspicion first, then fear. Her suspicion was that Connie had another friend or group of friends that she was secretly meeting. The mere idea of this hurt Meredith, but after a few minutes, Meredith rejected this theory. Connie had never mentioned other friends on Nantucket, and if she had had other friends, she would have called on them before now. This left Meredith with only fear, and her fear was that Connie's long absence meant she had met with foul play which had been intended for Meredith. Amy Rivers had run her car off the road, or someone had accosted her in the parking lot of Stop & Shop and hurt her somehow. She was in the hospital, or someone had kidnapped her and she was, at this very second, sitting in someone's kitchen bound by ropes to a Stephen Swift stool.

As soon as the Stephen Swift stool appeared in her field of vision, Meredith knew she was being ridiculous. Connie hadn't met with foul play. So where was she?

When Connie did eventually arrive home at two thirty and told Meredith that she had bumped into Dan at the grocery store and they had spent the day together, Meredith was furious. Here, Meredith had spent eight hours worrying while Connie was getting her heart's desire. Connie had been the one to drag Meredith along on both of her dates with Dan—one of them quite long— and not only had Meredith enjoyed herself but she had gotten used to the idea of the three of them being together. So to have them suddenly assert their couplehood was a shock.

Now, Connie had left for her date, dressed in a stunning pink and orange Herve Leger bandage dress that very few women even twenty years younger could pull off, and her new Vanessa Noel heels. She gave Meredith the novels that Meredith had requested from Bookworks—Connie had ridden her bike to Monomoy to get her car to go to the bookstore. She had made this effort because she felt guilty. Connie had also made Meredith supper: a chopped salad with hard-boiled eggs, bacon, blue cheese, avocado, and grilled shrimp. Before she left, Connie locked all the doors and set the alarm. Then she hugged and kissed Meredith good-bye, and when Dan's Jeep pulled up, she disappeared out the front door.

Meredith felt resentful, mostly because Connie had left her nothing to complain about.

Alone, Meredith thought. *Alone, alone.*

The phone in the house rang, and Meredith gasped. She and Connie had watched too many scary movies as teenagers; all she could think was that someone out there knew she was alone. She forced herself to check the caller ID—because what if it was Connie or one of the boys?—and Meredith saw that it was the law firm.

She picked up the phone.

"Meredith, thank God."

"Hi, Dev," she said.

"I just called your cell phone three times, and I sent you a text. Did you get it?"

"No," Meredith said. "I—"

"You need to keep your phone *on,* Meredith," Dev said. "What's the point in having it otherwise?"

Should she try to explain to him that by turning it off, she saved herself twenty-three and a half hours of worry about who was or was not calling her?

"Thank God you gave me the landline," Dev said. "Because things are starting to happen."

"Like what?" Meredith said. She sat on the very edge of the sofa. She couldn't let herself get too comfortable.

"Well, I have good news and I have bad news."

Meredith clenched her fists. "What?"

"The good news is from Julie Schwarz. The Feds have determined that this guy Deacon Rapp, the so-called legitimate trader who was fingering Leo, was, in fact, in on the Ponzi scheme himself."

"You're kidding!" Meredith said.

"He was trying to feed Leo up to the Feds in his place, which was a logical move since Leo is Freddy's flesh and blood. But after examining the so-called hundred pieces of evidence, the Feds caught on to this guy. They have a paper trail on him now that's miles long, and without his deposition, there's nothing implicating Leo. Leo's computer was clean, and they found no communication between Leo's office and the fiends on the seventeenth floor."

"Thank God," Meredith said.

"Even better, they found this woman, Freddy's supposed secretary on the seventeenth, Mrs. Edith Misurelli. They got her arriving at JFK from Rome and took her in directly for questioning. She said straight out that Leo Delinn had been denied access to the seventeenth floor, by...guess who?"

Meredith was shaking. "Who?"

"Your husband. Freddy forbade Leo from ever entering the offices where the dirty deeds were done. According to Mrs. Misurelli, Leo never once set foot on that floor."

"Oh, my God," Meredith said. She felt a wash of relief, like cool water over her burning concern. "So Leo is off the hook?"

"Unless something unforeseen comes out, yes. The Feds are finished looking at Leo. They're looking at this Deacon Rapp kid who had *thirty-one million bucks* squirreled away. He was in cahoots with his uncle, who deposited the money in four banks in Queens."

"So I can talk to Leo?" Meredith said. "I can call him?"

"Now for the bad news," Dev said. "Leo has been cleared. And this pisses off the investors and their lawyers, why? Because they want to hold another Delinn accountable. So who are they going to focus on now?"

"Me," Meredith said.

"You."

She stood up. *The other investors are clamoring for your head.* She walked over to the bookshelves and stared at Wolf Flute's collection of barometers. Oh, the hours Meredith had spent acquiring and collecting things, instead of worrying about her own freedom.

But Leo is free, she thought. *Leo is free!* She allowed the massive weight of those worries to slide off her shoulders, which felt amazing, but nothing felt as good as dropping the insidious nugget of doubt that Meredith herself had felt about Leo. She had never believed that he'd been involved in the Ponzi scheme, but she'd feared, deep down, that he might have known about it and been too loyal to his father to turn him in.

This mysterious woman, a secretary of Freddy's that Meredith hadn't even known existed, had provided the only palatable answer: Freddy had forbidden Leo from visiting the seventeenth floor.

In light of this new information, did Meredith care about her own fate? Hadn't she said she would sacrifice herself if Leo was set free?

"That brings us to the sticking point," Dev said.

"The fifteen million," Meredith said. Her voice sagged. Hadn't they gone over this? "Are you going to ask me about the fifteen million?"

"Do you have anything else to say about it?" Dev asked. "Anything?"

"No," Meredith said.

"Are you sure?"

"I told them already," Meredith said.

"Okay," Dev said. "Then all you can do is to keep thinking of places where that money might be, where the Feds might look. But you shouldn't contact Leo or Carver until you're cleared. It's more imperative now than ever, okay?" He paused. "Hey, but the good news is that Leo is free."

Meredith closed her eyes. She had refused to say the words before, but she would say them now. "Yes," she said. "That is good news."

Meredith set down the phone. Leo was free. There would be a quiet celebration at Carver's house tonight, possibly just Carver and Leo and Anais sharing a meal, listening to music, and laughing for the first time in months.

Meredith poured herself a glass of wine. She yearned to step out onto the deck, but she couldn't risk the exposure. Leo was free, but she was still in peril, possibly more so than before. Meredith wished Connie were here. Meredith looked obliquely out the glass doors. She saw Harold's dark head emerge in the smooth green glass of a cresting wave, then disappear. Only one seal.

Meredith's new novels were lying on the table. She could allow herself the pleasure of cracking one open, but the experience would be wasted on her. There was too much to think about.

The Feds thought they knew her, the investors thought they knew her, the American media thought they knew her: Meredith Delinn, wife of financial giant Frederick Xavier Delinn, mother of two privileged sons, socialite. They thought she sat on boards, they thought she organized charity galas, they thought she shopped. And whereas she had indeed done those things, there had been other things as well. Worthy things.

Meredith had taught English at Samuel Gompers High School in the Bronx for five years. It had been hard work, frightening work, frustrating work—Meredith challenged any federal agent or any soft-handed cubicle-sitter at the SEC to give it a try. She had forced tenth graders to read; some of them she had *taught* to read. She had thrown Carson McCullers's novel *The Member of the Wedding* at them. For some kids, the book was like a blanket over their heads—they couldn't see a thing. But for some kids, that book was a bright portal that led them to other books. Meredith read a poem to her classes every day, and some days no one was listening—they were too busy talking about the Knicks or Hector Alvarez's new Corvette or doing smack. And some days they said, *We don't give a shit about no red wheelbarrow or no white fucking chickens.* But some days, Meredith read Gwendolyn Brooks or Nikki Giovanni, and more than half the class looked mildly engaged. "A Boy Died in My Alley" got a response of *Hey, man, that's like Lippy Magee getting knifed behind the free clinic.* And Meredith said, "Okay, everybody take out a pencil."

She made a pittance, she took the subway, she was exhausted when she got home to the apartment—and sometimes Freddy was still at work. When Meredith got pregnant, she worried as she rode the 6 train uptown, and she was more exhausted when she climbed the four flights of stairs with bags from D'Agostino's. She thought about quitting, but then Freddy announced that he was leaving Prudential and starting his own hedge fund. Why should he be working so hard to make money for a huge corporation when he could be making money for himself?

Meredith stayed at Gompers another year, then another year after that. They needed the health insurance. Freddy was having a hard time making the new business fly. Meredith got pregnant again. They didn't have space for another child, and they couldn't afford to move.

One night, with her belly hugely swollen, and Leo, at eighteen months, wailing in his crib, and Freddy out with some potential investors, who in the end never seemed to want to invest, Meredith lay in the bathtub and cried. She thought of her father saying, *Brilliant and talented, that girl can do no wrong.* Had he been lying? And if he was telling the truth, then what on earth was she doing here?

Meredith drained her glass of wine and stared at her beautiful salad. Could she bring herself to eat anything?

It was getting dark, and Meredith knew she should turn on some lights, but she had the dreadful feeling that if she turned on the lights, the person who was watching her would see her in the illuminated room eating alone. She picked at the salad in the gathering dark—not because she was hungry, but because Connie had made it for her. Connie was such a good cook, a good friend, a good person. Meredith had said all those beastly things to her years ago, but Connie hadn't mentioned it once. Meredith hoped Connie was having fun tonight; she and Dan would still be at dinner. If Meredith had a legitimate scare, she could still call Connie's cell phone. She could call now, but not later.

In those years, Leo and Carver went to day care, which bothered Freddy, but there was no money for a nanny. They moved to a two-bedroom apartment on East 82nd Street, but it was still a walk-up. Freddy used to leave the apartment before the boys were awake and get home after they were asleep. He lost weight. Meredith begged him to have a milkshake with his lunch, she begged him to see a doctor, but for Freddy there was only work and more work. Getting the company up and running. Attracting clients. How would he attract clients? He worked on the weekends. Meredith was left to handle everything at home. She couldn't do it. She couldn't have two little kids and run a household and grade thirty essays and do lesson plans. Carver was already showing signs of anxiety disorder; he screamed and cried when Meredith dropped him off at day care, and he screamed and cried when she picked him up.

And then Meredith got pregnant again.

She was waiting for Freddy in the apartment when he got home from work, waving the pregnancy test in her hand like a wand: a wand that was going to reveal everything that was wrong with their life. She wanted things to be easier; she wanted things to be different. Her job was hard. That very day Meredith had come across two girls fighting in the bathroom, and one of the girls had a razor blade concealed inside her lower lip. The most disturbing thing was that Meredith had known how to restrain the girl and where to look for the blade. Why should she know such things?

She wanted to leave Gompers at the end of the year. She hated the commute on the subway. She hated dropping the boys off at the dreaded day care. Carver clung to the front of Meredith's shirt; he clawed for her glasses. The workers had to peel him off her. And now she was having a baby.

She stared Freddy down. She loved him, but this was not the life she'd expected.

"I'm taking the children," she said. "And I'm going to my mother's." She was disappointed at how cliché this sounded, but what was *not* cliché was the thought of sleeping in her childhood home, the big white Colonial in Villanova with the expansive back yard where the boys could run through the sprinkler and play on the swings. Meredith would have an extra set of hands. She would enroll the boys at Tarleton.

Freddy, Meredith remembered, had seemed to shrink. Then, he smiled. "Another baby?" he said.

"Another baby," Meredith said, and she smiled, too, in spite of herself. But then she hardened. "I mean it, Fred. I'm leaving. Until things change, I'm going home."

"You're not going anywhere," Fred said. "You're going to stay right here, and I'll make things better. I will take care of everything."

The SEC and the Feds postulated that Freddy had been operating his Ponzi scheme for at least a decade, but when Meredith looked back, she knew with gut-rotting certainty that it had started the year after Meredith threatened to leave. Because Freddy was good to his word: everything got better. Instead of schlepping all the way to the Bronx every morning, Meredith stayed home with the boys. She delivered Leo to a summer preschool program at the Catholic church, she took Carver for a chocolate milk at E.A.T. Café, then home to play blocks, watch *Sesame Street*, take a nap. One sweltering day in the middle of the summer, Meredith was headed down the building's stairs in her flip-flops, and she missed a step. She fell all the way to the landing. She was hurt, but not *hurt* hurt; however, she decided to call off their outing to the deliciously cool, air-conditioned halls of the Museum of Natural History. By the time she got upstairs to the apartment, she was bleeding.

She was only twelve weeks along, and she'd barely told anyone about the pregnancy (her mother, Connie, the principal at Gompers, who asked why she wasn't coming back), but still, the miscarriage struck Meredith as a tremendous loss. She was positive the baby would have been a girl, whom she would have named Annabeth Carson after her grandmother and Ms. McCullers.

Freddy had taken the miscarriage in stride, and when Meredith accused him of being unfeeling, he said, "We can't both be basket cases. We have the boys to think about. And we'll get pregnant again, sweetheart. Don't worry. We'll have our little girl." He held Meredith, and he said these encouraging things, but when his cell phone rang, he switched right into work mode.

It was that autumn, Meredith remembered, that the money started rolling in. They got full coverage with Blue Cross and Blue Shield. They pulled Leo out of the Catholic preschool and sent him to Saint Bernard's. Freddy wasn't home any more often, but when he was home, he was happier. He had solved the problem of attracting clients. It seemed the way to attract clients was to tell them they *couldn't* invest in Delinn Enterprises. Delinn Enterprises was only looking for certain kinds of investors; many people got turned away. Freddy had investors banging down the door. He put back on the weight he'd lost, and twenty pounds besides. He ordered lunch in every day: reuben sandwiches, lobster bisque, omelets with goat cheese and smoked salmon. He had business dinners at Gallagher's and Smith & Wollensky. He had no time for exercise. He got his first gray hair at age twenty-nine. Meredith had wanted to pluck it, but he wouldn't let her. He wanted to look older, he said. He needed gravitas, he said.

After the New Year, they moved to a three-bedroom apartment

with an eat-in kitchen in the East Sixties. It was a doorman building. They bought a car and kept it in the garage. They began renting a house in Southampton for two weeks a summer.

In September, Carver joined Leo at Saint Bernard's. Meredith
tried to get pregnant again but didn't have any luck. She suspected
that Freddy's sperm were too stressed to swim. Freddy gave Meredith carte blanche to hire a nanny and a cook, even though they
ate out almost every night. With both kids in school and a Filipino
nanny, Meredith was free to go back to work. Gompers, or any
other public school suddenly seemed out of the question, and
before she knew it, working at all seemed out of the question.
Freddy declared that business was gangbusters, and he whisked
Meredith down to Palm Beach for the weekend, leaving the kids
with Cecelia, and they loved Palm Beach so much that Freddy
wanted to look at property. *To buy.*

Meredith's life became consumed with managing all that she
suddenly had: The boys, their needs, their sports, their school func-
tions. There was yet another new apartment—the penthouse at
824 Park Avenue—that they had bought, as well as a house in
Palm Beach, the Pulitzers' former house. Freddy had snapped this
up at auction "for a steal," he said. (As a testament to her remove
from Freddy's financial dealings, Meredith never learned how
much the Pulitzer house had cost them.) The Frick Collection
asked Meredith to serve on its board of directors, and she was on
the Parent Action Committee at the boys' school, which allowed
Meredith to meet other busy, important people who each seemed
to want to get her involved in something else. She and Freddy had
things to attend—events, benefits, dinner parties, nights at the
symphony and the Metropolitan Opera. There wasn't time for
Meredith to work. She was too busy being Mrs. Freddy Delinn.

Meredith washed her dinner dishes. The house was dark now; she
had to use the light over the sink or risk breaking a glass.

She saw that there was a single cupcake under plastic wrap resting on a saucer. It looked suspiciously like a vanilla-bean cupcake with strawberry icing from the bakery at the Sconset Market. *Connie is an angel,* Meredith thought. Or Connie felt worse about leaving Meredith alone than Meredith realized.

Meredith ate the cupcake standing up at the counter, wondering about the moment when she'd realized they were really... rich. It was probably a quiet moment—a nondescript afternoon walking home from lunch at Le Cirque with the likes of Astrid Cassel or Mary Rose Garth, when Meredith stopped in to Bergdorf's and bought—who knows?—a $2,000 powder-pink Chanel cardigan and didn't keep the receipt. Or it was something more momentous, such as her first trip to Paris with Freddy since their backpacking adventure. He had booked a suite at the Hôtel de Crillon. They had eaten at Taillevent, and in the Jules Verne restaurant at the top of the Eiffel Tower (Meredith could have skipped the Eiffel Tower, but not Freddy). The highlight of that trip wasn't the hotel (though they laughed, remembering the hostel they had stayed at in the sleazy eighteenth *arrondissement* their first time through) or the dining (they remembered how they ate a baguette and Camembert while sitting on the floor of their room in said hostel), but a private tour that Freddy had arranged at the Musée d'Orsay. When he told Meredith they were going on a private tour, she thought that meant they would have their very own English-speaking guide. But what it meant was that at six thirty, half an hour after the museum closed, they stepped through a discreet door and were met by the museum's curator, who was trailed by a waiter with a bottle of vintage Krug. The curator proceeded to give Meredith and Freddy a *private tour* of the museum, with special emphasis on Pissarro, who had been Meredith's favorite painter ever since she attended a Pissarro exhibit with her father at the Philadelphia Museum of Art when she was fifteen years old.

Champagne, the whole museum hushed and waiting for them, the erudite curator with his elegantly accented English. Yes, on that day, Meredith understood that they had become rich.

*   *   *

Meredith checked the back door: locked. She checked the front door: locked. She checked the alarm: activated. The windows were shut and locked; the air-conditioning was on. Meredith toyed with the idea of turning on the TV. Other voices in the room might ease her anxiety. But Connie never turned on the TV and Meredith wouldn't, either. She might inadvertently come across something in the news she didn't want to see, or "Frederick Xavier Delinn: The Real Story" on E!

She went upstairs.

She couldn't help feeling like a woman in a horror film, one who met her unsuspecting end in the doorway of a dark room. She wasn't sure how to shed this feeling and relax. She was safe. Nothing had happened to the house or the car in weeks. It was now August; for all Meredith knew, Amy Rivers was gone. She, Meredith, was safe. The doors were locked, the alarm set.

She needed to sleep. And what that really meant was that she needed a sleeping pill. She knew Connie had something. Meredith had seen the prescription bottles.

She felt her way into Connie's bathroom. She needed to turn on the light. But this was okay, this was Connie's light. Whoever was watching from outside would see Connie's light go on and believe that Connie was home. Meredith switched on the light. The prescription bottles were right there where Meredith remembered seeing them. She checked the labels: Ambien, Lunesta, Ativan, Prozac, Seraquil, Zoloft. Connie had cornered the sleep-aid/anti-anxiety market. Meredith shook each bottle; they were all full.

Meredith debated between the Ambien and the Lunesta. She chose Ambien; she took two pills. She took two Ativan as well, for a later time when she might really need them. She took the Ambien immediately, with tap water.

This was stealing. God, how she *hated* that word. She would make this right; she would tell Connie she'd taken two Ambien and then it would be borrowing. She told herself that she would also confess to Connie about the Ativan, although she knew she wouldn't. Unless Connie counted her pills, she would never know, and plus it was only two Ativan, completely harmless.

So that was how stealing worked, right, Freddy? You "borrowed" a little something, no one would ever know; you were dealing out returns of 22, 23, 25 percent, everyone was happy. You could roll on like this indefinitely. You would be dead before anyone caught you.

Meredith acted like a thief, putting the bottles back exactly as she had found them, lifting them again to see if there was a noticeable difference in their weight.

As she tiptoed back down the hallway, she heard a *thump, thump, thump* and a squeak. She stopped in her tracks. Squeak. A prolonged squeak. A squeaky wheel.

Blood hammered in Meredith's ears. She was hot with panic and afraid she would vomit up her dinner—as well as the pills she'd just taken. She sucked in a breath. She was either imagining things, or Connie was home, or the police were wandering around, doing a check. (Had the police continued to do their surveillance? Meredith should have asked Connie to call them.)

She heard another thump, a definite thump this time, and Meredith thought, *Okay, now what do I do?* Her instinct, as when she saw Amy Rivers at the bookstore, was to freeze. She closed her eyes and remained as silent and still as an animal in the woods and hoped that the predator moved on.

Another thump, more squeaking. The noise was coming from outside. There were people outside, people at this house, way out in deserted Tom Nevers. Part of Meredith wanted to look out the window and find out what was going on. It might be the police, and if it wasn't the police, it would be something she would have to describe to the police. But Meredith was afraid of being seen.

The hallway, she decided, was safe. It had no windows, and the rug was velvety soft. Meredith laid her head down. She wanted a pillow, but she was too afraid to venture into her room or back into Connie's room to fetch one. They were coming to get her. And didn't she deserve it? Three days before Delinn Enterprises was exposed as a Ponzi scheme, Meredith had transferred $15 million from the company slush fund to her and Freddy's personal brokerage account. Meredith had made it clear in her deposition: Freddy had asked her to transfer the money, and she had transferred it. She had thought nothing of it—until that afternoon, freshly home from the bank, when she saw Freddy throwing back the 1926 Macallan. At that moment she realized the $15 million wasn't meant for a house in Aspen (Carver had been pressuring Freddy because he loved to snowboard) or for a Roy Lichtenstein (Samantha had a line on one for sale), as Meredith had believed it might be. The $15 million was a levee against the flood. But by the time Meredith realized this, the money had been moved. Meredith had done it at Freddy's behest; he had made her an unwitting conspirator. And now, investors were clamoring for her head. And now, quite possibly, she was going to prison.

But Meredith's first crime was that she had threatened to leave Freddy; she had threatened to take his children away. She had attacked his manhood; she had made it clear the life he was providing wasn't good enough. She didn't want to work; she wanted to stay home. She didn't want to drop her kids at day care; she wanted a nanny. She didn't want to ride the subway; she wanted cabs. That wasn't what she'd been saying, but that was what Freddy heard— and he set out to find a way to give those things to her.

There was another noise, louder than the others, that came from out front. A *BAM,* that was how Meredith would describe it; it sounded as though someone had dropped a large package on the front porch. But maybe that was Connie? Meredith waited. It was quiet for one minute, then two.

Meredith felt the sleeping pills sprinkle their fairy dust over her graying head. Her eyes drifted closed. The rug was velvety soft.

*   *   *

Meredith awoke to the first pink light of day. Her body ached from sleeping in a pile on the floor, but she noted the daylight with relief. She had made it to the morning.

She felt okay to move around the house. The terror of the night before had faded, although there was still some residual fear, worry, concern, anxiety, something picking at Meredith's corners. She had survived, but she wasn't safe. Something had happened in the night, she was sure of it, though it might have been her imagination. It had *not* been her imagination. But it if *were* her imagination, how grateful she would be!

She descended the stairs. At least she hadn't interrupted Connie and Dan's romantic evening.

The downstairs was clean and unchanged, the great room suffused with light. With trepidation, Meredith peered out at the back deck. It looked okay, right? But there was a trail of something dark, something Meredith didn't like the looks of. Meredith felt groggy and cottonmouthed. She needed water first, then coffee. Connie always made the coffee and, sure enough, when Meredith checked, the coffee machine was all set up and ready to go.

There was a trail of something dark on the deck. Oil, she thought. Though she knew better.

She didn't like the way she was feeling. She should call the police. And say what? That she'd heard noises? That there was a suspicious trail on the deck?

Have you looked around? the police would ask.

And Meredith would say, *No, I'm too afraid.*

She picked up her cell phone and turned it on. It chimed three times with messages. But when Meredith checked, she saw these were the messages left by Dev the previous evening. So there was nothing new. She got a glass of ice water, which she drank to the bottom. The coffee was brewing; the sunlight was filling up this room exactly the way Wolf Flute had intended.

Meredith moved toward the front door. But no, the front door was too scary. Meredith was thinking of the worst, and the worst she was thinking about was a bomb. Something had been dumped or thrown on the front porch, of that she was fairly sure. Special delivery for Meredith Delinn.

Call the police! Nantucket had little or no crime (or at least this had been the case before she arrived); the police would welcome something to do on this Thursday morning.

Have you looked around?

The front door was too scary. If she opened the front door, the bomb would detonate. There would be a fiery explosion or a lethal spray of nails or a leak of radioactive waste.

Meredith peered out the window of the sitting room, from which she could see part of the front porch obliquely. And yes, Meredith saw a spill of something dark. *Oh, God!* She was really shaking now, she was moving to the front door, she would open it just a crack, she would peek through her fingers, not enough to see, just enough to confirm her awful suspicions.

The door was triple locked, and she had to disengage the alarm before she could open it. That required the code, which was Ashlyn's birthday: 040283, a date Meredith had known for, well, nearly thirty years, but had trouble remembering in her present state. She turned the alarm off; the house was unsealed. She stood behind the door and pulled it open with a sucking sound, and she peeked—her eyes were mostly closed—but she saw what she needed to see. Flippers, whiskers, a ghastly, gaping red smile.

Harold lay on the front porch with his throat cut.

Meredith slammed the door shut and locked it. She was hyperventilating. Not a bomb, but in many ways worse. From her cell phone, she called the police and gave the address, then she said, "I have found a dead sea mammal on my front porch."

"On your front porch?" The dispatcher said.

"A seal," Meredith said.

"A dead seal?" The dispatcher said. "Really? On your porch?"

"Can you send someone, please?" Meredith said. And then she

said, "This is Meredith Delinn." She wasn't sure if the dispatcher would know her name, but of course she did, everyone in American knew her name.

The dispatcher said, "Yes, Mrs. Delinn. We'll send a car out now."

Meredith slid to the floor and understood that her mistake wasn't in threatening to leave Freddy. Her mistake was in not leaving.

PART TWO

CONNIE

Connie drove to the town pier alone, thinking that she had another fifteen minutes of peace before her summer detonated. When she'd told Dan what she'd done—or, more accurately, *not* done—he'd said, *Don't worry about it. With what we've been through, it can't be a big deal, can it?* But he might only have been saying that to make Connie feel better.

Town pier, eleven o'clock in the morning on a stunning summer day. The pier was crawling with families carrying coolers and fishing poles and clam rakes, clambering aboard motor boats to putter out to Coatue and Great Point. Connie was astonished how relaxed and happy these people seemed. Connie was sick with anxiety. Sick! She had followed her gut, and now she had to hope for the best.

Eleven o'clock, he'd said. But she didn't see him anywhere. Typical. It was Veronica's gene passed down: *Late for my own funeral.*

Connie walked the dock, checking out this boat and that boat, looking but not seeing, her heart thundering, her stomach sour like she'd eaten a dozen lemons for breakfast. Then she saw him, the square shoulders, the bowlegged lope. Unmistakable. The sun was a bright halo around his head.

Toby!

He was wearing a green polo shirt, a pair of khaki shorts, deck shoes without socks (did Toby even *own* socks?), aviator sun-glasses. He was tan. (Toby and Connie were alike in many ways, but Connie freckled while Toby was now, and always had been, a bronze god.) He still had a full head of sandy hair, and his weight seemed stable. In the past, Connie had seen him both gaunt and underfed, and bloated and heavy. He whooped and gave her a big hug, lifting her right off the dock, and Connie was reminded that, when sober, he was just like a Saint Bernard puppy, all boundless love and enthusiasm. He had been sober now for nearly two years—or so he claimed.

"I called your bluff!" he said. "I'm here!"

"Hey, brother," Connie said. He set her down and they kissed. He tasted clean, he smelled clean—not too minty the way he used to when he was drinking.

"This weather is amazing!" he said. He hoisted the canvas duffel bag he had owned literally his entire adult life over his shoulder. It was sky-blue with his monogram; it had traveled with Toby all over the world. "Maryland is brutally hot. We haven't had a lick of wind all summer. So I took that as a sign. This guy Roy Weedon has been asking me about my boat for years, and when the offer came from the Naval Academy, I thought, Now's the time to sell her."

"I can't believe she's gone," Connie said. Toby had saved for *Bird's Nest* for nearly ten years, and she was the most exquisite sail-boat Connie had ever seen. A classic. The Jackie O of sailboats, the Audrey Hepburn of sailboats. Toby had run the number one sailing charter in the state of Maryland, which gave him the free-dom and the cash to island-hop in the Caribbean all winter long. "I can't believe you sold her. You know you'll never be able to get her back, right? You know you'll never find another boat like her?"

"I do know that," Toby said. "But I can't be at the mercy of the wind or the economy, anymore, Con. And the gig at the Naval Academy was too choice to turn down. The premier collegiate sailors in the country will soon be under my tutelage."

Right. When they'd talked on the phone the day before, Toby

had confessed that the charter business had suited him because it left him free to do other things—primarily drink and chase after other men's wives. He needed something more stable, more serious. He had to think of his son, Michael. He needed health insurance, retirement benefits. He needed to grow up, finally.

"Want to take one last look at her?" Toby asked.

"Won't that be sad for you?" Connie asked.

"I've made my peace with it," Toby said. "Come on, she's down here."

Connie was grateful for anything that delayed their arrival back at home. She followed Toby down the dock. And there she was—*Bird's Nest*—thirty-three feet of polished wood, rope, canvas, and nickel. There was a guy on her, tying up the sails. He looked too young to be the new owner.

"Is that the man from Nantucket?" Connie asked.

Toby laughed. "You're funny, Con."

They ambled back to the car. He was going to think she was funny for another second or two. "So how are you doing?" Connie asked. The ride to Tom Nevers would only take twelve or thirteen minutes, so she had to work fast. "Are you sober?"

"Sure," Toby said.

"Sure?" Connie said. "What kind of answer is that?"

"Geez, Con," Toby said. "Are you riding me already? Can't we just ease into it?"

"No," Connie said. "We can't just ease into it." She wouldn't be lulled by his boyish, gee-whiz charm, though this seemed to work on everyone else. Wolf, despite the fact that he had seen Toby at his very drunkest and most pathetic, had absolutely adored his brother-in-law. The two of them could tell sailing stories for hours, and when Toby visited Nantucket, they used to race each other in Indians. It was the highlight of Wolf's summer—chasing Toby up the harbor and back again—and then settling with a cold beer at the Rope Walk so they could talk about the sail, tack by tack, afterward.

"Okay," Toby said. "I've been sober for twenty-two months. But

I don't take it for granted. I fell off the wagon once, early on." He squinted out the side window. "The evil combination of Marlowe Jones and the Treaty of Paris."

"Ah," Connie said. The Treaty of Paris was Toby's former watering hole. Marlowe Jones was the lonely wife of the Annapolis district attorney. Evil combination indeed.

"But like I said, that was nearly two years ago. I've come to terms with my relationship with alcohol. I inherited the disease. You're lucky you didn't."

Connie felt a complicated mix of emotions. She was ashamed, thinking of how drunk she'd gotten the day of the boat ride with Dan. But what that had taught her was that she *wasn't* immune; she had to watch herself. A part of Connie stupidly mourned the old Toby, the Toby who had been Connie's boozy, fun-loving comrade. Two years earlier, when Toby had come for Wolf's memorial service, he'd hit every bar downtown and had been dropped off at Connie's house in a cab, a sloppy-if-happy drunken mess. Then he and Connie had stayed up drinking wine on the deck until sunrise. Jake and Iris had found them passed out on the outdoor furniture in a dead-on reprise of their own parents.

Toby's not good for you, Iris, with her degree in psychology, had said. *You're not good for each other.*

"Are you dating anyone?" Connie asked him. "Other than Marlowe Jones?"

"I'm not dating Marlowe," he said.

"She's still married to Bart?"

"Still married to Bart. It's one of the worst marriages I've ever seen, but it just won't die."

"Like mom and dad," Connie murmured.

"Exactly," Toby said.

"And there's no one else?" Connie asked.

"No," he said. "Nobody special."

It might have been better if he'd been dating someone, Connie thought. But Toby's romantic life was impossible to keep track of.

There were always women, but rarely anyone who lasted more than a few weeks. Toby had been married twice. He'd met his first wife, Shelden, crewing on the boat *Cascade,* which was the boat he captained before *Excelsior.* Shelden had family money, much of which she spent financing Toby's lifestyle—the drinking and carousing in places like Portofino and Ios and Monaco. It wasn't hard to see why Shelden left—at that time, Toby was at his most uncontrollable and irresponsible, and Shelden was bankrolling all of his bad behavior. He would go to the most popular waterfront bar, buy a round for everyone in the place, and then arrive back at *Excelsior* with fifteen people ready to party until three in the morning.

Several years later while working in Norfolk, Virginia, Toby met Rosalie, who was a shore-bound single mother of two small children. Toby was like some kind of romantic hero who sailed in to save her—though "saving" her turned into getting her pregnant, marrying her, then making her so miserable and doing such a piss-poor job as a father and stepfather that Rosalie fled back to her family in New Orleans. Toby's son, Michael, was now ten. Rosalie had remarried a coach with the New Orleans Saints, a guy who Toby liked and admired. "The guy is so responsible," Toby said, "I want him to be *my* dad." There had been trips to New Orleans where the whole blended family—Rosalie and the coach had children of their own now—went to JazzFest and took river cruises.

"How's Michael?" Connie asked.

"He's great," Toby said. He flipped open his phone to show Connie a picture. She glanced at it quickly: Michael in a baseball hat. "He's a U-eleven all-star in Little League, and he's doing Pop Warner again in the fall. Starting QB. Kid's a natural athlete. Quick hands."

"Takes after his aunt," Connie said. She saw Toby staring at the picture. "Do you wish you saw more of him?"

"Huh?" Toby said. He flipped the phone closed. "Yeah, of course. I lobbied for him to come to Annapolis for two weeks, but he had camp."

"He still could have come for a little while," Connie said. "Did you ask Rosalie?"

"Of course I asked Rosalie," Toby said. "She said he had camp."

Connie shook her head, thinking, *Did you not fight to see your son?*

Toby said, "Michael's fine; he's happy, I'm happy he's happy. We Skype each other."

"Skype?" Connie said.

"Connie, it's fine," Toby said. And he did, indeed, sound fine.

Growing up, Toby had always been the better kid, at least in Connie's mind; possibly, this was a notion she'd gotten from her parents. Toby was the golden-haired son, the gifted athlete. He'd shown promise as a sailor during their summers at Cape May, but there was also football, basketball, and lacrosse. At Radnor, he'd been captain of all three varsity teams. He had always been kind and generous to Connie, perhaps because he understood that Connie wasn't as lucky as he was. She was smart, but he was smarter and better liked by his teachers. Connie was beautiful, but because she was a girl, this beauty was seen as a problem and not as a positive as it was for Toby. Connie's beauty required that she go to Merion Mercy, an all-girls Catholic school, instead of the super fun, incredibly social, less stringent public school that Toby attended. Connie's beauty led to boys sniffing around the house, none of whom her parents approved of.

When, in high school, Toby started drinking—going to keg parties out in the fields or stealing fifths of gin from their parents' liquor cabinet and drinking in the car on the way to South Street—it was treated as a rite of passage. When Connie started drinking, she was grounded for weeks, and she heard incessantly about the damage to her "reputation" from, of all people, her mother.

In general, growing up, Connie had resented Toby and worshipped him, hated him and wanted, more than anything, to *be* him.

Connie thought, *I have to tell him. Now.* But then Toby said, "How are you, Con? Are things any better?"

Are things any better? Connie didn't love the phrasing of this question, acknowledging as it did that things for Connie had been pretty bad. Well, they *had* been bad. Connie had been depressed about Wolf and about Ashlyn. But she resented the accusation that her life needed improvement—because, as an adult, Connie had been happy. She had the glowing marriage, the gracious home, the prestigious husband, the brilliant child.

"They're better," Connie said. The good news was, she could say this honestly.

"Are you seeing anyone?" Toby asked.

"Sort of," Connie said. She felt that as soon as she came right out and said, yes, she was seeing someone, the bubble would burst and Dan Flynn would vanish into thin air.

Because of the incident with Harold, her date with Dan had been overshadowed. But now she grew warm just thinking about it—Dan at dinner, holding her hand; Dan in bed, bringing her back to life. She felt Toby eyeing her.

" 'Sort of?' " he said. "What does that mean?"

They climbed into Connie's car, and Toby threw his duffel bag in the backseat. "It means yes, there's someone, but I don't know what's what yet, okay?"

Toby said, "Okay, sorry. Don't get all touchy on me."

"Oh, God," Connie said. She managed to fit the key in the ignition, but she didn't turn it. "There's something I have to tell you."

Toby raised his eyebrows at her. There was the look, so familiar, so condescending, as though he were sure she was about to make something out of nothing, typical female member of the family, drama queen like their mother. *Well, let's see then,* Connie thought. *Let's see how he likes it.*

"Meredith's at the house."

Yep, she got him. His eyes widened. The whole arrangement of his face changed. But she could tell he didn't quite believe her.

"You're fucking kidding me."

"Not kidding."

"Meredith Martin?"

"Meredith Delinn, yes."

Toby jerked his head, like he was trying to get water out of his ears. "She's..." He looked out the passenger-side window at the hot, shimmering grid of the town parking lot. "Wow."

"Yeah, I'm sorry," Connie said. "I was afraid if I told you, you wouldn't come."

"How long has she been staying with you?"

"All summer."

"You're fucking kidding me."

"Not kidding."

"So... I mean, the husband's in jail. So what is Meredith doing?"

"She's trying to figure out what to do. She's under investigation, I guess; she talks to her lawyer all the time. But the thing is... she's still *Meredith*."

"So you're telling me she didn't know what the husband was up to?"

"I'm telling you that, yes."

"I never met the guy."

"I think that was probably by design."

"But I could tell he was a class-A jerk. Typical Wall Street greedy banker hotshot."

"He was anything but typical," Connie said. And then, because it sounded like she was defending Freddy Delinn, she redirected the conversation. "So, are you okay with seeing Meredith?"

"Am I okay with seeing Meredith? Sure, of course." Toby's face was coloring. He was flustered.

"The last time you saw her was...?"

"Mom's funeral," Toby said. "And that ended badly. Are you sure Meredith is okay with seeing me?"

Connie rested her forehead against the top of the steering wheel. She turned on the car; she needed the air-conditioning. "She doesn't know you're coming."

Toby stared at her. "You're fucking kidding me."

"Not kidding." Connie backed out of her parking spot, thinking, *This whole situation is a tightrope walk.*

"Her head is going to spin," Toby said. "I hope you're ready."

"Don't flatter yourself," Connie said.

"I'm serious."

"After what we've been through this summer, seeing you will come as a very minor shock," Connie said. God, how she prayed this was true. She pulled out onto the road. "I'm sorry if that's a blow to your ego."

Connie spent her minutes on Milestone Road telling Toby about the highlights of the summer. Spray paint, slashed tires, Harold, their beloved seal, dead.

"You should have called me, Con," Toby said. "I would have come up sooner."

"We've been managing," Connie said.

"That sounds like a lie," Toby said.

"Only a partial lie," Connie said. She pulled into the driveway. "Here we are." Toby was looking at the front of the house. There was still a faint outline of the word *CROOK* on the shingles, but a few weeks of sun and sand had done its work. And Dan had used his power washer on the front porch to blast away all vestiges of Harold's blood and bodily fluids. All outward signs of terror had been wiped clean.

Toby adjusted his sunglasses and touched his hair, and with what sounded like a deep breath, he grabbed his old blue duffel bag out of the backseat. How did he feel? Did he have butterflies? Connie thought Toby might mask his nerves with small talk — *the house looks great* — but he was as silent as a monk.

When they walked in, Meredith was sitting at the head of the table. She saw them and stood up. She was wearing white shorts and a black tank top and she was in bare feet. Her hair was in a ponytail. She wasn't wearing any makeup, but her face was tan. She looked, graying hair aside, like she was sixteen years old — tiny and compact, a blue-eyed elf.

When she saw Toby, her eyes narrowed. She poked at her glasses, and Connie wanted to say, *Sorry, he's real.* Meredith looked at Connie, and then back at Toby. Connie had known Meredith since the age of four, but she had no idea how the woman was feeling right now.

Connie said, "Look who I found at the town pier."

Toby dropped his duffel and took a few strides toward her.

Meredith glared at Connie. "Do I seem like a woman who needs more surprise news?"

Toby stopped in his tracks.

Connie opened her mouth.

Meredith raised her face to the ceiling and let out a squawk. "Waaahhhhhh!!" Then she faced Toby. "Hello," she said.

He smiled nervously. "Hello, Meredith."

She took a baby step forward, and he opened his arms and they hugged. The hug was brief, but Connie thought it was real. Knowing each other for nearly fifty years counted for something. Connie wanted them both here, and somehow, by virtue of her own scatterbrained negligence, she had managed to get them in the same room.

She was proud of herself for that.

MEREDITH

Meredith felt the same way now that she'd felt at Connie's wedding. And Veronica's funeral. She couldn't bear to be near him; she only wanted to be near him. She was at a standoff with herself.

"How long are you staying?" she asked him.

"I don't know," he said. "How long are you staying?"

"I don't know," she said. She was angry enough at Connie to threaten to leave right that second—but where on earth would she go?

"Does anyone want lunch?" Connie asked brightly.

He looked good, but this only vexed Meredith further. She couldn't find her balance. There was so much she was dealing with already, and now Toby. Here, in person. He was wearing a green shirt and khaki shorts. His hair was the same, his face was the same but older, with lines and sun spots, but he was still a gorgeous golden lion of a man. Were they actually the same people who had kissed against the tree on Robinhood Road? Were they the same people who had made love in the Martin family library? There were two answers to that as well: They were. And they weren't.

"I'd love some lunch," Toby said.

"Meredith?" Connie asked.

"No, thanks," Meredith said. She could barely breathe, much less eat. "I might go up and lie down."

"Don't let me chase you away," Toby said.

"You're not..." Meredith wasn't quite sure what to say. *You're not chasing me away. You don't have the power to chase me away. You don't have power over me at all.* She was light-headed now. She said, "We've had a rough couple of days, as I'm sure Connie's told you. I'm exhausted."

"Stay down here with us," Connie said. She was already in the kitchen, toasting bread for sandwiches, slicing a lemon for the iced tea. "Even if you're not going to eat, come sit outside."

"You guys enjoy your lunch," Meredith said. "Catch up with each other. Do the brother-sister thing."

"Meredith," Connie said. "Stop it."

Toby put his hands on both her shoulders. Meredith closed her eyes and tried not to think. "Come out with us," he said. "Please."

The three of them sat at the outside table. Connie and Toby were eating sandwiches worthy of the front cover of *Bon Appétit.*

Meredith's stomach complained, but she would sustain her hunger strike. She sipped at her iced tea. Her back was to the ocean. She couldn't stand to look at the water. Thoughts of Harold with his throat slit, blood everywhere, as thick and viscous as an oil spill, pervaded.

"So...I'm here because I sold my boat," Toby said.

Meredith nodded.

"I've had her almost twenty years, so it was hard," he said. "But I tell myself that, ultimately, she was just a thing."

Just a thing. Well, Meredith could identify there. She had lost so many things: the Range Rover, the Calder mobile, the Dior gown. Did she miss any of them? Not one bit.

"It's hard imagining you without a boat," Connie said.

Meredith nodded again. Whenever she'd thought of Toby over the years, she'd thought of him in the cockpit of a sailboat, ropes in hand, the sun on his face. She'd thought of him toting all of his worldly possessions in the very same blue duffel bag he'd walked into the house with today. His parents had given him that duffel bag when he graduated from high school; Meredith had been sitting right beside him when he opened it. Little did she know then, it would become a symbol for Toby's life: He wanted to be able to carry everything he owned with him in that bag, so that he was free to get up and leave, move on to a new place, new people. No commitments.

But yes, one commitment, right?

"Tell me about your son," Meredith said.

"Michael is ten now," Toby said. "He lives in New Orleans with his mother and her new husband."

"Ten is the best age," Meredith said. All of her ached: her past, her present, her future. Because, suddenly, there were her memories of Leo and Carver at ten. Leo had asked Meredith and Freddy for a pair of Ray-Ban sunglasses, and Freddy had made him earn the hundred and thirty-nine dollars by doing jobs for Father Morrissey at the church. Meredith had gone to check on him and found him on his hands and knees, scraping candle wax off the wooden floors. Meredith had instinctively gotten down on her hands and knees to help, and Leo had said, *Don't, Mom. This is my job.* And reluctantly, Meredith had stood up and left him to it.

Carver had started surfing at age ten. He wore a leather choker with a white shell woven into it, and green and black board shorts that reached past his knees. Meredith could picture him so clearly—his young, tanned back, the emerging muscles under the smooth, clear skin of a boy, a boy whose voice had yet to change, a boy who still called her Mommy.

Mommy! Watch me!

"How old are your sons now?" Toby asked.

"Leo is twenty-six and Carver is twenty-four. They're in Connecticut. Leo has a girlfriend named Anais."

Toby nodded. The shirt made his eyes look very green.

Mommy! Watch me!

"Leo was working for Freddy, and he was under investigation for months. But my lawyer called a couple of days ago to say he's been cleared."

"That's good news," Toby said.

"The best news," Connie said. She swatted Toby. "Leo's my godson, remember."

"I'm sure you did a great job with the spiritual guidance through this crisis, Aunt Connie," Toby said.

"I was a basket case about it," Meredith said. "Your kids come first, you know."

"I know," Toby said.

"I'm still under investigation, however," Meredith said. She smiled weakly. "So enjoy me now, because I might be whisked off to jail at any moment."

"Meredith," Connie said.

"I don't mean to be maudlin. We've been having a pretty good summer, considering."

"Except for the dead seal," Toby said.

"Harold," Meredith said. "He was like our pet and they murdered him."

"And don't forget the slashed tires and the spray paint," Connie said. "Meredith spent the first part of the summer hiding inside."

"Wow!" Toby said. "There's a lot to talk about, but it's all really painful!"

Meredith stood up. Every time he opened his mouth, she thought about what had happened at Veronica's funeral. It made her dizzy. "I'm going upstairs to nap," she said.

"Please stay," Connie said.

"I can't," Meredith said. She realized this sounded harsh, so she said, "I can hardly keep my eyes open."

"Okay," Connie said. "If you're sure." She reached for Meredith's hand. Connie was being very sweet. Certainly she was worried that Meredith would be mad. Was Meredith mad? She was something. She needed time to process this.

She went upstairs to her bedroom, and cracked open the doors of her Romeo and Juliet balcony. She could hear the murmur of Toby's and Connie's voices. What were they saying? Meredith wanted to know. She stood in the stripe of sunlight between the doors and listened. Connie said, "Well, you didn't show up at Chick's funeral..."

"...always felt bad about that. But I was a kid..."

Meredith flopped on the bed. Her memories of Toby and her father were all jumbled up. One moment, she'd had them both. She lost one first, then the other, and like that, her childhood ended. She thought about her father and Toby in the front yard raking leaves, or in the den watching football. She thought about her father taking Toby aside for "the talk." *Respect my daughter. Be a gentleman.* She thought about Chick inviting Toby to sit in on the poker game and how thrilled Toby was to be included. It had been his passage into manhood. She thought about Chick and Toby heading off to the roast-beef station during brunch at the Hotel du Pont. She thought about her graduation from Merion Mercy. She had stood at the podium to deliver her salutatorian's speech, and when she gazed out at the audience, she found Veronica and Bill O'Brien, Toby, and her father and mother, all in a row. She'd day-dreamed about her wedding day at that moment. Her inevitable marriage to Toby. But less than twenty-four hours later, Toby had packed up his proverbial bag and announced that he was moving on, leaving Meredith behind. Meredith remembered the driving lessons with her father in the gathering dusk of the Villanova parking lot. The smell of hot asphalt and cut grass, the shouts of the few university students who remained for the summer, the unbearable knowledge that Toby was at the beach, and that the mainsail and the jib and his freedom were more important to him than she was. Chick Martin had said, "I can't stand to see you hurt like this," and at a loss for further words, he'd played the Simon and Garfunkel song over and over again. *Sail on Silvergirl, Sail on by.*

Meredith sat up. She couldn't sleep. She yanked her lone cardboard box from the closet and unfolded the flaps. On top were the photographs. Meredith pulled out the one of her and Freddy at the Dial holiday formal. They looked like kids. Freddy had weighed 165 pounds, and his black curly hair went past his shirt collar. There was a picture from their wedding day. Freddy's hair was cut short then, in the manner of all stockbrokers. Those were the days of his first suit from Brooks Brothers, a huge extravagance. For their wedding, he'd rented a tux. When federal marshals stormed their penthouse on the first of July, they would have found six tuxedos and fourteen dinner jackets in Freddy's closet.

Meredith could have spent all day on the photos, but she was looking for something else. She dug down to the paperback novels that were on top of the boys' yearbooks that were on top of the copy of her Simon and Garfunkel album. Meredith pulled out the record sleeve and there, in her father's handwriting, it said: *For my daughter, Meredith, on her sixteenth birthday. You always have been and always will be my Silver Girl. Love, Dad, October 24, 1977.*

She'd had her wedding to Toby all planned. Her first dance with Toby was going to be to "The Best of Times," and her dance with her father was going to be to "Bridge Over Troubled Water."

Meredith stared into the dim, nearly empty closet. She couldn't remember what song she and Freddy had danced to at their wedding. Freddy didn't care much about music. Freddy only cared about money.

And yet, years and years later, he'd bought her a star and he'd named it Silver Girl, after the song. It had always bothered Meredith that he named the star Silver Girl — because he never knew her father, and he'd never heard her father play that song for her. The name and the song and the story were Meredith's, Freddy was only a guest to it, and yet in buying that star, he co-opted the song and made it his own. He stole the name from Meredith in order to give it back to her as something else.

Meredith rummaged through the cardboard box to the bottom, where she found a manila envelope that held her important documents. She had taken only the lasting things: the children's birth certificates, her marriage license, her Princeton diploma — and, for some reason, the certificate for her star. She pulled it out. It was on official-looking cream-colored paper and it said "NASA" across the top.

She had received the star for her forty-fifth birthday. Freddy had booked a private room at Daniel. He had invited thirty people — New York friends only — Samantha and Trent Deuce, Richard Cassel and his new girlfriend (young), Mary Rose Garth and her new boyfriend (younger), their favorite neighbors from the building, and some people that Meredith and Freddy didn't know all that well but whom Fred had probably invited in order to fill the room. The dinner had been elegant, everyone else got bombed on the extraordinary wines, but Meredith stuck to her glass and a half of red, and Freddy stuck to mineral water. And yet, he had been more effusive than usual, a manic, overeager master of ceremonies. Something was happening after the meal, Meredith picked up on that, and it had to do with her birthday present. Meredith experienced a flutter of curiosity; for her fortieth birthday, Freddy had arranged for Jimmy Buffett to sing to her on the beach in Saint Barth's. She thought this year would be something like that—Elton John, Tony Bennett. They had all the tea in China and so purchasing gifts for each other was a challenge. What could Freddy give her that would be creative and meaningful and unique, that she wouldn't just go out and buy for herself?

Right after Meredith blew out her candles, Freddy chimed his spoon against his water glass.

"Attention, attention!" Everyone quieted down to listen.

"It's Meredith's birthday," Freddy said. He mugged, the room chuckled. Meredith thought about the things she really wanted. She wanted her children to be happy and successful. She wanted more time with Freddy. She remembered looking up at his salt and pepper curls, his piercing blue eyes, his fine-cut suit, and thinking, *I never see this man. I never spend time alone with him.* She remembered hoping that her present was everyone else in the room going home.

But no. There was some elaborate presentation of an envelope on a silver tray by one of the waiters, which Freddy opened with the nervous suspense of an Oscar presenter, and he announced that he had bought his wife, Meredith Martin Delinn, a star in Bode's Galaxy. He had named the star "Silver Girl," after a song Meredith's father had sung to her as a child.

Teenager, Meredith thought.

A star? she thought.

Where is Bode's Galaxy? she wondered.

"So when you look up in the sky," Freddy said, "you'll know that one of those stars out there belongs to Meredith."

He kissed Meredith and presented her with a certificate from NASA, and everyone in the room applauded, and the waiters moved around the room with star-shaped chocolate truffles and bottles of port from the year of Meredith's birth.

Meredith kissed Freddy and thanked him.

He said, "What do you think? I promise you are the only woman on the Upper East Side with her own star."

Meredith had kept the NASA certificate, although in truth, she had barely glanced at it. She was ambivalent about the name of the star, and she felt abashed at the grandiosity of the gesture, and in front of all those people, some of them perfect strangers. How much money had Freddy spent on this star? She wondered. A hundred thousand dollars? More? Wasn't it the equivalent of throwing money away, since the star wasn't something Meredith would ever see in this lifetime? Wasn't Freddy basically announcing that since they could afford anything on God's green earth, he had to move into the heavens to find a surprise for Meredith?

These things had all bothered Meredith, but what had bothered her the most was the way he'd acted. His posturing, his showmanship. There were times—and this was one of them—when Freddy came across as a charlatan, rolling into town with his cart of magic potions meant to cure this or that, tricking the innocent townspeople, disappearing with their money, leaving them with a handful of placebos and a vial of sugar water.

Meredith studied the certificate. There was no seal on it, nothing engraved or embossed. Meredith hadn't wondered about this at the time Freddy gave it to her, although now it seemed clear that this *wasn't* a NASA document at all—but, rather, something that Freddy had printed up himself on his computer. She shook the paper in fury. How had she not *seen* this? She hadn't studied the document closely at all. As with everything else Freddy told her, she'd accepted it on blind faith.

And now it was painfully clear that it was a fake. If she had only *looked at it,* if she had only *opened her eyes,* she would have seen that. This was something Freddy did himself on the computer. She wanted to rip up the certificate—*Goddamn you, Freddy!* She thought (zillionth and sixth). But it might be evidence. Meredith pulled out her cell phone and called Dev.

"I think I have it this time," she said. "Check for the name 'Silver Girl.' " Then she caught herself. "Or, that may be the name of a star registered with NASA."

"Huh?" Dev said.

"Freddy said he bought me a star," Meredith said. "But now I think he was lying about it." Of course, he was lying about it: the certificate had been printed on ivory cotton bond paper, the same paper Freddy kept in his office.

"When was this?" Dev asked.

"Two thousand and six," she said. "Did you find Thad Orlo?"

"I'm not allowed to say," Dev said.

"Not allowed to say? I gave you the information."

"We're getting closer, we think," Dev said.

Meredith noted how he now included himself as a "we" with the Feds. "Well, use the name 'Silver Girl,' and cross-reference it with what you've already got. Or what the Feds have got."

"Does the certificate say anything else?" Dev said. "Does it have a number on it? The Feds are looking for account numbers. Preferably nine digits."

"Yes, it has a number," Meredith said. In the upper-right corner, in Freddy's own handwriting, was a number—ten figures, not nine, and three of the figures were letters. In Freddy's own handwriting, in Flair pen. This was it, this was a real clue, this stupid star, her supposed *birthday present!* Freddy had hidden information here. He had given the information to her, but had he ever expected her to figure it out? God, Meredith was a dismal failure at seeing what was right there in front of her face. Meredith read the number off to Dev. "Zero, zero, zero, four, H,N, P, six, nine, nine."

He said, "Do those numbers mean anything to you?"

"Nope," Meredith said.

"It's probably just an account number from the bank. Maybe one of the zeros is extraneous; maybe one of the numbers is a dummy number. Thank you for this, Meredith. This is good stuff."

"But you don't know for sure if it's good stuff," Meredith said. "The Feds have to check it out, right? But can you please tell them I'm trying?"

"Oh, Meredith," he said. "We all know you're trying."

CONNIE

Meredith and Toby had been under Connie's roof for nearly twenty-four hours—and was it awkward?

Yes.

There had been a strained exchange at lunch. Meredith had lasted ten or twelve minutes before she went to hide out upstairs.

Toby had said, "Should I just leave? I have an open-ended ticket back to BWI. I can go anytime."

Connie said, "You just got here. I haven't seen you in aeons. I want you to stay."

"Okay," Toby said uncertainly.

"She'll get over it," Connie said.

"You think?" Toby said.

When Meredith descended at five o'clock, she looked even more unglued than she had at noon.

Connie said, "Everything okay?"

Meredith turned on her. "Okay?" she said.

"I'm sorry," Connie said. "I didn't mean to spring it on you. I honestly didn't think he'd show. You know how unreliable he is."

"That I do."

At that moment, Toby materialized out of nowhere. "Who's unreliable?" he said.

They had to do something about dinner. Connie didn't feel like cooking, Meredith didn't want to go out, Dan called to say he was spending the night at home with his boys but that he'd come by in the morning to take the three of them to Great Point. Connie told Meredith this. Meredith had been talking about going to Great Point for weeks, but Meredith just frowned and said, "Fine."

They decided to order pizza with sausage and onion, which was the kind of pizza they'd eaten all through high school. If Connie closed her eyes, she could see their booth at Padrino's, herself and Matt Klein on one side, Meredith and Toby on the other, the pitcher of birch beer and four brown pebbled plastic glasses between them, Orleans on the jukebox singing "You're Still the One."

Connie whipped up a salad, and when the pizza came, they sat down to eat. But the conversation was stilted; Meredith was off in her own thoughts someplace. It was as different from Connie's memories of Padrino's as a dinner could be.

Not to be defeated, Connie suggested that they go into the sitting room to watch a movie. Was this too obvious? How many hundreds of movies had the three of them watched together in the O'Brien basement? Toby was game, and Meredith agreed reluctantly. Connie took the easy chair and Toby sat on the sofa, and Meredith glanced at the spot on the sofa next to Toby. Toby patted the cushion. "Come sit here."

But Meredith said, "I'll be fine on the floor." She sat cross-legged on the Claire Murray rug, her back straight, her chin high. Annabeth Martin's influence, or all that diving.

Connie said, "Meredith, you *can't* be comfortable."

Meredith said, "I'm fine."

They deliberated over which film to watch, which was to say that Connie and Toby deliberated with the understanding that whatever they picked, Meredith would deem it "fine." They had agreed on *The Shawshank Redemption,* but then at the last minute, Toby cried out, "Oh, no, let's watch *Animal House.*"

Very slowly, Meredith turned to him. "You're kidding, right?"

"Come on," he said. "Don't you remember?"

"Yes," Meredith said. "I do remember." And then, slowly as smoke, she rose and drifted out of the room. "Good night," she said, once she was on the stairs. "I'm going to bed."

Connie waited until she heard the door of Meredith's bedroom click. "Do I even ask?"

"First date," he said.

"Why are you torturing her?" Connie said.

"I'm not torturing her," he said. "I thought she'd find it funny."

"Yeah, she was just cracking up."

Toby said, "So what happened between the two of you?"

"What happened between the two of *you?*" Connie said.

"Work in progress," Toby said.

Connie shook her head.

Toby said, "I know the two of you had a big fight. I noticed she didn't show up at Wolf's funeral, but you never told me what happened. And I was too much of a drunk to ask."

"It's water under the bridge," Connie said.

"Tell me," Toby said.

"Oh..." Connie said. She hadn't talked to anyone about her fight with Meredith except for Wolf. Ashlyn and Iris and her friend Lizbet knew there had been a rift, but Connie hadn't wanted to share the details. It was nobody's business, and the break from Meredith had been exquisitely painful. But Connie was sick to death of taboo subjects. If she had told Dan what happened with Ashlyn at the funeral, then she could tell Toby about her phone call with Meredith.

"A few months before Wolf died," Connie said—Wolf had still been working, but the doctors weren't pulling any punches; this was it, Wolf wouldn't be getting any better—"he scrutinized all of our financial paperwork." Wolf had pored over the statements and stock reports for most of a Sunday afternoon, and Connie remembered feeling annoyed and churlish. It had been a glorious September day, and she had wanted to go for a walk with Wolf while he was still able, but he was tied to the paperwork spread out all over the dining-room table. They should go out and embrace the day; they had Gene, their accountant, to worry about the finances, didn't they? Wolf had long since given up reading—the effort made his eyes ache—and even at job sites, he had an assistant read him the measurements off the plans. So how much of those columns of figures did Wolf understand? But he was determined. Connie went for the walk by herself and came home watery eyed and sneezing from hay fever.

"Wolf asked me to sit down. He presented me with a pile of statements from Delinn Enterprises, which had been printed on a dot-matrix printer. I had never laid eyes on the actual statements before. I said to Wolf, 'Jesus, we should donate these to the Smithsonian.'"

We're going to pull this money out tomorrow, Wolf said.

What?

Get out of Freddy's thing. Gene loves it, but he can't explain to me how it's done, and in all the years I've known Freddy, he's never been able to explain it to me in any way that makes sense.

It's black magic, Connie had said lightly. This was Freddy's answer whenever someone asked him about the formula for such fantastic returns, even in years when there was a down market.

It's black all right, Wolf said. *I'm sure he's breaking the law.*

Freddy?

Yes, Freddy. I like the guy; I've always liked him. God knows, he's generous to a fault. And I love Meredith and the boys, but something isn't right with that business. Whatever he's doing, the SEC is going to catch him, but we're not waiting around for that to happen. We're getting out of this tomorrow.

Tomorrow? Really? Don't you want to talk to Gene about it before…

Connie. Wolf had put his hand over her hand and tried to look at her, but his gaze had been off, as it occasionally was then. He couldn't always focus. Connie's eyes had filled with hot tears that had nothing to do with ragweed. She was losing him. The liquidation of the Delinn Enterprises account was one step taken in preparation for Wolf's death. *We're getting out of that fund tomorrow.*

Okay, Connie said, though she was skeptical. The returns were so good and they had been so lucky to be allowed to invest when so many others had been turned away. But she had backed Wolf on more radical decisions that this; she would back him now. *Do you think Freddy will be mad?*

Mad? Wolf said. He had seemed amused by this idea. *We only have three million in our account. That's a drop of water in the ocean of Delinn Enterprises. Freddy won't even notice.*

"But as it turned out," Connie said to Toby, "Freddy *did* notice. He left messages at Wolf's office—and then once he found out that Wolf was on-site all the time, he ambushed Wolf's cell phone." But Connie had only discovered this days later when, reaching a point of extreme frustration, Freddy called the house.

Pulling out your money? Freddy ranted. *What the hell?*

Freddy had sounded livid, which perplexed Connie. It was only $3 million. Why did he care? She said, *We have so little money with you. Compared to other clients of yours, I mean. You won't miss us.*

Won't miss you? Freddy said. *Do you know how proud I am to be able to tell people that Washington architect Wolf Flute is a client of mine? I have hundreds of clients in Hollywood—I have Clooney's money and Belushi family money—but I get more pleasure out of mentioning Wolf Flute's name than anybody else's.*

Really? Connie said. She hadn't known how to react to this. Freddy wanted Wolf to stay invested so Freddy could drop his name and lure other architects, or other prominent Washingtonians, to invest? Could this possibly be true? And if it were true, would Wolf be flattered or annoyed?

"So I hung up with Freddy, promising that Wolf would call to explain. Wolf then told me that he didn't want to explain. It was a free country, he said, and he was pulling our money out of Delinn Enterprises. I had no choice but to throw the Meredith friendship card. And Wolf told me that if I was worried about what Meredith thought, I would have to call her myself."

"So what did you do?" Toby asked.

"I called her," Connie said.

Meredith had answered on the first ring, as though she had been standing around her apartment waiting for the call.

Meredith?

Constance.

You heard?

I heard something, Meredith said. *But I didn't believe it.*

Connie had sighed. She had hoped that Meredith would make this easier. She had hoped that Meredith would take the news in stride and do her part to smooth things over with Freddy. *Wolf really felt we had to pull our money.*

That's what Freddy told me. But why?

Well, Connie said. Did she tell Meredith the truth here? Certainly not. *I don't know why, exactly.*

You're lying to me, Constance, Meredith said.

I'm not lying, Connie said. *Wolf has his reasons, but I'm not sure what they are.*

Wolf is sick, Meredith said.

Connie raised her hackles. *Yes,* she said. *I know.*

He has brain cancer, Meredith said.

Well, that doesn't mean he's stupid, Connie said.

He's making a stupid mistake, Freddy says.

Of course, Freddy would say that, Connie said. *It's Freddy's fund. Freddy wants us to stay in. He made that perfectly clear.*

So then, what's the problem? Are the returns not good enough?

They're good enough, Connie said. *Wolf feels like they're too good.*

What does that mean? Meredith asked.

Our accountant can't explain how Freddy's doing it, Connie said. *Nobody can.*

Well, of course not, Meredith said. *Otherwise, they'd be doing it themselves. Freddy is a genius, Connie.* Here, Connie could mouth along to Meredith's words, they were so predictable. *He was an econ whiz at Princeton. He understands the market like nobody else. Do you know how many people who ask to invest with Freddy he turns down?*

Wolf thinks it smells funny, Connie admitted.

Smells funny? Meredith said. *Are you accusing my husband of something?*

I don't know, Connie said. She had used an apologetic voice when she said this. She used a please-don't-let-our-husbands'- business-tear-us-apart voice. *Wolf's just concerned.*

Because he thinks Freddy is breaking the law, Meredith said.

I said, I don't know.

You do know that Freddy works in a highly regulated industry?

Connie opened her mouth to speak, but Meredith said, *God, I HATE it when people call Freddy a crook. He's excellent at what he does, he's better at it than anyone else, and that makes him a crook?*

All I'm saying is that Wolf wants our money out. Connie's voice was tougher with that statement. She had never put herself up against Freddy in Meredith's eyes, and now, she could see, she was going to lose. If Meredith was going to champion Freddy, then fine—Connie would defend Wolf. She thought of sitting on Wolf's shoulders during the chicken fights at the Madequecham Jam. Hadn't she been ruthless? Hadn't they won every single time? *We want our money out. We want a check in the morning!*

A check in the morning? Meredith said. *So that's your decision? You're done with Freddy?*

Done with Delinn Enterprises, yes, Connie said. She said this to make a distinction between the business and the friendship. The awkward fact was that Connie and Wolf had a vacation planned to Cap d'Antibes with Meredith and Freddy two weeks hence. What would they do about that?

Meredith was the one to ask. *What about France?*

The trip to France would most likely be Wolf and Connie's last trip together, and Connie had been desperately looking forward to it. But how could they go to France now?

We're not coming to France, Connie said.

Here, Meredith paused. *You're not coming to France?*

I don't see how we can…now, Connie said. What she meant was: *How can we all sit around and eat pâté and drink wine when you've both made such a brouhaha about us pulling out our money? How can we accept hospitality from a man whom we've essentially labeled a crook?*

Meredith's voice was very quiet. Perhaps if they had both still been yelling, they would have resolved things differently. But Meredith took a resigned breath and said, *Okay, Connie, if that's the way you want to play it, fine. But you're making a big mistake.*

And Connie, incredulous that the Meredith she had known for over forty years, a woman she considered as close as a sister, would let their friendship asphyxiate because of money, said, *Actually, I don't think I am.*

I'll tell Freddy you want a check tomorrow, Meredith said.

Thank you, Connie said.

And they both hung up.

"And that was that?" Toby said.

"That was that," Connie said. "Weeks went by, then months, and I didn't hear from her. I kept thinking she would call to apologize."

"But you didn't call her to apologize," Toby said.

"What did *I* have to apologize for?" Connie said.

When Wolf died, Meredith sent flowers and wrote a $10,000

check to the American Cancer Society in Wolf's honor. Connie wrote to say thank you. She thought that maybe she and Meredith could mend the fence, but she didn't hear back from Meredith. Connie knew this was because of Freddy.

And then Wolf was proved right: Freddy was arrested. The Ponzi scheme was revealed.

"I'm lucky we got out when we did," Connie said. "If Wolf hadn't pulled our money, I would have been forced to sell the Nantucket house. And maybe the Bethesda house, too. I would have had nothing left."

She would have been just like Meredith.

The next day was Sunday, and as soon as Connie woke up, she called Ashlyn.

She was shuttled right into voice mail.

"Hi, honey, it's me," Connie said. "I'm still on Nantucket, and guess what? Uncle Toby is visiting!" Connie paused, as if waiting for Ashlyn to respond. For all Connie knew, Toby talked to Ashlyn on a regular basis. As desperately as Connie wanted news of her daughter, she couldn't bring herself to ask. "Anyway, call me back when you get this. I love you, Ashlyn. It's Mom."

Connie packed as carefully for their trip to Great Point as she might have for a trip to Paris. She wore a bathing suit and a sheer white cover-up that she hadn't worn since the summer Wolf was sick. Even with his failing eyesight, he'd said, *You look like an angel in that white dress, my love.* That comment alone had made Connie unwilling to wear the cover-up for anyone else. But now she saw how silly that was. The cover-up had been expensive, and it looked good on her. She would wear it. She packed her book, sunscreen, towels, and a sweater. In her overnight bag, she packed her toothbrush, face lotion, and her brush, a nightgown.

She packed food in the cooler, and a thermos of iced tea, but no wine. It would be fine. Of course, she could pack a bottle of wine and simply choose not to drink it—but who was she kidding? If the wine was there, she would be too tempted.

She heard a horn beeping outside. Dan!

"Dan, this is my brother, Toby. Toby, this is Dan Flynn."

"Dan the man!" Toby said, shaking Dan's hand.

Dan grinned. "Nice to meet you. You and Connie look alike."

"We do?" Connie said. She could see right away that everything was going to be fine. Toby was used to charming everyone he came in contact with, and Dan would be no exception. Dan and Toby were alike; they were men of the outdoors. Neither of them cared about money or prestige or about leaving behind a legacy. They cared about being free to do as they liked. They were a perfect match.

Dan kissed Meredith on the cheek. He said, "I like the way you did your hair."

Meredith was wearing a red baseball hat with sorority letters on it. It had been Ashlyn's, long abandoned to the dusty shelf of the front closet. Connie had initially been shocked to see Meredith wearing it, then she thought, *Oh, what the hell.* No more taboos. And Meredith seemed marginally more cheerful this morning.

"Thanks," Meredith said.

"I meant, no wig," Dan said.

"Wait a minute," Toby said. "Do you actually wear a wig?"

"I've been traveling incognito," Meredith said. "But not today."

Dan touched Meredith's shoulder. "You won't need a disguise today."

"Great Point!" Toby said, rubbing his hands together.

"Let's go!" Dan said.

They drove through the town of Sconset, stopping at the market for sandwiches and bags of chips, pretzels, and marshmallows. Connie had made a fruit salad, potato salad, and coleslaw, and Dan said he had the rest of their provisions covered.

The top was down on the strawberry Jeep, and the sun shone on the four of them as they drove out of Sconset along the Polpis Road, past Sankaty Lighthouse and the golf course, past the flat blue oval of Sesachacha Pond, to the Wauwinet turnoff. Here, the road grew winding and rural—there were farmhouses surrounded by open land, and then there was a thicket of green, leafy trees before they reached the gatehouse at the Wauwinet inn. Dan stopped the Jeep and hopped out to let the air out of the tires. Toby said, "Can I help?"

"I'd love it," Dan said. He tossed Toby the tire gauge and worked with the car key.

Connie was up front, Meredith directly behind her. Connie turned around and smiled at Meredith.

"You okay?" she said.

"Great," Meredith said. She had her big, dark sunglasses on, so Connie couldn't tell if this was a real "great" or a sarcastic "great."

Connie listened to the hiss of air escaping the tires. It was like a double date, she thought. Having Toby here balanced things out. She remembered her last double date with Meredith—and Wolf and Freddy—in the south of France. Freddy had arranged for a car trip to the picturesque village of Annecy. They had traveled in a 1956 Renault; they had a driver in a military-blue chauffeur cap who spoke only French. Meredith had been the one who communicated with him. Connie remembered being envious of Meredith's French and feeling angry at herself for taking four years of useless Latin. The four of them had gone to an elegant lunch at a Michelin-starred restaurant overlooking a lake. It was a place Meredith and Freddy went often; they knew the owner, a distinguished, olive-skinned gentleman in an immaculate suit. The man had reminded Connie of Oscar de la Renta; he had kissed Connie's hand and brought both her and Meredith glasses of rose champagne. Krug. The lunch must have cost five hundred euros, though no bill ever came to the table. It had been like that with Freddy and Meredith—you had these amazing experiences that just seemed to magically happen—though, of course, Freddy had paid for lunch somehow. The lunch had probably cost more like a thousand euros because there had been at least two bottles of the Krug. There had been lobster and mango salad, and microgreens with marinated artichokes that were grown at a local farm. There had been a whole poached fish with sauce on the side and these special potatoes braised in olive oil, and a cheese platter with figs and tiny champagne grapes. And then, at the end of the meal, chocolate truffles and espresso. It had been the lunch of a lifetime. Freddy, Connie remembered, had drunk only mineral water. He had sat at the head of the table, the undisputed king, ordering up this dish and that, while Connie and Wolf and Meredith grew giddy on the Krug. Freddy's tee-totaling, Connie saw now, had been a way of controlling them all. And hadn't this car trip to Annecy and this lunch occurred the day after Freddy had kissed Connie on the terrace? Yes, she remembered feeling Freddy's eyes on her during that lunch; she had felt his admiration and his desire. She had, if she could be perfectly honest, basked in it.

He had kissed her, touched her.

Connie nearly turned around to ask Meredith the name of that restaurant—it was the kind of thing one was meant to remember—but Connie decided she wouldn't bring it up. For all she knew, the owner of the restaurant had been an investor; for all she knew, the restaurant was now gone, one more casualty of Delinn Enterprises.

You are an incredibly beautiful woman, Constance.

The attendant from the gatehouse came out to check their beach sticker. He was an older gentleman with a gray buzz cut and a stern demeanor. Ex-military for sure. A retired lieutenant. That was who was needed for this job: someone who could keep the unregistered riffraff off the hallowed conservation acres of Great Point.

The attendant brightened when he saw Dan. "Hello there, young Flynn," he said. "How goes it this fine day?"

The two men shook hands.

"It goes," Dan said. He looked at Toby, then back at the Jeep. "These are some friends of mine..."

Be careful! Connie thought.

"From Maryland."

Toby, never one to shy from an introduction, offered his hand. "Toby O'Brien."

"Bud Attatash," the attendant said. He looked past Toby at the Jeep.

Don't introduce us! Connie thought.

"You ladies ready to go have some fun?" Bud asked.

Connie waved. She couldn't see what Meredith was doing.

"How is it up there today?" Dan asked. Connie thought, *Get in the car. Please, let's go.* But then she remembered that Dan's real job was to know everyone on this island and everything that went on. Clearly, he felt he had to take two minutes to chew the fat with Bud Attatash.

Bud said, "Well, it's August and the seals are finally off the point. They've made their way up the coast."

"It'll smell a lot better," Dan said.

"Got that right," Bud said. He scratched the back of his neck. His collar was as stiff as cardboard. "Hey, did you hear about a dead seal on the south shore? Murdered, they say. Dropped off special delivery for that Delinn woman."

Toby made a noise. Bud looked over.

Dan said, "Yes, I did hear about that. Awful stuff."

Connie's palms itched. Her shoulders were burning in the sun. She was afraid to turn around to check on Meredith. Toby, she saw, looked stricken. If he'd had three drinks in him, he would have socked Bud Attatash in the jaw.

"Awful is right," Bud said. "Killing an animal like that."

"Senseless violence," Dan said.

Get in the car! Connie thought. She cleared her throat. Toby read her mind and hopped into the backseat next to Meredith.

Dan took a step back with one foot but wasn't able to make the full commitment to leaving.

Bud said, "They'll never catch the guys who did it. That woman has too many enemies."

"It's a little more complicated than that, Bud," Dan said. "And if you don't believe me, you should talk to the chief about it." Even Dan seemed flustered now, and Connie felt a flash of irritation. How had he not been able to keep the conversation off this one topic? Jesus! "Well, we should be shoving off now."

"A poor, innocent sea creature," Bud said.

They pulled out onto the sand, leaving Bud Attatash in his khaki uniform staring after them at the gatehouse.

Dan said, "Sorry about that."

Nobody spoke. Connie checked on Meredith in the side-view mirror. Her expression, under the brim of the hat and behind the dark, saucer-size lenses of her sunglasses, was inscrutable.

"Bud is harmless," Dan said. "I've known him my whole life."

Again, no one spoke. Connie turned on the radio. It was a commercial, loud and grating. She pushed in the CD, thinking it would be the Beatles, but the music that came blaring out was even worse than the radio. Dan popped the CD back out with a proprietary air that made Connie feel like she shouldn't have presumed to touch the radio in the first place.

He said, "Sorry. I let Donovan borrow the car. That's his music."

Connie feared all the good karma she'd attached to this day was in danger of draining through the floorboards.

But the Jeep bounced over some bumps in the sand, and Toby whooped, and Connie was forced to grab hold of the roll bar. They drove past the last of the summer homes and headed out onto the pure sands of Great Point.

Suddenly, their silence seemed not due to the awkwardness with Bud Attatash back at the gatehouse but, rather, in deference to the stark beauty of the landscape around them. The sand up here was creamy white. The vegetation consisted of low-lying bushes—bayberry and sweet-scented *Rosa rugosa*. The ocean was a deep blue; the waves were gentler than the waves in Tom Nevers. In the distance, Connie saw Great Point Lighthouse. What was breathtaking was the purity of the surroundings. A few men were surf casting along the shore. Crabs scuttled past the seagulls and the oystercatchers.

Why had Connie never come out here before? The real answer, she supposed, was that the Flutes didn't come to Great Point; it wasn't in their repertoire of Nantucket excursions. Mrs. Flute, Wolf's mother, claimed she couldn't abide the thought of automobiles on the beach, but Wolf told Connie that what this really meant was that his parents—being stingy Yankee folk—didn't want to fork over the money for a beach sticker. (It had been seventy-five dollars back in the day; now, it was nearly twice that.)

Well, Connie thought, they had missed out. The place was a natural treasure.

Dan drove them through the sand tracks to the tip of the island. "There," he said. "You can see the riptide."

Toby stood up in his seat. "Man," he said. "Amazing."

Connie could see a demarcation in the water, a roiling, where the riptide was. This was the end of the island, or the beginning of it. The lighthouse was just behind them.

"Can we climb the lighthouse?" Meredith asked. She sounded a little closer to her normal self. Hopefully, she had chalked the encounter with Bud Attatash up to bad luck. More than anything, Connie wanted to keep Meredith happy.

"Yes, can we?" she asked Dan.

"We can," Dan said. He pulled the car around to the harbor side of the point and parked. There were sailboats scattered across the horizon.

They trudged through the hot sand toward the lighthouse. There was an antechamber with two wooden benches, but the door that led into the lighthouse was shut tight.

"You never used to know if the door would be locked," Dan said. He turned the knob.

"It's locked," Connie said. She was disappointed. She tried the knob herself.

"It's locked," Dan said. "But I have a key."

"You do?" Meredith said.

Dan pulled a key out of his pants pocket. It was the color of an old penny. "I've had this key since I was eighteen years old. Back then, the ranger out here was a man named Elton Vicar. And I dated his granddaughter, Dove Vicar."

"Dove?" Connie said.

"Dove stole this key from Elton and gave it to me, and I was smart enough to hold on to it. Because I knew it would come in handy someday."

"Are you sure it still works?" Connie said. How could a key that Dan had had for thirty years still work?

Dan slid the key into the knob. He had to wiggle it, but he fit it in and turned the knob and the door opened. "They'll never change the lock. Too much trouble. Plus, they have no reason to."

"So are we doing something illegal, then?" Meredith asked. She sounded nervous.

"Relax," Dan said. "The crime was committed long ago, by Dove Vicar, who is now Dove Somebody Else, living somewhere in New Mexico."

"But aren't we breaking and entering?" Meredith said.

"We have a key!" Dan said, and he stepped inside.

Connie had never been inside a lighthouse before, but this one was about what she expected. It was dark and dingy with a sandy concrete floor; it smelled like somebody's root cellar. In the middle of the room was a wrought-iron spiral staircase and Dan began marching up. Connie followed, thinking, *I am dating the only man on Nantucket with a key to the Great Point Lighthouse.* Meredith was behind Connie, and Toby brought up the rear. Connie watched her step; the only light was filtering down in dusty rays from above.

At the top of the stairs, there was a room of sorts — a floor and windows and a case that held the reflecting light, which was powered by solar panels.

Toby was impressed. "How long ago was this built?"

"Originally in seventeen eighty-five," Dan said. "Reconstructed in nineteen eighty-six."

There was a narrow balcony that encircled the top. Connie and Meredith stepped out and walked around the outside. Connie could see all the way across Nantucket Sound to Cape Cod. To the south, the island was spread out before them like a blanket — the houses and trees and ponds, sand dunes and dirt roads. Connie had been coming to Nantucket for twenty years, but today might have been the first day she truly saw it.

Dan parked the Jeep on the harbor side, and they unfolded chairs and laid out towels.

"This," Connie said, "is a breathtaking spot. Isn't it breathtaking, Meredith?"

Meredith hummed. "Mmmhmmm."

Dan opened a beer. "Does anybody want a drink?"

Connie said, "Toby, I brought iced tea."

Toby held up a hand. "I'm fine right now, thanks."

Dan said, "Meredith, how about you?"

"I'm all set."

"Connie?" Dan said. "Can I pour you a glass of wine?"

"I brought iced tea," she said.

"Really?" he said. "No wine?"

"Really," Connie said. She put on a wide-brimmed straw hat that she'd bought to keep the sun off her face but that she never bothered to wear. Time to start taking care of herself. Wear a hat, leave the chardonnay at home. "I'll have an iced tea."

"Okay," Dan said. He sounded surprised.

Toby said, "Meredith, do you want to go for a walk?"

Meredith said, "Connie, do you want to go for a walk?"

Connie said, "Not just yet. You two go."

Meredith didn't move. She said, "I'll wait for Connie."

Toby said in a very adult, very serious voice Connie couldn't remember ever hearing him use before, "Meredith, come for a walk with me. Please."

Meredith sat, still as a stone. "No," she said.

Connie thought, *Is today going to be a total disaster?*

Toby walked off in silence. Connie watched him go. Then, a few seconds later, Meredith got to her feet, and Connie thought, *Oh, thank God.* But Meredith took off in the opposite direction.

Dan settled in a chair next to Connie. He had a copy of *The Kite Runner* in his lap. "So, do I dare ask? What's their deal?"

"Oh, God," Connie said. "I have no idea."

"You have no idea?"

When Connie looked at Dan, she was overwhelmed by how little she knew him — and she was overwhelmed by how little he knew her. How did it happen, getting to know someone? It took time. It took days spent together, weeks, months. The thought of all the effort it would take to get to know Dan and to have Dan know her suddenly seemed exhausting. Why had she not just brought the wine? Everything was so much easier with wine.

"Meredith and Toby dated in high school," Connie said.

"Ah," Dan said, as if this explained everything. But how could he possibly understand?

"They were madly in love," Connie said. "It was irritating."

Dan laughed. "Irritating?"

"Well, you know, he was my brother; she was my best friend..."

"You felt left out?"

"Sort of, yes. At first, I was really bothered by it. I nearly put an end to it — I had the power to do that, I think, at least with Meredith. But I grew used to the idea, and I had boyfriends, too, always..."

"That doesn't surprise me," Dan said.

"So we used to double date. We went to the movies and to

dances at Radnor High School, where Toby went. We went roller skating." Connie laughed. It *was* funny thinking about her and Meredith and Toby and Matt Klein at the roller rink with the disco ball spinning, creating spots of multicolored light. They skated to Queen and Lynyrd Skynyrd and Earth, Wind & Fire. Connie and Meredith skated backward—they had spent hours practicing this in Meredith's basement—and Toby and Matt rested their hands on the girls' hips. Connie and Meredith both had feathered hair; they kept plastic combs in the back pockets of their designer jeans. Between skates, the four of them would sit at the plastic tables in the snack bar and drink suicides and eat bad nachos. "But, I don't know, my boyfriends were always just guys to pass the time with. Meredith and Toby were different. They were in love. They were very vocal about that, very smug about it."

"Irritating," Dan agreed.

"And then once I'd pretty much embraced the fact that they were probably going to get married and have five kids, Toby broke up with her."

"Did something happen?"

"He was nineteen years old, going off to college, and he wanted his freedom. Meredith was a wreck. I was surprised by that. She was always so tough, you know, so cool, and...impervious, like nothing could affect her. But when Toby broke up with her, she crumbled. She cried all the time, she leaned on her parents a lot, she was very close with her father...I remember right after it happened, I tried to take her mind off him, and it backfired."

Dan leaned forward. "Really? What happened?"

"I had been invited to this party at Villanova, and I convinced Meredith to go with me. I had to beg her, but she agreed, and once we got there, she started drinking this red punch. Kool-Aid and grain alcohol."

"Oh, God," Dan said.

"And the next thing I knew, everyone else in the room was jumping up and down to the Ramones, and Meredith was slumped over on the couch. Passed out. Dead weight." What Connie didn't say was that there was a minute or two when Connie had feared Meredith was actually dead. Connie had screamed until someone shut off the music. And then another partygoer, who claimed he was pre-med, determined that Meredith was breathing and had a pulse. Then the music was cranked back up, and it became Connie's responsibility to get Meredith out of there. "The problem was that we had walked to the party," Connie said. For the preceding two years, Toby had been their ride everywhere. Connie had failed her driver's test three times, and Meredith was still learning how to drive from her father, but Meredith spent more time crying than driving. "So my options were to call my parents for a ride, call Meredith's parents for a ride, or try to get Meredith home on my own."

"So...?" Dan said.

So, Connie's parents were always drunk themselves and could offer no assistance. And Connie hadn't wanted to call the Martins because they truly believed that Meredith hung the moon, and Connie couldn't stand the thought of being the one to inform them that their daughter was a human being, an eighteen-year-old girl with a broken heart and some pretty typical self-destructive impulses. And she couldn't call Toby.

"I carried her home," Connie said. "On my back."

Dan hooted. "You're kidding me."

Yes, it sounded funny—anyone who heard the story always laughed—but it hadn't been funny at the time. It had been sad—a sad, difficult, poignant night in Connie and Meredith's shared experience of growing up. Connie had managed to rouse Meredith enough to get her to cleave onto Connie's back. Connie held Meredith's legs, and Meredith wrapped her arms around Connie's neck, and rested the hot weight of her head on Connie's shoulder. How many times had they stopped so that Meredith could throw up? How long and loudly had Meredith cried because of Toby? And Connie thought, *Why do you need Toby when I'm right here?* But she held her tongue. She rubbed Meredith's back.

I know, I know it hurts, I know.

Connie knew where the Martins kept their extra key, and she knew the alarm code for the house. She got Meredith upstairs into her own bed without waking up Chick or Deidre. Connie filled the bathroom cup with water and put three Excedrin on Meredith's nightstand, where, Connie saw, Meredith still kept a picture of herself and Toby from Toby's prom at Radnor. Connie turned the picture facedown and whispered to Meredith's sleeping form that everything was going to be fine.

The epilogue to that story, which Connie didn't like to think about now, was that the following January, Meredith sent Connie a letter from Princeton. The letter said, *Guess what? You were right. I am going to be fine! I've met an amazing guy. His name is Fred.*

Meredith returned from her walk with a handful of shells that she set in a row along the edge of her towel like a prepubescent girl.

She gave Dan a teensy smile. "It's lovely here. Thank you for bringing us."

Dan said, "Meredith, you're welcome."

Connie thought, *Things are improving.*

Toby returned a little while later with an armload of driftwood, which he dropped in a noisy pile a few inches from where Meredith lay.

"For a fire," he said. "Later."

"Great!" Connie said.

Toby nudged Meredith's shoulder with his big toe. "You missed a great walk," he said.

"No, I didn't," Meredith said. "I took a great walk. I went that way."

Toby eyeballed her a second, then shook his head.

Connie closed her eyes and thought, *Things are not improving.* She thought, *Okay, the two of you don't have to fall back in love, no one expects that, but can't you be friends? And if you can't manage to be friends, could you at least be civil?*

Meredith stood up. "I'm going for a swim."

"Me, too," Toby said.

Meredith whipped around. "Stop it, Toby," she said.

Toby laughed. "The ocean is big enough for both of us."

"No," Meredith said. "I don't think it is." She waded in, and when the water was at her hips, she dove under. She was as natural to the water as a porpoise. Toby dove in after her, and Connie thought, *God, Toby, leave the woman alone.* But he swam right up to her and snapped the strap of her black tank suit, and Meredith splashed him in the face and said, "Get some new tricks."

And he said, "What's wrong with my old tricks?"

Meredith said, "What's *wrong* with your old tricks? Do I really need to answer that?" But if Connie wasn't mistaken, her voice was a little more elastic, and that was all Toby would need to wiggle into her good graces. Meredith swam down the shoreline, and Toby took off after her, undeterred.

"That looks like fun," Dan said. He stood up to join them, and Connie followed, although she hated being pressured into the water. But the water here was warm and shallow. Connie floated on her back and felt the sun on her face. Dan encouraged her out a little deeper where he cradled her in his arms and sang a James Taylor song in her ear. "Something in the Way She Moves." He had a wonderful voice—he was good enough to be a real singer—and Connie loved the buzz in her ear. When he finished, she said, "You are the man with the key."

"The key to what?" he said.

The lighthouse, silly! she nearly said. But instead, she said, "The key to my heart."

He seemed pleased by this. "Am I now?" he said.

She nodded. Then she felt guilty. Wolf! Wolf was the man with the key to her heart. It was foolish to believe she could love anybody else like that.

She swam back to shore.

* * *

After lunch, Meredith curled up on her blanket and fell asleep.
Toby leaned forward in his chair and watched the sailboats in the
distance. Connie wondered if he was thinking about *Bird's Nest*.
Of course he was. She had been more than a boat; she had been,
for Toby, a home. As Connie was studying him—she wanted to
say something, though she wasn't sure what—she saw him cast
his eyes at Meredith. He gazed at her for a long couple of seconds,
and Connie thought, *Oh, boy.*

Dan pushed himself up out of his chair. "I'm going to fish for a
little while. Connie?"

"I'll pass."

Toby hopped to his feet. "I'd love to join you."

Connie watched her lover and her brother amble down the
beach with their fishing poles. Meredith's breathing was audible;
she was fast asleep. Connie wondered what she was dreaming
about. Did she dream about her sons or Freddy or Connie or her
attorney or the angry woman at the salon? Did she dream about
Toby, and if so, was it Toby at eighteen, or Toby now, at fifty-one?
Connie's eyes drifted closed. She heard Dan singing a song without words, she felt the breeze lift the brim of her straw hat, she
wondered if seals went to heaven and decided they probably did.

When she woke, it was because Toby was shouting about a fish.
Dan yelled up the beach, "It's a keeper!" Connie squinted at them.
Meredith was still asleep. Connie decided to walk over and be
impressed. She recognized the dark markings on the scales—a
striped bass. Big one.

Dan said, "Now *that's* a beauty."

Toby said, "The sea has always provided for me."

Connie looked at Dan. "Are we going to eat it?"

"I brought my filet knife," he said. "And a bottle of olive oil and
my Lawry's seasoned salt. I knew we'd catch something. We'll
cook it over the fire."

Connie smiled and kissed her brother on the cheek. "Hunter-gatherer," she said. "Meredith will be so impressed."

They played horseshoes, and Dan won handily. They played Wiffle ball, and Connie hit the ball over everyone's heads into the eelgrass and they couldn't find it again. Although this ended their game prematurely, Dan was impressed by the hit, and Connie beamed.

Toby said, "You should have seen her play field hockey. She was a killer."

Connie and Dan went for a walk and stopped to kiss, which got so heated at one point, Connie thought they might...there was no one around, so...but Dan pulled away. He said, "If Bud comes driving around and sees us, he won't like it."

"Does Bud come driving around?" Connie asked.

"Oh, sure," Dan said, and he nibbled on Connie's ear.

The sun was setting. When Connie and Dan got back to the camp, Toby had dug a pit with a shovel he'd found in the back of Dan's Jeep. He piled in the wood and used the paper from their sandwich wrappings to start a fire. He was a man with survival skills. Two failed marriages, a lifelong battle with alcohol, a little boy he didn't see enough of. Connie had buried a husband and lost a daughter; Dan had buried a wife and lost a son. Meredith — well, Meredith had experienced difficulty the likes of which Connie couldn't begin to imagine. And yet, despite all of this collective suffering, the four of them gathered around the growing heat and light of the bonfire, and let it warm them.

God, human beings are resilient, Connie thought.

We are resilient!

Dan filleted the bass, and Connie set out cheese and crackers on a plate. Toby and Meredith were sitting side by side on the blanket, not touching, not talking, but they were definitely coexisting more peacefully now. Or was she imagining this?

It was high school over and over and over again.

There was a noise. Connie looked up to see a forest-green pickup truck coming their way. Although it had been a nearly perfect day, they had seen very few people—a couple of lone fishermen on foot, a handful of families in rental Jeeps who approached their spot then backed up, for fear of infringing. But this truck drove toward the camp, then stopped suddenly, spraying sand on Toby and Meredith's blanket. There was white writing on the side of the truck. *Trustees of the Reservation.* A man poked his head out the window. He was wearing a green cap. It was Bud Attatash.

He stepped out of the truck. "You folks doing all right?"

Dan was monitoring the progress of the striped bass on the grill. He said, "We're doing great, Bud. Couldn't have asked for a better day."

"I'll agree with you there," Bud said. He stood with his hands in his pockets, an uncomfortable air about him. He hadn't come to talk about the weather. Was he upset about the grill? Or about the fire? Dan had gotten a fire permit; it was in the glove compartment of the Jeep. Was he going to scold them for having an open container? One open beer?

"You headed home?" Dan asked. He had explained that, as ranger, Bud Attatash spent the summer living in a cottage out here on the point.

"Yep," Bud said. "I just wanted to stop by and see how you folks were doing."

"We're cooking up this striped bass," Dan said. "It was legal, half inch over."

"They've been big this summer," Bud said. He cleared his throat. "Listen, after you folks headed out, I got to thinking about what you said about that dead seal on the south shore being a more complicated issue than it appeared. So I called up Chief Kapenash, and he told me about it. He said that you, Dan, were a part of that whole thing." Here, he looked, not at Dan, but at Meredith, whose face had gone scary blank. "And I realized that I said some inappropriate things." He nodded at Meredith. "Are you Mrs. Delinn?"

Meredith stared. Toby said, "Please, sir, if you don't mind..."

"Well, Mrs. Delinn, I just want to apologize for my callous words earlier. And for perhaps sounding like I cared more about a dead seal than I did for your welfare. What those people did was inexcusable. No doubt, you've been through enough in your private life without these hooligans trying to scare you."

Meredith pressed her lips together. Toby said, "That's right, you're right, she's been through enough."

"So if anyone ever bothers you again, you let me know." He gazed out over the dark water at the twinkling lights of town. "Nantucket is supposed to be a safe haven."

Dan came over to shake Bud's hand. "Thanks, Bud. Thank you for coming all the way out here to say that. You didn't have to."

"Oh, I know, I know," Bud said. "But I didn't want any of you to get the wrong idea about me. I'm not coldhearted or vindictive."

"Well, thanks again," Dan said. "You have a good night."

Bud Attatash tipped his cap at Meredith and then again at Connie, and then he climbed into his truck and drove off into the darkness.

"Well," Meredith said after a minute. "That was a first."

They ate the grilled fish with some sliced fresh tomatoes that Dan had gotten at Bartlett's Farm. Then they each put a marshmallow on a stick and roasted it over the fire. Meredith went back in the water, and Toby stood to join her, but Meredith put a hand up and said, "Don't even think about it." Toby plopped back down on his towel. "Yeah," he said. "She wants me." Connie climbed into Dan's lap and listened to the splashing sound of Meredith swimming. Dan kissed her and said, "Let's get out of here."

Yes! she thought.

She and Dan started breaking down the camp and packing everything up. Meredith emerged from the water with her teeth chattering, and Connie handed her the last dry towel. She collected the trash and stowed everything in the coolers. She folded up the blankets and the chairs while Dan dealt with the cooling grill and doused the fire. Toby put away the fishing poles, and Meredith collected the horseshoes. A seagull landed for the remains of the striped bass. Connie found the plastic bat in the sand and tucked it into the back of the Jeep. The Wiffle ball was still out there somewhere, Connie thought, tucked into the eelgrass like a seagull's egg, a memento of one of the small triumphs of the day.

The days zipped by. Connie spent nearly every night at Dan's house. She left a toothbrush there, and she bought half-and-half for her coffee (Dan, health nut, had only skim milk) and kept it in the fridge. She had met both of Dan's younger sons—Donovan and Charlie—though they had little more to say to her than "Hey." Dan relayed the funny things they said to him after Connie left.

Donovan, who was sixteen, had said, "Glad you're getting laid on a regular basis again, Dad. Can I borrow the Jeep?"

Charlie, the youngest, said, "She's pretty hot for an older lady."

"Older lady!" Connie exclaimed.

"Older than him, he means," Dan said. "And he's fourteen."

On the days that Dan had to work, Connie and Meredith and Toby walked the beach and then sat on the deck and read their books and discussed what they wanted to do for dinner. These were the moments when Toby acted like an adult. But more and more often, there were moments when Toby acted like an adolescent. He would mess up Meredith's hair or throw stones at the door of the outdoor shower while she was in there, or he would steal her glasses, forcing her to come stumbling blindly after him.

"Look at you," he'd say to her. "You're *chasing* me."

Connie said to Dan, "I can't tell if that's going to happen or not."

Toby asked if he could stay another week.

"Another week?" Connie said. "Or longer?"

"I don't start at the Naval Academy until after Labor Day," he said.

"So what does that mean?" Connie asked. "You'll stay until Labor Day?"

"Another week," Toby said. "But maybe longer. If that's okay with you?"

"Of course, it's okay with me," Connie said. "I'm just wondering what I did to deserve the honor of your extended presence?" What she wanted him to say was that he was staying because of Meredith.

"This is Nantucket," Toby said, "Why would I want to be anywhere else?"

MEREDITH

On the morning of the twenty-third of August, Meredith was awakened by the phone. Was it the phone? She thought it was, but the phone was in Connie's room, far, far away, and Meredith was in the grip of a heavy, smothering sleep. Connie would answer it. The phone kept ringing. Really? Meredith tried to lift her head. The balcony doors were shut tight—even with Toby across the hall, she didn't feel safe enough to sleep with them open—and her room was sweltering. She couldn't move. She couldn't answer the phone.

A little while later, the phone rang again. Meredith woke with a start. Connie would get it. Then she remembered that Connie wasn't home. Connie was at Dan's.

Meredith got out of bed and padded down the hall. Toby probably hadn't even heard the phone; he slept like a corpse. Meredith liked to believe this was a sign that he had a clean conscience. Freddy had jolted awake at the slightest sound.

Connie didn't have an answering machine, and so the phone rang and rang. *It's probably Connie,* Meredith thought, *calling from Dan's house with some kind of plan for the day—a lunch picnic at Smith's Point or a trip to Tuckernuck in Dan's boat.* Meredith's heart quickened. She had fallen in love with Nantucket—and yet in a few weeks, she would have to leave. She was trying not to think about where she would go or what she would do.

The caller ID said, *NUMBER UNAVAILABLE,* and Meredith's brain shouted out a warning, even as she picked up the phone and said hello.

A female voice said, "Meredith?"

"Yes?" Meredith said. It wasn't Connie, but the voice sounded like she knew her, and Meredith thought, *Oh, my God. It's Ashlyn!*

The voice said, "This is Rae Riley-Moore? From the *New York Times?*"

Meredith was confused. Not Ashlyn. Someone else. Someone selling something? The paper? The voice sounded familiar to Meredith because that was how telemarketers did it now; they acted like you were an old friend. Meredith held the phone in two fingers, ready to drop it like a hot potato.

"I'm sorry to bother you at home," Rae Riley-Moore said.

At home. This wasn't Meredith's home. If this was a telemarketer, she wouldn't have asked for Meredith. She would have asked for Connie.

Meredith said nothing. Rae Riley-Moore was undeterred.

"And so early. I hope I didn't wake you."

Meredith swallowed. She looked down the hall to the closed door of Toby's room. He would still be fast asleep. But a few days ago, he'd said, *If you need to come into this room for any reason, just walk right in. I am here for you, Meredith. Whatever you need.*

At the time she had thought, *Here for me? Ha!*

Meredith said, "I'm sorry. What can I do for you?"

"I'm calling about the news that broke this morning?" Rae Riley-Moore said. "In regard to your husband?"

Meredith spoke without thinking. "Is he dead?" Suddenly, the world stopped. There was no bedroom, no old boyfriend, no beautiful island, no $50 billion Ponzi scheme. Meredith was suspended in a white-noise vacuum, waiting for an answer to come through the portal that was the phone in her hand.

"No," Rae said. "He's not dead. And he's not hurt."

Things came back into focus, though Meredith was still disoriented. This wasn't Ashlyn, and it wasn't a telemarketer trying to sell her a subscription. This was something about Freddy. Meredith sat down on the smooth, white cotton of Connie's bed. There, on the nightstand, was Connie's clock radio, its blue numbers said 7:16. Certainly, Meredith knew better than to answer the phone. If the phone rang at seven o'clock in the morning, it was for a terrible, awful, disturbing reason.

"What then?" Meredith asked. "What is it?"

"Federal investigators have found evidence of an affair between your husband and a Mrs. Samantha Deuce. Your interior designer?"

Decorator, Meredith thought automatically. Samantha wasn't certified in interior design.

"And at two a.m. this morning, Mrs. Deuce made a statement to the press confirming the affair. She said that she and your husband had been together for six and a half years."

Meredith gagged. She thought, *Oh, God, it's true.* She thought, *It's true, it's true, Samantha and Freddy, Samantha confessed, it's true!* She thought, *Hang up!* But Meredith couldn't bring herself to hang up.

"Is this news to you?" Rae asked.

Was it news to her? It was. And it wasn't. "Yes," Meredith whispered. Her lips were wet with saliva.

"I'm sorry," Rae said. And she did, Meredith had to admit, sound sorry. "I didn't realize...I thought you knew."

"Well, now I hope it's clear," Meredith said. She cleared her throat. "I hope it's clear...that I knew *nothing* about what Freddy did behind closed doors."

"Okay," Rae Riley-Moore said. "So it's fair to say you're shocked and hurt."

Shocked. Could she honestly say *shocked?* Hurt, yes. And nothing about this was fair.

"You're telling me Samantha *confessed* to this?" Meredith said. "You're telling me she said they'd been together for six and a half *years?*"

"Since the summer of 2004," Rae said.

Summer 2004: Meredith rummaged. Cap d'Antibes? No, Sam had never been with them to France, though she'd dropped hints, hadn't she? Southampton? Yes, Samantha had come to their house in Southampton all the time—she and Trent had a place in Bridgehampton. Samantha, it now seemed to Meredith, had always been around. She had decorated three of the Delinns' four homes, down to the teaspoons, down to the hatbox toilets. Samantha had been their tastemaker, their stylist. She and Meredith used to go shopping together; Samantha picked out clothes for Meredith and clothes for Meredith to buy Freddy. She had insisted on the Yankees memorabilia and the antique piggy banks for Freddy's den.

Meredith had *seen* them together in his den; Meredith had *seen* Freddy's hand on Samantha's lower back. But Meredith had turned a blind eye, thinking, *No, not Freddy. Never.*

"Were they...are they...in *love?*" Meredith asked. She couldn't believe she was asking a total stranger, but she had to have the answer. She tried to remember: Had Samantha been at the indictment? No. Had she been at the sentencing? Meredith wasn't sure, since she herself hadn't attended the sentencing. Meredith hadn't heard from Samantha when the news broke—not a phone call, not an e-mail—except for an invoice for a small piece of artwork that arrived after Freddy was already in the city jail. Meredith had handed the invoice over to her attorneys. She didn't have the money to pay for it; it was something for Freddy's office. It was, she remembered now, a photograph of an Asian city that Meredith hadn't recognized.

"Malacca," Freddy had said. Meredith had been visiting Fred at the office a few weeks before the collapse. She had noticed the photograph hanging behind his desk, and she'd asked about it. "It's the cultural capital of Malaysia."

The invoice had been for twelve hundred dollars.

Twelve hundred dollars, Meredith thought now. *For a photograph of a place we've never been.*

Meredith had thought the invoice might have a note written on it, an expression of sympathy or concern. But no.

"Did she say they were in love?" Meredith asked again, more forcefully. "Mrs. Deuce. Samantha. Did she say that?"

Down the hall, the door to Toby's room opened, and Toby stepped out. He stood, in boxers and a T-shirt, looking at her.

Meredith held up a finger. She needed to hear the answer.

"She said she was writing a book," Rae Riley-Moore said.

Meredith hung up the phone. She walked toward Toby, and Toby walked toward her, and they met in the middle of the hallway.

Toby said, "I have some bad news."

The bad news was that Toby had been awoken by a commotion outside. There were news vans lining the road at the edge of Connie's property.

"I assume they're here for you?" Toby said.

"Oh, my God." Meredith couldn't have felt more exposed if they'd caught her stepping out of the shower. How did they know where she was staying? The police dispatcher, maybe. Or someone at the salon. Or they'd been tipped off by the wretched person who was terrorizing her.

"Do you know what it's about?" Toby said.

Meredith peered out the window. "Oh, my God," she said. "I can't believe this. I can't believe it."

"Did something happen?" Toby asked. "Who was on the phone?"

"A reporter from the *New York Times,*" Meredith said.

Toby stared at her.

"Freddy had an affair with our decorator, Samantha, for six and a half years." Meredith said these words, but she didn't believe them. She understood they were, most likely, the truth, but she didn't *believe* them.

Toby reached out for her. Meredith closed her eyes. Toby smelled like warm sleep. If she were brutally honest with herself, she would admit that she'd been wanting Toby to hold her like this for days. She'd been pushing him away, scorning him at every opportunity— he was still a teenager in so many ways, he had never grown up— but the truth was, she yearned for a little piece of what they'd had back then. But now, with this news, the only man she could think about was Freddy. Was it possible that she still loved Freddy? And if that wasn't possible, then why did she feel this way?

"The guy is a bastard, Meredith," Toby said.

Right, Meredith thought. That was the predictable answer. Freddy had cheated so many people, why would he not cheat Meredith? He was a liar; why would he not lie to Meredith? Mmm, impossible to explain.

Meredith had believed that Freddy had adored her. Worshipped her.

The idea that she might have been wrong about that—so very, very wrong—made her dizzy and nauseous. She pulled away from Toby and bent at the waist, bringing her head to her knees. The pike position in diving. She thought, *Okay, this is where I crumble, where I dissolve. I fall to the floor and I...I cry.*

But no, she wouldn't. She took a breath and stood up.

"What do we do about the reporters?" she asked. "How do we make them leave?"

"Call the police?" he said.

"Are they breaking the law?" she asked.

"If they set foot on the property, they're trespassing."

"They won't set foot on the property," Meredith said. "Will they?"

"Call the police anyway?" Toby said, "Or...you could give them what they want. Give them a statement."

Right. They wanted a statement. They wanted Meredith to decry Freddy, call him a bastard, a liar, a cheater. She looked at Toby's face uncertainly, although it wasn't Toby's face she was seeing; it was Freddy's face. Just as Freddy had been unable to give Meredith certain things, so now Toby would be unable to give her the answer to...why.

Why? Had Meredith done something wrong? Was Samantha Deuce better than Meredith in some way? Was she able to give Freddy something Meredith couldn't give him? Meredith had given him everything. Everything.

Toby said, "I'll call the police anyway. And I have to call Connie. She'll want to know that there are barbarians at the gate. Okay?"

Meredith nodded. Toby went for his cell phone. Meredith went into her bathroom, where she retched into the toilet until there was nothing left inside of her.

Toby brought Meredith a mug of coffee that she couldn't even look at, much less drink, and his cell phone. He had Connie on the other line.

Meredith said, "Hello?"

Connie said, "Oh, honey. I'm so sorry."

Meredith was in the kitchen. She was in a bright, sunny room with a pack of wolves at her back. "It's a beautiful day," Meredith said. "You and Dan should do something fun. You should avoid the house until we figure out what to do about all these reporters."

"Dan called Ed Kapenash," Connie said. "They're sending someone out to disperse the crowd."

"I hope that works," Meredith said.

"Is there anything I can do?" Connie asked. "For you?"

Take me back to yesterday, Meredith thought. "No," she said. Everything that had to be done, she had to do herself.

"You don't even sound angry," Connie said. "Aren't you *angry,* Meredith?"

Angry, Meredith thought.

"You're not going to let him off the hook for this, too, are you?" Connie said.

"I haven't let him off the hook for any of his actions, Connie," Meredith said. She heard something confrontational in her voice. She didn't want to fight. She didn't want to feel. She wanted to *think.* She wanted to *know.* She said, "I'll call you later, okay?"

"Okay," Connie said. "I love you, you know."

Meredith had been waiting all summer to hear Connie speak those words. Meredith hoped she was sincere and not saying them out of pity. "I love you, too."

She managed to wash her face and change into clothes. She put on a very comfortable white skirt and a soft pink T-shirt. She brushed her hair and her teeth. But something about all of these simple actions felt final, as though she were doing them for the last time. How could she go on?

Toby knocked at the door. He poked his head in. "How are you doing? Are you okay?"

She wanted to be left alone. But she was terrified of being left alone. She said, "They're still out there?"

"Yes, but the police are coming any minute. I'm going down to wait for them. Will you be okay?"

Okay? she thought.

Meredith tried to be calm and rational. Unlike the eighth of December, when she was forced to deal with a situation of such enormous proportions her mind could scarcely comprehend it, today was simple. Today was a man cheating on his wife. She, Meredith, was the wife.

She didn't feel any pain yet; she was suspended in a kind of breathless shock. Why shock? She had seen Samantha and Freddy together in Freddy's den. She had caught Freddy with his hand on Samantha's back. Meredith had witnessed them together, but she had dismissed it. It was a piece of dandelion fuzz that she'd blown off her palm into the wind. And why? If she ignored it, then it wasn't real? What she didn't know couldn't hurt her? Was that true, also, of Freddy's heinous crimes? Hadn't she been staring them right in the face but been refusing to see?

Toby was still downstairs. Meredith crept along the hall, to Connie's master suite. She opened the door to Connie's bathroom.

The pills were there. Six amber bottles in a line. Meredith checked the label of each one, as though she'd forgotten the exact names of the drugs or the exact order she would find them in or the exact heft of each bottle in her hand. Connie hadn't been taking the pills.

Meredith wanted the Ativan. And, yes, it occurred to her to take the whole bottle and end her life right there in Connie's room. If what Samantha had told the press was true, if she and Fred had been *lovers*—at the thought of this word, Meredith gagged again—then what choice would Meredith have but to end her life?

She counted out three Ativan. She already had two, in a pill box in her bathroom. If she took all five, would that be too many? Maybe. She would save the two that she had and take three right here, right now. She knew what she was after: Something more than sleep, something less than death. She wanted to be knocked out, unconscious, unaware, unreachable, untouchable.

She made it back to her bedroom, shut the door, checked that the balcony doors were secure, climbed into bed, and buried her face in the sweet pink covers. It was too bad, she thought. It was such a beautiful day.

They had met Samantha when they bought the penthouse apartment at 824 Park Avenue. Samantha had seemed to come with the building. She was decorating three other apartments, and so her presence had been nearly as steady as that of Giancarlo the doorman. Meredith and Freddy kept bumping into Samantha in the elevator. Either she was holding great big books of fabric swatches, or she was accompanied by plasterers and painters. They bumped into her in the service elevator carrying a pair of blue and white Chinese vases once, and an exquisite Murano glass chandelier another time.

It was finally Freddy who said, "Maybe we should have that woman decorate our place."

Meredith said, "Who?"

"That blonde we keep seeing around here. I mean, our place could use some help."

What year would that have been? Ninety-seven? Ninety-eight? Meredith had tried not to take offense at Freddy's comment. She had "decorated" the penthouse much the same way she'd "decorated" the other apartments they'd lived in, which was to say, eclectically. Meredith wanted to achieve the look of an apartment in a Woody Allen film—lots and lots of books crammed on shelves, a few pieces of art, a ton of family photographs, old worn furniture in leather and suede and chintz, most of which had been inherited from her mother and grandmother. Meredith liked Annabeth Martin's silver tea service on a half-moon table next to a hundred-year-old Oxford dictionary that she'd found in a back room at the Strand. She liked a mishmash of objects that displayed her intellectual life and her broad range of tastes. But it was true that, compared to the apartments of the people the Delinns now socialized with, their penthouse seemed bohemian and cluttered. Unpolished. Undone. Meredith knew nothing about window treatments or fabrics or carpets or how to layer colors and textures or how to display the artwork they did have. As soon as Freddy suggested they hire a decorator, Meredith realized how pathetic her efforts had been in presenting what they owned. No one else had so many tattered paperback books on shelves; no one else had so many photographs of their children — it seemed immodest all of a sudden.

Furthermore, now that they had the penthouse, there were more rooms — whole rooms, in fact, that Meredith had no idea what to do with. The room that was to be Freddy's personal den had walnut library shelves with nothing on them but his and Meredith's matched framed diplomas from Princeton.

"It looks like a dentist's office," Freddy remarked.

And so, Meredith set out to introduce herself to this woman they kept seeing around, the decorator whose name (Meredith had discovered from eavesdropping) was Samantha Deuce. Meredith approached her one afternoon as she was standing under the building's awning in the rain, waiting for Giancarlo to hail her a cab. Meredith introduced herself — Meredith Delinn, the penthouse — and asked if Samantha would be willing to come up to the apartment sometime so they could talk about the decorating.

Samantha had made a wistful face — not a hundred percent genuine, Meredith didn't think — and said, "I wish I could. But I'm so slammed that I can't, in good conscience, take on another project. I'm sorry."

Meredith had immediately backpedaled, saying yes, of course, she understood. And then she'd retreated — shell-shocked and dejected — back into the building.

That night at dinner, she told Freddy that Samantha, the ubiquitous decorator, had turned her down.

"Turned you *down?*" Freddy said. "Who turns down a job like this? Were you clear, Meredith? Were you clear that we want her to do *the whole apartment?*"

"I was clear," Meredith said. "And she was clear. She doesn't have time for another project." There had been something about the look on Samantha's face that bugged Meredith. Her expression had been too *prepared,* as though she knew what Meredith was about to ask, as though she knew something about Meredith that Meredith had yet to figure out herself. Had Samantha heard unsavory things about the Delinns? And if so, what were those things? That they were nouveau riche? That they were without taste? That they were social climbers? Meredith and Freddy hadn't known anyone else in the building at that time; there was no one to speak for or against them.

"I'll talk to her," Freddy said, and Meredith remembered that his decision to step in had come as a relief. She was used to Freddy taking care of things. Nobody ever said no to him. And, in fact, two weeks later, Samantha was standing in their living room, gently caressing the back of Meredith's grandmother's sofa as though it were an elderly relative she was about to stick in a home. (Which was true in a way: Samantha relegated nearly all of Meredith's family furniture to storage first, and then, when it became clear that it would never be used, to the thrift shop.)

Meredith said brightly, "Oh, I'm glad you came up to see the apartment after all."

Samantha said, "Your husband convinced me."

Meredith thought, *He talked you right out of your good conscience?*

And now, it was clear that he had.

Samantha Champion Deuce was a brassy blonde, nearly six feet tall. She towered over Meredith. She had broad shoulders and large breasts and hazel eyes and a wide mouth. She wore lipstick in bright colors: fire-engine red, fuchsia, coral. She wasn't a beauty, though there were beautiful things about her. She captivated. She was always the dominant personality in the room. She had a sexy, raspy voice like Anne Bancroft or Demi Moore; once you heard it, you couldn't get enough of it. She would say to Meredith, "Buy this, it's fabulous." And Meredith would buy it. She would walk into a room and say, "We're going to do it this way." And that was how the room would be done. She never asked for Meredith's opinion. The few times that Meredith expressed disapproval, Samantha turned to her and said, "You mean you don't *like* it?"

Not as though her feelings were hurt, but as though she couldn't imagine anyone in the world not liking it.

Hmmpf, she'd say. As if Meredith's response had stumped her.

Samantha moved through her life with extreme self-confidence. It was so pronounced that Meredith was drawn to studying Samantha's mannerisms: her wicked smile, the way she swore to great, elegant effect ("fucking Scalamandré, I fucking love it!"), the way she shimmered in the presence of every man from Freddy Delinn to the Guatemalan plaster guy ("José, you are a beast and a god. I could *eat* you").

As Meredith got to know her better, she learned that Samantha had been raised with four older brothers in Dobbs Ferry, New York. Her family was middle-class royalty. The four brothers were the best high-school athletes the town had ever seen; they all received Division I athletic scholarships. Samantha herself had played basketball all the way through Colby College. She married her college sweetheart, the preppy, handsome, and completely underwhelming Trent Deuce. They had lived downtown on Great Jones Street until their first child was born, when they moved to Ridgewood, New Jersey. Trent had worked for Goldman Sachs, but he'd been canned after 9/11. He then worked for a buddy who had a smaller brokerage firm — really, the details of Trent's career were always presented vaguely by Samantha, though Freddy had gathered enough information to conclude that Trent Deuce was a loser and would be better off at a car dealership in Secaucus selling used Camaros. (Freddy rarely spoke badly of *anyone,* so hearing him say this was flabbergasting. Now, Freddy's dismissal of Trent made perfect sense.)

Somewhere during the course of Trent's peripatetic career, Samantha had deemed it necessary to go back to work. She decorated a friend's house in Ridgewood. (Here, it should be noted that Meredith and Freddy had never once been invited to Samantha's home in Ridgewood, and Meredith had been grateful for that. Who wanted to make the trip from Manhattan to the Jersey suburbs?

No one. In Meredith's mind, Ridgewood was soccer mom/Olive Garden hell.) After the success of the Ridgewood friend's home, Samantha decorated the Manhattan apartment of the Ridgewood friend's mother, who happened to be fantastically wealthy, have millions of friends, and entertain often and lavishly. This set Samantha's career on its way. By the time Meredith met Samantha, she was a wealthy woman in her own right.

But not quite.

There was a subtle class distinction between Samantha and the Delinns—always. On the surface, Samantha told Meredith and Freddy what to do and they did it. But there was the underlying fact that she worked for them.

The Yankees memorabilia, the antique piggy banks. A certain lavender Hermès tie, Freddy's favorite tie, had also been one of Samantha's picks. Even the pink and tangerine palette of the Palm Beach house—which Meredith had bucked against—Freddy had defended. Pink and tangerine? Seriously? Samantha had used a pair of Lilly Pulitzer golf pants as her inspiration.

She's the expert, Fred said.

Samantha had something that Freddy valued. A knowledge, a perspective. He was a rich man. They, Freddy and Meredith, were a rich couple. Samantha was the one who showed them how to be rich. She had shown them how to spend. Nearly every extravagance that Meredith indulged in, Samantha Deuce had introduced her to.

Six and a half years. The summer of 2004. Had Fred and Samantha been in love? *Think, Meredith! Remember!*

She remembered Samantha in Southampton, decorating the house in whites and ivories, despite Meredith's protests that she had two teenage boys who also lived in the house, and Meredith wanted Leo and Carver and their friends to be comfortable dragging sand in, or sitting on the sofa in damp bathing suits. But the Southampton house had been done to Samantha's specifications, in whites and ivories, including a white grand piano that Meredith found tacky. ("Don't you think a white grand piano just screams Liberace? Or bad Elton John?" Meredith said. Samantha's eyes widened. "You mean you don't *like* it?")

Fred and Meredith used to meet Trent and Samantha for dinner at Nick and Toni's; inevitably, Freddy and Samantha would be seated on one side of the table, and Meredith and Trent on the other. Meredith struggled with conversation with Trent. She tried to remember to read the sports section of *USA Today* before they all went out, so she would at least have that to fall back on. More and more often, Samantha showed up alone, claiming that Trent was stuck in the city "working," or that she'd left him at home to care for the kids, because he absolutely never saw them during the week. Trent was always dismissed in this way, and so there had been many nights where it was just the three of them—Meredith, Freddy, and Samantha. Freddy used to say, "I'm going out with my wife and my girlfriend." Meredith had laughed at this; she had found it innocent and charming. She had occasionally been suspicious of dark, exotic beauties—women who resembled Trina or the lovely Catalan university student—although, really, Meredith was so certain of Freddy's undying devotion that these worries had flickered, and then extinguished.

It was around 2004 when Freddy had started to take care of himself again. Like everyone else, he stopped eating carbs for a while, but that was too hard, especially since he couldn't resist the focaccia or the ravioli with truffle butter at Rinaldo's. But he ate more vegetables. He had salads for lunch instead of reubens and omelets. He started working out at the gym in their building. The first time he'd told Meredith he was going downstairs to work out, Meredith said, "You're going to do *what?*" Freddy had never been much of an athlete or an exerciser. His tennis game was adequate and he could swim, but he didn't have time for golf. He didn't even like tossing the lacrosse ball with the boys. Meredith could no sooner see him lifting weights than she could see him break dancing with the Harlem kids in Central Park. But he went at the workout regimen with a vengeance; he hired a personal trainer named Tom. Some days he spent more time with Tom than with Meredith. He lost weight, he developed muscles. He had to have a whole new set of suits made on his next trip to London. He let his hair grow longer. It was really gray by then, more salt than pepper, and his beard was coming in gray, and some days he went two or three days without shaving so he would have a scruff that Meredith found sexy but that she suspected was raising eyebrows at the office. She said, "Did you have a fight with your razor?" Freddy said he wanted to try something different. He grew a goatee.

Samantha had loved the goatee, Meredith remembered. She used to stroke it like a cat, and Meredith had found this funny. She had wanted Samantha to join her in teasing Freddy. *That's his midlife crisis,* Meredith said.

Could be worse, Samantha had said.

When Samantha was around, Freddy was looser, he laughed more, he occasionally had a glass of wine, he occasionally stayed out past nine thirty. Once, the three of them had even gone dancing at a nightclub. Samantha had been immediately absorbed by the crowd. When Meredith and Freddy found her, she was dancing with a bunch of the gorgeous, emaciated Bulgarian women whom Meredith had seen around town — working behind the counter at the fancy food store or babysitting the art galleries — and their hulking boyfriends. They all abandoned the dance floor for the bar, where they did shots of Patrón. Freddy had followed them to the bar, he magnanimously paid for ten shots of Patrón, and then he tried to convince Samantha to leave the club with him and Meredith. Nope, she didn't want to go.

Meredith said, *Come on, Freddy. We'll go. She can stay. She's going back to Bridgehampton tonight anyway.*

But Freddy didn't want Samantha to stay. He had words with her that turned into an argument. Meredith couldn't hear what they were saying to each other, though she did see Freddy take Samantha's arm and Samantha pull her arm back. Now, of course, it was clear that it had been a lover's spat. Freddy didn't want Samantha to stay with this group of young, Eastern European hedonists. She might do drugs, she might participate in group sex and find a younger, hotter lover. But at that time, all Meredith thought was that it was a good thing she and Freddy had never had a daughter. Freddy's concern for Samantha that night had struck Meredith as avuncular, bordering on fatherly, even though Samantha was only seven years younger than Meredith and nine years younger than Freddy.

They had left Samantha at the club. Freddy had been fuming. Meredith had said, *Come on now, Fred. She's a big girl. She can take care of herself.*

What an idiot Meredith had been!

Was the summer of 2004 when the nickname had surfaced? At some point, Freddy had started calling Samantha "Champ," a shortened form of her maiden name, Champion. Meredith had noticed the sudden use of the nickname, and she thought, *Hmmm, I wonder what precipitated that?* But she'd never asked. Samantha was a part of their lives; after the decorating was done, she became their lifestyle consultant. She was always around—in their homes, in Fred's office, on the phone. Meredith had assumed the nickname came about organically from some conversation between Freddy and Samantha.

Does the word "champ" mean anything to you?

When had they met for this affair? And where? Six and a half years. Safe to say they had met hundreds of times then, right? But in Meredith's mind, Freddy had spent every night in bed beside her. He had been in bed by nine thirty, asleep by ten, awake by five, in his home office until six thirty when he left for the office-office. Had Meredith and Freddy spent nights apart from each other? Well, yes: Freddy had to travel. He went to London to do business with the office there, and that was where he'd gotten his suits tailored. Had Samantha met him in London? It would be safe to say yes. She had probably introduced Freddy to the tailor whose name he would not disclose. That tailor probably thought Samantha was Freddy's wife. There were times when Meredith was in Palm Beach when Freddy had to fly back to New York. Lots of times—especially in recent years. Had he seen Samantha then? Yes; of course, the answer was yes. Where did they meet? (Why did Meredith have to know this? Why torture herself with the details? What did it matter now?) Did they meet at a hotel? If so, which hotel? Did they meet in Ridgewood? Certainly not. Did they meet in Meredith and Freddy's apartment? Did they have sex in Meredith and Freddy's *bed?* Meredith could see how awful and insidious this was going to get.

Did they rendezvous on the yacht *Bebe?* There had been plenty of times when Freddy had flown to "check out" one problem or another with *Bebe*—when the yacht was in the Mediterranean, and when she was in Newport or Bermuda. But *Bebe* had a crew and a captain. If Freddy had been on board with Samantha, certain people would have known about it.

So certain people knew about it. Billy, their captain knew, and Cameron, the first mate knew. They were complicit.

Samantha said she'd always wanted to see their property in Cap d'Antibes, but this may have been a smoke screen. She may have been quite familiar with the property.

As Meredith awoke from her stupor—someone was calling to her from the bottom of a deep hole, or she was the one in the deep hole and someone was calling to her from the top—she flashed on the photograph that Samantha had selected for Freddy's office. A photograph of Malacca, in Malaysia. As far as Meredith knew, Freddy had never been to Malaysia; he'd never been to Asia at all, except for his trip to Hong Kong before they were engaged. Or was Meredith wrong about that? Had Freddy and Samantha been to this place, Malacca, together? The photograph had been hanging right behind Freddy's desk. What had hung there previously? Meredith tried to think. Another photograph.

Toby had her by the shoulder. The room was dark; there was a light on in the hallway behind him and she could see the outline of Connie standing there.

"What time is it?" Meredith asked.

"Nine o'clock," Toby said. "At night. You slept all day."

Meredith was relieved. It was nighttime. She could go back to sleep. She closed her eyes. But the dark was terrifying. She was unmoored, in danger of floating away. She opened her eyes.

"Toby?" she whispered.

"Yes?"

She wanted to ask him something, but she didn't have to. She already knew the answer. Veronica's funeral had been in July of 2004. Meredith had been on Long Island, and Freddy had arranged for a helicopter to take Meredith to New York and then a private car to drive her down to Villanova. Meredith had asked Freddy to come with her. And what had he said? "I never met the woman, Meredith. This is your chance to be with Connie. Go be with Connie. I'll stay here and hold down the fort."

Hold down the fort?

"Never mind," Meredith said to Toby now.

Meredith felt Toby staring at her, then he retreated to the hallway and pulled the door closed.

Meredith awoke in the morning, dying of thirst. She slipped downstairs to the kitchen and poured herself a tall glass of ice water. She drank deeply and thought about how there were times when you were just grateful for cold, clean water, and this was one of those times.

Connie appeared in the kitchen, floating like a ghost or an angel in a white nightgown and robe. Meredith figured that Dan must be upstairs.

Connie hugged Meredith.

"Oh," Connie said. "I'm sorry." She pulled away. She had tears in her eyes. "I am so, so sorry."

Meredith nodded. It hurt to move her head. Everything hurt.

She hadn't thought that anything could hurt again after what she'd been through, but yes, this hurt. This hurt differently. God, she couldn't believe she was even thinking this: it hurt worse.

Connie said, "You slept for nearly twenty-four hours."

Meredith exhaled. She said, "I took three of your Ativan."

Connie hugged her again. "Oh, honey."

"I think maybe you'd better hide the rest of the pills. It did occur to me to take them all."

"Okay," Connie said. "Okay."

"I thought you'd be mad," Meredith said. "I snooped around your bathroom when I first got here. I've snuck five Ativan altogether and two Ambien. I stole them."

"I don't care about the pills," Connie said. "I care about you."

"I don't know what to do," Meredith said.

"What do you want to do?" Connie asked.

Meredith pulled away and eyed her friend. "I want to talk to Fred."

"Oh, honey, you're kidding."

"I'm not kidding. That's all I want. I don't want to read about their love affair in her book. I want to hear about it from my husband. I want him to confess to me. I want to hear the truth from him."

"What makes you think Freddy would tell you the truth?" Connie said.

Meredith had no answer for this.

A little while later, both Toby and Dan came downstairs. Connie made coffee. Meredith thought, miraculously, that the coffee smelled good. She was back to counting each small blessing: cold water, hot coffee with real cream and plenty of sugar.

Dan and Toby were concerned about the practical problem they faced.

"The reporters are still out there," Toby said. "In fact, they seem to have multiplied overnight."

Dan looked at Meredith apologetically. "I called Ed Kapenash yesterday morning, and by noon, the reporters were all gone. We could have gotten you out of here for a little while. But now they're back. I could call Eddie again, but..."

"Or we could try Bud Attatash," Toby said. "He seems like the type of guy who owns a shotgun and isn't afraid to use it."

"It's okay," Meredith said. She was embarrassed that Dan had to ask personal favors from the chief of police on her behalf. She sat down at the table with her coffee. Three months ago, she had been all alone. Now she had friends. She had a team. She added this to her list of things to be grateful for. "I'm going to enjoy this coffee, and then I have some phone calls to make."

"I'll make French toast," Connie said.

Upstairs, in the privacy of her bedroom — balcony doors still shut tight — Meredith called Dev at the office, while praying a Hail Mary.

The receptionist answered, and Meredith said, "This is Mrs. Delinn, calling for Devon Kasper."

And to Meredith's shock, the receptionist said, "Absolutely, Mrs. Delinn. Let me get him for you."

Dev came to the phone. "Holy shit, Meredith."

"I know."

"Once you gave me the name, the Feds did the rest. It was all right there. All over his date book, his planner..."

"Stop," Meredith said. "I didn't know they were having an affair."

"What?"

"I knew that 'champ' was Samantha. That was what Freddy called her. But I didn't know they were sleeping together."

"Meredith."

"Devon," Meredith said. "I didn't know that my husband and Samantha Deuce were having an affair."

There was silence. Then Dev said, "Okay, I believe you."

"Thank you." She sighed. "There are reporters all over the front lawn."

"Good," Dev said. "You should make a statement."

"No," Meredith said.

"Meredith," Dev said gently. "This could help you."

"The fact that my husband was betraying me, not honoring our vows, *for six and a half years,* could help me? I can see you know nothing about marriage. I can see you know *nothing* about the human heart."

Dev, wisely, changed tactics. "The information about the star was good information."

"Did you find the account?" Meredith asked. "Did you find Thad Orlo?"

"The Feds are still working on it," Dev said. "I can't tell you what they've uncovered."

"Even though it was my information to begin with?" Meredith said.

"Even though," Dev said. He paused. "Do you think this Champion woman knew what was going on with Fred and the business?"

"You'd have to ask her that," Meredith said. She wondered how she would feel if it turned out that Samantha *had* known about the Ponzi scheme. Would Meredith feel betrayed? Would Freddy have shared his biggest secret with Samantha, but not with his wife? Then again, wasn't *not* knowing its own kind of gift? But Meredith was the one who had lost everything. Samantha was still out walking around, still running a decorating business, still driving her children to Little League and dance, still cozy at home with her underwhelming husband, her community, and her friends. Samantha Deuce wasn't under investigation, her home wasn't being vandalized, she wasn't being stalked. She might be now, with this admission. Samantha must have had no choice. The Feds must have had ironclad evidence; they must have had phone records or eight-by-ten glossies or a video. Or, perhaps, Samantha had been so overwhelmed by her love for Fred that she decided to talk. Or an $8 million book deal sounded good.

"There's something else I want to tell you about," Meredith said. "There's a framed photograph in Freddy's office. It's a street scene in an Asian city. Freddy said the city is called Malacca. It's in Malaysia. It's the cultural capital of Malaysia."

"And this is relevant because..."

"Because to my knowledge, Freddy has never been to Malacca. Or Malaysia at all. And yet this was a photograph that Samantha bought for Fred's office. The invoice came after he went to jail: twelve hundred dollars. Freddy hung the photograph right behind his desk." At that instant, Meredith remembered. The street scene in Malacca had replaced a grainy photograph of Freddy with his brother, David: the two of them bare chested in cutoff shorts, standing in front of a Pontiac GTO that David had restored. It was the only surviving picture of the two brothers together, and Freddy had replaced it with Malacca? "This photograph had a secret meaning for Freddy, I think. I'm sure of it now."

"Like it was a place he trysted with the Deuce woman?" Dev said.

"Just find the photograph," Meredith said.

"Okay. I'll do that. Your instincts are good."

"And Dev?"

"Yes."

There was one last thing. The most important, vital thing. But she was having a hard time thinking of how to ask.

"I need to talk to Fred."

"Fred," Dev said flatly.

"I need to talk to him," Meredith said. "About this and about other things. Can I call him, or do I have to travel to Butner?"

"Traveling to Butner would be a waste of your time," Dev said.

Part of her was relieved to hear this. The thought of leaving Nantucket was debilitating enough. She couldn't imagine traveling to North Carolina in the brutal heat of August, or of suffering the dust and filth and indignity in order to visit the prison's most infamous inmate. There would be reporters everywhere like buzzards on fresh roadkill.

"Really?" she said. "A waste?"

"There's been no change in his demeanor," Dev said. "He won't speak to anyone. Not even the priest. It's unclear if he *can't* speak or if he's choosing not to speak."

"He might choose to speak to me, though," Meredith said. "Right?"

"He might," Dev said. "But it's a gamble."

"Can I call him?" Meredith asked.

"He's permitted one phone call a week."

Meredith swallowed. "Has he...? Has he taken any other phone calls?" What she wanted to know was if Freddy had talked to Samantha.

"No," Dev said. "No phone calls. He speaks to no one."

"Can you help me set up a phone call?" Meredith asked.

Dev sighed. It was the sigh of a much older man. Meredith was aging him. "I can try. Do you want me to try? Really, Meredith?"

"Really," Meredith said.

"Okay," Dev said. "I'll contact the prison and see what I can do."

"Thank you," Meredith said. "It's important to me."

"Make a statement, Meredith," Dev said. "Save yourself."

She had spent the whole summer wondering how to save herself, and now, she found, she didn't care. *Goddamn you, Freddy!* she thought (zillionth and seventh). She didn't care if she lived or died; she didn't care if she was dragged off to prison. She would, like Fred, fold herself into an origami beetle. She wouldn't speak to another human being as long as she lived.

And was that what Fred had wanted all along? Had he meant for them to be ruined together? Had he asked her to transfer the $15 million so that she would go to prison?

Save herself? For what?

Brilliant and talented. That girl owns my heart.

Mommy, watch me!

Sail on Silvergirl. Sail on by. Your time has come to shine. All your dreams are on their way.

Meredith sat on her bed and took a stab at writing a statement. She pictured herself marching out to the end of Connie's driveway to face the eager reporters; this would be the juiciest news since OJ drove off in the white Bronco. She imagined her face and graying hair on every TV screen in America. She couldn't do it.

But she wrote anyway.

I have been informed that my husband, Fred Delinn, who is serving one hundred and fifty years in federal prison for his financial crimes, had been conducting an affair with our decorator, Samantha Champion Deuce, for over six years. This news has come as a profound shock. I had no idea about the affair, and I am still ignorant of the most basic details. Please know that I am hurting, just the way that any spouse who discovers an infidelity hurts. My husband's financial crimes were a public matter. His infidelity, however, is a private matter, and I beg you to respect it as such. Thank you.

Meredith read her statement over. It was … minimalist, nearly cold. But would anyone be surprised by this? She had an opportunity here to say that she'd known nothing about Freddy's financial dealings. Should she add a line? *Clearly, my husband kept many secrets from me.* But that felt too confessional. *I knew nothing about Freddy's Ponzi scheme and nothing about this affair.* I didn't know Freddy was stealing everyone's money and I didn't know he was romancing Samantha Deuce, our best friend.

I didn't know Freddy.

"Jesus!" she said, to no one.

*   *   *

She took the statement down to the kitchen where Connie and Dan and Toby were still gathered around the table, finishing up plates of golden brown, cinnamony French toast.

"The *Post* is going to have a field day with this," Connie was saying. Then she saw Meredith and clammed up.

Meredith waved the paper at them. "I wrote a statement," she said.

"Read it," Connie said.

"I can't read it," Meredith said. "Here."

Connie read the statement, then passed it to Toby. Toby read it, then passed it to Dan. When they finished, Meredith said, "Well?"

"You're too nice," Connie said.

"The guy's a bastard," Toby said. His face was bright red— from the sun or from anger, Meredith couldn't tell. "Why don't you just align yourself with the rest of America and come right out and call the guy a bastard? If you aren't tougher on him, people are going to think you were conspiring with him."

"Is that what *you* think?" Meredith asked.

"No..." Toby said.

"I've been holding my tongue because that was how I was raised," Meredith said. "I don't feel like spilling my guts all over the evening news. I don't want the *details* of my *marriage* popping up across the Internet. I don't even want to make this statement. I think it's crass."

"Because you're a repressed Main Line snob," Toby said. "You're just like your parents, and your grandmother."

"Well, it's true my parents never battled it out on the front lawn," Meredith said. "They didn't hurl their wedding china at one another. But, for the record, I'm not 'repressed.' You know damn well I'm not 'repressed'! But I also didn't spread my love and affection around the way you've apparently spent your life doing. And the way my husband did."

"Hey, now," Connie said. She put a hand on Meredith's arm.

Toby lowered his voice. "I just think you need to sound angrier."

"At who?" Meredith said. "You know what I thought when I met Freddy Delinn? I thought, here's a guy who's rock solid; this guy isn't going to ditch me so he can go off sailing in the Seychelles. You, Toby, you made Freddy look like a safe bet."

"Oh, boy," Dan said.

"But I never lied to you, Meredith," Toby said. "You have to give me that. I was insensitive when I was nineteen years old. I was possibly even worse than insensitive when I saw you a few years ago. I know I hurt you and I'm sorry. But I never lied to you."

Meredith stared at Toby, then at Connie and Dan. "You're right," she said. "He's right."

"The statement is what it is," Connie said. "It's a statement. It's classy and discreet, worthy of Annabeth Martin." Connie cut her eyes at Toby. "And that is a *good* thing. So, are you going out there to read it now?"

"I can't," Meredith said.

"You can't?"

"I want *you* to read it," Meredith said.

"Me?" Connie said.

"Please," Meredith said. "Be my spokesperson. Because I can't read it."

Connie got a strange expression on her face. In high school, every time Meredith had been sick, or at early diving practice, Connie had jumped at the chance to do the readings at morning chapel. She had been sick with jealousy when Meredith gave her salutatorian's speech at graduation. Something like 90 percent of Americans were afraid of public speaking—but not Connie.

"Me?" she said. "Your spokesperson?"

"Please," Meredith said. It would be better to have beautiful, serene, red-haired Connie read the statement. America would love Connie. People would see that Meredith did have someone who believed in her. But most important, Meredith wouldn't have to do it herself.

"Okay," Connie said, standing up.

"You're not going out like that?" Dan asked. Connie was still in her filmy nightgown and robe.

"No," Connie said. "I'll wear clothes."

A few minutes later, Connie was dressed in a pair of white linen pants and a green linen shirt and flat sandals. She looked like an ad for Eileen Fisher. With the paper in hand, she walked straight out to the end of the driveway, for the weirdest press conference ever. Flashbulbs started going off. Meredith closed the front door behind her.

Meredith wanted to watch Connie from the window, but she was certain she would be photographed if she did. So she sat at the oval dining table with Toby and Dan, and waited. She imagined all of the people across the country who would hear Meredith's words come out of Connie's mouth.

Well, for starters, Ashlyn would see Connie on TV. Had Connie thought of this? Leo and Carver would see Connie. Gwen Marbury would see Connie, Amy Rivers, Connie's friend Lizbet, Toby's ex-wife in New Orleans, Dustin Leavitt, Trina Didem, Giancarlo the doorman, Julius Erving. Everyone in America would watch the footage. Samantha herself would watch it. Possibly even Freddy would watch it, on a TV in prison.

And what would he think?

A few minutes later, Connie stepped back into the house. The reporters, far from dispersing, were yelling things. What were they yelling?

Connie looked pink and winded, as if she had just finished a foot race. She was perspiring.

Dan said, "How'd it go?"

Toby said, "Water, Con?"

Connie nodded. "Please."

They all trekked into the kitchen, where Toby fixed his sister a glass of ice water with lemon.

"Why are they yelling?" Meredith asked.

"Questions," Connie said. "They have questions."

Meredith thought, They *have questions?*

Connie said, "Mostly, they want to know if you're going to divorce him."

"Divorce him?" Meredith said.

"Leave him."

"Leave him?" Meredith didn't get it. Or she thought maybe the reporters didn't get it. The man was in jail for 150 years. He was never getting out. Maybe people thought Meredith would move to North Carolina, would visit him every week, would lobby her congressman and pray and wait for ten or twelve years for possible conjugal visitation rights. Meredith and Freddy making love in some tin-roofed trailer. Maybe that was what Meredith had envisioned for herself. But no—Meredith had envisioned nothing of the sort. The present was so overwhelming, she'd had no energy or imagination for any kind of future, with or without Freddy.

Would she divorce him?

She didn't know.

She was Catholic, she believed in the sacrament of marriage, she believed in the vows—till death do us part. Her parents had remained married, and her grandparents. She and Freddy would never live together as husband and wife again, so what would be the point of getting divorced?

Across the kitchen, she and Toby locked eyes.

The point of getting divorced was that Meredith would be free to get an annulment and marry again. Start over.

The notion was exhausting.

"I can't answer any of those questions," Meredith said. "I don't know what I'm doing."

Connie hugged Meredith so hard, Meredith nearly tipped over.

"It's going to be okay," Connie said. "I think the statement worked, or it will work, once they realize it's all they're going to get."

"So you didn't say anything else?" Meredith said. "You didn't answer for me?"

"It was hard," Connie said. "But I just stood there with a plastic smile on my face. "

"We should see what it looks like on TV," Toby said.

Connie jumped at this idea, and Meredith couldn't blame her, though Meredith didn't want to see the statement broadcast on TV; she wanted three more Ativan and a dark bedroom. She wanted to talk to Freddy; her throat ached with the need. *Tell me everything. Tell me who you really were.*

Toby and Dan and Connie went into the sitting room and turned on the television. Meredith lingered in the hallway, not committing to watching, not committing to hiding upstairs. She was dangerously close to the front door; anyone might see her through the sidelights. She stepped into the sitting room. She heard Connie reading her words: *Please know that I am hurting…* She saw Connie on the screen, looking natural and calm and poised. The channel was CNN. The banner at the bottom of the screen read: *Meredith Delinn spokesperson, Constance Flute, responds to the news of love affair between Freddy Delinn and the couple's decorator, Samantha Deuce.*

In the background, Meredith could see Connie's house.

The banner changed to read: *Meredith Delinn seeking refuge on Nantucket Island.*

It was her they were talking about, her life. That was her best friend speaking her words. They showed the house—this very house where they were now watching TV. It was weirdly reflexive.

Connie said, "I look awful."

Toby said, "It's not really about you, Con."

Dan said, "You look great."

Meredith needed to thank Connie for going out there on her behalf and reading the statement, but she couldn't find the words.

And then the phone rang.

*   *   *

Toby answered. He said, "May I ask who's calling?"

Meredith started to shake. She clung to the soft material of her skirt.

Toby put a hand over the receiver. "It's your attorney."

Meredith took the phone upstairs to her room. She reminded herself to breathe. She was light-headed; the caffeine from the coffee darted through her like lightning bolts. She felt a pressure in her bowels. But not now, with Dev on the phone. She lay down on her bed.

"Two things," Dev said. He sounded more chipper than he had earlier. Maybe his coffee had kicked in, too. "I just saw the statement on TV."

"Already?" Meredith said.

"We have a twenty-four-hour news feed in the office," Dev said. "Everyone does these days."

"And…?" she said.

"You could have said more," he said. "And you could have said it yourself."

Meredith nodded, though of course he couldn't see this. "I couldn't…"

"Because you know what people's response will be. Is already."

"What?"

"That you hired someone to do it for you. A spokesperson."

"I didn't *hire* Connie. She's my friend. I didn't have the guts to do it myself. She offered."

"I'm just telling you the perception. What people will think."

"I don't care what people think," Meredith said.

"You do, though," Dev said.

Meredith thought, *He's right. I do.*

Taking pity on her, he said, "But it was better than nothing. You communicated *something.* That's what matters."

"The second thing?" Meredith said. The caffeine high was fading. She was suddenly exhausted.

"I spoke to the warden at Butner," Dev said.

Her bowels squelched. She put a hand to her abdomen.

"He's looking into it for you," Dev said. "The phone call."

Dan had to leave the house to go to work. He asked if anyone was up for steaks that night at his house.

Toby said, "Not tonight, man."

Meredith said nothing. She was now the fun-sucker Dan had feared she would be.

Connie said, "Maybe. Call later."

"You guys should go," Meredith said. Dan was leaving soon for a three-day camping trip to New Hampshire with his sons. And by the time he returned, there would be less than a week left before Labor Day. It was all going to end; there was nothing Meredith could do to stop it.

Connie and Meredith and Toby retreated to the back deck. It was hot; Meredith wanted to swim, but she was afraid if she tried to swim, she would drown. Her limbs felt light and useless. She was a husk. She was a bladder filled with the hot, stinking air of anxiety.

Toby said, "You should divorce him, Meredith."

"Leave her be, Toby," Connie scolded. Then a few seconds later, she said, "You *should* divorce him. I'll pay for it."

Meredith laughed a sad, dry laugh. She hadn't even considered cost.

Toby swam. Meredith moved in and out of consciousness. She felt sluggish, then jumpy; the Ativan were exacting revenge. Toby became Harold, Harold had been brutally killed, and it was Meredith's fault. It was like Meredith had a hex on her, why not blame her for everything, the oil spill in the Gulf, the bloodshed in the

Middle East. Why, oh why, had Samantha spoken? Everyone would hate Samantha now, too, her life would be ruined. She must have loved Freddy, must love him still if she was going to allow him to destroy her life. She still had young kids, one of them only ten. Her business would go kaput, or maybe not. Maybe infidelity boosted a decorator's cachet. What did Meredith know? Samantha was writing a book. Meredith could write a book, should write a book, but what would that book say? *I wasn't paying attention. I was moving blithely through my days. I accepted what Freddy told me as the truth. I had never been exposed to lying or liars growing up; I didn't know what to look for.*

Connie said, "What are you thinking about?"

Meredith said, "Nothing."

The phone in the house rang. Meredith nearly leapt out of her chair at the sound. She knew she shouldn't answer it, but she hoped it was Dev calling back with an answer from the warden. She checked the caller ID: *NUMBER UNAVAILABLE.* Meredith couldn't help herself: she picked up.

A woman's voice said, "Meredith?"

Meredith felt like someone's hands were around her neck. She felt like she had a golf ball stuck in her throat, or one of the gobstoppers the boys used to buy at the candy store in Southampton.

"It's Samantha," the woman said, though of course Meredith knew this.

"No," Meredith said.

"Meredith, please."

Please what? What did Samantha want? Did she expect to bond with Meredith now that she had been exposed as Freddy's lover? Did she think that she and Meredith would be sister-wives, do the blended family thing the way Toby was so content doing? Meredith as some sort of ersatz aunt to Samantha's children? Meredith and Samantha joining forces to appeal Freddy's sentence?

"No," Meredith said, and she hung up.

*　　*　　*

The phone rang again an hour and six minutes later. Meredith was hyperaware of time passing. She thought of Samantha stroking Freddy's goatee. He had grown the goatee for Samantha, he had started going to the gym for Samantha. Everything had been for Samantha.

Meredith believed that it had all started when she went to Veronica's funeral. Or shortly after. Because Freddy sensed something, because Meredith came back addled and distracted. Freddy had asked her how the funeral was, and she had said, "Oh, it was fine," though it hadn't been fine; it had been an emotional sweat bath, but Meredith had stayed true to Freddy. She had stayed true, but not Freddy. He had stepped out of bounds. He had called Samantha, or something had sparked between the two of them in person. Meredith understood that. Because of what had happened between her and Toby at the funeral, she understood. But when you're married, you smother those sparks. You step on them, you extinguish them.

Meredith felt like she was going to vomit again. When she checked the caller ID, it gave the name of the law firm.

"Hello?" Meredith said.

"Meredith?" It was Dev.

"Yes," she said.

"Boy, do I have news for you," he said. "Sit down and fasten your seatbelt."

Meredith didn't like the way this sounded. At all. She said warily, "What is it?"

"Listen to this: There were four numbered accounts at the bank in Switzerland where Thad Orlo was most recently employed that looked like they might have links to Delinn Enterprises. Each of the accounts had the same numbers and letters as the one on your supposed NASA certificate, only in a different order. These accounts were all "managed" by Thad Orlo, and each account contained either a little over or a little under a billion dollars. But these were holding accounts; there was no action on them."

Meredith said nothing. She hated to say it, but she no longer cared about Thad Orlo or the missing money. Still, she had the wherewithal to ask, "Whose accounts were they?"

"All four accounts were under the name of Kirby Delarest."

Meredith gasped.

Dev said, "Wait, it gets better."

"But you know who Kirby Delarest is, right?" Meredith asked. "He lived near us in Palm Beach. He was an investor."

"Not an investor," Dev said. "He was Freddy's henchman. He was the one responsible for hiding the money and moving it around."

"He's dead," Meredith said. She thought of Amy Rivers, her lip curled in disgust. "He killed himself."

"He killed himself," Dev said, "because he was in so deep. Because he was afraid he was going to get caught. But Meredith…" Here, Dev paused. Meredith could picture him pushing back his floppy bangs or adjusting his glasses. "He was not only investing with Thad Orlo. He *was* Thad Orlo."

"What?" Meredith said.

"Kirby Delarest and Thad Orlo were the same person. He held two passports—one American, Kirby Delarest, and one Danish, Thad Orlo. Thad Orlo had an apartment in Switzerland where he worked for the Swiss bank and managed four accounts, which contained a total of four billion dollars. Kirby Delarest of Palm Beach, Florida, owned three large condo buildings in West Palm as well as a P.F. Chang's restaurant and a couple of rinky-dink strip malls. His real action, though, was overseas. He hid Freddy's clients' money and kept it safe. Four billion dollars. Can you believe it?"

Meredith reminded herself to breathe. She saw Connie coming up the stairs from the beach rubbing her wet hair with a towel, and she prayed that Connie wouldn't come inside and ask if Meredith wanted a turkey sandwich for lunch. Meredith needed to process what she'd just heard; she felt like she was torn between two worlds. There was this world, Nantucket, with the ocean and the outdoor shower and lunch on the deck, and then there was the world of international banking and double identities and lies. Kirby Delarest was Thad Orlo. Kirby had been tall and blond and lean, and he'd had that accent, which he'd claimed he'd acquired growing up in Wisconsin. Meredith knew something was wrong with that answer, but she hadn't questioned him. What had Freddy always said? Midwesterners were the most honest people on earth. Ha! Kirby Delarest had been in cahoots with Freddy. His daughters always wore those beautiful matching Bonpoint dresses. Meredith thought of the afternoon when she had discovered Freddy and Kirby Delarest by the pool, the bottle of Petrus consumed by two men on a Wednesday afternoon to celebrate the fact that they were robbing the whole world blind. Kirby Delarest had shot himself in the head rather than face Freddy's fate.

Meredith's eyes burned like she was in the desert. The account numbers had all been variations on the phony NASA star. These were Silver Girl accounts. Did that implicate her further? Please, she prayed, no.

"So you found the money, then?" she said. "Four billion? That's a lot of money."

"No, no," Dev said. "The money was withdrawn last October. All of it—gone, vanished. Moved, most likely in cash, to another location."

"When in October?" Meredith asked, dreading the answer.

"October seventeenth."

Meredith shut her eyes. Connie tapped on the glass door. Meredith opened her eyes. Connie mouthed, *Are you okay?*

"That's ..." Meredith said.

"What?" Dev said.

"You're sure it was the seventeenth?" Meredith said. "The seventeenth of October?"

"What is it?" Dev said. "What is the seventeenth of October?"

"Samantha Deuce's birthday," Meredith said.

"Okay," Dev said. "Okay, okay, okay. Could be a coincidence. But probably not. Let me call you back."

"Wait!" Meredith said. "I have to know...Have you heard from the warden? At Butner? Can I speak to Fred?"

"Fred?" Dev said, as though he wasn't sure who Meredith meant. Then he said, "Oh. No, I haven't heard back."

"I really need to..."

"I'll let you know if I do," Dev said. "When I do." And he hung up.

Meredith lowered herself onto a chair. She thought about Kirby Delarest, his wife Janine, those little blond girls, as perfect and precious as the von Trapps. She thought of Kirby Delarest's brains splattered all over his garage. Meredith remembered Otto, the folk sculpture in Thad Orlo's Manhattan apartment with his gray cottony hair and the piece of wire twisted to make spectacles. She remembered how carefully she had watered the Norfolk pine, terrified it would turn brown and lose its branches in their custody. She had never met Thad Orlo, though she had lived among his things. Those fancy knives, the blond wood rocking chair. She had felt she'd known him.

The phone rang at ten minutes past six.

The evening news, Meredith thought. America was now watching the evening news.

Connie was there to check the caller ID. "Number unavailable," she said. "Should I answer?"

"I'll answer," Toby said. He had just come downstairs in fresh clothes. Meredith had been unable to tell him or Connie about the Thad Orlo/Kirby Delarest story, partly because it was so bizarre that Meredith couldn't believe it was true, though of course it was true. Freddy hadn't acted alone; he'd had helpers, *henchmen,* Dev had called them, people helping him to dig a mass financial

344   Elin Hilderbrand

grave—and it made sense that Meredith would know some of these people. *Kirby Delarest was Thad Orlo.* All of the things that hadn't made sense about Kirby Delarest were now explained. Meredith had been right about Thad Orlo, and she had been right about the phony NASA star, and yet she worried about just how right she had been. The $4 billion in those accounts were, however tangentially, connected to her. Had Freddy hidden the money there for her? He'd moved it on October seventeenth—*Samantha's birthday*—but what did that mean? Was it a coincidence, or was the money for Samantha?

Meredith was afraid to think any further.

She also didn't tell Connie or Toby because she wanted to keep the noxious fumes of the story out of this house. This house was Meredith's only safe place. But she couldn't keep the phone from ringing.

"*I'll* get it," Connie said, and she picked up. "Hello?"

Meredith watched Connie's face, trying to gauge friend or foe, but she couldn't tell. Connie looked surprised; her mouth formed a small, tight "o." Her eyes popped, then mysteriously, filled with tears. Were these sad tears, happy tears, angry tears, a little of each? Meredith couldn't tell.

Connie held out the phone. "It's for you," she whispered. She blinked. Tears spilled down her pretty, tanned face. Meredith took the phone, and Connie moved away with purpose.

"Hello?" Meredith said, thinking, *What has Connie just handed me?*

"Mom?"

Oh, my God. She nearly dropped the phone. It was Carver.

What did he say? What did she say? She could only remember the conversation in snippets afterwards.

"I saw the news," he said.

"Did you?" she said.

"Jesus, Mom. I can't believe it."

She didn't want to talk about this. She had her son on the phone. Her baby, her beloved child.

"How are you? What are you doing? How is your brother? Are you making it? Are you okay?" She would have said there was nothing bigger inside her than her hurt, but yes, this was bigger. Her love for her sons was bigger.

But Carver was stuck back on this other thing. "He cheated on you, Mom. Now do you see? Please tell me you see him for what he really is...a shallow, empty person who fills himself up with lies and things that he can take from other people. You get it now, right?"

"I get it," she said, though she was lying. She didn't get it. "I need to talk to him."

"Who?"

"Your father."

"No!" Carver shouted. "Forget him, leave him, divorce him, get him out of your life. This is your chance."

"Okay," Meredith said. "Yes, you're right. You're right. How are you? How are you?"

Carver's voice softened. "But he did love you, Mom. That's what blows me away about all of this. He really did love you. He revered you, like a queen or a goddess. Leo agrees with me. He knows it, too."

Leo! Meredith thought. She wanted to talk to Leo. He was such a straight arrow, such a good kid, on his hands and knees scraping wax off the hard wood floor of the church, refusing Meredith's help. There had been one time when Meredith had shot up to Choate in the middle of the week to see Leo's lacrosse game. Meredith broke the speed limit in the Jaguar, but she had made it there in time to surprise Leo, and he had scored the goal that won the game. Meredith had been there to cheer, and then afterward, she took Leo and Carver and two teammates to Carini's for pizza. She had made it back to the city before Freddy got home from work, but when he walked in, she told him what she'd done; she told him about the goal and how surprised Leo had been to see her, and how he'd kissed her through the car window before she pulled out of the gates, even though his buddies were watching.

Freddy had smiled wearily. "You're a wonderful mother, Meredith," he'd said. But his mind had been elsewhere.

"Are you okay?" Meredith asked. "Is Leo okay?"

Carver sighed. "We're doing okay, Mom."

But what did this *mean?* Was he really okay? Meredith had been picturing the two of them in a big, dusty Victorian house. She wanted to hear about the house, how they were refinishing the floors or painting the baseboards.

"We love you," Carver said. "But I'm calling to make sure you do the right thing. File for divorce. Please. Promise me."

She wanted to promise. But she couldn't promise. No one understood. She was absolutely alone. She panicked because she heard the end of the conversation encroaching in Carver's voice, and there was still so much to say. So much she wanted to know. He was going to hang up, and she didn't have a number for him. He would be lost to her again, as lost to her as Freddy was, as her father was.

"Wait!" she said. "Your number! Can I call you?"

Again, the sigh. Carver had become a sigher, like a disappointed parent.

"Julie Schwarz wants Leo to wait," he said. "Until the smoke clears a little more. Until a little more time has passed. And that goes for me, too. I shouldn't have called you now, but I had to. I had to talk to you."

"I know," Meredith said. "Thank you."

"You heard me, Mom, right?" Carver said.

"Right," Meredith whispered.

"I love you, Mom. Leo loves you, too," Carver said. And then he hung up.

Meredith said, "I love you, too. I love you, too!" She became aware that she was speaking to a dead phone, and she became aware that there were other people in the room: Toby, who was watching her, and Connie, who was watching Toby watch her.

CONNIE

She should have gone over to Dan's house for dinner. When she called him to say she was staying home, he told her he might just go out by himself. Connie pictured him eating at the bar at A.K. Diamond's, where he knew everyone and everyone knew him, where his old flames would find him, or the cute receptionist from the salon would be sitting on a neighboring bar stool. Connie desperately wanted to go with him, but she couldn't go out; her face was all over the news. Sure enough, when Connie checked her cell phone, she had missed calls from Iris and Lizbet; they had seen her on CNN. She couldn't go anywhere.

"Remember, I'm leaving for New Hampshire on Friday," Dan said.

Connie hesitated. Dan was taking Donovan and Charlie on a wilderness-survival camping trip for three days in the White Mountains. He wouldn't even be able to call her.

"I have to stay in," Connie said. She knew he was waiting for her to invite him over, but she couldn't do that, either. The emotions in this house were too raw. "Tomorrow for sure."

But now, she wished she'd gone. She watched Meredith hang up the phone. Meredith said, "That was Carver."

Connie could barely bring herself to nod. She was the one who had answered the phone, she was the one who had heard Carver say, "Hi, Aunt Connie? It's Carver. Is my mom there?" Connie had been consumed by an emotion she couldn't identify, though now she supposed it was just plain envy, concentrated envy, envy in its purest and most insidious form. Meredith's son had called her. He had heard the news and reached out. He had told her he loved her. Connie had felt both pierced and deflated. She could check her cell phone right now, but she knew that even though her face had been on TV all day, there would be no message or missed call from Ashlyn.

*   *   *

Meredith seemed a little lighter since the phone call from Carver—although she was quick to admit that Carver had barely said a word about himself. Meredith didn't know where he was living or what he was working on or if he still had friends or if he was dating anyone.

"He just called to make sure I was going to divorce Freddy," she said.

"And what did you tell him?" Connie asked.

Toby stared. Meredith said nothing.

"My offer stands," Connie said. "If you want to divorce Freddy, I'll pay for it."

Meredith said nothing. Connie could see the shine of the phone call wearing off. Meredith was very slowly slipping back down to her previous depths.

"He told me he loved me," Meredith said.

"Of course he loves you," Toby said. "He's your son."

The phone rang again, just as the sun was setting, at seven thirty. Setting sun at seven thirty? God, the summer was ending; they were running out of time. Dan was leaving the day after tomorrow for his camping trip, and when he got back, they would have a scant week left together. Last year, Connie remembered, she had been grateful for the end of summer. The sunshine and the beach and the forced cheerfulness had been trying for her. Last summer, she had been unable to look at the ocean without thinking of Wolf's ashes. So much had changed in one year; she should be happy for that.

Toby was over by the phone, checking the caller ID. "It's an unknown caller," he said. "Want me to answer it?"

"No," Connie said, but Meredith said, "Go ahead," and since Meredith's answer would always trump Connie's answer with Toby, he answered.

"Hello?" He paused. He looked at Meredith. He said, "May I

tell her who's calling?" He paused. He said, "I won't give her the phone unless you tell me who this is."

Then, to Meredith, he said, "It's her."

"Samantha?" Meredith said.

Toby nodded.

"No," Meredith said.

Toby hung up. Connie thought, *I told him not to answer.* But her insides were jumping. She hated to admit it, but it was exciting living through this kind of drama.

"Wait a minute," she said. "That was *Samantha?*"

"Samantha Deuce," Toby said.

Meredith slowly shook her head.

"You don't seem surprised," Connie said.

"She called earlier."

"She *did?*"

"I answered, and when I figured out it was her, I said, 'No,' and hung up."

"Wow," Connie said. "That woman has guts."

"Well, yeah," Meredith said.

Connie put out some crackers with bluefish pâté, but none of them ate. It grew dark in the room, and Connie thought, *I should turn on some lights,* but lights seemed too harsh, or perhaps too optimistic, so Connie lit candles, as she might have during an electrical storm. It was too bad it wasn't raining, she thought. A storm would fit the mood.

Connie wanted wine. If this had been three weeks ago, she would already be on her third glass. And Dan wasn't here, so... Connie poured herself some.

She said, "Meredith, do you want wine?"

Meredith said, "Do I want wine? Yes. But I shouldn't. I won't."

Connie shouldn't either, but she was going to anyway. She took in a mouthful, thinking, *Deliver me.* But the wine tasted sour; it tasted like a headache. She poured it down the drain. She got herself a glass of ice water with lemon. She knew they should do something about dinner. Meredith was in the armchair, folded into herself like an injured bird, and Toby was sprawled across the sofa, keeping vigil on Meredith. He loved her. It was as plain as the nose on his face.

But Meredith wouldn't divorce Freddy. The man had done despicable things, both publicly and privately, and yet Meredith still loved him. Any other woman would have left Freddy Delinn in the dust, but not Meredith.

Dinner, they needed to eat dinner, Connie thought, *something simple — sandwiches, salad, scrambled eggs, even. But she wasn't hungry.*

She said, "Meredith, are you hungry?"

Meredith said, "I'll never eat again."

At that second, Toby's cell phone rang. He said, "It's Michael," and he bounded up the stairs to his bedroom.

Meredith said, "I can't believe Samantha called here twice."

"I'm sure she wants to talk to you," Connie said.

"I'm sure she does," Meredith said.

They sat for a second, listening to the mantel clock tick. Connie could hear the strains of Toby's voice. "Hey, buddy." Everyone was talking to their children tonight, except for her.

Meredith must have heard Toby, too, because she said, "It was good to talk to Carver. It was magical to hear his voice, just to hear him call me 'Mom,' you know? Just to hear him say he loves me. I can't see him, I can't touch him, but at least I know he's alive out in the world somewhere. Thinking of me."

Connie was suddenly too sad for tears. This, she realized, must have been how Meredith felt. Her sadness took on a sharp, shining edge.

She said, "Do you think Samantha was the only one?"

"What?" Meredith said.

"Well, we know Freddy did things in a big way."

"What are you saying?" Meredith asked. "That there might have been other lovers?"

"There might have been," Connie said. "I mean, you know how Freddy was."

"No," Meredith said. Her voice was cold stone. "How was Freddy?"

"He was flirtatious," Connie said. "And at times, he was more than flirtatious."

"Did he ever make a pass at you?" Meredith asked. She sat up in the armchair, her spine straight, her chin lifted as though there were a string from the top of her head to the ceiling. Meredith was so small in stature, she looked like a ventriloquist's dummy. "He did, didn't he?"

"He did," Connie said. She couldn't believe she was saying this. She had decided there would be no more taboo subjects, but really, to bring *this* up? *Stop, Connie, stop! Shut up!* But there was something inside driving her. She couldn't say what. An urge to *tell.* "He made a pass at me in Cap d'Antibes. He told me I was a beautiful woman, and then he kissed me."

"He kissed you."

"And he, sort of, touched my breast. Cupped it."

Meredith nodded once, succinctly. "I see. Where was Wolf?"

"Running."

"And where was I?"

"Shopping."

"So the two of you were alone in the house, then," Meredith said. "Did you sleep with him?"

"No, Meredith, I did not sleep with him."

"This was...when?" Meredith said. "What year?"

Connie tried to think. She couldn't think. "It was the year we had lunch at that restaurant in Annecy. Do you remember that lunch?"

"Yes," Meredith said. "So...two thousand three. Does that sound right?"

"I don't know," Connie said. "I guess so."

"Before Samantha," Meredith said. She slapped her hands against her thighs. "So maybe there were others, then. Safe to assume there were others. Dozens, maybe, or hundreds..."

"Meredith..." Connie said.

"Why," Meredith said. She shut her mouth and swallowed. "Why on earth didn't you tell me?"

God, what was the answer to that question? Freddy had made a pass; Connie had deflected it. There was, essentially, nothing to tell. Maybe she had kept quiet about it because it was a private moment between her and Freddy; he was paying her a compliment, and it had made Connie feel good. It had made her feel *desired*. She didn't want to ruin that feeling by turning it into something else. Maybe she hadn't wanted to spoil the week in Cap d'Antibes by making a mountain out of a molehill. Maybe she hadn't had access to the kind of language it would require to tell Meredith what had happened without implicating herself. It hadn't been Connie's fault. Except, she had worn the clingy patio dress that put her breasts on display. But a woman should be able to dress however she wanted. It wasn't an invitation for men to act inappropriately.

"I don't know why I didn't tell you," Connie said. "It didn't seem like a big deal."

"My husband kissed you and touched you, and you remember it all these years later, but it didn't seem like a big deal?"

"It was alarming," Connie said. "Of course it was. But I backed away. In my mind, I minimalized it. I guess because I was embarrassed."

Meredith stared. She had an arsenal of cold, scary looks. "I can't believe you."

"Meredith, I'm sorry..."

"You're my best friend. And after you, my closest friend was Samantha."

"I didn't sleep with Freddy," Connie said. "I didn't encourage Freddy or invite any further attention. I did nothing wrong."

"You didn't tell me," Meredith said.

It suddenly felt like a question pulled from a woman's magazine: If your best friend's husband makes a pass at you, do you tell her? Certainly the answer was no. But maybe the answer was yes. Maybe Connie should have told Meredith. One thing was for sure: Connie should *not* have told Meredith about it tonight. She had done so out of meanness; she had wanted to hurt Meredith, when Meredith was already hurting so badly. *Do I look like a woman who needs more surprise news?* But why? And then Connie knew: she was jealous about the phone call from Carver. Now look at the mess. If Connie had intended to keep her moment with Freddy a secret, it should have remained a secret forever.

"I'm sorry," Connie said. "I should have told you, I guess."

"You *guess?*" Meredith said. "You *guess?*" Her voice was shrill and righteous. Connie stood up. She needed a glass of wine; she didn't care if it tasted like Drano. She took a glass from the cabinet and opened the fridge.

Meredith said, "That's right. Pour yourself some wine. That'll fix everything."

Connie slammed the refrigerator door shut, then she threw the wine glass into the kitchen sink and the glass shattered. The noise was startling. Her anger and upset were unbelievable, and she knew that Meredith's anger and upset matched, if not surpassed, hers. Was there room in one house for so much agony? Connie looked at the broken glass—and she spotted a chip in her enamel sink. Her gorgeous farmer's sink, of which she had once been so proud.

Wolf, she thought. *Ashlyn.* Lost to her. Lost.

She thought, *Dan. I should have gone to Dan's.*

She said, "Well, while we're at it."

"While we're at it, what?" Meredith said.

"While we're at it, I'm not the only one who made a mistake. I'm not the only one in the wrong here."

"What are you talking about?" Meredith said.

She was standing with her hands on her hips, her graying hair tucked behind her ears, her horn-rimmed glasses slipping to the end of her nose. She had gotten those glasses in the eighth grade. Connie remembered her walking into American History class and showing off the glasses, and then in lunch and study hall, passing them around for other girls to try on. Connie had been the first one to try them on; they had turned the cafeteria into a blurry, swarming mass of color. Connie had almost vomited. And yet, she had been jealous of Meredith's glasses, and of Meredith, since childhood. Practically her entire life.

"I'm talking about the things you said about Wolf," Connie said. "The horrible things. You insinuated that we were pulling our money because Wolf had brain cancer and didn't know any better."

Meredith said, "You basically came right out and called Freddy a crook."

"Meredith," Connie said. "He was a crook."

Meredith pushed her glasses up her nose. "You're right," she said. "He was a crook." She stared at Connie. She seemed to be waiting for something. "And what I said about Wolf was ruthless. I'm sorry. I don't know how I could have been so awful."

"And you didn't come to Wolf's funeral," Connie said. "And you knew that I needed you there."

"I was on my way," Meredith said. "I was at the door of the apartment, wearing a charcoal-gray suit, I remember. And Freddy talked me out of it." She bit her lower lip. "I don't know how he did it, but he did. You know Freddy."

"Whatever Freddy told you to do, you did," Connie said.

"That's why I'm in trouble with the Feds," Meredith said. "Freddy asked me to transfer fifteen million dollars from the business to our personal account three days before he was exposed, and I did it. I thought he was going to buy a house in Aspen." She laughed. "I thought I was going to Aspen, but instead I'm going to jail."

So that was why she was under investigation, Connie thought. She hadn't been brave enough to ask. Another taboo shattered. She said, "You were supposed to come visit me here in nineteen eighty-two, but you didn't come because of Freddy. Because Freddy had sent that telegram. He'd proposed, remember? And I said, 'That's great, we can celebrate your engagement.' But you only wanted to celebrate with Freddy."

"That was thirty years ago," Meredith said.

"Exactly," Connie said. "He's been holding you hostage for thirty years."

"I still don't understand why you didn't tell me what happened in France," Meredith said. "Did our friendship mean nothing?"

"Wait a minute," Connie said. "We've both done damage to the friendship. It wasn't just me. I didn't tell you about Freddy because, at the time, my best judgment told me to let it go. I'm sorry I brought it up."

"Not as sorry as I am," Meredith said.

"I'm not Samantha Deuce," Connie said. "You're angry with Samantha. Not with me."

At that moment, Toby came downstairs. "What's going on?" he said. "Did someone break a glass?"

"Connie," Meredith said.

Toby turned to Connie. Connie could speak, but Toby wouldn't hear her. This was her house—where, it might be pointed out, both Meredith and Toby were guests—but she had no voice.

"I'm going to bed," Connie said. *Dinner,* she thought. She foraged through the pantry and selected a Something Natural herb roll, which she took a bite out of like an apple.

Meredith said, "No, the two of you stay up. *I'm* going to bed."

Old habits die hard, Connie thought. It was exactly nine thirty.

*   *   *

Connie spent the night on the living-room sofa. After growing accustomed to sleeping in a real bed, she felt that the sofa offered as much comfort as an old door laid across sawhorses, and when she woke up, Connie felt like she had fallen from a ten-story building. Her breath stank of onions from the herb roll. She had forgotten to pour herself a glass of water, and her lips were cracked. She needed lip balm. She needed to brush her teeth.

She stood up, gingerly. She decided she wouldn't think about anything else until she took care of these small tasks.

Water. Chapstick. Toothbrush.

She cleaned out the sink—carefully removing the shards of glass with rubber gloves. She made a pot of coffee. She was okay. Her heart hurt but she was functioning.

Her cell phone was there on the counter, charging, and because she couldn't help herself, she checked for missed calls or messages. She was thinking of Dan, but really she was thinking of Ashlyn. There was nothing new. The voice mails from Iris and Lizbet lingered, unheard.

The coffee machine gurgled. Connie got a mug and poured in half-and-half and warmed it up in the microwave. She poured in the coffee and added sugar. She could remember drinking coffee for the first time with Meredith and Annabeth Martin in Annabeth's fancy drawing room at the house in Wynnewood. Connie and Meredith were wearing long dresses. Connie's dress had been red gingham with a white eyelet panel down the front that was embroidered with strawberries. Connie remembered thinking, *Coffee?* That was something adults drank. But that was what Annabeth Martin had served; there was no lemonade or fruit punch. Annabeth had poured cream out of a tiny silver pitcher and offered the girls sugar cubes, stacked like crystalline blocks of ice, from a silver bowl. Connie's coffee had spilled into her saucer and Annabeth had said, "Two hands, Constance."

And then, when Connie got home and told her mother that Annabeth had served them coffee, Veronica had said, "That woman is trying to stunt your growth."

Connie smiled now, remembering. Then she felt a heaviness gather inside her. She and Meredith had been connected since her earliest memories. She didn't want Meredith to be upset with her. She couldn't lose another person.

She took her coffee out to the deck. There were a few clouds on the horizon, but the rest of the sky was brilliant blue. Nantucket was the kind of place that was so beautiful it broke your heart, because you couldn't keep it. The seasons passed, the weather changed, you had to leave — and return to the city or the suburbs, your school, your job, your real life.

Connie drank her coffee. She thought, *I can't lose anyone else.*

She turned and saw Meredith standing in the doorway, holding a cup of coffee. She was in a short white nightgown. She looked like a doll. Her hair was lighter.

Connie spoke without thinking. "Your hair is lighter."

Meredith said, "You're just saying that because I'm mad."

"I'm saying that because it's true. It's lighter. It's blonder."

Meredith took the seat next to Connie and reached for her hand. "I'm sorry," she said.

"I'm sorry," Connie said.

Meredith narrowed her eyes at the view. Her face was tanned, and she had a spray of freckles across her nose. She said, "I would have died without you."

Connie squeezed her hand. "Shhh," she said.

Later that morning, the phone rang. Toby said, "Geez, the phone has rung more in the past two days than it has in the past two weeks."

Connie threw him a look. Meredith was upstairs getting dressed. There were no reporters out front, so Connie and Meredith were going to run to the grocery store, and if that went well, to Nantucket

Bookworks to stock up on novels. Dan had called; he was taking Connie to the Pearl for dinner, so Meredith and Toby would be on their own at home.

Connie checked the caller ID. It was the law firm. Connie picked it up. The fifteen-year-old attorney asked for Meredith.

Connie said, "Just a moment, please."

Connie caught Meredith coming down the stairs. She said, "It's your counsel."

Meredith said, "I wish we'd left five minutes ago."

Connie said, "I'm going to run up and brush my teeth. We'll go when you're off the phone?"

"Okay," Meredith said. She had her wig in one hand. They were back to the wig.

Goddamn you, Freddy, Connie thought.

She climbed the stairs slowly because she wanted to listen. Toby was right there in the room, probably unabashedly eavesdropping. Connie heard Meredith say, "Hello?" Pause. "I'm doing okay. Do you have any news for me?"

Connie stopped in her tracks, but she was near the top of the stairs, and she didn't hear anything more.

MEREDITH

He wouldn't talk to her.

"I asked everyone in the system at Butner," Dev said. "Everyone gave the same answer: Fred Delinn won't take your phone call, and they can't make him. They can't even make him listen while you talk."

Meredith felt her cheeks burn. She was embarrassed. Humiliated. She was dying a living death. "Why won't he talk to me?"

"It's anyone's guess, Meredith," Dev said. "The guy is a sociopath, and he's deteriorated mentally since he's been in. Everyone at the prison knows what happened with Mrs. Deuce. They understand why you want an audience. Mrs. Briggs, the warden's secretary, personally pushed for Fred to face you on Skype and at least be forced to listen to what you have to say, but that idea was shot down. It's against prisoner's rights. They can lock him up, they can make him go to meals, they can make him go out into the yard at nine a.m. and come in from the yard at ten a.m., they can make him take his meds. But they can't make him talk, and they can't make him talk to you."

Meredith reminded herself to breathe. Toby was somewhere in the room, though she wasn't sure where. Her right knee was knocking into the table leg. "I should go down there and see him in person."

"He won't see you," Dev said, "and they can't make him. You'll go down there for nothing, Meredith. It's a romantic idea, like in the movies. I get it. You go down there, he sees you, something clicks, he offers up all kinds of explanations and apologies. That isn't going to happen. He's a sick man, Meredith. He's not the man you once knew."

She was tired of this idea, even though she knew it to be true.

"So you're telling me I can't go?"

"I'm telling you you shouldn't go," Dev said. "Because he won't see you. You can travel down there to hot and desolate Butner, you can plan on enduring a media circus, you can meet with Nancy Briggs and Cal Green, the warden, but they're just going to tell you the same thing that I'm telling you. He won't see you. He won't talk to you."

"I'm not going to yell at him," Meredith said. "I'm not going to hurt him. I'm not going to go on some kind of crazed jealous-wife rampage. I just want answers."

"You won't get answers," Dev said.

She couldn't believe what she was hearing. She had thought that perhaps the prison would make it difficult for her to talk to Fred.

But from the sound of it, they wanted to facilitate the phone call but couldn't—because Freddy refused. It was the very worst thing: He had stolen everybody's money, he had lied to the SEC and single-handedly put the nation's economy in the toilet. He had cheated on Meredith for six and a half years with a woman she considered to be their closest friend. He had lied to Meredith tens of thousands of times—fine. But what she couldn't forgive was this, now. What she couldn't forgive was this stonewalled silence. He *owed* her a conversation. He *owed her the truth*—as egregious as it might be. But the truth was going to stay locked up in Butner. It was going to stay locked up in the sooty black recesses of Freddy's disturbed mind.

"Fine," Meredith said. She slammed down the phone. She was furious. Furious! She would make a statement to the press vilifying the man. She would take down Freddy and the undisputed harlot who was Samantha Champion Deuce. (She wrote her own *Post* headlines: *CHAMPION HOMEWRECKER, CHAMPION TWO-FACED LIAR.*) Meredith *would* file for divorce, and three hundred million Americans would support her; they would raise her up. She would regain her position in society; she would hit the lecture circuit.

She turned around. Toby was standing there, and something about the look on his face made Meredith's anger pop like a soap bubble.

She said, "He won't talk to me. He refuses. And they can't make him."

Toby nodded slowly. Meredith expected him to take this opportunity to say, *He's a rat bastard, Meredith. A piece of shit. What further proof do you need?* But instead, Toby said, "Maybe he'll change his mind."

Meredith smiled sadly and headed for the front door to meet Connie in the Escalade. They were going to the store. Meredith had planned on wearing her wig, but this suddenly seemed pointless. The wig was meant to protect her, but she had just suffered the ultimate blow. Nothing anyone did could affect her now; the wig had been rendered useless. Meredith left it on the stairs. When she got home, she would throw it away.

Toby was being kind about Freddy because he could afford to be. He knew, as Meredith did, that Freddy would never change his mind.

That night, before she left for her date with Dan, Connie made dinner for Meredith and Toby. It was a crabmeat pasta with sautéed zucchini in a lemon tarragon cream sauce, a stacked salad of heirloom tomatoes, Maytag blue cheese, and basil, sprinkled with toasted pine nuts and drizzled with hot bacon dressing, and homemade Parker House rolls with seasoned butter.

Unbelievable, Meredith thought. Connie had showered and dressed. She looked absolutely gorgeous, and she had made this meal.

"I feel guilty," Meredith said. "You should have served this meal to Dan."

"I offered," Connie said. "But he really wanted to go out."

Without us, Meredith thought.

"And I wanted to cook for you," Connie said.

Because she feels sorry for me, Meredith thought. *Again.* But there was something almost comforting about reaching this point. Nothing left to lose, nothing left to care about, nothing left to want.

The outdoor table was set with a tablecloth and candles. There was a breeze off the ocean that held a hint of chill.

Fall was coming.

Connie wrapped herself up in a pashmina and said, "Bon appétit! I'm off for my date. I'll be back tomorrow morning. Dan's on the noon boat."

"This is lovely," Meredith said. "Thank you."

"And there's dessert in the fridge," Connie said.

"Have fun," Toby said, pushing her gently to the front door.

She left, and Meredith had the feeling that Connie was the parent, and she and Toby were teenagers on a date. It was supposed to be romantic — the candlelight, the delicious food, the ocean before them like a Broadway show. Meredith should have dressed up, but she was in the same clothes she'd put on that morning: a ratty old T-shirt from Choate that Carver had worn his senior year, and her navy-blue gym shorts. She knew it was possible that she would sleep in these clothes and wear them again the next day. She didn't care how she looked. She didn't even care, anymore, about her hair.

Thirty years of marriage, and he wouldn't talk to her. So many dinners at Rinaldo's she had sat with Freddy the way she was now sitting with Toby, and she had talked about her day, and Freddy had nodded and asked questions, and when Meredith asked him about work, he'd run his hands through his hair and check his BlackBerry as if a pithy answer would be displayed there, and then he'd say something about the stress and unpredictability of his business. Meredith had no idea that Freddy was printing out fake statements on an ancient dot-matrix printer, or that he was spending his lunch hours with Samantha Deuce at the Stanhope Hotel. Freddy had pretended to live in awe of Meredith, but what he really must have been thinking was how blind and gullible and stupid she was. She was like…his mother, Mrs. Delinn, who toiled at providing for Freddy and giving him love. *He'll pretend like he can get along without it, but he can't. Freddy needs his love.* And Meredith had been only too happy to take over the care and maintenance of Freddy Delinn. He was a rich man, but she was the one who rubbed his back and kissed his eyelids and defended him tooth and nail to those who said he was corrupt.

There had been one time in early December when Freddy had called out in the night. He had shuddered in bed, and when Meredith rolled over, she saw his eyes fly open. She touched his silvering hair and said, "What? What is it?"

He didn't speak, though his eyes widened. Was he awake?

He said, "David."

And Meredith thought, "David? Who is David?" Then she realized he meant his brother.

"It's okay," Meredith said. "I'm here."

And he had turned to her and said, "You're never going to leave me, Meredith, right? Promise me. No matter what?"

"No matter what," she'd said.

Freddy's eyes had closed then, though Meredith could see manic activity beneath his twitching lids. She had stayed awake as long as she could, watching him, thinking, *David. I wonder what made him dream of David?*

But now she suspected he hadn't been thinking about David at all. He'd been thinking about money, the SEC, a looming investigation, being caught, discovered, indicted, imprisoned. He had invoked his brother's name to throw Meredith off the trail of his real worries. He had known how to lie to her, even when he was only semiconscious.

No matter what, Meredith had promised. But she hadn't known what kind of "what" he was talking about.

"I don't think I can eat," Meredith said. Toby was very patiently holding his utensils in the hover position over his plate, waiting for her.

Toby's face darkened. "The guy is the biggest creep on earth," he said. "He didn't deserve you."

It was confounding hearing these words from Toby. Quite possibly, Freddy had said something similar about Toby so many years ago, when Meredith told him about how Toby broke up with her on the night of her high-school graduation. *You're better off without him. He didn't deserve you.*

Toby put a forkful of pasta in his mouth and chewed sadly, if such a thing was possible.

"You're luckier than Freddy," Meredith said. "You got me at my best. Sixteen, seventeen, eighteen. That was the best Meredith, Toby, and she was yours."

Toby swallowed and looked at her. "You're at your best right now." He fingered the fraying sleeve of her ancient T-shirt. "You're the best Meredith right now."

Meredith thought back to the day of Veronica O'Brien's funeral. Meredith had arrived at the church nearly an hour early, and the only person there was Toby. He was sitting in the back pew, and Meredith had tapped his shoulder and he turned and they looked at each other and—what could Meredith say? She hadn't seen Toby in nearly twenty years at that point, but the sight of his face brought her to her knees. He stood up and took her in his arms. It started out as a condolence hug. His mother had, after all, just died. The indomitable Veronica O'Brien was gone.

Meredith said into his chest, "I'm so sorry, Toby."

He tightened his grip on her, and she felt her body temperature rise. She thought she was imagining it. Of course, she was imagining it. She was married, married to rich and powerful Freddy Delinn. Freddy gave her everything her heart desired, so what could she possibly want from Toby now? But the human heart, as Meredith learned then, rarely paid attention to the rules. She felt Toby's arms tense around her, she felt his leg nudge up against her leg, she felt his breath in her hair.

"Meredith," he said. "My Meredith."

The next thing Meredith knew, Toby was leading her out of the church, leading her to the shady spot under a majestic tree where his car was parked. He opened the passenger-side door for her and she got in.

She stared out the windshield at the trunk of the hundred-year-old tree, and when Toby got into the car, Meredith said, "Where are we going?"

"I want to take you somewhere," he said. "I want to make love to you."

"Toby," Meredith said.

"Did you feel it back there?" he asked. "Tell me you did."

"I did."

"You did, right? Look at me, I'm shaking."

Yes, Meredith was shaking, too. She tried to think of Freddy, who had hired a helicopter and a private car to get her here, but who had not given her the most precious thing—and that was his time. He hadn't come with her.

Meredith said, "This is insane."

"I should have been more persistent at Connie's wedding," he said. "I knew then that I'd made a mistake with you."

"You broke my heart," Meredith said. "I thought we would get married."

"I want to take you somewhere."

"But the *funeral*..."

"We have time," he said. He started the engine and drove out of the churchyard

"We should turn around," Meredith said.

"Tell me you don't want me."

"I can't tell you that," Meredith said.

"So you do want me?"

She was glowing with arousal, but it wasn't just sexual. A part of Meredith had been yearning for this moment —Toby wanting her back—since she was eighteen years old.

He drove through the town of Villanova to the O'Brien house. He screeched into the driveway, and he and Meredith got out. The day was hot, Meredith was wearing a black lace Collette Dinnigan dress; it was too fancy for the Main Line, and now it was plastered to her, and itching. Toby led Meredith into the O'Briens' garage, which smelled exactly the same as it had twenty-five years earlier—like cut grass and gasoline from Bill O'Brien's riding mower. A tennis ball hung from a string over one of the bays; it had been placed there when Veronica smashed her Cutlass Supreme into the garage's back wall after too many gimlets at Aronimink. As soon as they were shut in the cool dim of the garage, Toby took Meredith's face in his hands, and he kissed her.

And oh, what a kiss it had been. It had gone on and on, Meredith *could not* get enough, it had been so long since someone had kissed her like that. Freddy loved her, but there were a hundred things more important to him than sex and romance. Money, money, money, his business, his reputation, his clients, his profile in *Forbes,* his appearance, his yacht, his suits, his early bedtime — all of those rated with him in a way that kissing Meredith did not.

"Come upstairs with me," Toby said. "To my room."

She thought of parking with Toby in the Nova. *The best of times are when I'm alone with you.* She tried to think of Freddy, but she couldn't conjure his face. So, she would go upstairs with Toby. She would have him again, just this once.

They hurried through the house, up the stairs. It was so familiar, it played tricks on Meredith's sense of time and place. She had started her day in Southampton 2004, but now it was three o'clock in the afternoon and she was in Villanova 1978. Toby's room was exactly the same — why hadn't Veronica turned it into an exercise room or a study like every other empty nester? There was Toby's lava lamp, his poster of Jimmy Page, his water bed. The heels of Meredith's Manolos got caught in the shag rug. She stumbled and Toby caught her, then somehow they both crashed onto the water bed, and this knocked Meredith back into her present self. She stared up at the ceiling, and there were the tape marks from where Toby had hung his Farrah Fawcett poster.

He started to kiss her again. She said, "Toby, stop. I can't."

"What?" he said. "Why not?"

She rolled onto her side, creating wave motion in the mattress. She looked into his green eyes. "I'm married, Toby."

"Please, Meredith," he said. "Please?" He looked like he might cry. She reached out to wipe away the first tear with her thumb.

"I'm sorry, Toby," she said. "I can't."

He watched her for a second, perhaps to see if she was bluffing. She hoisted herself up off the bed and straightened her dress.

"So that's it?" he said.

"We should go back," she said. "It's your mother's funeral."

"Is it the man you love?" Toby asked. "Or is it the money?"

Meredith stared.

"Is it the houses? Is it the place in France? Is it the behemoth boat? I saw her once, you know, in the Mediterranean. Saint Tropez."

"Toby, let's go."

"Does he make you laugh?" Toby asked.

"No," Meredith said honestly. "But you're not very funny right now, either. Let's go back."

"I can't believe you're doing this to me."

Meredith turned on him. "What am I supposed to do? Allow you to make love to me, allow the feelings to come back, and then watch you take off tomorrow for... where? Where, Toby?"

"Spain," he said. "On Tuesday."

"See?" she said.

"You wouldn't come with me even if I asked you," he said. "Because you're married to money."

Meredith shook her head. "I wouldn't come with you even if you asked me because you wouldn't ask me."

On the way back to the church, Toby wept silently, and Meredith felt bad. He had just lost his mother. But Meredith was angry, too—for so many reasons.

Connie and Wolf had been ascending the church stairs. Connie waved to Toby to hurry up; they were to follow the casket inside. She herded Meredith along, too, but Meredith demurred. She wasn't family. Connie studied her critically and said, "Did you two go somewhere together?"

Meredith kissed the side of Connie's face. She said, "I have to leave right after. I'm sorry, Con. I can't stay for the..."

"You can't stay?" Connie said.

"I have to get back," Meredith said.

Toby appeared then, over Meredith's shoulder. "Yeah," he said. "She has to get back."

Now, Meredith smiled sadly at Toby. "At your mother's funeral..."

"You did the right thing," he said. "Then."

"Yes," she said. "I suppose I did. Then."

Meredith reached a hand out to him, and he grabbed it and brought it to his mouth. They rose from their chairs and faced each other and Meredith thought, *My God, what am I doing?* And in a flash, it came back: the greedy, hungry desire for this man. Did Toby understand? Did he feel it? Toby lifted her up by the hips, and she rubbed against the length of his body. He was more powerful than Freddy; Meredith felt featherlight, no more substantial than a wish or a hope. Toby kissed her, his mouth was warm and buttery, tender at first, then fierce. She wanted fierce. She wanted fire.

She had wanted to kiss Freddy good-bye before the FBI dragged him away last December, but when she'd taken his arm, he'd looked at her in wild confusion.

Toby's hands were in her hair. It was the tree on Robinhood Road all over again; something so old it was new. She could feel him hard against her leg, an occurrence that had confused her at age fifteen and that, truth be told, confused her now. Was she finally going to make love to Toby O'Brien again? His hands shifted to her back, his hands were up inside her T-shirt, unhooking her bra. Meredith thought of Freddy with his hand on Samantha's back. Was Meredith acting out of anger, out of retribution? If so, she should stop right now. But she didn't want to stop. She was pulsing with heat and light; she was experiencing an arousal that was as cutting and bordering on painful as it had been in her new body. This was a different kind of sexual awakening. It was electrifying in its utter wrongness. *Stop!* she thought. But she had no intention of stopping. It felt like Toby was going to tear her T-shirt in two just to get at her.

She twisted and darted inside the house.

"Meredith?" Toby said. He thought she was running away.

"Come on!" she screamed.

They made love on Toby's bed amid his rumpled sheets, which smelled like him. The sex was urgent, quick, rough, and desperate. Afterward, Meredith lay panting; the inside of her elbow hurt from where Toby had pinned her. Toby touched Meredith's hair, her graying hair, she was so much older now, but there was something fountain of youth–like about this summer. Meredith felt seventeen. She grabbed Toby's hand—the thought of being touched gently unnerved her—and she brought his hand to her mouth and kissed it first, then bit it.

"Ouch!" he said.

"I'm starving," she said.

That night, she feared she might dream about Freddy or Samantha or the warden at Butner—but instead she dreamed about their dog, Buttons. In Meredith's dream, Buttons was Toby's dog. He was standing on the bow of Toby's boat, eating a striped bass. Meredith was yelling at him—*No! Please Buttons. No, you'll get sick!* Toby was dressed in a white naval cadet's uniform, with the brass buttons and flat-top hat. He tried to pull the fish away from Buttons, but Buttons fought back like a junkyard dog and Toby ended up reeling backward and falling into the water. Meredith checked over the edge, but there was no sign of him, except for his floating hat. He had disappeared.

She woke up. Toby was propped on one elbow, watching her. She had inhaled the plate of food that Connie had made her, as well as a dish of panna cotta with berries, which Toby had brought to her in bed. She had left the smeared dishes on Toby's nightstand, and she'd fallen asleep without brushing her teeth. Now, she felt louche and irresponsible. Her elbow still hurt, and there was a dull soreness between her legs.

She couldn't help wondering if Freddy had ever gazed at her like this. She wanted so badly to believe that he had, but it was probably time to admit that Freddy had only adored himself. And money. And, possibly, Samantha. Meredith almost hoped he had adored Samantha, because that, at least, would mean Freddy was human.

She said to Toby, "I dreamed I lost you."

"I'm right here," he said.

Later, Meredith tiptoed naked across the hallway to her bedroom and climbed out onto her Juliet balcony for one quick second, almost daring the paparazzi to come get her. *You're the best Meredith right now.* She nearly laughed at the thought. She could do so much better than this.

Meredith slipped on a robe and padded down to the outdoor shower. She stayed in as long as she could in good conscience, and then she went back upstairs to dress. Toby was asleep in his bed, snoring. Meredith gently closed his door.

She retreated to her room. She pulled the cardboard box out of the closet. In that box was the spiral-bound notebook that she had been taking notes in on the day that Trina Didem interrupted her anthropology class to tell Meredith that her father was dead. Meredith had kept the notebook.

It still had plenty of empty pages. Meredith lay across her bed the way she used to as a schoolgirl. She meant to write Freddy a long letter that would elicit all the answers she needed, but the only two words that came to her, which she traced over and over again until the letters were heavy and dark, were **OBLIVION** and **LOVE**.

These were her crimes.

CONNIE

Dan would be gone for three days. Four, really, because he was coming back on the late boat on Monday, so Connie wouldn't see him until Tuesday. When she said good-bye to him, she felt a sick kind of desperation, which she tried to hide.

It was Dan who said, "I can't believe how much I'm going to miss you."

"And it's only three days," Connie said. What she meant was: *Think how bad it will be a week from now when I go back to Maryland.*

But then, too, Dan was excited about his camping trip with the boys. Connie had taken a gander at all their equipment: the three-season tent, the Coleman stove, the sleeping bags and air mattresses, the fishing poles and tackle box overflowing with flies, the generator and heavy-duty flashlights, the grocery bags of ramen noodles and peanut butter and instant oatmeal.

"We're going to catch fish and fry it up," Dan said. "We're going to hike and swim in waterfalls. We are going to *survive.*"

Connie pretended to be excited for him. He would be consumed with the wilderness, leaving little time to pine for Connie.

She kissed him good-bye in his driveway—self-consciously, because the boys were in the house—and then she drove away.

She needed something to keep her mind occupied. But what? And then it came to her. She would teach Meredith to cook.

"You're going to teach me to cook?" Meredith said. "Me?"

"I'm going to teach you the basics," Connie said. "So when you're..."

"Living alone..."

"You can feed yourself," Connie said.

"Cheaply," Meredith said.

"Right," Connie said. She smiled uneasily. She wanted to ask Meredith what her plans were once Labor Day arrived, but she didn't want to cause Meredith any additional anxiety. But really, what was she planning on doing? Where would she go? To Connecticut, to live near her boys? Before the most recent development with Freddy, Connie had feared that Meredith would move to North Carolina. That wouldn't happen now, thank God. Meredith needed to *cut bait*—Dan's term—and set herself free from that man. It was Connie's opinion that, in refusing to see her or talk to her on the phone, Freddy was doing Meredith a favor. He was giving her a chance to liberate herself. Really, Freddy was acting out of kindness—either that, or he was too much of a coward to answer for his actions.

"You can stay here, you know," Connie said. The house had heat. Connie had toyed with the idea of staying here herself. What reason did she have to go back to Bethesda? The powers that be had asked her to serve on the board of directors at the VA, so she could look forward to a lifetime of meetings in the building that had been more important to Wolf than his own life. She would go back to Bethesda because that was where her life was—her friends, her Whole Foods, her UPS man. She would go back to Bethesda because that house was where Ashlyn had grown up, and Connie would keep it for her, in case she ever decided to come back. Pointless? Probably.

"I can't stay here," Meredith said. "I've imposed on you long enough."

"You know better than to say that."

"I still have time to think about it," Meredith said. "I don't have to decide today. And there's still a chance that I'll be..."

Connie held up a hand. She couldn't stand to hear Meredith say it. She turned to her cutting board. "The first thing I'm going to teach you is how to chop an onion."

They chopped onion, shallot, garlic. They sautéed the shallot in butter. Connie showed Meredith how to move the shallot around the sauté pan with a wooden spoon. They added white wine and reduced it. They added Dijon mustard. They added heavy cream, salt and pepper, and a handful of fresh herbs.

"There," Connie said. "We have just made a mustard and herb cream sauce. You can add grilled sausage and serve this over pasta. You can substitute lemon juice for the Dijon and add shrimp."

Meredith was taking notes. It was so elementary, who needed notes? But Meredith had always been that kind of student.

Connie poached some chicken breasts in water, white wine, and celery leaves. She let the chicken cool, then shredded it with two forks.

"You don't even need a food processor," Connie said.

"That's good," Meredith said. "Because I can't afford one."

"You can probably buy one on eBay for cheap," Connie said.

"And which computer will I be using when I bid on eBay?" Meredith said, "And which credit card will I use?" She smiled. "I'm only kidding. I still have some money. Very little, but some. All I need is the guts to apply for a new credit card. All I need is the courage to walk into the public library and ask to use the Internet."

"Correct," Connie said. "You're a free citizen. You can do these things, and no one — *no one,* Meredith — can stop you."

They did eggs next. Eggs were cheap. Connie mixed three eggs with a little milk and some salt and pepper. She threw some butter in the frying pan.

"Scrambled eggs," Connie said. "Low heat, slow motion. You can add any kind of cheese you want. I like cheddar or Gruyère."

"Does my future include Gruyère cheese?" Meredith asked.

"Cheddar, then," Connie said.

"Government cheese," Meredith said. She laughed. "Do you think the government would even give me cheese? If they don't indict me, maybe they will give me cheese."

Connie turned off the burner under the eggs; they were rich and creamy. She threw in a handful of fresh thyme, and the aroma enveloped them. "Do I need to worry about you?" she asked.

"Yes," Meredith said. She smiled, then she reached out to hug Connie. "This is amazing, Con. You're helping me."

"No," Connie said. "You're helping me."

They ate the scrambled eggs right out of the pan, and then they moved on to quiche. Connie used a prepared pie shell — Meredith wasn't ready to make her own pastry dough—and mixed up a basic custard of eggs, half-and-half, and salt and pepper.

"You can add anything you want," Connie said. "Bacon, sausage, chopped ham, chopped Spam, government cheese, scallions, chives, wild onions you find on the side of the road, diced tomatoes, diced zucchini, mushrooms, you name it. Then you pour it into the crust like this, and bake it at three fifty for fifty minutes."

Meredith took notes. Connie shredded some Emmental cheese and added chopped deli salami and some diced tomatoes and snipped chives. She slid the quiche into the oven. They would eat it for lunch.

Dan had been gone for only an hour. Connie wasn't sure how she was going to make it through the next three days.

"Now," she said, "I'm going to teach you the most important lesson of all."

"What's that?" Meredith said. She seemed genuinely interested, and Connie wondered how Meredith could be so focused—nearly happy—when she was doomed to read about Freddy's affair in a book written by Samantha Deuce.

Just then, Toby walked into the kitchen and said, "Something smells good." He kissed Meredith on the back of her neck and grabbed her around the waist. Meredith cast her eyes down, and Connie thought, *All right, what's going on?*

She said, "Did something happen last night?"

Meredith elbowed Toby in the ribs. "Connie was just about to teach me the most important lesson of all."

Toby said, "Dinner was delicious. When we finally ate it."

Connie glanced at her brother. He kept a straight face, then broke out into a beautiful smile. Meredith turned around and kissed Toby in a way that evoked 1979, and Connie nearly groaned. This would be a lot easier to stomach if Dan were here.

"Out of the kitchen," Connie said to Toby. "I'll call you when lunch is ready."

"But I want to learn the most important lesson," Toby said. "What is it?"

Connie felt like she should give a profound answer. What *was* the most important lesson? Was it love? Was it forgiveness? Was it honesty? Was it perseverance?

She wielded her whisk. "Vinaigrette," she said.

They ate a late lunch of quiche and perfectly dressed salad greens. After lunch, Meredith and Toby wanted to go for a bike ride—probably they wanted to be alone—but if Connie sat around the house by herself she would lose her mind, so she tagged along with them. They biked out to Sconset. The climbing roses were in their second bloom, even more lush and lavish than they had been in July—and then they decided to bike Polpis Road. This was nine miles on top of the two they had already done. Connie was in terrible shape, but the bike ride invigorated her. Her heart was pumping and her legs were warm and tingling, and she filled with a kind of euphoria from the fresh air and the endorphins. It was ideal weather—low seventies with low humidity and mellow sunshine. Autumn was coming. Maybe it was this thought that made Connie suggest that they head into town instead of home to Tom Nevers.

"Town?" Toby said. "You're sure?"

"We can get ice cream," Connie said.

They biked an additional two miles into town, at which point Connie was wiped out. She collapsed on a stool at the counter of the Nantucket Pharmacy. Meredith and Toby flanked her and the three of them ordered chocolate frappes. There were lots of other people in the pharmacy—primarily older people who had come to get their prescriptions filled and harried-looking mothers with recalcitrant children demanding jimmies, but none of them seemed to notice Meredith, and more unusual still was the fact that Meredith didn't seem to mind if she was noticed or not. She interacted with one little girl whose scoop of peppermint-stick ice cream was threatening to topple into the lap of her hand-embroidered sundress. The little girl was about six years old and had a perfect blond bob. The little girl *was* Meredith Martin at age six.

"Let me help you with that," Meredith said, and she secured the ice cream onto the cone with a spoon.

"Thank you," the girl's mother said.

Meredith smiled. To Connie, she murmured, "She looks like one of these little girls I knew in Palm Beach." Her expression darkened, the demons were encroaching, and Connie thought, *We have to get out of here while things are still okay.*

She eased back off her stool; even that made her legs ache. She said, "I'm never going to make it back home. We have to call a cab."

"Thank God you said that, Nance Armstrong," Toby said.

They called a cab that could accommodate the bikes, and rode home in exhausted silence.

It was six o'clock. They took turns in the outdoor shower, with Meredith slated to go last.

"So you can stay in as long as you want," Connie said.

"You're so good to me," Meredith said.

"Who's the little girl in Palm Beach?" Connie asked.

"Long story," Meredith said.

Connie wanted to pour a glass of wine—oh, boy, did she—and she had earned it with nearly fifteen miles of biking and Dan away and Meredith and Toby in a state of bliss, but she decided against it. She prepared pasta and served it with the Dijon shallot cream sauce that she and Meredith had made earlier, and a salad with vinaigrette, and some leftover Parker House rolls. It was a good dinner, and the three of them ate outside. After, they cleaned up, and Toby asked if they wanted to watch a movie. Meredith said yes, but Connie said she was tired and thought she would go upstairs to read.

"But reading might not last long," Connie said. "I'm beat."

"It was a good day," Meredith said.

"Dinner was delicious," Toby said. "Thank you."

Once in the master suite with the door shut, Connie thought, *I survived the first day without Dan.* But how would she make it through three more days? And how, how, *how* would she leave the island?

She loved him.

She sat on the edge of her bed. Okay, wait. She was unprepared to love anyone but Wolf Flute. So she didn't love Danforth Flynn. But God, her heart was splintering at the prospect of even three days without him. The clock radio was on the nightstand. Connie reached over to turn it on, and then she got an idea.

No, the idea was stupid. It was so cliché. But before she could stop herself, Connie had her cell phone in her hand and she was dialing. With all those hours of avid listening, she knew the number by heart.

At first, the line was busy. Of course, it was busy; Delilah had millions of listeners who all wanted to send songs out to their loved ones. Connie hit redial.

And on her sixteenth try, someone answered. Not Delilah, but a screener.

"Tell me your story," the screener said. The screener was male; he sounded as young as Meredith's attorney. Was this some college kid earning extra money by screening for Delilah? Connie found this amusing.

She thought, *My story? My story will take all night.*

She said, "My husband died two years ago of brain cancer, and I never thought I'd find love again." Here, Connie walked over to her dressing table. She pointed to herself in the mirror and thought, *You, Constance Flute, are made for Delilah!* "But this summer, I've met a wonderful man named Dan, and my life has changed. I've changed. Dan is away this weekend, on a camping trip with his sons, but I'd like to send out a song to him so he knows I'm thinking of him."

"What's the song?" the screener asked.

"'Something in the Way She Moves' by James Taylor," Connie said. The song Dan sang in her ear up at Great Point.

"Good stuff," the screener said. "I'm going to get you on."

The next day, Connie taught Meredith how to make a cream soup from scratch.

"Once I show you the basics," Connie said, "you can do this with any vegetable: broccoli, asparagus, carrot, tomato, mushroom."

"Right," Meredith said. "But what's going to keep me from reaching for a can of Campbell's for a dollar forty-nine instead?"

"You'll see once you taste it," Connie said. "First, you sauté an onion in four tablespoons of butter until the onion is soft." She moved the onion around the stock pot as the butter foamed. Connie had done so well on the radio that now she was thinking TV, she was thinking the Food Network, her own cooking show! "Then, add three tablespoons of flour and cook for one minute. Cooking the flour a little eliminates the starchiness." If Toby could go to the Naval Academy, why couldn't Connie do the Food Network? "Add the vegetable next—in this case, four cups of *sliced summer squash.*" Connie enunciated clearly, mugged for an imaginary camera, then dumped the squash into the pot. Meredith didn't notice the theatrics; she was bent over her little notebook, writing down every step. Would she really make her own soup? Connie wondered. Or was she destined for Campbell's? "Pour in six cups of chicken broth, a cup of white wine, and a teaspoon of fresh thyme. Put the top on the pot and simmer for twenty minutes."

Connie set the timer. She turned to Meredith. She was unable to hold it in any longer. "I was on Delilah last night."

Meredith's brow crinkled. "Huh?"

"I called in to Delilah and sent a song out to Dan."

"You did not."

"I did so. I was on the radio."

"Why didn't you tell us?" Meredith said. "Oh, my God, what I would have given to hear that. What song did you ask her to play?"

" 'Something in the Way She Moves.' " Connie said. "By James Taylor."

A shadow crossed Meredith's face.

Connie said, "Don't even think about it."

Meredith turned away. Connie absently stirred the squash in the pot.

"Okay, do think about it," she said. "What song would you send out to Freddy?"

"I don't know," Meredith said. " 'I Will Survive'?"

"And you will," Connie said. "You will, Meredith."

Meredith walked over to the sliding-glass doors. "I'm going to sit in the sun," she said. "You know, we only have nine days left."

Nine days. A ticking started in Connie's head, like a time bomb.

When the squash had cooked and cooled to room temperature, Connie went outside to grab Meredith. "Time to finish the soup."

Connie poured the cooled contents of the pot into her food processor. When she turned it on, the mixture became a smooth, sunny-colored liquid. Connie poured it back into the pot and added salt, pepper, and a cup of heavy cream. She lifted a spoonful for Meredith to taste, then she tasted it herself.

Sublime. It was fresh, sweet, and squashlike. This was why Meredith couldn't simply pick a can off the shelf.

"You have to promise me that you'll try this yourself," Connie said. "With some really good produce."

"I'll try," Meredith said. "But I can't promise. How can I promise?"

That evening, they ate the soup with a fresh, piping hot baguette— the crevices filled with melting sweet butter—and a green salad with vinaigrette that Meredith had made herself, as a final exam of sorts. It tasted just like Connie's vinaigrette, and Meredith was thrilled. They did a cheers with their water glasses. The cooking lessons had been a success, Meredith was a quick study, and it was a good thing because Dan would be home soon enough, and Connie would have other things to do.

In the middle of the night, Connie was awakened by a noise. At first, she thought it was the radio; she had fallen asleep listening to Delilah. But it was a rattling, coming from downstairs. It was a pounding.

The vandal, Connie thought. There had been nothing for weeks, nothing since Toby arrived, but now, yes—someone was outside. Connie slipped out of bed. She was wearing only a T-shirt and underwear. She needed shorts.

She called out, "Toby!" The man slept like the dead. She might have to splash him with cold water to wake him up.

But when she got out to the hallway, Toby and Meredith were standing at the top of the stairs.

"Someone's outside," Connie said.

"I'll take care of it," Toby said.

"It sounds like the person is trying to get in," Meredith said. "What if it's Samantha? What if she came here to confront me?"

"Is that possible?" Connie asked. Of course, it was possible, but was it likely? It did sound like the person was knocking, then shaking the doorknob, trying to force the door. What if it was the FBI, come to take Meredith away?

Toby turned on the hall light. Connie peered down the stairs at the clock. It was only five after eleven.

Toby said, "Who is it?"

Connie and Meredith were creeping down the stairs one at a time. Connie tried to look out the sidelights.

A muffled voice said, "Itzashalan."

Connie said, "It's Ashlyn!"

Toby unlocked the door, and Connie heard herself cry, "Wait, wait!" Because they had to punch in the security code first, Ashlyn's birthday, Connie did it automatically, her whole body was shaking like she had a fever, and she thought, "Is it Ashlyn? Is it?"

And they opened the door and Connie looked, and there was her baby girl.

Connie didn't know whether to laugh or cry. She did both. She was a hysterical, sobbing mess, but it didn't matter, did it? She had her daughter, her very own daughter, in her arms. Toby's eyes were brimming, and Meredith—well, Connie didn't expect tears from Meredith and she didn't find any. Meredith was smiling and nodding her head. Meredith was level-headed enough to get everyone inside and Ashlyn's luggage in and the cabbie paid. She shepherded everybody into the kitchen, and Connie sat at the table and encouraged Ashlyn to sit, but she wouldn't let go of Ashlyn's hand. No way.

Meredith said, "Ashlyn, are you hungry? Would you like some summer-squash soup? It's homemade."

Ashlyn looked at Meredith, then at Toby, then at Connie, and she burst into tears.

Connie said, "Honey, what's wrong?" She realized then that something horrible must have happened. Ashlyn wouldn't have shown up here out of the blue for Connie's sake.

"Bridget and I..." She tried to get air in. "Bridget and I..."

"Split up?" Connie said.

Ashlyn nodded. "For good this time!" she wailed and dropped her head to the table.

Oh, no. Oh, dear. Connie wasn't sure what to do. She touched the top of Ashlyn's head, the pale hair. "Oh, honey. I'm sorry."

Eventually, Ashlyn raised her head. Her nose was red and running. "We split earlier this summer..."

"When you called me before?" Connie said.

"When I called you before," Ashlyn said.

"But...?"

"But then we got back together, and I didn't feel like I could talk to you about it. Because of what happened at the funeral."

"Ashlyn," Connie said. "I'm sorry about what happened at the funeral."

"I love Bridget so much," Ashlyn said. "And she was my best friend besides." They all waited, watching Ashlyn cry, and Connie thought, *I'd do anything to make her feel better.* But there was nothing. Of course, there was nothing any of them could do.

"What happened?" Connie asked.

"I wanted a baby," Ashlyn said.

Instinctively, Connie made a noise. She pressed her lips together.

"And Bridget didn't," Ashlyn said. "I really did and she really didn't. And two months ago when she found out that I'd been to a donation center and had put myself on the list for insemination, she told me she was leaving. She moved out. Our separation lasted two and a half days, then I went to her and said I couldn't stand to be away from her, and I said I would give up the idea of having children."

"She doesn't want children right now?" Connie asked. "Or not ever?"

"Not ever," Ashlyn said. "She's on track to be the best female pediatric heart surgeon in the state of Florida. She wants to be the best pediatric heart surgeon, man or woman, in the country some-day. She said she was around children enough to know that she wasn't capable of raising her own. She thinks she's too selfish, too driven."

"But lots of men are like that," Connie said. "If you agreed to stay at home..."

"She still wouldn't do it," Ashlyn said. She started crying again.

Connie squeezed Ashlyn's hand, thinking, *This is my daughter's hand. This is all I've been wishing for.*

Meredith set down a bowl of warm soup and a hunk of baguette and a glass of water. Toby cleared his throat. He said, "So then why did you break up?"

Ashlyn wiped at her red eyes. Her hair was in a messy bun. It didn't look like she'd seen the sun all summer. But she was, absolutely, the most beautiful creature Connie had ever laid eyes on.

Ashlyn said, "I'm pregnant. Due in April."

Toby jumped in surprise. Meredith said, "Oh, Ashlyn, that's wonderful."

Connie thought, *Wolf! Wolf! Did you hear that?*

Ashlyn was still crying. "And I thought news of a baby, a real live baby, would change Bridget's mind." She sniffled. Meredith brought a box of Kleenex. Ashlyn blew her nose. "But it didn't."

"So here you are," Toby said.

She crumpled the Kleenex in her hand. "So here I am." She looked at Connie with bleary eyes. "I've been a terrible daughter, and I know I don't deserve a second chance, but I came here because I didn't have anywhere else to go."

"That sounds familiar," Meredith said. She rested her hands on Toby's shoulders.

Connie thought, *What is the most important lesson of all? Perseverance? Honesty? Forgiveness? Love?*

Wolf, Ashlyn, Toby, Meredith, Dan. Ashlyn, Ashlyn, Ashlyn — Connie and Wolf's daughter, their only child, conceived so many years ago in the back of a pickup truck a few miles away, beneath a sky filled with stars. Ashlyn was going to have a baby. Ashlyn had been so angry — she had been silent and seething — but she had come back to Connie because Connie hadn't stopped loving Ashlyn even for a second. Ashlyn would soon know it herself: parents didn't stop loving their children for any reason.

Love, then, Connie decided. *The most important lesson is love.*

MEREDITH

Meredith felt like they were all graduating from college, and everyone knew what the next step was but her.

In the span of sixteen or seventeen hours, Connie's life had transformed as dramatically (almost) as Meredith's life had the previous December—only for the better. Connie would return to Bethesda the Tuesday after Labor Day. That was as planned. What was different now was that Ashlyn was putting her house in Tallahassee on the market and moving back up to Bethesda, into Connie's house. Ashlyn would live with Connie indefinitely. She would have the baby, and Connie would care for it while Ashlyn went back to work. Ashlyn had applied for a job in the ped onc department at WHC, and if she didn't get that job, she would look elsewhere.

"Lots of good hospitals in Washington," Connie said to Meredith and Toby. "And just think, next summer when we're all here, we'll have a baby!"

Next summer when we're all here: These words were a balm to Meredith. She had been invited back. It took some of the sting out of leaving, although it did nothing to help her sense of floundering, about where to go or what to do in the next ten months.

Toby was going back to Annapolis. A brand-new freshman class of cadets awaited.

"Now I wish I hadn't sold my boat," Toby said. "Now I wish I could just sail with you around the world."

Sailing with Toby around the world: it was appealing, Meredith had to admit.

"I know you," Meredith said. "You have to have your freedom."

"I'd like to share that freedom with you," he said. "Give you a little sip of it. It's the most intoxicating thing on earth."

But Meredith's freedom was still in the firm grip of federal investigators.

*   *   *

They all sat on the back deck, enjoying the sun: Connie, Ashlyn, Toby, Meredith. They had a pitcher of iced tea (decaf, for Ashlyn) and a bowl of Bing cherries, which they passed around. Ashlyn was nauseous; every half hour or so, she'd go into the house to throw up.

"I can't believe how lousy I feel," she said.

"I could tell you stories," Connie said. "About you."

Meredith squinted at the ocean. She decided to speak the words that were on everyone's mind. "I never want to leave here."

"You don't have to," Connie said. "You know you don't have to go anywhere."

The phone rang inside. The phone, the phone. Meredith's shoulders tensed. "Maybe that's Dan," she said.

"Not for another thirty-two hours," Connie said.

"I'll get it," Toby said. He heaved himself up and out of his chaise. A second later, he poked his head out and said, "Meredith, it's for you."

"Of course," Connie said.

"Is it Dev?" Meredith asked.

"I don't believe so," Toby said.

Leo, Carver, Freddy? Freddy, Freddy, Freddy? It was official: Meredith hated the telephone. The phone terrified her.

It was Ed Kapenash, chief of police. He wanted Meredith to come down to the station.

"I think we've found our man," he said. "And our woman."

Meredith and Connie went to the police station together. Although it was Meredith who was being terrorized, the property belonged to Connie. She was the only one who could press charges.

"Who do you think it is?" Connie said. "Do you think it's someone you know? Do you think it's your friend from Palm Beach?"

"I don't know," Meredith said. She was in a hazy daze. It was hot outside. She wanted to be on the deck. She wanted to go for a swim. She wanted to whip up more vinaigrette. She wanted Freddy to call. Most of all, that was what she wanted. She didn't want to be going into the police station to meet her own personal terrorist.

"Right down the hall," the secretary said. She stared grimly at Meredith for an extra second, and Meredith guessed that this was the kind of person who would dress up as "Meredith Delinn" for Halloween. "First door on the left."

Connie led, Meredith followed. The first door on the left was unmarked.

"This one?" Connie said.

"That's what the lovely woman said."

Connie knocked, and Ed Kapenash opened the door.

"Come in," he said. He ushered them in to what looked like a classroom. There was a long particleboard table, ten folding chairs, a green blackboard coated with yellow chalk dust. Two people sat at the table already, two people whom Meredith could only describe as hungry-looking. The man was beefy with a thick neck, a buzz cut of dirt brown hair, a gold hoop earring, and a T-shirt that appeared to be advertising Russian beer. He looked familiar to Meredith. She felt like she had seen that T-shirt before. Meredith-got a hot, leaky feeling of fear. The woman, probably in her midthirties, had very short hair dyed jet black. She wore jeans shorts and a sleeveless yellow blouse. She had a bruise on one cheek. Meredith couldn't believe these two were just sitting at the table, as though they had arrived early for dinner.

"Mikhail Vetsilyn and Dmitria Sorchev," the chief said. "They were stopped on Milestone Road for speeding at two o'clock this morning. They said they were headed to Tom Nevers to see 'an old friend.' The van reeked of marijuana smoke. The officer on duty, Sergeant Dickson, asked them to step out of the van. He then proceeded to check the back of the van. He found three five-gallon jugs of gasoline and fourteen empty cans of electric-green spray paint. He called in reinforcements and did a full check of the van, and they found this." The chief held up a plastic bag containing a medieval-looking curved dagger, covered with blood and hair. Meredith looked down into her lap.

"Have they confessed?" Connie asked.

"They've confessed," the chief said. "Two acts of vandalism for her. That, plus the unlawful slaying of a sea mammal for him. God only knows what they were going to do with the gasoline."

"Burn the house down," the man said.

"Hey!" The chief's voice was like a whip. Meredith looked up in alarm. There was the chief, being chieflike. "I'm happy to book you with attempted arson," he said. He turned to Connie and Meredith. "I assume you want to press charges."

"Burn my house down?" Connie said. "My husband designed that house. God, yes, I want to press charges."

"But wait," Meredith said. "Who are they?" She lowered her voice, trying to convince herself they wouldn't hear her, and if they did hear her that they wouldn't understand. "Are they Russian?" Were these the assassins the Russian mob had sent? Two people who looked like they'd escaped from the gulag?

"They're from Belarus," the chief said. "Minsk."

Minsk. Meredith looked at the woman. *Like me, also from Minsk.* "Are you a housekeeper?" she said. "Do you clean houses?"

The young woman nodded.

Yes, okay. Meredith said, "Did you give your life savings to your employer to invest with Delinn Enterprises? A hundred and thirty-seven thousand dollars?"

The girl twitched her head. "Yes," she said. "How you know?"

"I met a friend of yours," Meredith said.

Connie eyed her quizzically.

"At the salon."

"Ahhh," Connie said.

Meredith studied the man. She had seen him before. *Burn the house down.* She had heard his voice before. And then she remembered: She had seen him on the ferry. He had been in line with her when she went to get coffee for her and Connie. He must have recognized her then. He must have followed Connie's Escalade out to Tom Nevers.

"We can drop the two vandalism charges on her," the chief said, "but the unlawful slaying of a sea mammal will stick with him regardless, as well as a marijuana-possession charge."

"Drop the vandalism charges," Meredith whispered.

"What?" Connie said.

"She lost her life savings."

"So?" Connie said. "It's *my* house. *My* car."

"Would you ladies like to talk about this out in the hallway?" the chief asked.

"No," Meredith said. She smiled at Connie, then whispered, "She lost a lot of money, Con. She lost everything."

Connie shook her head, unconvinced.

"And here's the other thing," Meredith said. "If they hadn't spray painted the house, you wouldn't have met Dan."

"Oh, come on," Connie said.

"You should be *thanking* them," Meredith said.

Connie rolled her eyes. She turned to the chief. "Okay, we're out of it. You'll punish him for killing Harold? And you'll make sure neither one of them does anything like this again?"

"That's our job," the chief said.

Meredith and Connie stood to leave. Meredith approached the woman, Dmitria Sorchev, and said, "I want you to know how sorry I am. I'm sorry about your money. Your savings."

The young woman pulled her lips back to reveal grayish teeth. "Fuck Freddy Delinn."

Meredith sighed and looked at Connie over the top of her glasses. Connie smiled. She liked the girl a little better now.

Connie turned to the chief. "Thank you for calling us."

"I'm glad we settled this," the chief said. He escorted the ladies out to the hallway. "There will be paperwork for you to sign, probably sometime tomorrow."

Connie and Meredith shook his hand. The secretary, thankfully, had left for lunch. Meredith stepped outside into the sun.

"I'm going to take you up on your offer," Meredith said as they climbed into the Escalade. About eight weeks earlier, Meredith had climbed into this car for the first time, running through a dark alley, dodging the flash of the hidden photographer. "I'm going to stay on Nantucket this winter."

"Atta girl," Connie said. And she started the engine.

No sooner had Meredith and Connie settled into their chaise lounges on the deck next to Toby and Ashlyn than the phone rang again.

"You answer it," Connie said. "I want to tell these guys what happened with Boris and Natasha."

"Did anything happen here?" Meredith asked. She didn't want to answer it.

"Just napping and puking," Ashlyn said. But she seemed marginally more cheerful.

Anything but a ringing phone. *Leo, Carver, Freddy. Freddy, Freddy, Freddy! Goddamn you, Freddy!* she thought (zillionth and eighth). That poor girl, her gray teeth, her life's savings; she might as well have poured gasoline on the money and set it on fire herself.

Meredith dragged her feet for so long that the phone stopped ringing. She exhaled. Then it started ringing again. The starting up again was worse: whoever it was really wanted to talk to her.

But maybe the call wasn't for her. Maybe it was Bridget, calling for Ashlyn.

Meredith checked the display. It was the law firm.

Meredith picked up the phone, saying a Hail Mary in her head. Now that she had decided to stay on Nantucket, the most devastating thing she could think of was for someone to take her away. *Please don't take me away.* "Hello?"

"Meredith?"

"Dev?"

"Thank *God* you answered," he said. "I tried a second ago and no one answered."

"I just walked in," she said.

"We found the money!" Dev said. He sounded amped up, triumphant; he was *crowing*. "And you were right! It was in a bank in Malaysia—nearly four billion dollars in Samantha Champion's name. That money had been transferred from the four numbered accounts in Switzerland on Mrs. Champion's birthday last October."

"Four billion dollars," Meredith said. For Samantha, on Samantha's birthday, which was exactly one week before Meredith's birthday.

"The word 'champ' was all over Freddy's confidential papers, and so, thanks to you, the Feds brought Mrs. Deuce in. And when the Feds questioned her, she copped to the affair. I think she thought if she confessed to the sexual stuff that we'd be thrown off the trail of her financial involvement. But the information you gave us really helped."

"Great," Meredith said, but her voice was flat. On the one hand, she no longer cared about money. On the other hand, she couldn't believe Freddy had transferred $4 billion to Samantha on Samantha's birthday and had left Meredith with nothing.

"And we found eight billion dollars in other accounts at the same bank...in the name of David Delinn."

David Delinn.

"His brother," Meredith said.

"His brother."

"But his brother *is* dead, right?" Meredith said. God, what if Freddy had been lying from the very beginning? From their first walk together, their first conversation?

"His brother was shot and killed in a training exercise outside of Fort Huachuca in nineteen seventy-eight. Freddy used an existing account of David's from the nineteen sixties. Freddy had been depositing money into that account for decades. He was listed as trustee. The money was transferred out in nineteen ninety-two, then, apparently, transferred again. It was a web that was almost impossible to untangle."

Meredith shut her eyes. It was a web of lies involving David, Samantha, Kirby Delarest, and Thad Orlo, but not her. Not her. They knew that, right? Not her.

"So, that twelve billion dollars was recovered," Dev said, "largely thanks to you. This is going to help out a lot with the restitution to investors."

"Right," Meredith said. She wondered if Amy Rivers would get any money back. Or the poor girl from Minsk, who would need it now for her comrade's legal fees.

"The Feds are going to issue a statement at five o'clock today," Dev said. "And they will include mention that information provided by Meredith Delinn was instrumental in the investigation."

"So I'm not in trouble anymore?" Meredith said. "I can call my children?"

"The SEC is going to be sifting through the rubble of this for years, Meredith," Dev said. "But for now, the Feds are satisfied that you had no knowledge of the Ponzi scheme. They now believe what you said in your deposition: Freddy asked you to transfer the fifteen million dollars, and you transferred it. You were his pawn, but that's not a crime. So, yes, you can call your children."

"Thank you," Meredith whispered. She took a huge breath. She was getting her kids back! Leo! Carver! As soon as Meredith hung up, she would call Carver's cell phone. It would ring in the pocket of his Carhartt overalls. Meredith imagined him standing on a ladder leaning against the great big beautiful old house that he was restoring. He would answer the phone, and it would be Meredith. And after she'd told him about what had happened, she would ask to speak to Leo. Carver would call out, "Hey, Leo? It's Mom." He would toss the phone down to Leo, and Leo would grin, and he would say, "Hey, Mom."

*   *   *

In the days that remained of the summer, news of Freddy Delinn and the spoils of his kingdom hit the front page of every paper in the country. All reports mentioned that Meredith Delinn had been working with federal investigators to help locate the missing money.

Dennis Stamm, the head of the SEC's investigative team, was quoted as saying, "We couldn't have found this money without salient bits of information provided by Mrs. Delinn. She showed herself to be a truly great citizen with the effort she put forth in cracking the code and recovering this money for Mr. Delinn's former investors."

Meredith fully expected the reporters to reappear, but they didn't. Maybe because Ed Kapenash was an effective police chief who had finally learned how to protect the island's most notorious summer resident, or maybe because the *Post* only followed trails of blood. Girl Scouts didn't make the front page.

Meredith didn't want to waste the final days of summer watching reports about the rediscovered money on TV, and luckily, she didn't have to. She and Toby went kayaking in the Monomoy creeks, where the only sounds were the water lapping against their paddles and the cries of seabirds. When they got home, they found Connie and Ashlyn sitting together on the sofa, Ashlyn weeping, Connie rubbing Ashlyn's feet.

"Everything all right with the baby?" Meredith asked quietly later.

"Everything's all right with the baby," Connie said. "She misses Bridget."

And Meredith thought about how it felt to yearn for something that you absolutely knew you weren't going to get—in her case, a phone call from Butner. "Yes," Meredith said. "I bet she does."

They managed to get Ashlyn out of the house the next day. Dan took everybody on an expedition to Smith's Point, where Toby and Dan caught eight inedible bluefish—so they ended up having fish tacos on the outdoor deck of Millie's as the sun went down. The next morning, Meredith and Toby and Connie and Dan biked to Bartlett's Farm and found themselves on a road that cut through two resplendent fields of flowers. As far as the eye could see, there were snapdragons and zinnias and marigolds and lilies, a palette of color upon color such as Meredith hadn't seen since she viewed the Pissarros during her private tour of the Musée d'Orsay.

Meredith stopped her bike and inhaled. It was an intoxicating sip of freedom.

On their final afternoon, Meredith and Connie sojourned into town. Meredith bought two novels, which she would read after the others had left the island, and Connie bought a white baby blanket that had the word "Nantucket" embroidered across the bottom in navy thread. Then Connie wanted to zip into the kitchen store, and Meredith took the opportunity to light candles at the church.

The interior seemed brighter than it had the last time; muted light shone through the stained glass windows. Meredith stuck ten dollars into the slot, a small fortune, for despite all that had happened, she still believed.

She lit a candle for Connie first, then Toby, then Dan. She lit candles for Leo and Carver. Then she lit a candle for heartbroken Ashlyn and one for the baby inside her. Then Meredith lit a candle for her mother and her father. She had one candle left. She thought about lighting it for Dev or for Amy Rivers or for Samantha. She considered lighting it for herself. Of everyone she knew, she needed a candle the most. One thing was for sure: she was *not* going to light a candle for Freddy.

She pushed the button and thought, *For Dev.* He had been so good to her.

She slipped through the double doors into the vestibule, but she couldn't bring herself to leave the church. She rummaged through her purse for another dollar bill and went back and lit another candle—for Freddy.

Because that was how she was. She couldn't seem to abandon him.

No matter what.

Out in the sunny world, Connie waited on a bench.

Connie said, "Did that go okay?"

Meredith said, "I lit candles." She didn't tell Connie that she'd lit a candle for Freddy—but who was she kidding? Connie already knew.

"I got you something," Connie said. She handed Meredith a big white shopping bag with cord handles from Nantucket Gourmet. "Sorry it's not wrapped."

Meredith peered inside. It was an eleven-cup Cuisinart food processor. "Of course you can use the one in my kitchen," Connie said. "But this is one of your very own. A graduation present."

Meredith was so overwhelmed by the perfection of the gift that she closed her eyes. She thought back to the cruel summer weeks right after Toby had broken up with her. Connie had dragged her to a party at Villanova, and Meredith had drunk too much, and Connie had carried Meredith home on her back. This summer was like that night times fifty billion (this was the largest real number Meredith could think of). This summer, Connie had carried Meredith on her back once again. She had carried Meredith all the way to safety.

"I almost lit a candle for myself in there," Meredith said, nodding at the church. "But then I realized I didn't need to."

Connie put a hand up. "Don't say it, Meredith. You'll make me cry."

Meredith said, "Because you, Constance—you are my candle."

Connie sniffed; tears leaked out from beneath her sunglasses. Meredith pulled her to her feet, and they crossed the cobblestone street to Connie's car.

Endings were like this. You could see them coming from far away, but there was one more thing (dinner at Le Languedoc) and one more thing (ice cream at the Juice Bar) and one more thing (a stroll down the dock to see the yachts) and one more thing (an hour with Toby out on the deck, looking at the stars, knowing, finally, that not a single one of them was especially for you) and one more thing (lovemaking, tender and bittersweet) and one more thing (watching the sunrise on the Juliet balcony) and one more thing (a trip to the Sconset Market for snickerdoodle coffee and peach muffins, only they didn't have peach anymore; fall was coming, they'd switched to cranberry) and one more thing…

Endings, when anticipated, took forever.

And one more thing: Toby and Meredith sat on the floor of Meredith's room, sifting through the possessions in her one cardboard box. Downstairs, Connie and Ashlyn were packing, and Dan was helping them load the car, which was going back to Hyannis on the noon boat. Dan was taking Toby to the airport at eleven. Toby's sky-blue duffel bag was packed fat, waiting at the top of the stairs. Meredith was torn between wanting the ending to be over with—just everyone go—and wanting to squeeze the life out of every remaining second.

The first thing out of Meredith's box were the photographs, which Meredith placed facedown. Too painful. Next, were the boys' yearbooks and Meredith's favorite paperbacks—*Goodbye, Columbus* and *The Heart Is a Lonely Hunter.* There was her record album, *Bridge Over Troubled Water.* And finally, her anthropology notebook. Meredith paged through the notebook, ogling her eighteen-year-old handwriting. There was so much knowledge here, completely forgotten.

Toby studied the Simon and Garfunkel album. He pulled out the record sleeve and read her father's note. "Wow," he said. "No wonder you kept this."

Stay with me, Meredith almost said. *Live here with me for the winter.* It was ironic that Toby would have been free to do that in the past, but now he had a steady job. And, of course, his son. Toby promised he would bring Michael to Nantucket for

Thanksgiving, along with Connie and Ashlyn. Dan would come, too, with his sons.

"And when you realize that you can't live without me," Toby had said the night before, "you can come and live with me in Annapolis. It's not Park Avenue and it's not Palm Beach, but we will live an honest life."

"Dunbar's number," Meredith said, reading from her anthropology notebook. "It says here that human beings can have stable social relationships with a maximum of one hundred and fifty people. One hundred and fifty is Dunbar's number."

"Stable social relationships?" Toby said.

Meredith said, "My own personal Dunbar's number is four. On a good day, seven. You, Connie, Dan, Ashlyn, Leo, Carver, and…"

The phone rang in the house.

Meredith heard Ashlyn cry out, "I'll get it!" Meredith knew that Ashlyn would be hoping and praying it was Bridget.

A second later, Ashlyn called out. "Meredith?"

Was there any doubt? Meredith looked at Toby, and Toby pulled her to her feet. Out in the hallway, Ashlyn offered up the phone, a look of crushed disappointment on her face.

"Thank you," Meredith whispered. And then, into the phone, "Hello?"

"Meredith?"

It was Dev. He sounded excited again. Another insidious discovery? More money uncovered? Hidden with the jihadists perhaps, in the Middle East?

"Hi, Dev," Meredith said. He was her seventh stable social relationship.

"Somehow this woman, Nancy Briggs? At the prison? At Butner?"

"Yes?"

"Somehow she worked it out. Her and the priest. Or her through the priest—maybe that's what it was, since I'm sure the warden's secretary doesn't have any contact with the actual prisoners. But she convinced the priest, and the priest convinced Freddy, and he's agreed to take your call."

"He's agreed to take my call," Meredith said.

"He'll take your call," Dev said. He paused. "That was what you wanted, right? That was what you asked me for?"

"It was," Meredith said. Toby squeezed her hand, and then he left the room. He knew that there were some things that Meredith had to deal with alone.

Freddy would take her call. What did that mean? That meant he would sit in a room, and someone would hold the phone to his ear or he would hold the phone himself, and Meredith would speak. She would go down her list of eighty-four questions, as though she were giving Freddy a test. Where? When? How? Why? Why? Why? Why?

She was never going to get the answers she was looking for. Freddy wouldn't tell her the truth, or he would tell her the truth and she wouldn't believe him. There was no truth with Freddy. Freddy's own personal Dunbar's number was zero. It had always been zero.

"Oh, Dev," she said.

"Don't tell me," he said. "You've changed your mind."

"I can't believe it," Meredith said. "I'm sorry."

"You don't want to talk to Freddy."

"That's right," Meredith said. "In fact, I don't want any news of Freddy at all, from this point on. Unless, well, unless he dies. You can call me when he dies." Meredith fidgeted with her grand-mother's engagement ring. This was the ring that she had given Freddy to give to her, a strange transaction in its own right, but now, more than anything, Meredith wanted it off her finger.

Dev said, "Okay, Meredith, are you sure? You want me to call the people at Butner back and tell them to forget about it?"

Was that what she wanted? She imagined prison officials saying to Fred, *You know what? Your wife doesn't want to talk to you, after all.* What would Freddy think? Meredith didn't care what he thought. She was going to save herself. She was going to swim to shore.

"I'm sure," Meredith said.

"Fine," Dev said. He paused, and then he added. "Good for you."

"Thanks, Dev," Meredith said, and she hung up. Downstairs, she heard Ashlyn and Connie and Dan and Toby talking about taking a picture before they all left. Who had a camera? It was one more thing, and Meredith was grateful.

She hurried downstairs to join them.

EPILOGUE

Autumn on Nantucket was serene and shockingly beautiful. Meredith was able to swim until the twenty-fifth of September. She kept hoping for the company of another seal—a brother of Harold's, perhaps, or a son or daughter, or a friend or lover—but none came.

Dan Flynn, whose real job it was to know everyone on Nantucket and everything that was happening, found Meredith a beat-up Jeep for $2,000 cash.

"The thing will probably leave a trail of sand all the way down the Milestone Road," he said. "But at least you'll be able to get around."

Meredith loved the Jeep much more than she had loved any of her other, fancier vehicles. It made her feel younger, wilder, freer; it made her feel like a person she had never been. She had taken taxis until she was twenty-eight; then, she and Freddy bought a Volvo wagon, which was quickly traded in for a BMW and so on and so on.

The Jeep already had a beach sticker, so Meredith packed herself a lunch—chicken salad that she'd made herself, a ripe, juicy pear, and a whole-wheat baguette from the Sconset Market—and she headed up to Great Point on a sparkling Thursday afternoon. The foliage on the Wauwinet Road was burnt orange and brilliant yellow. Meredith wanted to internalize the colors of the leaves, much like the flower fields of Bartlett's Farm. She wanted to keep the beauty, even as she knew that it was, and only could be, ephemeral. Time would pass, the leaves would fall, children would grow up. Thinking this made Meredith feel unspeakably lonely.

But there, at the gatehouse, was Bud Attatash. He peered at Meredith and the derelict Jeep suspiciously. Then, once he recognized her, he saluted.

Meredith slowed to a stop and shifted into first gear. "Hello, Mr. Attatash."

"Bud, please. You make me feel like I'm a million years old."

Meredith smiled at him. He was checking out the car.

"You're sure that's going to make it?" he said.

"If you don't see me by sundown, you'll come out and get me?"

"That I will," Bud said. He cleared his throat. "Young Flynn tells me that you're staying on island through the winter, and that you're looking for a job. Something out of the public eye?"

"That's right," Meredith said. She needed a job—for the money, certainly, but also as a reason to get out of the house.

"Well, my wife is looking for someone to shelve books after-hours at the Atheneum. They had plenty of help this summer, but everyone has gone back to school."

"Really?" Meredith said. "I'd love to do it."

"It doesn't pay a fortune," Bud said.

Meredith blushed. "Oh," she said. "I don't need a fortune."

And so, Meredith worked Tuesday through Saturday from 5 to 9 p.m., shelving books at the Nantucket Atheneum. She worked alone; most times, the only other person in the echoing historic building was the Salvadoran janitor.

Louisa, Meredith's housekeeper and cook, had been from El Salvador. Flashes of Meredith's previous life surprised her like this.

One day, she read a collection of Gwendolyn Brooks poems before she shelved it. *My God,* she thought.

Her favorite thing about the job was everything. She liked the quiet hush of the building; she liked its dusty museum smell. She loved the Great Hall upstairs — its volumes of Nantucket whaling history, its old New England cookery books. She loved handling books, putting them back where they belonged, in their indisputable proper place. When her workload was light, she would sit and read a chapter or two of books she'd read years before, and they seemed brand-new to her. She always poked her head into the children's section, which was dark and calm, the wooden trucks put away in their garages, the picture books fanned open on display. Children still read *Goodnight Moon,* they still read Carver's favorite, *Lyle Lyle Crocodile.* There was a colorful area rug and huge, plush chairs in the shape of zoo animals. Meredith wondered if she would have grandchildren someday.

Those grandchildren would never know Freddy. Thoughts like this haunted her.

She talked to Leo and Carver several times a week. Meredith asked Leo if he wanted Annabeth Martin's diamond ring, and he said yes. He was planning to propose to Anais sometime in the spring. The house that Meredith had been imagining them in had been sold for profit, and the boys had put a bid on a dilapidated Victorian in Saratoga Springs. They had promised they would come to Nantucket to see Meredith at Thanksgiving.

Meredith bought butternut squash at Bartlett's Farm and made soup, with Connie on the phone as a consultant. Meredith froze what she couldn't eat. She met Dan every Monday night at A.K. Diamond's, and he introduced her to his year-round friends, the carpenters and firemen and insurance agents, and whereas Meredith imagined that his friends would be interested in her lurid back story, most of them just wanted to know how she liked driving that funky Jeep.

The larger world began to open its doors to her once again. Notes arrived at Dev's office from people who had received their restitution checks, and Dev forwarded these letters to Meredith, though Meredith would sometimes let them sit for as long as a week without opening them. It was difficult to accept praise or thanks when so many people had lost so much. Meredith received a letter from an elderly woman in Sioux City, Iowa, who had received a check for a quarter of a million dollars, only 60 percent of what she'd invested—but still the woman was grateful to Meredith, and at the end of the note, told her to hold her head high. *You did the right thing,* she said.

What right thing was that? Meredith wondered.

A letter came from Michael Arrow in Broome, Australia, saying that the US government had promised him restitution of $1.3 million. It wouldn't be enough to buy back his family's pearl farm, but with the favorable exchange rate, it would be plenty to buy a holiday home somewhere in the south—maybe in Geraldton, maybe in Margaret River. The letter was friendly and informative; at the end of the letter, he invited Meredith to come visit him in Western Australia "anytime."

She folded the letter back up, baffled. Where had Michael Arrow been before the restitution was promised, when Meredith was living in the dark and didn't have a friend in the world?

There was no communication from Amy Rivers.

Through Dev, Meredith was informed of interview requests from Diane Sawyer and Meredith Vieira. The manager who had once handled Oliver North wanted to put Meredith on the lecture circuit. Big bucks to be made there, this manager told Dev.

Meredith turned everything down. She didn't want to make a single penny from her connection to Freddy.

A book offer came in. Undisclosed millions. More than the advance that Samantha had gotten, because Meredith was the wife. No.

Her passport arrived in the mail. She could go anywhere in the world.

But she didn't want to be anywhere else.

*   *   *

Meredith talked to Toby on the phone, she talked to Connie. She and Dev discussed how to go about changing her name back to Meredith Martin. It was easier than she thought it might be— fifty dollars, a stack of paperwork at the town clerk's office, five minutes in front of a very sympathetic judge. Once Meredith had shed the name Delinn like a diseased skin, she thought she might feel like a different person.

But she didn't. She felt the same. Although she had decided not to talk to Freddy, she sometimes found herself talking to him in her mind.

I let go of your name, she said. Like it was a balloon that she'd sent soaring up into the air.

Meredith was lonely some nights, and sadness cropped up in her like a virus. It made her sick, it went away, it made her sick again. On cold nights, she lit a fire and she tried to read—she would always have reading—but she wanted someone beside her. *Goddamn you, Freddy,* she thought (zillionth and ninth, tenth, eleventh). One particularly bad night, she checked in Connie's bathroom for the pills, but Connie had taken them all with her.

Meredith felt like she was waiting for something. She thought perhaps she was waiting for Freddy to die. He would be murdered by the Russian mob, or he would do the job himself by eating rat poison or slicing his wrists with a shiv. Prison officials would find a scrap of paper next to his bed with a single letter on it. The letter M.

And then, one afternoon, there was a thump on the front porch, and Meredith, who was on the sofa in front of the fire reading a Penelope Lively novel, sat straight up.

Call 911? she thought. Or Ed Kapenash's cell phone?

She tiptoed to the front of the house. The sun was hanging low in the sky, casting a mellow autumn glow across the front porch.

A package.

Meredith was suspicious. *Bomb,* she thought. *Crate of rattle-snakes. Raw sewage.* She stepped out onto the porch and, without touching the box, looked at the label.

It was from Toby. And then, Meredith realized that it was October twenty-third, and that the next day was her birthday.

She lugged the package inside. She knew she should save it for the following day, but her life had been devoid of small, happy surprises like this one for so long that she went ahead and opened it.

It was a record player. A pearlescent blue Bakelite record player with a black rubber turntable and an extension cord snaking out the back. It had a grooved white plastic knob, off/on, volume one through ten. She plugged it in. Would it work? Meredith ran upstairs and grabbed her Simon and Garfunkel album, which until that moment had been as useful as a pocketful of Confederate money. She dashed downstairs and put the record on the turntable. She turned the knob and a tiny red light came on and Meredith lowered the arm until the needle fit in the groove of the first song.

The song filled the house; the music had that crackling, staticky sound that Meredith remembered from childhood. Meredith turned the music up as loud as it would go, which was, surprisingly, pretty darn loud. Meredith braced herself against Connie's beautiful kitchen counter. As the operatic strains of the song progressed through the verses, she felt something happening to her chest, her head, her face.

> *Sail on Silvergirl,*
> *Sail on by*
> *Your time has come to shine*
> *All your dreams are on their way*

There was a slow burning in her eyes, a buzzing in her nose, and then, her cheeks were wet.

She was astonished. She felt like she was standing at the refrigerator watching herself. *Look, Meredith's crying!* Then she let go. She sobbed and wailed and gasped for breath. She took off her glasses and set them on the counter. She didn't care how out of control she was; no one was around to hear her. She thought of Ashlyn's swollen belly, and she thought that these tears had been gestating in her for a long, long time.

> *See how they shine*
> *Oh, if you need a friend, I'm sailing right behind*
> *Like a bridge over troubled water*
> *I will ease your mind*

Meredith Martin Delinn was crying. Her tears were coming from someplace old and far away. They were coming from the beginning of this story—the uneaten lobster roll, the weekly poker games, the driving lessons in the Villanova parking lot. Meredith was crying because she missed her father. It was the pain that never went away.

Tomorrow was her fiftieth birthday.

When the song was over, Meredith did the only thing she could do. She picked up the arm of the record player, and she started the song again.

ACKNOWLEDGMENTS

Some books are tougher than others; this one was very tough. I have to start by thanking my editor, Reagan Arthur, for her wise direction in revising this novel. Also, the brilliant and compassionate team at Inkwell Management, led by two of my favorite men in all the world, Michael Carlisle and David Forrer. Thanks also to Lauren Smythe and Kristen Palmer, whose input was invaluable.

I wouldn't have gotten a word written without my nanny, Stephanie McGrath, who covered for me in all ways with my three kids, and who bestowed her radiant smile on our household. Thank you, again, to Anne and Whitney Gifford for use of the house on Barnabas, my refuge, and to my mother, Sally Hilderbrand, for allowing me to come home and live like a moody teenager in my childhood bedroom while I revised this novel. Thank you to Anne Fitzgerald and Laurie Richards for always making me look good.

For shining their light on my life in any number of different ways, I'd like to thank Rebecca Bartlett, Elizabeth and Beau Almodobar, Richard Congdon, Wendy Hudson and Randy "Manskills" Hudson, Shelly and Roy Weedon, Evelyn(!) and Matthew MacEachern, Jill and Paul Surprenant (couldn't have done Little League without you!), Wendy Rouillard and Illya Kagan, Mark,

Eithne, and Michaela Yelle, Jennifer and Norman Frazee, John Bartlett, Rocky Fox (for constantly replacing my gold card), and Heidi and Fred Holdgate (the pool is my happy place). To my darlings whom I don't see nearly enough: Margie and Chuck Marino, Debbie Bennett (33!), Manda and West Riggs, David Rattner and Andrew Law, John and Nancy Swayne, Tal and Jonnie Smith (who taught me a lobster dinner should always be followed by blueberry pie), Fred and Irene Shabel, Tim and Mary Schoettle, Bob and Mindy Rich (Happy 70th, Bubba!), Catherine Ashby, and Sean and Milena Lennon (Freo forever!).

Among other things, this book is about my late father, Robert H. Hilderbrand Jr. I'd like to thank those people in my family who keep his laughter and loving memories alive: my stepmother, Judith Hilderbrand Thurman, my brothers Eric Hilderbrand and Douglas Hilderbrand, my stepbrother Randall Osteen, and my best friend in all the world whose over-the-top joyful energy and belief in me keep me going, my stepsister, Heather Osteen Thorpe. A huge hug goes out to Duane Thurman for captaining the ship and keeping us on course.

Last, I'd like to thank my husband, Chip Cunningham, who skillfully and compassionately dealt with the parts of author-under-stress-of-deadline that no one else sees, and my three children who are the coolest people I know: Maxwell, Dawson, and Shelby.

ABOUT THE AUTHOR

ELIN HILDERBRAND lives on Nantucket with her husband and their three children. She grew up in Collegeville, Pennsylvania, and is an enthusiastic Philadelphia Eagles fan. She has traveled extensively through six continents, but loves no place better than Nantucket, where she enjoys jogging, cooking, and watching her sons play Little League Baseball. Hilderbrand is a graduate of Johns Hopkins University and the graduate fiction workshop at the University of Iowa.